Horrible death of the maniac's wife on board the pirate vessel.

GILBERT COPLEY,

THE REPROBATE.

A DOMESTIC ROMANCE.

BY THE AUTHOR OF

"THE HEBREW MAIDEN; OR, THE JEW'S DAUGHTER;" "THERESE; OR, THE ORPHAN
OF GENEVA;" "FATHERLESS FANNY;" "KATHLEEN; OR, THE SECRET
MARRIAGE;" ETC., ETC., ETC.

Man is the real enemy of man,
When his perverted nature, rank with hate,
Destroys the purpose of creative love,
And makes this earth a theatre of woe,
Which else had been a paradise of bliss.

W. L. THOMAS.

LONDON:
E. LLOYD, 12, SALISBURY SQUARE, FLEET STREET.

1844.

PREFACE.

It is usual to write a preface, though it must be confessed the custom would frequently be more honoured in the breach than in the observance. It is, however, an excellent medium whenever an author is desirous of returning thanks for the kindness with which his labours have been received; and with that view the writer of the following pages has been induced to take upon himself a task to which he feels inadequate. Were he, however, to omit the opportunity thus offered he might be deemed ungrateful for the favours that have been so frequently and so liberally bestowed upon him on every occasion that he has appeared before the public.

"Gilbert Copley" may lay a fair claim to originality, though it is but justice to add, that it is founded on a short tale which appeared a few years since in one of the popular periodicals. The author saw that there was plot and incident enough on which to construct a narrative of greater extent, and, by adding largely to the original source, he has constructed a story which, if he may judge by its extensive sale, has afforded satisfaction to his numerous readers.

This explanation appears to be necessary in order to avoid the charge of having borrowed an idea without having also the courage and honesty to avow it. The writer admits his obligation, but fearlessly asserts, that though the plot has been taken from the source above-mentioned, the language is entirely his own.

June, 1844.

GILBERT COPLEY,

THE REPROBATE.

BY THE AUTHOR OF "THE HEBREW MAIDEN; OR, THE LOST DIAMOND," "KATHLEEN," ETC.

A ROMANCE OF THRILLING INTEREST.

CHAPTER I.

THE FUGITIVE.—THE ANNOUNCEMENT.—THE FAMILY PARTY.

IT was a dark night in the month of December, and though the snow was lying deep upon the ground Simon Stripes, parish-clerk and schoolmaster, buttoned himself up in his great coat and left home to go on an errand of some importance to the mansion of Sir Lionel Dacre. It must be confessed he would rather have postponed the business till the morning, but " delays are dangerous," was a copy he had so often given his scholars, that he could not forget the injunction, and taking good heart he groped his way along, muttering now and then to himself at the cause which had led to the unpleasant journey he had undertaken.

On arriving at the end of his journey he was in no humour to answer the questions of Mr. Launcelot Cramp, the steward, with whom he was generally upon very gracious terms, and, having been ushered into a room where a cheerful fire was blazing, he seated himself on one side of the chimney till it should please the owner of the mansion to give him an audience. Luckily for his patience Sir Lionel soon made his appearance.

No. 1

" Your visit is rather a late one, Mr. Stripes," said the baronet, as he seated himself at the opposite side of the table, " and, judging from your disturbed looks, I am afraid the subject of it is not altogether an agreeable one."

" So you will say when I have told you all," replied Simon Stripes, " for the truth is, the youngster has made himself scarce, and ——"

" Who are you speaking of ?" interrupted the baronet, impatiently.

" Of your graceless nephew," replied Simon ; " in short, Gilbert Copley has taken to his legs, and Heaven only knows where or when he will be found."

" The thankless scoundrel !" exclaimed Sir Lionel ; " and did he leave no letter or message by which I may learn what course he intends pursuing ?"

" I have not heard of any," replied Stripes, " and so I suppose he don't want anybody to find out where he is."

" Perhaps, after all," said Sir Lionel, " there is not much cause for alarm. I dare say it is some sudden freak of his, and we shall see him again before long."

" I don't much think you will," answered Simon ; " for if there was not something in this more than we know of, he would have told me he was going away for a little time, and not have run away like a thief in the night."

" You are severe upon him, my good friend."

" And not without good cause," replied Simon. " He has been a great trouble to me, and I always said if his manners didn't mend he would meet with a bad fate."

" Are you a believer in fate, Mr. Stripes ?" asked the baronet, after a pause.

" Why, to tell the truth, Sir Lionel, I have never given the subject much thought," answered Simon ; " but to my mind it don't seem a very difficult thing to predict that Gilbert Copley will not come to any good end."

" It seems, then, that I go somewhat beyond you in my belief," exclaimed Sir Lionel, " for it was foretold to me many years ago that I should be stung by the serpent I had fostered, and for years past I have always expected that Gilbert was alluded to in the prophecy."

" Very singular, indeed," said the other.

" It is singular," returned Sir Lionel, thoughtfully ; " and, should my suspicions about this youth be confirmed, you must admit that the gift of prophecy has not yet passed away from us."

" And it's likely enough they will be confirmed," answered Stripes, " for it has always been my opinion that Gilbert Copley would turn out a bad fellow, and his running away in this sort of manner proves that I was not much out in my notions."

" You think he will not return then ?"

" Yes ; that's my opinion."

" And do you know of any reason that he could have had for such ingratitude ?"

" I have not had much time to reflect upon it yet," replied Simon; " but I dare say that it won't be very long before the murder's out. In the morning I'll make all inquiries, and you shall know all particulars as soon as I can collect them."

" Remember my anxiety, and use all diligence to relieve it," answered Sir Lionel. " To-morrow I will expect to see you again, and let me hope the news you bring will serve to remove from Gilbert the suspicions his conduct has given rise to."

Simon left the room, and, on his way towards the hall-door, was met by Launcelot Cramp, who, with remarkable hospitality, invited him to take a draught of ale, and then, with exceeding ingenuity, began to question him upon the object of his visit at so late an hour of the night. Simon Stripes, however, was too old a bird to be caught with chaff, and warding off the inquiries as well as he could, he at length succeeded in quitting the house, leaving the steward no wiser than he was at the beginning of the interview.

In the meanwhile, Sir Lionel returned to the drawing-room where he had left Lady Dacre and the Reverend Matthew Podger; the latter was the clergyman of the parish, and, as his invitations to the mansion were unlimited, he was pretty frequently to be found in the enjoyment of the host's hospitality. Rarely, indeed, was he an unwelcome visitor, but upon the present occasion Sir Lionel was too much occupied with his own thoughts to pay the usual attention to him, and it was not till Mr. Podger had thrice inquired whether anything unpleasant had occurred, that he turned his eyes from the fire upon which he had been gazing, to ask his guest if he knew anything of Simon Stripes.

"Oh, yes," replied the other; "he is my clerk, and, of course, I know a little of him."

"And you believe him to be an honest, respectable man, I suppose?"

"I do," replied the parson; "and now, having answered your questions, may I ask what is it that seems to perplex you so much to-night?"

"We shall come to that presently," said the baronet. "The truth is, I have heard bad news of Gilbert ——"

"Of Gilbert?" interrupted Lady Dacre.

"Yes," replied her husband; "he has thought proper to leave the house of Simon Stripes, and there is but too much reason to fear he is wilfully rushing to his own destruction."

"Has any search been made for him?" inquired the clergyman.

"There has been no time for it at present," replied Sir Lionel, "for it is only within the last hour that the news has been brought to me. Indeed, I have some notion that he is scarcely worth the trouble of trying to seek after."

"It seems, then," said Lady Dacre, "that you are beginning to think of him as I have done; I was always afraid the boy would give you a great deal of trouble, and now it is likely you will see reason to be sorry that you gave him so much of your regard. However, I am grieved to hear he has behaved with so much ingratitude, and if you will take my advice in the matter you will bestow no pains in trying to seek after him."

"And yet, perhaps, the fault has been in a great measure my own," returned the baronet. "Gilbert may have been anxious for active employment, and I have kept him in an obscure, retired village, when he was yearning to enter upon the more bustling scenes of the world. This I should have thought of before, and I hope that even now it is not too late to retrieve an error which might lead to serious mischief."

"For my own part," observed her ladyship, "I never could discover what Gilbert was fit for. He seemed to be naturally of an indolent disposition, and with a young man of that description it is not easy to say what course should be pursued."

"Under any circumstances," added the rector, "I think it will be necessary to let him feel that his ingratitude is not to pass unpunished. He has chosen to leave the protection of a good friend, and the endurance of a little hardship may serve as a wholesome corrective in after life."

"But by following your advice," said the baronet, "may I not so harden his heart that he will never become what you and I should wish to see him?"

"That will entirely depend upon his disposition," replied Podger. "It must be admitted that all tempers are not to be managed in the same way, and as you know the nature of this young man better than I do, it would be presumption in me to offer any further opinion upon the subject."

"For my own part, I am only afraid all further kindness will be thrown away upon him," said Lady Dacre. "He has proved himself to be unworthy another thought, and having once become disobedient to his benefactor, there is no hope of his amending a fault that has been committed at a period of his life when he was well able to judge between right and wrong."

"Yet I have known instances," observed Sir Lionel, "of men turning out well who have been a little wild and refractory in their youth."

"The subject," said the clergyman, "is one that requires reflection, and I would therefore advise you to sleep on it. To-morrow you will have had time to turn it over in your mind, and you will then be able to judge how far kindness may be beneficial to this headstrong youth. Lady Dacre, too, will, I dare say, give the matter a calm consideration, and with the aid of her counsel I have no doubt your decision will be a good and just one."

Having delivered himself thus, the Reverend Matthew Podger took leave of his host and hostess, and, promising to pay them another visit at the earliest opportunity, he left the mansion to wend his cheerless way along the roads, which, by this time, were deep in snow.

CHAPTER II.

THE REPROBATE.—A MODEST DEMAND.—MYSTERY.

MONTHS glided away after the events related in the last chapter, and still no tidings were heard of Gilbert Copley. No steps, indeed, were taken by Sir Lionel to discover what had become of him, and if it cannot be said that he was entirely forgotten, it may be asserted that his name was rarely mentioned by those who, for various reasons, were not sorry that he had left them. Lady Dacre had never liked the youth, nor had she sought to disguise the feeling with which she regarded him, and Sir Lionel, who could easily guess the cause, took care never to mention a name which generally gave rise to bickerings and recriminations.

Affairs were in this situation, when, one morning, a servant entered the breakfast parlour to announce that Hugh Darnton, a tenant of Sir Lionel's, was below, and desired an immediate audience. Now this, of all men, was the last whom the baronet would have wished to see; but there were reasons why he should not give offence to his unwelcome visitor, and looking towards Lady Dacre, as if wishing she had been absent, he desired the servant to shew Hugh Darnton into the room.

"I wonder you have patience to see that man, Sir Lionel," said her ladyship, as the domestic retired. "His conduct is always insolent, and it seems to me that he possesses a degree of control over you that I must confess is quite inexplicable."

"It would be far better were you less suspicious of your husband," exclaimed the baronet, in an angry tone of displeasure. "The truth is, Hugh Darnton has been a tenant of mine many years, and I do not think proper to turn my back upon him because of late his rent has been getting a little in arrears."

"Nor would I wish you to be severe with an honest man," answered Lady Dacre; "but the person we are speaking of bears the impress of villany upon his countenance, and, from all I hear, his looks do not belie him. You, however, seem to stand in fear of him, and I ——"

"Hush!" interrupted Sir Lionel; "he comes, and it is my request that you do not treat him with incivility. In a few moments I shall have gone through the long account of Cramp's, and, if it is your pleasure, you may then hear what passes between us."

He had scarcely finished speaking when Hugh Darnton, a coarse, ruffianly-looking fellow, entered the room. His gaze was directed towards Sir Lionel, but seeing that he was just then busily occupied, he turned towards Lady Dacre, nodded familiarly, and then seated himself at the table.

"You wish to see Sir Lionel?" she said.

"I do, my lady," replied Hugh ;—" times are hard with me, and I want to see if something can't be done for a poor fellow that has a family depending upon him for support."

"Have you many to feed?"

"Seven of 'em, my lady, *that's all*," replied Hugh. "Sometimes they get a bit to eat, and sometimes they don't. I see them almost starving about me, and it's now time that something should be done to get out of this misery."

"I know not how it is," returned Lady Dacre, "that you, among all our tenants, are the only one who ever complains. The rest are regular in their payments, whilst you have been frequently excused, though your farm is certainly not inferior to any of them."

"Well, it can't be helped if I am a little behind hand," replied Hugh, doggedly. "It's not to be denied that my rent has sometimes been excused, but Sir Lionel knows whether there may not be some reason for treating me with a little favour."

"And what reason should there be for it?" said the baronet, throwing down the paper he was perusing, and directing an angry glance towards the man.

"The reason need not be given now, I suppose," answered Hugh, with composure. "However, there is no occasion for anger, Sir Lionel ;—I'm here on a little matter of business, and the sooner it's settled the sooner you will be rid of me."

"You would ask for time, I suppose?"

"Time would be of very little use to a man that's over head and ears in difficulties," replied Hugh. "I've been struggling hard enough against bad luck, and now I must think of doing something else."

"What do you propose?"

"Why, in the first place, I must give up my farm," replied Hugh Darnton ; "I've had no luck in it, and so the best thing you can do, Sir Lionel, is to take it back into your own hands."

"But your situation will be still worse," said the baronet, "if you give up your only means of support."

"Oh, no," replied Hugh, "I have thought of something that will answer my purpose better, and it now depends upon you, Sir Lionel, whether I am to starve or get my living like an honest man."

"The arrears you are indebted to me I shall not be urgent for," answered Sir Lionel, "but in no other way shall I feel inclined to assist you."

"Humph!" ejaculated Hugh, and then directing a look of peculiar meaning towards the baronet he said with a half sneer—" May I make so bold, Sir Lionel, as to inquire if you know what has become of a certain young man, named Gilbert Copley?"

"I know nothing of him," replied Sir Lionel, in evident trepidation. "He quitted the village secretly, and I therefore have not thought it worth while to make any inquiries respecting him ; you are now answered, and may leave the room."

"Not before I have told you what I have to say" returned the other. "I told you just now that it's my intention to give up the farm, and, of course, if I do that you must help me in some other way."

"*Must* help you !"

"Ay, those were my very words," answered Hugh, "a man won't starve while he can help it, and so, to make my story as short as possible, I shall want fifty pounds of you."

"Of me ?"

"Yes ; where else can I get it ?"

"You certainly might apply elsewhere than to the man to whom you are so much indebted."

"But I might apply for a long time without getting it," answered Hugh. "People are not so apt to part with money unless there is good reason for it. Others would refuse me, but *you* will not."

"Insolent !"

"I am sorry we should fall out, Sir Lionel," exclaimed Hugh ; "but you have heard me, and I'm not a man to be refused where I can make a demand."

"But the sum might have been more moderate."

"Not if you consider my necessities," replied the other ; "so be brief with your answer, for I have already waited long enough to know whether I am to have the money."

"If it is to improve or stock your farm," said the baronet, "the sum asked for shall be yours."

"Well, then, I'll not deceive you about the matter," exclaimed Hugh. "The money is not either to improve or stock my farm ; I have a relative that lives some few miles away from here, and if he sees that I'm not quite a beggar, he will help to put me forward in the world."

"It is a vain hope," said the baronet ; "for I have known you years enough to be convinced that the reckless course you have pursued will never be altered."

"Did you never hear of a man giving up his bad ways then ?"

"Now and then I have heard of such an instance," replied Sir Lionel, "but the present instance, I fear, is quite a hopeless one."

"You don't mean to let me have the money I ask for, then, it seems ?" said the other, threateningly.

"I have not yet refused it," replied Sir Lionel, after a brief pause. "Indeed I am inclined to serve you, Darnton, if I could only be assured that the sum you have named will be of real and lasting benefit to your family.'

"I have told you that it will," returned Hugh, sullenly. "Besides, you needn't have been so particular about the money, since I dare say it will be in my power to repay it some day or other."

"And on condition that I comply with your request this time, you will not come on the same errand again ?"

"Oh, yes, I promise that."

"Then the money shall be advanced."

"How soon ?"

"In the course of a week."

"That will not do," exclaimed Hugh ; "I must have it this very day, so there's an end of the matter."

"Well, well, you are an importunate fellow," said the baronet, "and I will e'en comply with your demand to be rid of you. Come at eight o'clock this evening, and the money shall be ready."

"You will not play any trick, I suppose ?" exclaimed the other ; and then seeming to recollect himself, he added, "but I know you will not do that, because there's good reason against it. So I'll take your word, Sir Lionel, and at the hour you have appointed I shall not fail to be here."

He left the room as he uttered these words, and Lady Dacre, who had been a silent auditor of all that had passed, ventured to inquire how it was that fifty pounds had been so readily promised to a man who was already considerably in debt.

"Why the truth is," answered Sir Lionel, who was sorely perplexed what reply to make, "this man has long been an incumbrance to us, and, even at a sacrifice, it will be advisable to get rid of him."

"Which might have been done," she observed, "by sending him to a prison. It seems, however, that you are in fear of him, from what cause I am unable to guess. The mystery, I suppose, you are not inclined just now to clear up."

"There is no mystery," replied Sir Lionel, "beyond what your own fancy supplies."

"You will have a difficulty," answered her ladyship, "to convince the world that there is not some powerful motive for giving money to a man of worthless character, like this Hugh Darnton. It has been remarked before that you favoured him more than any of your other tenants, and when it becomes known that you have bestowed this further gratuity upon him, it will confirm all previous rumours."

"And what have I to do with rumours?" demanded the baronet. "I am master of my own actions, and my neighbours have no right to question my motives for relieving a poor man by an act of charity. It is true, Darnton bears not the best of characters, but he has a helpless family, and they, at least, deserve some little commiseration."

"But people will talk," answered Lady Dacre, "and they will naturally wonder why you are so generous to that worthless fellow."

"It really seems to me," exclaimed Sir Lionel, "that *you* are the most inquisitive about an affair that really need excite no wonder."

"And is there not sufficient to excite my doubts?" cried her ladyship. "His words were spoken threateningly, and you evidently yielded through fear."

"Fear!"

"Yes, Sir Lionel," she replied; "deny it as you will, I am not to be deceived. The man who has just left us possesses a secret that you would not have disclosed, and he practices upon your fears whenever he requires money. I observed the almost fiendish expression of his countenance when he asked about Gilbert Copley, and your own trepidation was not unnoticed."

"Hah! am I to be doubted thus?"

"There is but too much reason for it," replied Lady Dacre, "and it is to put you on your guard that I have spoken thus freely. Hugh Darnton is not to be trusted, even though half your fortune should be spent to purchase his silence. He will exultingly tell his comrades how easily he can obtain money whenever it is required, and though he may not tell the secret itself, through fear of losing his hold upon you, he will afford opportunities for the spreading of rumours that may be fatal to your character."

"I will have no more of this," exclaimed Sir Lionel; "you have no reason for these suspicions, and yet I find myself debased in the opinion of one who should be the last to side with my enemies."

"It is to vindicate your honour that I have spoken thus freely," she replied. "The man should have been dismissed with scorn, and if there is really no secret, you could have had little to fear from the threats which I could not fail to observe."

"I will hear no more upon this subject," exclaimed Sir Lionel. "That there is a secret I will not attempt to deny, but it is of no importance, and at some other time I may perhaps be induced to make you my confidant. At present, however, I am in no humour to speak further upon the matter, and you will best consult both your own happiness and mine by thinking no more of what has just passed, till I inform you of the trivial circumstance which has thus been magnified into importance."

He strode from the room at these words with a proud and angry step and Lady Dacre, far from being convinced, was more assured than ever that some terrible secret existed in which the honour and happiness of her husband were involved. The character usually given to Hugh Darnton was of itself sufficient to keep him from the house, unless there were reasons for his being admitted to it, and the words he had given utterance to in the recent interview were such as he would not have dared to speak had Sir Lionel been indifferent to the consequences.

Exactly at the appointed time, Hugh Darnton once more made his appearance at the mansion, and was instantly conducted to the room where the baronet was awaiting his arrival.

" I suppose," he said, " you have not changed your mind about what we were talking of this morning ?"

" I have not," replied Sir Lionel; " but I must warn you against speaking in presence of a third party. Lady Dacre heard all that passed, and her suspicions have been excited."

" That was your own fault, Sir Lionel," answered the other, " for I should not have said half so much if you had been more ready to agree with my just demands. I was forced to speak out a little, you know, or this business would never have been settled."

" And now," said the baronet, " on condition that I let you have the money, you will not come here to trouble me any more ?"

" Oh! certainly not," replied Hugh, with a cunning look, " unless I come to repay you the money."

" Which there will not be any occasion to do for some time to come," returned the baronet. " I have drawn a memorandum to the effect that it shall not be demanded for a certain number of years, and it will depend upon yourself whether it is ever asked for. Act faithfully by me, and the fifty pounds will never be asked for."

" And what am I to do with the paper, or memorandum, as you call it ?"

" Sign it," replied Sir Lionel, " and when that is done, here is the money I have promised."

" Oh! very well," said Hugh, taking up a pen and scrawling his name at the bottom of the paper; " that is soon done, you see; so now give me the money and I'll be off."

" It is here," answered the baronet, handing him the notes; " and now, Hugh, having fulfilled my promise, I have a few questions to ask of you."

" Why, as to that," exclaimed the other, as he buttoned up the pocket in which he had deposited the money, " you can ask as many questions as you please, but I don't know that I shall be fool enough to answer them ; I've got what I came for, and you know well enough that you didn't dare refuse me, so now we stand upon fair ground, and I shall decline saying anything till we meet again. The cash will be enough for me at present, but I don't promise that I shall not pay you another visit before long."

With a swaggering step he left the mansion, and, as his clattering steps descended the stairs, Sir Lionel bitterly cursed his own folly for having suffered himself to be thus tricked. On the following morning, however. he sent a message, desiring Hugh Darnton to call upon him without delay ; but the fellow had in the interim made the best use of his time, for, having previously converted all he possessed into cash, he had left the place with one of his daughters, leaving the rest of his family to the merciful consideration of the parish.

CHAPTER III.

FRIENDSHIP.—THE DYING SOLDIER.—THE PROTEGE.

The few angry words that had passed between Sir Lionel and Lady Dacre were soon forgotten,—or at least not referred to,—and matters went on for some weeks with as much harmony as if nothing had ever occurred to disturb their usual good understanding. At last news was brought them that their neighbour, Captain Evered, was taken seriously ill, and from that period a messenger was sent daily to inquire how he was going on. Each time, however, the answers sent back were more unfavourable, and then either Lady Dacre or some of the family called themselves to see him and console his daughter Agnes, whose grief at the danger of her father was excessive. Sir Lionel was himself deeply concerned at the probability of losing an old and valued friend, and it was not without visible emotion that one morning, after having received a very unfavourable account on the preceding night, he inquired of her ladyship if any news had been heard of his friend.

"I have not yet sent," replied her ladyship, "for it was my intention to go there with Eleanor in order that we might see if anything could be done to assist poor Agnes, who seems nearly to have worn herself out with constant watching and nursing."

"I am afraid he is in a very dangerous state," said Sir Lionel, "and that a short time will deprive Agnes of her only remaining parent."

"And in that case I know not what is to become of her," sighed Lady Dacre, "for her father's pay dies with him, and I fear he has not been able to make much provision for his child."

"She must come and make one of our family," replied Sir Lionel;
No. 2

"both Eleanor and Alice have ever expressed a sisterly affection for her, and she shall share our roof as if she had been a daughter of our own. You, I am sure, will offer no objection to such an arrangement, for I know she has been an especial favourite, and the certainty that his daughter will not be left unprotected will afford consolation in the last hours of our friend."

"Your suggestion has but anticipated mine," said Lady Dacre, "and most happy do I feel that the proposal has first proceeded from yourself. Poor Agnes will at least find a home when affliction falls upon her, and our daughters will thus be enabled to alleviate the grief of a highly valued friend."

"I have been thinking," said Sir Lionel, "that his apothecary, Mr. Burton—though esteemed an able practitioner—may not exactly understand the captain's complaint. If such should be the case a hope remains, and I will call round on our physician, Doctor Morley, and take him with me to the patient's house. At all events it is a last resource, and can do no harm even if no good should result from it."

In fulfilment of this plan Sir Lionel set out without delay, and having found Doctor Morley at home he took him to see Captain Evered, who was found to be in a more alarming state than had been expected. Sir Lionel waited for the doctor in a room below, and when the latter took his departure he accompanied him to inquire whether any hopes of recovery could be given.

"It would be wrong to excite hopes where none can be held out," answered the physician, "and I therefore declare that no skill can save your friend, who is now sinking rapidly."

"And is he aware of his danger?"

"I thought it my duty to tell him of it."

"How did he receive the announcement?"

"Like a good man who has no fear of death," replied the doctor. "He spoke of his daughter with concern, and his only wish to live that he might have seen her placed safely under the protection of a husband."

"Agnes Evered shall find a home beneath our roof," exclaimed Sir Lionel, "and my only concern is that no friendship, no protection can replace that of her father. She shall, however, find that there are those who yet care for her in spite of the desolation that has fallen upon her heart."

"She will feel the blow heavily at first," replied the other, "but being possessed of strength of mind I doubt not that her grief will yield to the mild persuasions of her friends. She is indeed fortunate in having found such generous protection, and gratitude alone will be sufficient to withdraw her from the despair into which she might otherwise have fallen."

Having by this time reached the part of the road where they were to separate, Doctor Morley took his leave, and Sir Lionel returned home to communicate the melancholy news of which he was the bearer.

Poor Agnes had but too plainly discovered in the countenance of the physician the fatal secret of her father's danger, and sinking with apprehension she entered the chamber in which the sick man was lying. Even during her brief absence a visible alteration had taken place in his appearance, and sinking into a seat beside his couch she gave way to those tears of filial affection which it was impossible to control. He had fallen into a disturbed slumber at the departure of Doctor Morley, but the half suppressed sobs of his daughter served to rouse him, and taking her hand he attempted to murmur forth his blessing. The effort, however, was for a few minutes in vain, but at length recovering himself he faintly pronounced her name, and then, as if weakened by the effort, was once more exhausted and speechless.

She would have called for assistance, but the effort to do this appeared again to arouse him, and retaining her hand within his own he said in an almost inaudible whisper—

"I would have none present till I have spoken to you. I am dying, Agnes ; exhausted nature cannot much longer support me, yet are there things which I left to be told when my last hour should come. It is here ere I expected it, and not half that I would have said can be uttered."

"For mine. for your own sake," said the weeping girl, "do not exert yourself."

"My dear Agnes," he sighed, "death has no terrors for me ; yet, for your sake, I have sometimes wished to live a few years longer. To have seen you happy was the only wish of my heart, but it has been denied me ; and I can bow with meekness to the will of Heaven."

He paused for a few seconds, and having recovered himself again addressed her :—

"I have reason to believe that after my death you will be offered an asylum in the mansion of Lady Dacre. It affords me happiness to know that you will thus find a friend in whom you may place the firmest reliance. There at least you will remain for a time, and should it be necessary to remove, I am not without hopes that you will find protection in your mother's family. They have been bitter enemies, but when those they hated are dead, their hearts may turn with pity towards their innocent offspring. On my own side there is little friendship to be expected, unless it be from a brother who went abroad, of whose existence I have been for some time uncertain."

"Dear, dear father," she cried, "you do but exhaust yourself when nature has so much need of repose."

"The little I have to say must be spoken," he replied. "At my death your means will be much diminished, yet enough will be left to save you from falling into absolute poverty. More ought to have been yours, but injustice has robbed you of your rights. Search my papers, and you will learn more than I have space to tell you—you will there see how your mother ——"

His voice failed and the hue of death spread itself over his countenance. Agnes with a scream of terror rose from her seat, and was only prevented falling to the ground by the entrance of Lady Dacre and Eleanor, who at that moment had reached the house of their dying friend. A hasty glance served to convince them that all was nearly over ; and Eleanor leading her young friend from the room left Lady Dacre and the housekeeper to remain by the death-bed of the veteran. From that moment Captain Evered was unable to utter another syllable ; power and consciousness seemed alike to be taken away from him, and in another half an hour of the time that Agnes was led from the room he breathed his last.

To break the mournful intelligence to her was a task that Lady Dacre would have shrunk from had she not been afraid that the duty might have been more roughly performed by the domestic. She therefore went to the room to which the sorrowing daughter had been conveyed, but the announcement she had to make was rendered unnecessary by the agitation she displayed, for Agnes at once perceived that all was over, and sinking back into a chair with a suppressed cry of agony, she gave way to those tears which alone could assuage her anguish. It was now the time for Lady Dacre to offer that consolation which was so much needed, and though her efforts were at first unheeded she at length succeeded in so far tranquillizing her grief as to obtain a hearing. Agnes then expressed the gratitude she felt at the kindly interest that had been taken in her behalf, and eventually she yielded to the kind solicitations of her friends.

After the funeral of her parent Agnes gradually, though by slow degrees, regained a portion of those spirits for which in happier days she had been remarkable. This she considered as being in some respect due to the affectionate attention bestowed upon her by those who had offered her an asylum, and though her heart was yet depressed by its afflictions she contrived to exhibit an outward show of happiness that was indeed foreign to it.

Eleanor Dacre never suffered her young friend to dwell for any length of time upon past miseries, but sought by every means in her power to banish from her thoughts all the reflection which might serve to recal painful images of the loss she had sustained. Agnes yielded passively to the kindness thus manifested, and, in appearance at least, she was soon restored to her accustomed cheerfulness.

CHAPTER IV.

AN EVIL COUNSELLOR.—THE QUEER COMPANION.—THE START.

It is now necessary to the clear development of our story that we should follow Gilbert Copley, who was spoken of at the opening of this narrative as having mysteriously disappeared from the village. For some time previously to this step he had observed that his visits to his uncle were regarded with suspicion and dislike by Lady Dacre, and possessing too proud a spirit to thrust himself upon those who were not inclined to receive him with cordiality, he totally abstained from paying his accustomed visits to the hall.

This change could not fail to be observed by Sir Lionel, who readily guessed the cause of it, for he knew the antipathy felt by Lady Dacre towards his nephew, and was also perfectly well assured of the reason which had given rise to her prejudice. Even then he would fain have prevailed upon Gilbert Copley to resume his visits as usual, but the young man was resolute in the determination he had formed, and as no other alternative remained he would frequently call upon our hero at the house of Simon Stripes, and by engaging him in conversation, endeavour to find out the course of life for which he was best adapted. At last having satisfied himself upon that point, he accompanied Gilbert in a walk, and telling him it was necessary that he should now enter upon the active scenes of life, he proposed that he should accept a situation till something more adapted to his own views should offer itself. Gilbert offered no objection to this arrangement, and it is certain that he would have acceded to the terms had it not been for Hugh Darnton, who had contrived some time before to worm himself into his friendship and thus exercise a control over him that was altogether unaccountable. His first impulse on receiving the intimation from his uncle, was to call Darnton and inform him of what had passed, expressing at the same time a repugnance to the drudgery it was proposed for him to commence with. The rustic heard him with a concealed feeling of scorn, and having reflected for a few moments he inquired if he was prepared to take a bold step.

"I am," replied our hero.

"Will you quit this place for a time?"

"Ay, for ever if there is need for it."

"But will you go," asked Darnton, "where no one but myself can find you?"

"Your proposition is a strange one," said Gilbert, "but as I believe your intentions towards me are friendly and honourable, I shall offer no objection."

"You have done well in deciding so," exclaimed the other, "and I am glad to find my motives are not doubted. You must leave this place without delay, and your escape must be so skilfully contrived that no one will be able to discover which route you have taken."

"Which can be done easily enough," said Gilbert, "but you have not yet told me where I am to seek concealment?"

"That will be known all in good time," answered the other. "Something, however, must be done quickly, for I suppose your uncle has determined on your immediate departure for London?"

"I believe he has."

"In that case," said Hugh Darnton, "we have no time to waste in delay. Sir Lionel, in his anxiety, will no doubt strike while the iron is hot, and if you would escape the disgrace of being made a drudge you must take French leave at once."

"Directly if you think it best."

"Why that's well said," exclaimed Darnton; "you were always a fellow after my own heart, and I dare say I shall be able to make something of you yet. I have watched you, Gilbert Copley, for many a long month, and it's only because I saw you were a bold, resolute fellow, that I determined to try if something better than mere slavery couldn't be your lot."

"And where do you propose for me to go?"

"That must be thought of by and by," answered Hugh Darnton. "I suppose Sir Lionel won't be in a hurry to get you out of the way just yet, but if he should you can let me know, and I'll take care to find some place for your concealment. You'll not be afraid to trust me, I hope?"

"Oh, no," replied Gilbert, "with you I shall feel myself safe anywhere."

"Ay," exclaimed the other, "but it wouldn't be wise for us to be together just yet. You must contrive to give them the slip first, and I can follow when all the consternation is at an end. They must not fancy we are together, or perhaps a reward would be offered for our discovery, which would not be very pleasant for either of us."

"True, but how long will it be before you will be able to join me?"

"No longer than will be necessary to get a little money together," answered Darnton. "I have some by me already, and I dare say it will not be long before I can borrow some more from a certain person that I will not name at present."

"Well, your plan suits me amazingly," exclaimed Gilbert Copley; "for, to tell you truth, I was not best pleased at the idea of being cooped up in a dingy counting-house, where there's nothing to be seen but desks and stools, and files of musty bills. I have always looked forward to a life of enterprise, and the greater the danger the better will it suit with my humour."

"If that's the sort of thing you like, I can promise you plenty of it," said Hugh Dornton; "I have a scheme in my head, lad, that will suit you to a hair, and I would tell you what it is at once, only that I'm afraid to trust a youngster with such a secret."

"If you suspect my prudence," exclaimed Gilbert, sharply; "it will, perhaps be better that we have nothing more to do with each other."

"What! you are growing nettled are you?" cried the other; "but never mind; I like a lad of spirit, and we won't fall out about trifles. You shall see that I'm a man of my word, and by and bye you will acknowledge that it was far better to trust Hugh Darnton than an uncle that would have made a mere earth-worm of you. So now, away to your home, my boy, and in less than a week the matter shall all be comfortably arranged."

Gilbert Copley saw that no good was to be gained by arguing the subject any further just then, and desiring his companions not to forget his promise, he returned to the house of Simon Stripes, to reflect on the projected alteration in his circumstances. His disposition was naturally an adventurous one, and he looked forward with pleasure to a roving life, instead of being buried alive in London, so that the more he thought over the affair the greater was his pleasure at contemplating a change so congenial to his feelings.

The intervening period was one of intense anxiety to our hero, who ardently longed to ascertain the course he was to pursue, and could scarcely refrain from calling upon Darnton to inquire if his arrangements were yet complete. On the morning, however, that exactly completed the week since their last meeting, he strolled out towards the spot where they usually saw each other, and scarcely had he reached the place when Hugh, issuing from a thicket, suddenly presented himself before him.

"Well done, my fine fellow," he exclaimed, grasping the hand of his young companion, as if it had been in a vice; "this is better even than I expected, for it seems you are still in the same mind as when we last met each other."

"I am more pleased than ever with your proposition," answered Gilbert; "and shall, no doubt, readily enough fall into any plan that you may have to propose."

"Don't speak so loud, then, lest anybody should happen to overhear us," whispered Hugh; "it would spoil all should we happen to be seen together, so we must meet at some other place, where we can talk this matter over by ourselves."

"Lead the way, and I will follow you."

"We must part company at present, and afterwards meet as if by accident," replied the other.

"Where?"

"At the little public-house, down in yonder hollow," answered Hugh Darnton. "Of course you know the place well enough?"

"I do."

"Well, then, get there as fast as you can; take the lane that leads from the cross-roads, and I'll go through the wood, which is rather a nearer way. Lose no time about it, my boy, and over a glass of ale you shall hear what a good plan I've formed for getting you out of this humdrum life."

He darted off as these words were uttered, and Gilbert was left to his own reflections upon the appointment he had so inconsiderately made. It seemed to him that he had gone too far to retreat, and that circumstance, added to his own desire to burst the trammels of home, confirmed the determination to hear the proposition of his reckless associate. He, therefore, resolved to proceed without delay to the public-house spoken of, and, on reaching it, was shown into a little, dark, dingy apartment, where he found Hugh Darnton, and a man of rather suspicious appearance, who he had never seen before. They were both of them smoking and drinking, and from the freedom of their manners to each other, it was quite evident that they were old acquaintances.

Harrowby—for such was the stranger's name—glanced a suspicious look towards Gilbert as he entered the room, but on a few words being muttered in his ear by Hugh Darnton, he saluted the young man with a familiar nod, and pushing a chair towards him, desired that he would seat himself. The young man then observed that the stranger had taken especial care to conceal his features as much as possible; but in spite of the pains he had bestowed for that purpose, there was quite enough of his face to be seen to show that he was possessed of no small share of cunning and roguery.

"Is this the chap you were speaking about?" he said to Hugh Darnton, after taking three or four long whiffs at his pipe.

"Yes," replied his companion, "and from what I know of the youngster, don't think we shall find him a very bad sort."

"That remains to be proved," said the stranger, "for I'm not apt to form an opinion of people at first sight." Then glancing sullenly towards Gilbert he added, "You seem to be a strong, hale young fellow enough ; but, perhaps, couldn't endure the fatigue of a long journey on horseback ?"

"Why, for that matter," answered the young man, "I can do as much in that way as most people, I am fond of riding, and let our journey be as long as it may, I don't think I shall be the first to complain of fatigue."

"Spoken like a lad of mettle," exclaimed Harrowby, in a tone of greater freedom.

"Humph !" ejaculated Darnton, "you are convinced now, I hope, that have not deceived you in the description I gave you of him ?"

"Oh, yes, he'll do well enough, I dare say," replied the other ; "but I shall be able to judge better when we have been longer acquainted."

"May I ask what you are going to do with me, gentlemen ?" inquired Gilbert during the pause that now occurred in the conversation.

"All in good time, if you'll only have a little patience," answered Harrowby. "It seems, however, that you don't exactly approve of certain plans that have been formed by your friends, and as I am a good-natured fellow, Darnton has asked me to lend a helping hand towards putting you in a way to get plenty of money without having the trouble to drudge for it."

"And will the course you are about to propose be an honourable one ?" demanded Gilbert, in a tone of anxiety.

"Why, to be sure it will," replied Harrowby, with a sly wink towards Darnton. "We are your friends, and wouldn't persuade you to do wrong on any consideration."

"Then there can be no occasion for all this mystery."

"Yes there is," answered the other. "We don't want everybody to know what's going to be done, and if you are at all suspicious about the matter, the best way will be to say at once that you don't mean to trust us."

"Psha ! you are too sharp with the youngster," interposed Darnton. "He is a little bit taken by surprise at first ; but when you've known him as long as I have, you'll own him to be a regular thorough-going chap, that will enter heart and soul into the business."

"Pray, what is the business you are speaking of ?" asked Gilbert.

"A very good one for making plenty of money at," replied Harrowby. "Your life will be free and happy, and as there'll be but little work to do, there can't be much to grumble at after you've been let into the secret."

"But the profession may happen to be one that I cannot approve of."

"Then stay where you are, and submit to any disgrace that your friends may think proper to bring on you," answered Harrowby. "Sir Lionel, I believe, wants to make a mere drudging clerk of you, and if that's more agreeable to your own grubbing notions, say so at once, and there's an end of the matter."

"You are a fool for your pains, Harrowby, to talk in this way," exclaimed Darnton. "The young fellow has made up his mind to put himself under our guidance, and yet you must be the first to tell him to break with us."

"Then, he should plainly say what he means to do in the matter."

"So he will, if you only give him a minute or two to make up his mind," answered Hugh Darnton. "He has determined not to be made a fool of by Sir Lionel, and at any rate I should by all means persuade him to accept our plan, and then, if the life shouldn't suit him after a trial, he can easily give it up, and return to the place he comes from."

"What say you to that, young man ?" demanded Harrowby. "Will you go with us on liking, as Darnton has proposed ?"

"I will," replied Gilbert ; "but let me understand that it must be on condition that no attempt is made to restrain me should I afterwards see any reason to break up the connection that has been formed between us."

" Oh, you may rely upon our honour in that respect."

" Then I no longer hesitate," replied Gilbert. " I will follow wherever you lead, and for the present will place myself entirely under your direction."

" So far all goes very well," said Harrowby ; " but we may get ourselves into trouble if it should be supposed that Darnton and I have persuaded you to do this for our own advantage, and you must, therefore, put your own name to this bit of paper that I have drawn up ready for your signature."

" What is the nature of the document you would have me put my name to ?" inquired Gilbert Copley, after a pause.

" There is nothing in it that you need be afraid to sign," replied Harrowby.

" Can I not be allowed to read it first ?" inquired the young man.

" There's no occasion for taking so much trouble," replied the other. " It is only an acknowledgment that you leave home of your own free will, and may spare us the inconvenience of being searched after by your guardian, Sir Lionel Dacre."

Gilbert did not feel exactly satisfied with this reason, yet the thought of a change in his destiny overcame his scruples, and taking the pen which was offered him, he put his signature to the document, and then threw the paper across the table ; Hugh Darnton, however, thought proper to add his signa- ture, and those forms having been gone through, the document was folded up with great care, and placed in the side-pocket of Harrowby's coat.

" And now," said Darnton to our hero, " it follows, as a matter of course, that you will not be able to do much in the world without money. I am not very rich, as you know, but here is a purse with a few guineas in it, and be- fore they are gone, I dare say you will be on the high road to fortune. Mark Harrowby will, I know, be a constant friend to you, and as soon as I can get rid of the farm, I shall hasten to join you at the place where he will lead you to."

With great apparent friendship Hugh Darnton shook hands with our hero, and having whispered a few words to Harrowby, he left the room to return home.

" Now, young gentleman," said Mark, " I think it's time we should be going, for there's a long journey before us, and I should like to get out of this neighbourhood as quickly as possible. Horses are already saddled for us in the stable, and the road to fame and fortune lies before you."

These were high sounding words to Gilbert Copley, and rising from his seat, he followed the man into the back premises, where they found the horses in readiness. Full of hope and buoyancy, our hero leaped into the saddle, and in another minute their journey had commenced.

CHAPTER V.

THE JOURNEY.—SUSPICIOUS CIRCUMSTANCES.—THE RETREAT.

GILBERT and his companion rode on for some miles in silence, for the latter would not deign to make a reply, though questions were repeatedly put to him. As they approached London, however, he began to exhibit symptoms of being a little more sociable upon every subject except those which related to the place they were going to. In the morning they rested, and at night resumed their journey, in the course of which certain adventures occurred that filled the younger traveller with amazement.

In one instance they met an elderly gentleman on horseback, and having passed him some little distance, Harrowby informed his companion that he was almost certain the person was an old acquaintance, and desiring him to

ride slowly onwards, he turned his own horse, and retraced his steps at the utmost speed. There was nothing very remarkable in this, it is true, but presently Mark came galloping back as if pursuers were at his heels, and shouting out to his companion, he bade him follow with all his speed. Gilbert obeyed; but when he afterwards asked what made him use such extraordinary haste, he changed the subject to something else, telling him that he should know more when they reached the end of their journey.

On another occasion they met a carriage, and again desiring Gilbert to proceed forward about a mile, and then wait for him, he galloped after the vehicle as if he had some message to deliver, upon which life and death depended. This was all very strange to our hero, and he was still pondering upon the circumstance, when Mark Harrowby again came rushing along with the swiftness of a tempest, and making a sign for Gilbert to follow, he turned down a bye lane, and did not lessen his speed till they had ridden at least six miles. At length, when they did proceed at a gentler pace, our hero ventured to inquire of his companion why he followed the carriage, and the reason of his making such extraordinary haste back.

"I'll tell you what it is, young man," replied the other, "it's hardly proper for a youth to question his elders; but since you seem to be inquisitive you must know, that I thought when I passed the carriage, that the people in it were some of my former acquaintances."

"Humph!" ejaculated our hero, "you must know a great many people I think, for you fancied the gentleman on horseback was some one that you had seen before."

"There's no helping mistakes at times," replied the other. "The gentleman was a perfect stranger to me; but he behaved so exceedingly well, that I have no reason to regret having followed him."

"And I suppose you made a similar mistake with the people in the carriage."

No. 3

"Ah!" replied the other, "and the mistake had like to have been a very serious one, for the people pretended to be alarmed, and declared that I was a highwayman come to rob them."

"A highwayman!"

"Yes, that's what they called me," replied Harrowby, "and if it had not been for the brace of pistols I wear, the cowardly knaves of servants would have run me through with their swords. However, I managed to get clear off, though they pursued me some distance, and now I leave you to judge whether there was not reason for my returning to you in such haste."

"How could they have made such a mistake," said Gilbert, "as to believe you were a highwayman?"

"The truth is, the most innocent of us are liable to the foulest suspicions," replied Mark, with well dissembled humility. "I was mounted, and had pistols, so of course they must at once set me down for one of the gentlemen of the road."

"But even if you had fallen into their hands," observed Gilbert, "it would have been easy to prove that they were mistaken."

"It would not have been as easy as you imagine," replied Mark, "for our scurvy magistrates will not take a man's own word for his innocence, and I've known many a fine fellow to be hanged, because he couldn't get the judge and jury to believe he wasn't guilty of what they were trying him for."

"You have been acquainted with people that have been hanged then?" cried Gilbert, with surprise.

"To be sure I have," answered the other, "and it don't follow that I'm any the worse for it. If we had time to go a little out of the road, I could show you a couple of them that are still swinging on their gibbet. There ain't much of 'em left now but bones, but there they are, and though the world say they deserved their fate, I say there's a good many left behind that deserve hanging a great deal more."

"But I suppose there was no doubt of their guilt?" observed Gilbert.

"Why, the fact is, there's no denying it," replied Mark, "but one cannot help feeling sorry when a friend is taken off in his prime."

"And yet," said our hero, "if it was not for such examples there would be no end to violence."

"Very true," answered Harrowby, significantly, "but you would not like it if such a fate was ever to come to your turn."

"I'll take care it never does."

"Don't make too sure of it," replied the other, "for a man sometimes gets his neck into a noose before he's aware of it. You can't tell what's to happen any more than I can, and if you get into queer company, there's no saying how soon it may be your lot to ornament a gibbet."

"But suppose I take care to avoid the sort of company you speak of?"

"Psha!" exclaimed Harrowby, "it's not so easy to avoid as you may think for. You have made the first step by leaving the protection of your friends, and ——"

"Ah!" cried Gilbert, "there is some dreadful meaning in your words. But it is not too late to retrieve my error, by returning to the place I came from."

"And throw yourself upon the mercy of those who will not easily pardon what you have done."

"Sir Lionel Dacre," replied our hero, "is not the vindictive man you take him for."

"Ah!" cried Harrowby, "you speak like an inexperienced fellow as you are. Now I know the world somewhat better, and you may take my word for it, that if he was to receive you kindly, it would be all sham

Hugh Darnton has told me that the baronet don't like you, and it has been his intention for some time past to get you out of the way, and his plan of sending you off to London was only that he might pack you off abroad at the first opportunity."

" And even if it was so," exclaimed Gilbert, " anything would be better than risking the fate you just now spoke of."

" What!" cried the other, " I have frightened you, my young spark, have I ?"

" I am not to be so easily frightened as you think," replied the youth. " Give me any bold task to do, and I'll not shrink from it, but my character shall not be forfeited while I can help it."

" Well, there's no fear of that while you have me for a companion," replied Harrowby. " I shall keep a strict watch over you, depend upon it, and after being a little time at the place I am going to take you to, I shall be able to explain myself more fully, and to point out a course that will enable you to obtain renown."

" Have we much further to go ?" asked Gilbert.

" No," answered the other, " we are approaching the sea-coast, and the place where you are to seek concealment, commands a delightful view over the ocean. You will be as happy as the days are long, and Sir Lionel, inquire as he may, will never be able to discover your retreat."

" Do you live there, alone ?"

" Humph!" returned Harrowby, " you are a little bit inquisitive, I see ; but it's a part of my present business to be rather close. All will be known in good time, and take my word for it, you will see no reason to be sorry that chance has made me your friend."

" That," said Gilbert, thoughtfully, " remains to be proved."

" So it does," answered the other ; " but I know you have a great respect for Darnton ; he's an honest fellow, and would not have trusted you to the care of any one that was not as good as himself. But look ! the sea is now before us, and it will not be long before we arrive at our journey's end."

" Is the house in view ?" asked Gilbert, looking anxiously before him.

" No, we can't see it yet," replied Harrowby, " because yonder high rock is in the way. We have got to wind round a narrow path that leads almost to the summit, and then we shall find ourselves in comfortable quarters."

" It seems rather a strange place to choose for a residence," observed our hero, with surprise.

" It's exactly the sort of place where nobody will be able to find you," answered the other. " A month or two there will do you no harm, and by that time Sir Lionel will have given up all further inquiries as useless. Then we may think of stirring a bit, and I'll answer for it, you will enter into just such a bustling life as you like."

" But will it be an honourable one ?" inquired Gilbert Copley.

" Why, to be sure it will," replied Harrowby. " You may make your name famous in story ; and that, I take it, is just what you want to do. Pray, young sir, what may your age be ?"

" Eighteen."

" Ah!" returned the other, " that's just the time when a young man ought to place himself under the guidance of his friends. I will be your counsellor, and if you will only be guided by me, everything will turn out as may be wished. Darnton, too, will come to live with us by-and-by, so that you will have no lack of companions."

" But, perhaps," said Gilbert, " he may not find it so easy to get rid of his farm as he expects."

" There won't be much trouble about that," replied Harrowby, " for he
don't very often trouble himself about paying his rent, and Sir Lionel will
not be sorry to get rid of a queer tenant. But this is the rock we have got to
climb, and, as the path is rather narrow and slippery, I would advise you
to dismount, as I intend to do, and lead your horse gently up, lest an
accident should happen."

Gilbert Copley was not long in following this suggestion, and with the
greatest difficulty he slowly ascended the path, which was rendered the more
dangerous by the snow that had lately fallen. He, however, was not de-
ficient in resolution, and keeping as close as possible behind his companion,
he at length reached a level place of some extent, at the farther end of which
was a cottage, so situated as not to be seen, except from the spot they had
reached.

" We have reached the end of our journey," said Harrowby, " and we
shall find comforts within yonder house that will repay us for the trouble we
have had to get at it."

" 'Tis a strange place to build a cottage in," said Gilbert, with surprise.

" At any rate, it will answer your purpose well enough, young man,"
replied the other. " No one will ever be able to find you out here, and by-
and-by you may go to some better place."

He then approached the door, knocked gently at it, and listened to hear
if any one was within. A voice demanded who was there, and a reply being
given, they were admitted into the house.

CHAPTER VI.

THE NEW HOME.—ROUGH ASSOCIATES.—A CAROUSE.

THE person who had admitted them to the cottage was a masculine, re-
pulsive-looking female, who, after having eyed Gilbert with a scrutinizing
glance, welcomed the return of Mark Harrowby in a most cordial manner.
He, however, seemed in no humour to answer all the questions that were
put to him, and having sullenly desired her to put something to eat before
them, he and our hero sat down to partake of a meal which their long journey had given them an appetite for. During the repast Mark spoke very
little, but, his hunger being at length appeased, he demanded of Deborah,
for that was the name of the singular-looking female, what she could bring
him to drink.

" What can you have better than brandy?" she asked. " There's some
left that was in the place when you went away, and you know how you
praised the quality before you left us to go on your journey."

So saying she left the room, and returned in a minute or two afterwards
with a bottle of the liquor she had spoken of, which, with a couple of
glasses, she placed before Harrowby and his guest.

" Try that, young gentleman," said Mark, as he tossed off his own
quantum and prepared to repeat the dose. " You'll find it some of the
right sort, and not like the wishy-washy you've been used to get. It's
strong, and will serve to warm you this bitter night."

Gilbert tried to follow the example that had been set him, but it was like
swallowing liquid fire, and having nearly choked himself in the effort, he
asked for water to mix with it.

" Water!" exclaimed Harrowby, with surprise ; " would you spoil it by
so base a mixture?"

" The truth is," replied the other, " I have never been much used to
drinking spirits, and I'm afraid this will be too much for my head."

"The young gentleman has a lady's stomach," said Deborah, sneeringly, "and can't take his drops as you and I can. But, after he's been with us a little while, he'll grow more used to it, and take off his glass as well as I do myself."

Suiting the action to the word, she swallowed the potent draught without wincing, and was about to wash it down with a second, when Mark Harrowby snatched the bottle from her hand.

"Come, come, old woman," he exclaimed, "it won't do to let you take too much of this. You are apt to grow quarrelsome in your cups, and I don't want to see you make a fool of yourself before this young stranger."

"A fool, Mark Harrowby!"

"Ay," he replied. "What's the use of mincing words? But no more of this. Have you had anybody here since I have been away?"

"People don't come when the master's absent," answered Deborah. "I've been lonesome enough, and I have looked as anxiously for your return as if you had been my young lover."

"Hark!" exclaimed Harrowby; "there's a knocking at the door. The boys seem to know that I've come back again. Go, Deborah, let them in, for I long to know what they have been doing."

Gilbert listened to the woman as she unfastened the door, and it was evident to him that she had let in several persons. A good deal of whispering followed their admittance, and, as a sudden exclamation of surprise burst from them, they hurried towards the room, and welcomed the return of Mark Harrowby most boisterously. They were a strange-looking set of fellows, and their appearance was anything but in their favour; yet they greeted their companion with hearty good will, and seemed to be delighted at seeing him once more among them.

"What made you so long gone?" demanded one of them. "I began to think you had grown tired of us, and forsaken your friends altogether."

"I went on business," replied Mark, "and could not return till it was finished."

"And have brought a companion with you, I see," observed another.

"He's one," whispered Harrowby, "that I think you'll all like, when you come to know him. He's a lad of mettle; one that don't fancy your dull, plodding, every-day sort of life. His friends wanted to set him down to a desk for the remainder of his days; but he had a soul above ledgers, and he has run away to take shelter here, till they've done looking after him."

"Are you sure he's one of the right sort?"

"To be sure I am," was the reply, "or he would never have found his way to this place. Besides," he added, in a still lower whisper, "we have him safe here, and if anything should happen to make me alter my opinion, we shall know what to do with him."

"Why, that's very true," returned the other; "but we must not let him know too much till we can judge what sort of chap he is. Keep him dark, and I don't know that there's much to be afraid of."

"Afraid of!" said another. "Why he is but a stripling, and if I thought there was any danger from him, I'd ——"

"Hush," whispered Mark Harrowby; "he's looking towards us, as if he thought we were talking about him. Seat yourselves at the table, and over a cup of liquor, we can speak of things that won't open his eyes too much."

The men obeyed this suggestion, and one of them, addressing Gilbert, asked him how he liked the long ride he had had.

"I liked it well enough," he replied; "but there were two or three little adventures that, I must confess, I would rather had been avoided."

"Ha! ha! ha!" shouted Mark. "The fact is, I thought I knew two or three persons that we met on the road, and it led to some awkward mistakes. In one instance I was charged with being a highwayman, and, if our horses had not been good ones, I don't know that you would have seen us here to-night."

"And was this youngster with you," demanded one of the men, "when you went up to the people you speak of ?"

"No," replied Harrowby ; "I left him a little distance off ; but, when I scampered away, he followed, and we didn't slacken our pace till we had ridden a good ten miles."

"What did you think of it, young sir ?" asked one of the fellows.

"Why, it so happens that I like a smart pace as well as anybody," answered Gilbert, "so it proved very good sport to me ; but, it must be confessed, I felt rather surprised how any one could have taken your friend for a highwayman."

"It was strange, indeed," exclaimed the man ; "but the truth is, a great many robberies have been committed of late, and people are apt to take everybody they meet on the road for highwaymen. I have had the same cry raised against myself ; and, on one occasion, was taken hold of, and taken off to prison."

"And of course your innocence was proved ?"

"I didn't give twelve men a chance of saying to the contrary," replied the man, "for at the first opportunity I gave 'em leg bail."

"You escaped from jail ?"

"Yes ; I broke away a couple of iron stancheons that barred my window, and, with the assistance of the bed-clothes, let myself down about five-and-twenty feet to the ground."

"But, by running away," said Gilbert, "you gave room for your enemies to believe you were guilty."

"I don't care what they think," he replied, "for I know a man's better on the outside than the inside of a prison. How could I tell what enemies I might have to swear against me ; and, if once the jury had pronounced me guilty, there would have been very little chance of escaping the gallows."

"When you know more of the world, young man," said Mark Harrowby, "you will not be much inclined to trust to the good nature of people. Juries may be wrong as well as other folks, and more instances than one have happened of innocent people being sent out of the world before their time."

"Ah !" cried Deborah, "you may go no farther for one instance than poor Tom Bellingham, who ——"

"Silence, beldame !" roared one of the fellows. "Do you think we want one of your long-winded stories to amuse this youngster ? Tom Bellingham was an old sweetheart of yours ; and, if the truth must be told, he met with no more than his deserts."

"To your bed, Deborah," exclaimed Harrowby ; "go to your kennel, slut, and let us see nothing more of you till the morning. We mean to keep up a roistering night, and women are not wanted here, to join in with their croaking."

The woman went grumbling from the room, and, every cup being filled, the company drank long life and success to their companion, Mark Harrowby.

"Thank you, my friends, thank you," exclaimed Mark, as soon as their boisterous applause was finished. "We have managed to live together in harmony, and destruction fall upon the man that first attempts to disturb it. This youngster will, I have no doubt, fall in with our ways ; and, I dare say, the more he sees of them, the better he'll like 'em. Here's the health of our new companion, Gilbert Copley."

"Gilbert Copley," pronounced every voice ; and, on their cups being drained to the very bottom, a repetition of the boisterous applause took place.

"Gentlemen," exclaimed Gilbert, whose head began to feel the effect of the strong potations he had been indulging in, "this kind reception is so un-expected, that I am unable to express my thanks. I have sought shelter among you, and never shall any act of mine give cause for any one here to re-gret my appearance here."

"Bravo—bravo!" shouted the company, and half a dozen hands [were held out to him in friendship.

"I thought there would be no mistake among us," exclaimed Mark Har-rowby, "for the youngster was recommended to our protection by Hugh Darnton, and he's not a fellow that would send any one among us that was not of the right sort."

"Is Hugh Darnton likely to pay us a visit?" asked one of the men.

"Ay, and that may be soon, too," answered Harrowby; "he's going to *borrow* a little money of a friend of his, and, when his pockets are comfortably lined, we shall have him among us again. He's a fellow after our own heart, and it's through his good advice that our jocund friend yonder left a life of slavery to follow one of freedom and jollity."

"And pray what is the life I am to lead?" inquired Gilbert Copley.

"Ah, you will know all about it in good time," replied Harrowby. "At present we have not quite settled what will be best for you; and, indeed, there's no hurry about it, for Sir Lionel may take it into his head to inquire after you; and it's only by remaining close here that you'll have a chance of escaping him."

"Perhaps I have done wrong in leaving him," exclaimed our hero.

"Psha! are you going to grow melancholy over your cups?" returned Mark Harrowby. "Drink deeper, my man of mettle; the stuff you've been swallowing is good for the doldrums, when you take enough of it, and, as for ourselves, we don't mean to part company for at least a couple of hours to come."

Gilbert was at all times easily persuaded, and on the present occasion he was not inclined to draw upon himself the ridicule of his companions. He, therefore, partook more freely of the liquor than he ought to have done, and at length, yielding to its powerful influence, he sank, completely stupified, with his head upon the table. A loud laugh followed this, and, in a state of utter unconsciousness, he was carried by some of the men to his bed.

CHAPTER VII.

THE COLLEGIANS.—THE MANIAC.—THE RETURN.

LEAVING Gilbert Copley to his sleep, we must now beg the reader to accompany us to Cambridge, where Sir Lionel's only son, Vivian, and his friend, Henry Markham, were preparing to set out for Dacre Hall, where the latter had been invited to spend the vacation with his fellow-collegian. It was a cold, sharp winter's morning when they left the university, and, with buoyant spirits, the two young men rode onwards, exulting in the liberty which they now enjoyed. Various was the conversation that passed between them, for both of them were exhilarated by the brightest anticipations, and Henry Markham was in a transport of joy at the prospect of being introduced to the two Miss Dacres, of whom he had so often heard Vivian speak.

"I have already pictured them in my mind's eye," he exclaimed, "and can believe them to be possessed of beauty, amiability, and every virtue that can adorn woman; nay, more, I have almost made up my mind to fall despe-rately in love with one of them, if it were only for the sake of calling you brother-in-law."

"But what if the girls' hearts are already engaged?" asked Vivian, laughingly.

" Why, then I must try to get rid of my rival in the best way I can," answered the other. "Some people would say pick up a quarrel, challenge your man, and shoot him; but I have a suspicion that the days of romance are gone by, and that ladies' love is not to be purchased, as it used to be, at the price of blood. I must, therefore, find some other way to send the gentleman to the right about, and you shall be my chief adviser upon the subject.''

" And what," asked Vivian, "if neither of the girls should happen to favour your views?"

"Why, then, I must lay a vigorous siege to the heart of one of them," replied his friend.

"But you have not yet seen either of them," exclaimed the other; "and it is not yet by any means certain that they will come up to your expectations."

"Have I not heard you describe them?" asked Henry Markham; "and can I not take the word of a friend, though he may have been a little partial in describing those who are so dear to him? But you were speaking of a rival just now; pray is there anything to fear from a certain Gilbert Copley that I have sometimes heard you speak of?"

"I believe not," answered Vivian, "for though twelve months have elapsed since he mysteriously disappeared, we have never heard anything of him. Indeed, I have sometimes heard my father say that my cousin must have perished soon after he left home."

"Did he go away of his own free will?"

"There is every reason to believe he did," answered Vivian, "for he was alone when he quitted the house where he had been living, and he was not known to have associated with any one that was likely to give him bad counsel. Some people, indeed, said that he had been seen occasionally with a man named Hugh Darnton, but the fellow's character was so notoriously bad that I can scarcely give credit to the rumour."

" And what sort of a disposition was this Gilbert Copley?" asked the other.

"Somewhat stubborn and headstrong," replied Vivian; "in fact, one of those sort of fellows that will never be deterred from a course that he has taken, whether it be right or wrong. His disposition is daring in the extreme, yet were there points in his character which obtained for him the regard of my father."

"But if I have understood you rightly," observed the other, "he was not a great favourite with every part of your family?"

"My mother had a prejudice against him," replied Vivian, "for which I could never account. Gilbert was aware of it, and for some time before he left never paid his visits to our house. He grew moody and melancholy, I have heard, and it's likely enough the circumstances may have had the effect of urging him to take his unexpected departure. My father, I really believe, was sorry for the wilfulness that had induced him to desert his friends, and had just before made arrangements for placing him in a mercantile house, where it is likely he would have attained a very honourable eminence."

"Perhaps the course of life was not one that he could approve of?" said Markham.

"I have no doubt it was mortifying to his proud spirit," replied Vivian; " but what was to be done with him, when he had neither fortune nor expectancies? A good start was all he had a right to look for from my father, and I am afraid, if he still lives, he will yet repent the folly that induced him to throw away his only chance."

"And yet, on the other hand," said Henry Markham, "if he is a lad of spirit he may make his way through the world much better than if he had friends to depend on. A bad beginning sometimes makes a good ending, and

who knows but that may eventually be the case with your cousin, Gilbert Copley?"

They now rode on for some distance in silence, which, indeed, was not broken till they arrived at a roadside hotel, where they stopped to rest their horses and partake of refreshments. Their lunch, however, was scarcely finished, when a well-dressed young man intruded himself into the room, the wildness and singularity of whose manner at once convinced the two friends that he must be insane, and Vivian rose to ring the bell for the landlord to expel the intruder from their presence. He, however, seemed to guess his purpose, and rushing forward, he seized the young man in his arms, and carried him forcibly back to his seat.

"Ha! ha!" he exclaimed, wildly, "I have found you at last, have I? You are the conspirators that would slay me; you would have my blood— you would murder me!"

"Believe me, my good sir," returned Henry Markham, "we are your friends, and would ——"

"Friends!" he exclaimed; "'tis false; I never had but one, and she they slew."

"Will you be kind enough to tell us, sir, where you live?" asked Vivian. "We see you are agitated, and would see you home."

"I have no home," he replied; "I wander the wide world—sleep beneath the hedges—feed upon the berry, and drink from the green, slimy ditch. I took you for conspirators, yet you would fain make me believe you are friends."

"You seem to have walked far, sir," exclaimed Vivian; "shall we call for refreshments?"

"No," he replied, abruptly; "you are frightened because I've found you out; you want to call for assistance, but I warn you not to stir from your seat, for I am armed, and will defend myself to the last."

No. 4

With that he flourished a stick as if it had been a sword, and once or twice brought his weapon so near to the heads of Vivian and his friend, that they began to think it necessary to make a simultaneous rush upon the maniac, in order to disarm him. They were, however, unwilling to exert any violence towards the unfortunate man, so long as it could be avoided, and presently afterwards the madman ceased his frantic flourishes, and looking earnestly at Vivian, exclaimed :—

"Whence comes that blood that's upon your hand—is it *her* blood? Speak—are you the murderer of all that I held dearest in the world?"

"By Heaven, I am not!"

"That word has saved you," he said, dropping the stick, which had been raised to inflict a desperate blow. "I took you for the villains I am in search of, but if you are not guilty of bloodshed, you may go. Flee from me, for my brain burns like molten lead. Away! away! Leave me, or my heavy wrath may fall upon and consume ye!"

Luckily for the two travellers, the door was at this moment thrown open, and a couple of men rushed into the room, one of whom seized the madman and forced him into a seat

"For Heaven's sake, sir, be pacified," said the man; "we have had a long race after you; but never mind, we have found you safe and sound, which is better luck than I expected."

"And who is it that has dared lay his hand upon me?" demanded the madman.

"Your father's old and faithful servant," replied the man; "don't you recollect me, sir?"

"Ay, for a villain."

"Heaven help his wits!" exclaimed the man; "he didn't call me such hard names before this terrible malady came on. Then I was his favourite, and a good reason was there for it, for I brought him up in his father's house, from a child." Then, turning towards the two friends, he said, "Has he been very violent to you, gentlemen?"

"Why, it must be confessed he was rather so," replied Vivian. "We, however, perceived the malady with which he is afflicted, and tried to soothe him in the best manner we could."

"Has he been long in this state?" asked Markham.

"Yes, sir, some time," replied the man; "his wife, to whom he had not long been married, was murdered before his eyes by some pirates, as they were returning home from abroad."

"What is his name?" whispered Vivian.

"He is the son of Mr. Blundell, the rich nabob," answered the man. "Poor young gentleman, he's heir to a princely fortune, but I'm afraid he'll never be able to enjoy it. Come, sir," he added to his young master, "your father is dreadfully alarmed at your remaining away from him,—you'll return with us. won't you now, to relieve his mind?"

"Psha! talk to the winds, fellow," exclaimed the maniac; "I am my own master—the world is my home, and I am free to wander where I choose."

"I rather think," observed Markham, "from the state of his mind at present, you will do little good by trying to persuade him to return home. At this house you will be able to obtain a carriage, and I should advise you to get him back as soon as possible."

"But he won't get into a carriage without being forced there," said the man, "and I must confess I shouldn't like to hurt the poor young gentleman, for he was always a special favourite of mine."

"Yet where a little violence is necessary," returned Markham, "it would be wrong to let your good-natured feelings interfere with your duty.

He seems now to have sunk into a sort of lethargy from over exertion, and the task, I rather think, will not be so difficult as you imagine."

"We'll try it at any rate," said the man; and beckoning to his companion, he, in a whisper, desired him to hire a carriage for the conveyance of his master. The person returned almost directly, and in the course of ten minutes the vehicle was announced as being in readiness.

"Now, sir," exclaimed the servant to his master, "if you'll please to go with us, we'll take you home to your father. The poor old gentleman is in terrible trouble about your leaving him, and I'm sure you wouldn't let him fret on your account."

These words seemed to have the effect of soothing him, and rising from his seat, he permitted them to conduct him from the room. Upon seeing the carriage, however, he again grew violent, and had nearly succeeded in breaking away from his attendants, who, finding that no other alternative remained, forced him into the vehicle, and seating themselves one on each side of him, they were driven from the inn towards the residence of Mr. Blundell.

Somewhat disconcerted by the adventure, Vivian and Henry Markham resumed their journey. They felt deeply interested in the fate of the young man whose afflictions had overturned his reason, and as they rode onwards they could converse upon no other subject than the one which engrossed all their thoughts.

At length, however, they reached the hospitable mansion of Sir Lionel Dacre, and the reception they there met with soon drove from their minds all recollection of the adventure that had befallen them on their journey.

CHAPTER VIII.

A BOLD DEMAND.—THE CONFERENCE.—THE CAPTURE.

A FEW mornings after the return of Vivian to his home, he received a message from his father, desiring to see him in his study without delay. This the more surprised him, as he had parted from Sir Lionel only a very short time before, and hastening to the place he found the baronet a good deal agitated, whilst before him stood a coarse-looking fellow, whose careless expression of countenance seemed to denote the most complete indifference to the anger he had given rise to.

"You sent for me, I believe, sir?" exclaimed Vivian, and he turned his hasty glance from the stranger to his father.

"I did," answered Sir Lionel, "for this person has brought me a note that I shall require your advice upon. The writer of it is a scoundrel whom I have too often served, and he would now extort more by threats of future vengeance."

"Who is the writer?" asked Vivian.

"Hugh Darnton."

"And he demands money of you?"

"He does," replied Sir Lionel; "I lent him fifty pounds some months ago, and now he demands another fifty, threatening me with his future wrath in the event of my refusing it."

"I can't wait here all day," exclaimed the messenger, insolently; "I've been sent here on an errand, and want my answer."

"Then you may take him back my most decided refusal," said Sir Lionel. "I have been too often imposed upon by the scoundrel, and here, in the presence of my son, I declare that no more will I assist a profligate villain,"

" And that's what I'm to tell Hugh Darnton ?" said the fellow.

" It is," replied the baronet ; " and you may further add that should his place of abode ever come to my knowledge, I will take care that he meets with his just deserts."

" Oh," replied the other, " he don't want to make any secret of his whereabouts ; you'll be able to find him at any time at ——"

" I have no wish to hear where he is," interrupted the baronet. " You have heard my answer, and have now only to return to him and say that I will neither give nor lend him another shilling."

" Are you quite sure of that ?" exclaimed the messenger, with a cunning leer.

" It is my determination."

" And you won't give me the money he has written to you for ?"

" This insolence is not to be endured !" exclaimed Vivian, angrily. " Hence, fellow, and deliver the message you have been charged with."

" I don't want to be told by you, sir, what I'm to do," retorted the fellow ; " I've been sent on an errand to your father, and he ought to be the best judge whether it wouldn't be wiser for him to think a second time before he sends me away."

" Will you leave the house, sirrah ?" exclaimed Sir Lionel, fiercely.

" When I've done all I was told to do," replied the man, with the greatest coolness. " Darnton said he shouldn't wonder if you rode rusty about it, and in that case he bade me give you this other note, which might perhaps bring you to your senses. Will you read it, Sir Lionel ?" he added, handing him another letter.

" Villain !" exclaimed Vivian, " leave the house, or I'll thrust you forth like a dog as you are."

" Be calm, Vivian," said the baronet, with an emotion that he could not conceal. " It must be my part to chastise the fellow's insolence ; but I have first a few questions to ask, and you may therefore leave the room for the present. Go into the next room and be ready if I should require your presence."

Vivian reluctantly obeyed this command, and when he had disappeared, Sir Lionel, fixing his eyes sternly upon the messenger, inquired if he knew the subject of the second letter.

" Oh, yes," replied the other ; " Hugh Darnton don't keep many of his secrets from me."

" But do you know all the circumstances of which the writer of that letter speaks ?"

" Ay, to be sure I do," he replied ; " I know all about it, so you needn't be afraid of speaking out boldly before me."

" And will you keep your knowledge a secret ?"

" That will depend upon the answer you send back to Hugh Darnton," replied the fellow ; " I can keep a secret as well as anybody when it's proper to do so, but I'm not bound to keep my mouth shut when people don't behave as they ought. You know what's wanted, and all I've got to do is to perform my errand."

" I would first know how far you are in this secret," returned Sir Lionel.

" And that's just exactly what I don't mean to tell you," replied the man, doggedly. " I've given my word to do nothing more than deliver my message, and having done so, I've only got to wait your answer to it."

" Your insolence, scoundrel, almost tempts me to give you into custody."

" That you dare not do."

" Dare not ?"

"No," replied the fellow; "because I should talk too much if you did, and, in that case, I should like to know who would come worst off."

"Will a sum of money induce you to tell me what you know?" demanded Sir Lionel, who began to see that threats would avail him nothing.

"A thousand pounds wouldn't buy me," replied the other; "for the truth is, I never want anything except from hand to mouth; and if I had as much money as you have, I should not know what to do with it. So, now, having told you my mind freely, I ask once more whether you mean to send Hugh Darnton the fifty pounds he's asked for?"

"There is one thing mentioned in this note that I feel deeply interested in," exclaimed Sir Lionel. "Your friend alludes to a young man named Gilbert Copley, who disappeared from this neighbourhood about twelve months ago, and I would know whether you can give me any information respecting him?"

"You need hardly ask me that question," said the man, "for I have already told you that I know everything that's mentioned in the letter."

"Then you can relieve my mind by telling me where the young fellow is to be found?"

"To be sure I can," answered the fellow; "but promises are not to be broken, so I shall not say anything about it till I know whether Darnton is willing that you should hear of the youngster."

"Darnton must beware what he does," exclaimed Sir Lionel, "or I may be driven to seek other means that will compel him to make the disclosure."

"Perhaps you'll think twice, though, before you do anything of that kind," returned the man, with a malicious sneer. "Darnton has been very quiet so far, but he may be driven to do something you would not like if matters should begin to run cross between you. But I can't be waiting all the day with you, so tell me at once whether you mean to do what my friend has asked?"

"You must call again," replied Sir Lionel; "at present I have not made up my mind what I shall do in the matter."

"That's as much as to say you will not lend him the fifty pounds. I suppose I may tell him so?"

"You have heard me," exclaimed the baronet; "I must think of the matter, but to-morrow you may call for your answer."

"Ay," returned the other, "and when I come to-morrow you'll have an officer or two in readiness to take me into custody. It won't do, Sir Lionel, for I'm a plain, straight-forward fellow in my way, and this business must be settled now or never."

"You must give me time for consideration."

"Not another moment," replied the man; "I've been kept here too long already, and I shall now return to Hugh Darnton, and tell him that you are determined not to let him have the money he would borrow. It's a pity, too, for fifty pounds is not much in comparison with the mischief a few words may do you. So I wish you a good morning, Sir Lionel, and if anything unpleasant comes of this, you must blame yourself for it—that's all I know about the matter."

"Sit down again for a moment," exclaimed Sir Lionel, as he saw the man was preparing to leave the room. "Hugh Darnton knows my weak side, and has not failed to take advantage of it. Already is he deeply in my debt, yet would he extort more money from me by threats of secret disclosures."

"I'm sure he wouldn't threaten you for the world," replied the other; "and as for the money you make such a fuss about, he don't ask it as a gift, but will return it to you, with interest, whenever it is in his power to do so."

" And he knows he will never have the means of repaying it," answered the baronet; "however, I can see no alternative just at present, and the money he demands shall be sent to him."

" By my hands ?"

" Yes.   Here is a note to the amount he requires."

" A note won't do," replied the fellow; "it's evidence against us, if you should afterwards turn round to play us false. I must have gold, for it ain't so easily sworn to."

" Even as you please," exclaimed Sir Lionel, opening his desk, and taking out the required sum, which he handed over to the messenger. " There is the money, and you may tell Darnton from me that it is the last he will be able to extort from me."

" I tell you he don't extort it," replied the other, as he composedly deposited the gold in his pocket. " Hugh Darnton has a conscience as well as his betters, and that there should be no mistake about it, he wrote a memorandum on this piece of paper, acknowledging the loan, and promising to return it as soon as he can. There it is, Sir Lionel, and now, as our business is comfortably settled, there's no occasion for me to remain here any longer. So I wish you a very good morning, and perhaps when Hugh Darnton wants to ask a favour again he'll come here himself about it."

The fellow, bowing with mock humility, left the room, and before Sir Lionel could well recover from the agitation into which he had been thrown, Vivian once more presented himself before him.

" The scoundrel is gone, I see, sir," he exclaimed; " and I only wish you had given me a hint to kick him from the door without ceremony. My blood boiled at the coolness of the villain, and I can only wonder how you endured such insolence from a low-bred ruffian like him."

" I almost wish," said the baronet, " that I had not interrupted him when he was going to tell me where Hugh Darnton is to be found."

" That cannot matter much," returned Vivian, " for I have no doubt he would have given you a false direction. The fellow seems to be playing at hide-and-seek, and it is scarcely likely he would let you know where he is to be found. It is strange, too, that a man who once bore a tolerable character, should turn out to be such a hardened villain, without any apparent cause."

" I believe idleness and bad company have been the cause of his ruin," answered the baronet. " For the last three or four years he has been getting worse and worse, and I was not sorry when he at length threw up the farm and left the neighbourhood. He *borrowed*, as he calls it, money of me then, and taking with him one of his daughters, he left his wife and the other children to starve or depend on the parish for a miserable existence."

" That, I suppose, may account for his not having paid you a personal visit," observed Vivian. " However, be that as it may, I'm afraid he is too incorrigible a villain to amend his bad ways, and now that he has began to find that he can extort money, he will soon spend what you have sent, and before long you will receive another message from him demanding a further sum of money."

" I am afraid, Vivian," exclaimed his father, " that my conduct must give rise to suspicions in your mind that I am ashamed to reveal. There is, indeed, a secret that I would gladly confide to you, but at present you must be content to remain in darkness upon the subject. I may, however, observe that the chief source of my unhappiness has been occasioned through taking my nephew, Gilbert Copley, under my protection."

" He has indeed proved ungrateful," replied Vivian; " but I am at a loss to conceive why you should be unhappy, merely because he thought proper to withdraw himself from the kindness of one who had proved himself a generous benefactor."

"The evil, my dear boy, lies deeper than you imagine," answered Sir Lionel. "It is true I felt greatly mortified at his leaving us in the way he did; but my anger has passed away, and I would make search for him, were it not that it would occasion unpleasant recriminations that it is better to avoid."

"Recriminations, sir!" cried the young man; "and from whom, I pray?"

"Your mother."

"Indeed! My mother, I am aware, never held Gilbert Copley in much esteem; but I was never conscious that he had been the occasion of any unhappiness between you."

"Gilbert has been a stumbling-block in my way," replied Sir Lionel, "and yet he is in no way to be blamed for it. Your mother affects to believe that he is not my nephew, and though absolute quarrels have not resulted from it, there has been a coldness in her manner towards me that showed she believed there was a secret that I had not thought proper to acquaint her with."

"Then who," demanded Vivian, "does my mother take Gilbert Copley to be if he is not my cousin?"

Sir Lionel paused a moment to reflect, and was about to reply, when the door opened, and Henry Markham entered the room.

"So you have been robbed, Sir Lionel!" he exclaimed; "but the villain has not been suffered to escape with impunity, for a couple of your men have just seized him, and he is now below waiting your leisure to enter upon his examination."

"Of whom do you speak?" demanded Sir Lionel Dacre, anxiously.

"I don't know the rascal's name," replied Markham; "but it appears that he was seen a little while ago sneaking away from the house, and as a couple of your servants suspected that he had been committing a robbery, they followed in pursuit."

"And have taken the man?"

"Oh, yes, they have him safe enough," replied Markham; "for though he run with all the speed he could, his pursuers were not to be defeated in their object, and at last they came up with him in the copse, where he had thrown himself behind a fallen tree for concealment."

"And have they any reason for believing that he has been guilty of a robbery?" demanded the baronet.

"Plenty," replied Henry Markham; "for, on searching his pockets, no less a sum than fifty pounds was found in his possession."

"Which may be his own," observed Sir Lionel, trying to conceal his chagrin.

"I must beg leave to differ from that opinion," said Markham, "for he is a miserable-looking object, and quite an unlikely fellow to be the honest possessor of so large a sum of money."

"Has he attempted to offer any explanation?" asked the baronet, anxiously.

"No," answered Markham; "the rascal takes it very coolly, and says it will be all right as soon as you see him."

"My servants have been over officious in this affair, I believe," observed Sir Lionel; "for the truth is the man has not been guilty of a robbery. Judging from the sum that was found upon him, I have no doubt it is a man to whom I just now entrusted fifty pounds to convey to a person who lives at some distance off."

"Humph! then it seems there has been a great deal of fuss without any cause."

"My servants have acted rashly," observed Sir Lionel, "and the man has reason to complain of the violence that has been offered him. You had better see him, Vivian," he added to his son. "Go down and see that he is instantly set at liberty, and bid him speed on his errand with all despatch, or the person who is waiting to receive the money will grow impatient."

"And shall I give him anything as a recompense for the inconvenience he has been put to?" inquired the young man.

"You may offer him anything you please," replied Sir Lionel; "but I rather think he will not accept of it. I just now proposed to reward him for the trouble he had been put to in coming here, but, in spite of his seeming poverty, he refused to accept of anything."

Vivian left the room, and Henry Markham, addressing himself to h e baronet, said,—

"You will excuse me, Sir Lionel, I hope, but would it not have been better for you to have seen this man yourself? He seemed to wish to be brought into your presence, and I fancy he has something that he would like to communicate."

"My son will do quite as well," replied Sir Lionel. "The man was here not half an hour ago, and had it not been for the interference of my servants, the errand he was sent upon would have been executed with the requisite speed."

"And yet the fellows are not to be blamed either," said Henry Markham, "for it certainly looked suspicious when they saw a stranger creeping from your house with marks of guilt upon his countenance. Then his flight on being perceived would naturally serve to increase their doubts, and the money that was found upon him fully justified them in bringing him back till an inquiry could be made."

"It is thus that officious persons often cause a great deal of unnecessary trouble," observed Sir Lionel. "However, I am not inclined to throw much blame upon my servants, who, I dare say, were prompted by their zeal in my behalf. The man they captured, too, seems to have endured his rough usage with a great deal of forbearance, and if money will make him any compensation, Vivian will know how to satisfy him."

"The fellow has refused to accept anything," exclaimed Vivian, who entered the room while his father was speaking. "I told him you were angry at his having been captured by your servants, and the rascal grinned, as much as to say you ought to be."

"Did he explain to the men," asked the baronet, "how he came possessed of so much money?"

"No," replied Vivian; "he disdained to make them any reply; and when I entered the room he said that to no one but yourself would he speak upon the subject."

"And is he gone?"

"Oh, yes," replied Vivian; "but as he was leaving, he whispered that he might pay you another visit soon, and it would be then time enough to recompense him for having been seized upon like a thief. But you were going to tell me something just now, and, with your permission, we'll retire to another room."

"The conversation that was broken off must be resumed on a future occasion," answered Sir Lionel. "At present I would be alone, and remember, it is my most earnest wish that you try to forget what passed between us just now. Another time you shall know more."

Vivian and his friend left the room, the former wondering in his own mind what the secret could possibly refer to.

CHAPTER IX.

THE RAVEN'S NEST.—A ROBBERY.—GLOOMY PROSPECTS.

WE must now return to Gilbert Copley, who did not rise till a late hour on the morning after his carouse, and finding that all had left the place except Deborah, he sat himself down to breakfast, and after some little time had passed away in silence, he inquired of the female where his host was.

"Gone out," she replied abruptly.

"And his friends?"

"Are with him."

"When do you expect them to return?"

"Can't say," she replied; "I never ask questions that don't concern me."

This was plain enough to convince Gilbert that he had little to expect from his companion, and for some minutes he sat in deep thought, wondering within himself how it would be possible for him to prevail on her to be more communicative. At last, in the most persuasive accents he could assume, he inquired of her if she could tell him how long he was likely to remain in his present place of concealment.

"Mark never tells me more than he can help," replied the woman; "but I suppose you'll stop with us till we have heard from Hugh Darnton, who seems to have the principal hand in this affair?"

"He is to follow us here as soon as possible," returned our hero; "but it may be some little time before he's able to get rid of his farm."

"It won't give him much trouble to do that," replied Deborah; "for he's a determined chap, when once he makes up his mind, and as he expects to make something of you, we shall see him here sooner than you expect."

"You know, then, what his views are respecting me?"

"I tell you I never know anything," she replied. "It's dangerous to open

No. 5

one's mouth here, so don't ask me so many questions, for I shall not answer them."

"At any rate," said Gilbert, "you can have no objection to tell me if you have been acquainted with Darnton any length of time?"

"I've known him long enough to make him afraid of me," replied Deborah. "We have had one quarrel, and it's not likely he'll ever seek another, for I could make his cheek grow pale by only whispering two or three little words in his ear."

"Has he committed crime?"

"You'll know all about that quite soon enough," replied the woman; "but let me advise you, young man, not to be too inquisitive while you remain among us."

"Which will not be very long, I believe," exclaimed Gilbert, "for though I have not been here many hours, I already begin to feel heartily tired of the sort of life you lead here."

"At any rate," replied Deborah, "you'll stay here as long as Mark Harrowby thinks proper."

"How!—am I then a prisoner?"

"Why, I don't know that you're exactly what may be called a prisoner," answered the woman; "but Mark says that there would be danger in your going out just yet, and so he's made up his mind that you shall not leave the Raven's Nest till the folks have done looking after you."

"I shall consider myself the best judge about that," said Gilbert Copley; "and he will find, that though I have placed myself under his care for a little while, I have not yet made him the master of my liberty. Your Raven's Nest, as you call it, is not built so high up but I may be able to take a flight from it whenever I grow weary of my quarters."

"Ah!" exclaimed Deborah, "you think, because there's no one but a woman left to guard you, it will be easy to get away whenever you please. But, hark you, young gentleman, I have a brace of loaded pistols within reach, and I can use them, too, if I should happen to see occasion for it."

"Would you commit murder," cried Gilbert, "and that, too, upon one who only seeks to obtain the liberty which no one has a right to deprive him of?"

"I've nothing to do with the right or the wrong of the business," answered the woman, "for I have sworn to obey the commands of Mark Harrowby, and I'll not break my oath to please any one."

"And in that case, I may feel inclined to risk my life, rather than be forced to stay here after I have determined to take my departure," exclaimed our hero. "That I have been deceived is apparent, and it is now high time that something should be done to retrieve the false step I have been foolish enough to take."

"You've heard me, young sir," exclaimed the woman, furiously, "and you may yet have to find out that I've a bit of the devil in me when my blood's put up. Mark Harrowby has given me this duty to perform, and, after being friends together so long, he shall not have it in his power to say that I neglected to do his bidding. Besides, he's your friend, so long as you don't try to make him otherwise, and as for your liberty, there's no fear of your losing it, so long as you continue to behave yourself in a quiet, orderly manner."

"Hugh Darnton, as well as myself, has been deceived in him and ——"

"Psha!" interrupted the woman, "Hugh Darnton and he are as thick as thieves; they row together in the same boat, and what one does the other knows of."

"You would make me believe, then, that Darnton ——"

"Is a villain," again interrupted Deborah. "The truth is, young man, I know him a little better than you seem to do, and for all his smooth tongue, I could tell you something of him that would make your blood run cold."

"Humph!" ejaculated Gilbert, "you could tell me, I suppose, that he has killed a few hares and partridges in the course of his life?"

"He has killed something more than hares and partridges," answered Deborah.

"Woman!" exclaimed our hero, "you would fain make me believe that he has raised his hand against the life of a fellow-creature!"

"Ask me no further questions," she exclaimed, "for I have already said a great deal more than I ought. It's treason to open one's mouth too wide in this place, so don't tell Mark Harrowby what we've been talking about, or I shall get in the black books with him, and then perhaps you may make an enemy of one who never forgets an injury."

"You threaten me, woman!"

"And it's well for you that I do so," she replied; "for now you know what to expect. Take my advice, young fellow, and though matters seem to run a little cross at present, everything will go smooth enough by-and-bye."

She left the room with these words, taking care, however, to fasten the door after her, and Gilbert Copley removing his seat nearer to the window, began to reflect upon the dangerous situation into which he had brought himself. Notwithstanding the threat that had been held out, he determined upon attempting to escape at the first opportunity that presented itself, and this he believed could not be very difficult, as the money which had been given him by Hugh Darnton would be amply sufficient to provide the means for returning to the house he had been imprudent enough to leave; but when he felt in his pocket for the purse, he found it was no longer there, and upon thoroughly searching his clothes, he became but too well convinced that foul play had been practiced upon him. His thoughts then naturally recurred to Mark Harrowby, and the rough associates with whom he had spent the preceding evening; but to have accused any of them, without sufficient proof, would have been madness, and he therefore determined to speak to Mark upon the subject, and inquire of him what course he should adopt to obtain the restoration of his money.

Whilst his mind was still occupied in these reflections, a loud knocking was heard at the outer door, which was at length opened by Deborah, but not before she had thoroughly ascertained who it was that demanded admittance. The voice of Mark Harrowby was then to be distinguished, and in a few minutes afterwards he entered the room.

"So, young fellow," he exclaimed, "Deborah tells me you have grown tired of your quarters already, and that you are wanting to show us a clean pair of heels."

"And why should I run away," demanded Gilbert, "when at any time I have a right to leave the house with as much freedom as I entered it? Besides, even if such a thought had come across me, I have been deprived of the means of travelling through a country to which I am an entire stranger."

"What mean you?" asked Mark Harrowby, with well affected surprise.

"Simply that the money given me by Hugh Darnton has been taken from me."

"Pshaw!" exclaimed the other; "why, you don't think you have entered a den of thieves?"

"I only know," answered Gilbert, "that the money was safe in my pocket yesterday, and to-day not a farthing of it remains."

"Why, then, I suppose you lost it coming along," returned Harrowby. "We rode at a pretty smart pace, as you may remember, and money is such a slippery article that it often gets out of our pockets without our being able to tell how. But let that be as it may, you surely can't suppose that you have lost it here where we are all friends together?'

"I accuse no one," replied Gilbert Copley; "but as I wish to return home, I must borrow enough of you to pay the expenses of my journey."

"What! Have you grown homesick already?"

"It is not home that I am anxious to see" replied the young man; "but the truth is, the life I am likely to lead here is not such as I expected."

"And pray what did you expect?" demanded Harrowby. "Your *friend*, Hugh Darnton, is one of our sort, and you have known him long, enough to give you a pretty good notion of what sort of fellow he is."

"I have known him only as a wild reckless man," answered Gilbert; "but, from what you have said, I begin to fear my opinion of him was too favourable."

"What, because I said he was one of our sort?"

"You have not yet condescended to tell me what pursuit you follow," returned the other.

"Patience, my good fellow, and you shall know all in good time," exclaimed Mark Harrowby. "We have not been acquainted with each other very long, but if it should appear that you are worthy of our confidence, you shall see reason to be glad that you left a dull home to become one of us."

"And am I to see no companions," asked Gilbert, "but such as were here last night?"

"What better fellows can you wish to see?" demanded the other.

"I expected," replied our hero, "to have met with men who were not inferior to myself."

"Well, then, you have not been disappointed," exclaimed Mark Harrowby. "They are all of them a good sort, and one of them in particular was brought up to be a fine gentlemen."

"You mean the one that was called Elliot?"

"Ay, that's the man," replied the other; "Dick Elliot will make a capital companion for you, and when you've known him a little while, we shall hear no more about your finding the place dull. They tell me he can talk Latin and Greek like a parson, but as I don't understand any lingo but my own, I'm obliged to take all that upon hearsay. You, however, will soon find it out, and then you and Dick will be the best friends in the world."

"Perhaps not," exclaimed Gilbert, "for he let out a few things last night that, in my opinion, would have been much better kept to himself."

"Tush, man—you are too particular by half," returned Harrowby. "The fact is, Dick's been a little wildish in his time, and has run through a mint of money, so that at last his friends turned their backs upon him. He then came to live with me, as you are doing now, and as he is a lad of spirit, there's no doubt he'll be able to make his way in the world."

"May I inquire what profession I am likely to follow?" demanded Gilbert.

"You shall know all about that in good time," replied Mark Harrowby.

"And why not now?"

"Because the thing's not yet decided on," answered the other. "Hugh Darnton must be consulted first, and when we know what his opinion is, I'll take care that you hear all about it without delay."

"But it may be some time before Hugh Darnton is able to join us here."

"That I grant," answered Harrowby, "but you are not such a child as to grow impatient before you have been with us four-and-twenty hours. Make friends with Dick Elliot, and you'll soon hear from him that the Raven's Nest is not so bad a place to live in as you seem to imagine

Besides, I shall always be at hand, so that you'll have friends enough to keep you from falling into the dumps. As for the money that's been lost, you have no occasion to fret about it, for I'll be your banker whenever you have any need of cash, which will not be while you remain here."

"And is it true that I am not to leave the place?" demanded Gilbert.

"My dear fellow, don't let that trouble you," replied the other. "A little confinement will do you no harm, but if you were to leave this place, who knows but you might be seen by those who have been sent out in search of the fugitive. And let me tell you, young gentleman, your home would not be quite so comfortable, now that you have once played them a slippery trick. So just think of what I've been telling you, and amuse yourself with a little reflection between now and when we meet together again."

Mark Harrowby left the room as he uttered these words, and our hero fell into a train of thought, that proved to be anything but agreeable. Escape, however, seemed at present to be impracticable, and he therefore determined to make friends with Elliot, and after sounding him upon the subject, prevail upon him to give the assistance that might be required.

CHAPTER X.

A VISITOR.—FAMILY DISCLOSURES.—THE TWO FRIENDS.

In the family of Sir Lionel Dacre, affairs remained for three or four weeks pretty much as we last left them. Vivian frequently tried to engage his father in a conversation upon the subject that had been so abruptly broken off, but each time that he made the attempt, something or other occurred to disturb them, and he began to fear that Sir Lionel seemed less anxious to relieve his mind from the burthen than he had formerly been. At length, just as he had resolved to make one more effort, and was leaving the room for the purpose, his friend, Henry Markham, hastily approached him.

"Vivian," he exclaimed, "I have news for you, my boy; a visitor has just arrived, and who do you imagine I think it is?"

"Nay," replied the other, "that is more than I can guess. But I suppose it's some of our neighbours come to make a formal call."

"You are mistaken," exclaimed Markham, "for I have seen the livery servant, and I could almost swear that he is one of the fellows who followed the madman, that we met with on our journey hither."

"A most unlikely circumstance, truly," returned Vivian, "for it so happens, that we have no acquaintance with the man's master, and as our names were not mentioned, he cannot have called to thank us for any attentions we may have shown the unfortunate maniac. Besides, even if it should be so, the call would be merely one of ceremony."

While he was speaking, Sir Lionel entered the room, and addressing himself to the young men, said,—

"I bring news that I think will be gratifying to you both, though perhaps more particularly as to you, Vivian. A Mr. Blundell has just arrived here, to see Agnes Evered, who, it appears, is his niece, he being the brother of the late Captain Evered."

"Humph!" ejaculated Markham; "methinks he has taken a tolerable long time to make up his mind to pay his orphan niece a visit."

"Why, the truth is," replied Sir Lionel, "the old gentleman is not so open to blame as you seem to imagine. He has not very long since returned to England, and having heard of his brother's death, it is only very lately that he has been able to trace Agnes to this house. He, however, seems to be very much delighted at having discovered his niece, and ——"

"We have a chance of losing her," interrupted Vivian, "after she has become almost like one of our own family."

"I don't know that," replied Sir Lionel, "for her uncle may not feel disposed to remove her from those who offered her a home when she had need of protection. For aught we know, he may be a bachelor, or ——"

"Nay," exclaimed Henry Markham, "that is a question that both Vivian and I can set at rest, for we happen to know that he has a son, and perhaps half a dozen other children besides."

"And how know you that?"

"Because the son I speak of," answered Markham, "happens to be the unfortunate maniac you have heard us speak of, and who we encountered on our journey from the university."

"How do you know that Mr. Blundell and your mad friend are so nearly related?"

"I think there is no doubt of it," replied Markham, "since his servant, who I just now saw below stairs, is one of of the men who came in pursuit of the fugitive. But, hark! I hear the carriage moving, and as I suppose the visitor has taken his departure, I shall run down to hear what sort of a reception he gave his niece, and whether he is likely to afford her an asylum in his own house."

The departure of Markham seemed to be a relief to Sir Lionel Dacre, and bidding his son be seated, he, after some little hesitation, said,—

"I have many times wished for an opportunity to speak with you upon a subject that has been so often broken in upon. I remember telling you that your mother always expressed a doubt as to the real relationship that exists between Gilbert Copley and myself, and the uneasiness her suspicions have caused me, you may well imagine."

"And is she deaf to your assertions, that he is actually your nephew?" asked Vivian.

"So much so," replied his father, "that I now despair of ever removing the fatal impression. I have tried to reason her out of this unfortunate prejudice, but though on every other point we live in the utmost harmony, she is still obstinate in this one error."

"And I believe," said Vivian, "she has always regarded him with a feeling of dislike?"

"She has," replied Sir Lionel, and for that reason I have thought it prudent to let him live out of the house. He was placed with Simon Stripes, at whose cottage I used to visit him, and you are aware of the manner in which he left a house where I had taken care he should be in the enjoyment of every comfort suited to his situation in life."

"It must be confessed," exclaimed Vivian, "that I was not at all surprised when I heard of his abrupt departure from this neighbourhood. It is true, I was not very often in his society, but I have seen quite enough of him to convince me that he possesses a restless disposition which is fitted only for a career of constant activity."

"Which is one cause of her ladyship's antipathy towards him," answered the baronet. "I would have brought about a reconciliation between them had it been in my power to do so, but her dislike towards the youth increased every day, and at last I avoided mentioning his name, except when absolutely compelled to do so."

"May I be allowed to ask," said Vivian, "in what degree of relationship you stand towards him?"

"He is the illegitimate son of my brother," replied Sir Lionel. "You ever saw much of your uncle, for he died abroad when you were very young."

"Gilbert, then, was not born in England ?"

"He was not," answered the baronet. "My brother, I believe, was very fond of the boy, and when he felt that death was approaching, he left him to the care of Hugh Darnton, who had been a servant of his, with strict injunctions to bring him to England, and place him under my guardianship."

"And that," exclaimed the young man, "was, I suppose, the origin of your acquaintance with Darnton?"

"It was," replied Sir Lionel, "and most bitterly do I regret the hour that threw the scheming villain in my way."

"Hugh Darnton certainly appears to exercise a great deal of control over you," observed Vivian, "and I cannot help feeling some surprise at the insolence you seem to endure from him. For my own part, I should long since have driven him from my presence, in spite of any threats he might choose to hold out."

"I have been afraid, my dear Vivian," exclaimed the baronet, "lest you should form erroneous opinions of the motives that have led me to endure the conduct of this scoundrel. Be assured, however, that I have no reason to dread anything he may say, and yet, strange as it may appear, I have never yet found resolution enough to refuse the extortionate demands he is in the frequent habit of making upon me."

"Will you allow me," asked the young man, "to rid you of a pest that I feel assured is continually harassing and perplexing you ?"

"There is no need for it, my dear boy," replied Sir Lionel, "for I have at length come to the determination to treat him in the way he deserves. He is now absent, but should he ever venture into my presence again, I will take care that he shall not fail to meet with his just punishment. The scoundrel has been like an incubus, but my patience is now worn out, and he shall find to his cost that I can be as resolute in my enmity as he has hitherto found me pliant to his demands. This I am the more inclined for, as your mother suspects there must be some reason for my submitting to his demands, and I am determined to convince her of her error, by daring the miscreant to do his worst."

"I am rejoiced to hear it," cried Vivian, "for the world, which is never very charitable in its constructions, may by-and-bye think there is some cause for your enduring this insolence, which ought long ago to have been punished as it deserves."

"The truth is," replied Sir Lionel, "I should have done so before now, but that I feared the consequences would fall upon Gilbert Copley."

"You think, then, he has been the cause of inducing my cousin to quit this neighbourhood ?"

"There can be no doubt of it," replied the baronet, "though, on the other hand, it must be admitted I have no proof of his having any participation in it. Hugh Darnton is aware of this, and, as you have witnessed, he carries on his system of extortion, by borrowing money, as he calls it, without any intention of ever repaying it."

"Ay," answered Vivian, "he is cunning enough to know that you can never proceed criminally against him, while the money is advanced to him as a loan. A little patience, however, may serve your purpose well, and if we can only get him to commit himself upon one of the occasions, there is some hope that Hugh Darnton will at length meet with the punishment he richly deserves."

Sir Lionel was prevented making any further reply, by the approach of Markham, whose brow appeared to be more troubled and overcast than on any previous occasion during his visit. Vivian observed it, and feeling really anxious on his friend's account, inquired the cause of his altered appearance.

"I have been vexed," he replied, "and, perhaps, when you hear my explanation, you will say it is not without sufficient cause. In short, I have received a letter from my father, desiring me to return home on some business or other, that he takes it into his head is of very great moment."

"And we are positively to lose your company?"

"For the present, we must endure a separation," answered Markham; "but, if my presence here is not a downright bore, I shall not be absent more than a few days. In fact, everything has been made so agreeable, that I doubt whether any other place will possess the same charms for me."

"That is to say," laughed Vivian, "there are certain parties here you are unwilling to take leave of. Nay, deny it not, Harry, for I am not blind, and if my penetration is as good as I believe it to be, there is one young lady in this house who will be as sorry as yourself at the idea of a separation."

"Really, my dear fellow," answered Markham, "I scarcely know what reply to make. There are three females to whom your remark may apply, but I am not aware that my attentions to any one of them in particular can have given rise to such an observation."

"Tut, man, there's no occasion for all this secrecy between friends. My father, you see, has left the room, and why should you not at once confess that your heart has been fairly caught in the meshes of love?"

"Why, I should be a dullard, indeed, could I see so much beauty without feeling some emotion," replied Markham, with a sigh.

"And pray, which of the ladies," demanded Vivian, "may claim the honour of having captivated the heart of the accomplished Henry Markham?"

"Your question is somewhat difficult to answer, in the present state of affairs," returned the other; "but, as it may relieve you from some anxiety, I will at once declare, that with all my admiration for Agnes Evered, I have never had a thought of preferring my own claims in preference to those of my riend."

"Ha! ha! you have fairly turned the tables upon me," exclaimed Vivian, "and, upon being thus forced, I will e'en confess that I have had some thoughts of popping the question to the young lady you have named. And, now, having thus far pleaded guilty, I may, perhaps, be allowed to ask which of my two sisters is likely to make me your brother-in-law?"

"Upon my word," cried Markham, "you question me so closely, that I find there is no way left but to confess the truth at once, and ——"

"I'll spare you the confession," interrupted Vivian, "for your marked attentions to Eleanor have not passed unnoticed by one who feels so deep an interest in her behalf. She is in every respect worthy of your love, Harry, and, to speak my mind freely, I rather think you will have no great difficulty in obtaining the encouragement you desire. Go to her at once, Harry, you will find her in the shrubbery, and I am a bad prophet, indeed, if you wear not a more joyous countenance when next we meet together."

Vivian left the room as he pronounced these words, and after a brief space his friend hurried off, determined to seek an interview with Eleanor Dacre, and hear from her lips his doom of happiness or disappointment.

CHAPTER XI.

AN AVOWAL.—FRIENDLY ADVICE.—THE DEPARTURE.

DIRECTING his way towards the shrubbery, Markham was not long before he met with Eleanor, who, startled at his sudden appearance before her,

would have fled from the place, had he not taken her hand, and earnestly entreated her to remain, lest he should imagine that some unconscious cause of offence had been given.

"Nay," she replied, timidly, "surely no offence can have been given where none has been offered."

"But, sometimes," answered Markham, "an unconscious word or action may mar the happiness we have fondly pictured to ourselves."

"Am I to believe, then," asked Eleanor, "that a frown from me can cause you uneasiness?"

"Ay, a whole life of bitterness," he replied, earnestly. "I was about to tell you, Eleanor, that a hard necessity compels me to leave your father's roof sooner than I had expected."

"We are to lose you, then?" she cried, with an emotion it was impossible to conceal.

"For the present," answered Markham, "there is no help for it; but it will depend upon yourself whether my absence will be temporary or eternal."

"If my entreaties are wanted in addition to those of my father," she replied, "I will at once confess that your absence will leave a void in our little society which all must feel alike."

"And is there no one," asked Markham, "who will regret my departure more than the rest? Nay, your changing countenance tells me I have spoken too freely, and I have to ask pardon for presuming too much on the friendship that subsisted between us. I have been over bold, and the penalty, I fear will be a heavier one than I have fortitude enough to endure."

"May I ask what the penalty is you so much dread?"

"Your anger," he replied, "and consequent banishment from the society of one I love."

Eleanor remained silent om emotion; words rose to her lips, but could not give them utterance, and it was not till Henry was about to speak again, that she could collect sufficient firmness to reply.

"I will not affect," she exclaimed, "to misunderstand words that are intended to convey an expression of the regard with which you have been pleased to honour me. I have perhaps done wrong in permitting this interview, yet, I feel assured Mr. Markham possesses too much generosity to urge me further upon a subject that I am not at present prepared to answer."

"Then I have offended past forgiveness?"

"Nay, I have not said so," she replied, "for my heart cannot but feel gratified at the fact of my having obtained the esteem of one whose worth is proved by the friendship with which he is regarded both by my father and my brother. Your presence here has added joy to our little domestic society, and I may say, without boldness, that to none will your absence occasion more sorrow than myself."

"It is enough," exclaimed Markham, rapturously; "your words inspire me with hope, and I may yet be blessed in the possession of a prize which it has been my most earnest desire to obtain. For a brief period we must part, Eleanor, yet, ere I go from hence, you will perhaps allow me to speak to your father upon a subject that so nearly concerns him?"

Before Eleanor could make any reply, footsteps were heard at some little distance off, and she hurried away, leaving Markham to curse the intrusion which had thus broken in upon a conversation on which the happiness of a whole life depended. He would have turned away to avoid the person who had thus disappointed him, and as he did so Vivian appeared from one of the cross-paths, and suddenly stood before him.

"So, so!" he exclaimed, "you have followed my advice, I see, and now, it is but fair that I should know how far your love affair succeeds. My sister just now passed me so absorbed in her own thoughts that she was unconscious of my being so near, and you know, my dear fellow, that absence of mind is one of the most certain signs of love."

"Your intrusion was most unfortunate," replied Markham; "for just when I was expecting an answer from your sister, she was frightened away by hearing your footsteps."

"Ay," exclaimed Vivian, "a third party is never required in these cases, and I am vexed with myself for having been such a marplot in the present instance. However, you must not mind it, my boy, for I feel almost as interested in the affair as yourself, and you may rely upon my friendly offices towards obtaining for you the hand of my sister."

"You think, then, I have no reason for giving way to despair?"

"Despair!" exclaimed Vivian, "are you beginning to grow melancholy already, as if she had given you a positive and downright refusal?"

"It is the weakness of lovers to do so," answered Markham. "I know not yet that Eleanor can regard me with any other feeling than that of friendship, and, much as I value her esteem, it is too cold a feeling for one who seeks to gain the entire possession of her heart."

"And that I dare say you have," replied Vivian; "but young ladies are sensitive creatures, and must not be expected to jump at an offer as if they were ready to have made the same proposition, if the rules of society would permit it. Take my word for it, Eleanor has no other lover, and, unless my discrimination deceives me, you will have no great difficulty in obtaining just such a reply as you desire."

"Has she ever said anything," asked Markham, "that may serve as an encouragement to my hopes?"

"Why, the truth is," replied Vivian, "when people are over head and ears in love, their manners and actions speak as eloquently as the tongue. Now, I have watched my sister narrowly, and I can take it upon myself to assert that you have captured her heart, though, of course, she tries to conceal the circumstance as much as possible. Her eyes always wander round the room in search of you, and if you are are not present, I can see that she feels a disappointment more than she dares express by words."

"So you may both think and wish," answered Markham; "but I must confess, my own thoughts upon the subject are less sanguine than yours appear to be."

"And yet but just now I thought you seemed to be full of hope."

"I am so still," replied the other, "but hopes are so often frustrated that I almost fear to believe that happiness is within my grasp. Besides, even if she favours my suit, there is still your father to be consulted, and he may have formed other views for his daughter, which he will not allow to be interfered with."

"This is self-inflicted torture," exclaimed Vivian, "and yet it is in your own power to set the affair at rest in a few minutes."

"How is that to be done?"

"Why you have been sufficiently explicit with Eleanor," replied the other, "and if she had had any decided objection to accepting your offer she would at once have given you an answer to that effect. You may, therefore, take it for granted that one party is safe, and now all you have to do is to see my father upon the subject, and I am much mistaken indeed if he does not give an immediate consent to your becoming the suitor of his daughter."

"And Lady Dacre?"

"Will throw no obstacle in the way of her child's happiness," replied Vivian. "You are a favourite of my mother's, I know, and nothing will afford her greater pleasure than the prospect of seeing you become a member of our family. So now, Harry, I have given you encouragement enough, and it will be your own fault if you leave this place otherwise than a happy man."

"Then you would advise me to seek an interview with Sir Lionel?"

"I would."

"But when?"

"Why before you are another hour older," replied Vivian. "It seems you are about to leave us for a brief period, and there's nothing like following these matters up closely lest anything should occur to occasion disappointment."

"I believe you are right," exclaimed Harry Markham after a pause; "yet you can scarcely wonder at my want of resolution when the uncertainty of my fate is taken into consideration. This asking the consent of a father and mother is an awkward sort of business, and to speak the truth I felt inclined to put it off as long as possible."

"Then see my father by himself," returned Vivian; "you will find him in the library, and take my word for it he will receive your announcement with all the respect so important a communication deserves. He is most anxious to see my sisters well settled in the world, and he can have no objection to you for a son-in-law since your family is fully equal to our's, both in respect to wealth and rank."

"And you think he will not reject my proposal with scorn?"

"My dear fellow," exclaimed Vivian, "you have the rare merit of undervaluing yourself! What on earth can make you think my father will receive your confession of love with anything else than courtesy and respect?"

"Why, the truth is," replied Markham, "I have seen that the fairest hopes are often blighted when we make most certain of success. I have, however, gained some confidence from what you have said, and, acting upon your advice, I will see Sir Lionel, and at once end this uncertainty by freely disclosing my thoughts to him."

"Why, now, that's fairly coming to the point," exclaimed his friend, "and take my word for it you will see no reason to regret taking my counsel. Eleanor I am sure regards you with favour, and the affair will be brought to as comfortable a conclusion as your heart can desire."

"But if ——"

"Psha! there you are with your eternal doubts again!" interrupted Vivian. "Why, man, the road lies straight before you, and you can only err by not following the directions I have given. Even at the very worst you can only have a damper thrown upon your love, and obstacles are nothing in the way of matrimony, for the more difficulties that are thrown in the way of your true lover the more resolute is he to carry off the prize."

"I should be unworthy of Eleanor were I to hesitate any longer," answered Markham. "You have counselled me well, Vivian, and though I must needs confess some little irresolution yet remains, I will dare even the displeasure of your father, and the consequent loss of Eleanor, rather than endure any longer the tortures of suspense."

"Then lose no more time about it, but seek this interview without delay. It only wants a little resolution, and take my word for it, you will have a lighter heart when you and I meet together again."

By this time they had reached the house, and whilst Vivian proceeded to the drawing-room, Henry Markham made his way towards the library, where he found Sir Lionel Dacre occupied in reading. The book, however, was immediately laid down and the baronet commenced a conversation upon various subjects, till observing the restlessness of his visiter, he abruptly broke off and inquired if he had sought him upon any particular business.

Now, therefore, was the time to make the desperate plunge, and recovering himself as well as he could, the young man confessed the secret of his heart, and perceiving that his announcement had not given any displeasure, he proceeded with increased ardour to describe the attachment he had conceived for Eleanor, and the hopes he had formed that his love would not be blasted through parental interference. Sir Lionel listened to him with attention, and having heard him to an end without interruption, he said,—

"You will, perhaps, be surprised, Mr. Markham, when I tell you that the object of your present visit to me was guessed as soon as you entered the room. The truth is, I have observed a growing regard between you and my daughter Eleanor, and observing you just now in earnest converse together, prepared me for the announcement you have just made."

"Then you are not displeased with me, Sir Lionel, for the course I have adopted?"

"Nay," answered the baronet. "I can see nothing to be displeased with at present, for your conduct has been candid, and I admire the honourable mode you have followed in the affair."

"May I hope then," asked Markham, "that there will be no obstacle in the way of my happiness?"

"There will certainly be none on my part," replied Sir Lionel, "though it must not be forgotten that there are others to be consulted besides myself. My daughter, I suppose, has not rejected your offer?"

"I have scarcely ventured so far," answered Markham, "as to engage a promise from her till I had first obtained the sanction of yourself and Lady Dacre."

"Very proper."

"Then I may consider that you will not offer any opposition to my hopes?"

"We must not hurry on unadvisedly in an affair of this importance," replied Sir Lionel; "for though I can see no objection to such a union as you have proposed, there are others to be consulted before the arrangements are completed. Your own friends, for instance, may not approve of the step you have proposed to take."

"It is impossible for them to raise any objection to such a marriage," exclaimed Henry.

"So you may think," replied the baronet, "but experience in the world tells me that these affairs require a great deal of caution before we involve ourselves too far. I have been told that there is a fair prospect of your inheriting a title and very large property, and it is, therefore, not unlikely that my daughter may be considered unworthy of such an alliance."

"Indeed, Sir Lionel," exclaimed Markham, "you do my friends an injustice, for they are anxious only to insure my happiness, and my choice is left unshackled as long as I disgrace not the name I bear, by seeking a union beneath myself. It is true I have some expectation of succeeding to a title, but an heir may yet be born to it, though the probabilities are certainly very much against such an event."

"Well, Mr. Markham," said the baronet, after a pause, "you have now heard my opinion upon the subject, and that it is not an unfavourable one, you must admit. I understand you are about to pay your father a visit, and during that time you will have ample opportunity to speak to him upon the matter. You are at liberty to tell him all that I have said about it, and if he raises no objection, I shall be proud of an alliance with your family."

Sir Lionel rose from his seat, as a signal that he wished the conversation to end for the present, and Markham left to rejoin Vivian, and inform him of all that had passed. It occurred to him, indeed, that every difficulty had vanished, and when at length the day arrived on which he was to take his departure, he bade farewell to his friends with a certainty that he should shortly return with news that all obstacles were removed.

CHAPTER XII.

THE SMUGGLERS.—THE KEEPSAKE.—A RE-APPEARANCE.

WE must now take leave of the quiet scenes, and return once more to the Raven's Nest, where Gilbert Copley was still sojourning, though a more willing guest than when we last left him. The smugglers—for such was the occupation followed by Mark Harrowby and his band—soon wrought upon the imagination of their younger companion so successfully that he willingly consented to join them in their voyages, and being naturally of a bold and fearless disposition, he gained the favour and applause of those who, in the beginning, had treated him with distrust.

It must be observed, however, that he knew not the full extent of crime to which these men went; that they were robbers on land, as well as smugglers on the ocean, and that the hands of all of them had been stained with human blood, in the pursuit of their lawless career. Had he been aware of all these things, he would have refused to join them even at the hazard of losing his life; but smuggling he had been persuaded to believe was no crime, and as it offered a wide field for adventure, he entered upon his new career with enthusiasm. He made several sucessful trips with them, and at the period at which our narrative has now reached, they were preparing for another voyage from the retreat in which they found concealment whenever they were obliged to be ashore.

Upon his first arrival at the Raven's Nest, our hero had been an object of the greatest antipathy to Deborah, and she took no pains to conceal the hatred she bore towards him. By degrees, however, she began to regard him with more favour, and, strange as it may seem, at length fell violently in love with him. This she manifested upon every opportunity that offered; but Gilbert either did not, or affected not to understand her, and at last, taking advantage of their having been left alone together, she presented him with a poniard of curious workmanship, bidding him keep it in remembrance of her.

"And why should I do so," said Gilbert, with surprise, "when I have had so many proofs that you regard me with feelings of the deepest hatred?"

"Ay," she replied; "but that was when I thought you would prove to be a spy upon the band, and betray us into the hands of the enemy. I distrusted you once, but it don't follow that I should do so for ever."

"And this poniard is given as a keepsake?"

"Yes," she replied; "but you must not let Mark see it, or he'll be jealous."

"Jealous!—and wherefore?"

"Because he don't like me to take notice of anybody but himself," answered Deborah. "He's a sort of lover of mine, you see, and wouldn't like me to make presents to any one else, especially to a young and comely fellow like you."

"Then you had better take back your gift," exclaimed Gilbert, "for I have no wish to draw down the anger of Mark Harrowby either upon you or myself."

"What!" cried Deborah, "will you break my heart by refusing to accept my keepsake?"

"It has always struck me," replied Gilbert, "that you have no heart to break, or, at any rate, if you have one, it is made of such hard materials that there's very little danger of any harm coming to it."

"Hard as it may be to others, it's not so towards you," exclaimed Deborah; "all the hatred I once bore towards you, is turned to love, and ——"

"Psha!" interrupted the other; "this is only some trick to lure me to destruction. I have never sought your favour, and, to speak the plain truth, would rather have your hatred than your love."

"And do you know what my hatred can do?"

"I know it may prompt you to deeds of violence against me," replied Gilbert; "but I also feel assured that you will not dare to hurl your vengeance against one that Mark Harrowby calls his friend."

"Mark himself is not safe from me if I once resolve upon his death," she exclaimed, savagely. "He fears me, in spite of all his boasted power in this place, or, long before this, he would have driven me from hence to seek a refuge somewhere else."

"Humph!" said Gilbert; "he thinks, I suppose, you would betray him to his enemies?"

"He knows better than that," exclaimed the woman; "for I'll never turn informer, however great my injuries may be. But there is another road to vengeance besides that, and if I'm once roused, the lives of Mark and all that own his authority would be sacrificed at the same instant."

"In what way?" demanded Gilbert.

"Oh, easily enough," she replied; "he has not told you, I suppose, that he has made up his mind never to fall into the hands of his enemies, and as

re can be no doubt that this place will some day or other be discovered, he
taken care to prevent being taken by surprise.''

" How ?''

" Why, the vault beneath is nearly filled with gunpowder,'' answered
borah, " and when the worst comes to the worst, a lighted torch thrown
wn yon trap-door, would send the band and those who come to seek them
o eternity. Now, I care as little about life as most people, and if ever
ark Harrowby gives me mortal offence, the mine shall be sprung, and away
all fly into the air together. So you see he's obliged to behave civilly to
; for if I was to be turned away from the Raven's Nest, he would always
in fear of my betraying the place.''

" But suppose,'' observed Gilbert, " his dagger should one night find its
ay to your heart ?''

" That's easier said than done,'' she replied, " for I am aware of my dan-
r, and always guard against it. I sleep with one eye open, boy, and those
ho aimed against my life would most likely lose their own for their pains.
ut we are going from the subject ;—I was saying just now what a faney I
ve taken to that comely face of yours, and yet it seems I am to be treated
ith scorn, because you don't think me young and handsome enough to
e your partner.''

" Come, come, Deborah,'' exclaimed Gilbert, " enough has been said upon
his subject for the present, and since you know my mind, don't speak any
ore about a foolish notion that ought never to have entered your head.''

" You know best about it, I suppose,'' muttered Deborah ; " but I'd advise
ou to recollect that I can be either a friend or an enemy ; and if I'm forced
o be the latter, you may yet live to repent your scorn.''

" Do you threaten me, woman ?''

" Ay, and I can do as well as threaten,'' she replied, fiercely, and then
uddenly altering her tone, she added, " but you are only saying this to try
ny patience ; and I can forgive you that, young sir, because in this place
've learned to govern my passion instead of giving way to it, as I used to do.
ay, then, that we part friends now, and I'll give you till to-morrow to con-
ider whether my proposal is to be refused.''

" Upon my word,'' said Gilbert, who could not help laughing outright at
he woman's pertinacity, " your conduct is altogether so extraordinary, that I
now not whether to take it as jest or earnest. And now, supposing I should
e inclined to marry you, what would Mark Harrowby say to it ?''

" We should leave Mark to his fate,'' answered the woman.

" What ! run away from the retreat ?''

" Yes,'' she replied, " and then I could take you to a place where you
night collect a band of your own. You may have a pretty company under
our command, and that will be a great deal better than living here like a
epedant, when you have spirit enough to be at the head of a brave set of
ellows.''

" And you,'' exclaimed Gilbert, " who profess to be so faithful to Mark
Harrowby, are the first to counsel me to be treacherous to him !''

" If I do so,'' she replied, " it is because I feel an interest in your behalf
hat is far greater than I ever felt for anybody else. I would not any longer
ee you obey the orders of another man when it is in your own power to take
ommand upon yourself, and earn a more terrible name than that of Mark
Harrowby.''

" But suppose I was not ambitious to attain such very unenviable notoriety.''

" Why then I should pronounce you to be a greater fool than I thought
or,'' replied Deborah ; and then, as a distant sound fell upon her ear, she
dded, hurriedly, " there's Mark's footsteps coming this way, and I must be
ff, lest he should suspect that you and I are plotting together. And mind,

youngster, not a word must be said of what has passed between us, for if I catch you blabbing secrets your own blood shall answer for it."

She disappeared as these menacing words were uttered, and scarcely had Gilbert been left alone, when Mark Harrowby entered the room.

"I have news for you, Gilbert," he exclaimed, " and that too which will gladden your heart, for an old friend is at hand that you've long been wishing to see."

"Why, you don't mean Hugh Darnton, do you?" exclaimed the other, with surprise.

"But I do mean him, though," replied Mark ; "and what's more, he don't come here alone."

"Who is his companion?"

"Why Martha, his pretty daughter, to be sure," returned Harrowby. "Little Patty and you used to be good friends before you left home, and I thought you'd be glad to hear that she was going to be a visiter here."

"This is not exactly the sort of place I should like to see her in," answered Gilbert. "She seemed to be a gentle creature enough when I knew her ; but if she stays long here she will learn no good among us."

"Psha! her father's the best judge about that," exclaimed Mark ; "besides, he's one of our sort, though we don't often see him at the Raven's Nest, and I dare say Patty knows more about smuggling than you seem to think for."

"That's more the pity," returned Gilbert, thoughtfully ; and then, after a pause, he inquired when she and her father might be expected.

"Oh, it will not be long first," answered Harrowby, "for I left them just as they turned off to the village where they are to leave their nags. They must be on their way by this time, so that we shall see 'em presently."

"But they will not stay with us very long, I suppose?"

"That's more than I can tell you," responded Mark Harrowby : "for Hugh hasn't told me the reason of his coming, although, from something that dropped, I rather think he's left his home for good and all ; and if that's the case, I suppose he'll come and live among us and be one of our society."

"Surely," exclaimed Gilbert, "if he had such an intention as that, he would not have brought his daughter to take up her abode in such a place as this?"

"And why the devil shouldn't he bring her here?" demanded the other ; "ain't the den a very comfortable one, and won't another woman in it make us all the more happy and cheerful?"

"That may be all very true," answered our hero ; "but the father ought to have considered well before he brought her to be the companion of such rough fellows as she is likely to find here."

"Tell him so yourself, then, for here he comes," exclaimed the other, as Hugh Darnton and his daughter presented themselves at the door.

Gilbert, however, was too well pleased at seeing his former friends, to enter upon the proposed subject just at present, and after the first cordial greeting was over, he asked Darnton how he had left Sir Lionel, and whether his disappearance had given rise to any anger on the part of the baronet.

"Anger!" exclaimed Darnton, whose object it was to impose upon the credulity of his young friend, "why he went almost raving mad when first he heard of your running away from old Stripes's house, and he has sworn that if ever you show your face there again, he'll have you turned away like a dog."

"He shall not have an opportunity of doing so," answered Gilbert, "for sooner would I starve by the roadside, than ask a favour of any man. I have my hands to labour with, and whilst I have the use of them Sir Lionel Dacre shall not have the gratification of insulting me with his scorn."

"That's spoken like a lad of spirit," exclaimed Darnton, " and I glory in

you for it. You are comfortable, of course, in your new quarters here?"

"Why, it must be confessed I begin to grow reconciled to the life I am leading," replied Gilbert; "at first I felt rather a dislike to it; but danger and enterprise always had charms for me, and it cannot be denied that there's enough of both to be found here. You, I suppose, mean to stay with us some little time?"

"I dare say I shall," returned Darnton; "for the truth is, I took French leave of home, and there's somebody left behind that would like to know where I'm to be found."

"You have been poaching again, I suppose?"

"Exactly so," answered Hugh.

"And it is known that you are the party?"

"Why, there's a strangish suspicion about it," replied Darnton, "and so I thought the safest way was to get clear off before anything worse became of it. I should tell you, too, that I contrived to get a small matter of money from Sir Lionel, and having found a customer for all the stock I had upon the farm, I bolted, bringing Patty with me by way of a companion."

"And your wife and the rest of the young ones?"

"Must do as well as they can without me," replied the ruffian. "The parish will take care of 'em, I suppose, and if not, Sir Lionel ain't a bad sort of a chap, and perhaps he'll put 'em into some way of getting a living."

"But surely you will not throw them on the pity of a heartless world?" cried Gilbert.

"How can a fellow like me help himself?" demanded the other. "I couldn't remain where I was with the chance of being thrown into prison for shooting a few hares and birds; and if I'd brought the whole family with me, I never should have been able to hide myself for any long time. But come,

No. 7

this is a subject I don't much like to talk about, so let's change it. You've had time enough to take a few trips with our friends here, and I suppose you're as good a smuggler as the best of 'em?"

"Ay, ay, he'll do," interposed Mark Harrowby; "he's not afraid of a little danger, and I've good hopes of bringing him up so that he'll be able to succeed me in the command, whenever death thinks proper to take me off."

"Didn't I always tell you I'd got something good in view for you," exclaimed Darnton. "This is a life to suit any lad of mettle, and is far better than wandering about at home without knowing what to do with yourself. Here's something to keep you upon the move, and he's a paltry hound that would prefer idleness to the bustle of a life like yours."

"I have no wish to exchange it at present," replied Gilbert; "but I must confess that, till within the last few minutes, I had a hope that something better would have turned up in my favour."

"What do you mean, lad?"

"Why, I fancied Sir Lionel would not have been quite so hard upon me, and that by-and-by he would be glad to see me return, if it was only for the sake of putting me in the way of getting an honourable living."

"An honourable living?" exclaimed Hugh Darnton, in a tone of scorn.

"Ay," replied the other; "I thought he might have got me a commission in the army or navy, and that by a life of exertion in my country's cause I might have wiped out the stain that has been brought upon my name by my early indiscretions."

"And do you really believe," asked Darnton, "that either the army or the navy would have received a fellow that has passed a great part of his time among some of the most daring smugglers that England ever produced? No, no, my lad, you have chosen your course, and must stick to it for the remainder of your days."

"So he will," exclaimed Mark Harrowby; "the young fellow takes to it as if it had been cut out for him, and he has only to go on as he has begun to make a name for himself that will never be forgotten. But come, this is dry work; and, as Deborah has produced some of our choicest brandy, let's sit down and make a night of it. Patty can go to bed if she likes, and then we may talk over our affairs, and arrange what shall be done for the future."

Martha Darnton, after conversing apart with her father for a little while, left the room, and as there was no longer any restraint upon them, Darnton, Gilbert, and Harrowby sat themselves down to drink strong potations, and form schemes for further operations. So earnestly, indeed, were they engaged, that the morning's light dawned upon them before they retired to their beds.

CHAPTER XIII.

AN ALARM.—PLANS ARRANGED.—THE MURDER.

WEEKS passed away, and still Hugh Darnton and his daughter remained at the Raven's Nest, no hint was given of their intention to depart, and it seemed that they meant to pass the remainder of their days in the lonely spot which afforded them a shelter. This circumstance afforded no little uneasiness to Deborah, who, from the first, had been jealous of the superior attractions of Patty, and the consequent probability that she had lost all chance of obtaining a husband in the person of Gilbert Copley. On various occasions she tried to draw him into another conversation upon the subject; but he guessed the object she had in view, and always effected his escape from her presence whenever he saw there was a probability of their being left alone together.

It was while Hugh Darnton was still in concealment at the Raven's Nest, that one of the band was despatched to Sir Lionel Dacre, demanding fifty pounds of him, and threatening him with disclosures in the event of his refusing to comply with the terms. The man sent on this errand was one of the most ruffianly in the band, and orders were given him to murder the baronet in the event of any violence being offered him. Fortunately, however, as has been seen, Sir Lionel complied with the extortion, and the messenger returned to his employers with the money which had been required to fit them out for the next voyage.

In the midst of the bustle, however, that was consequent upon their proposed departure, news was brought that one of the band had been captured and sent to prison with every certainty of meeting the punishment due to his lawless career. This was an event that rarely occurred among them, and as there was some reason to fear the fellow would confess and bring his comrades into trouble, schemes were devised by which he might be liberated from prison, and though the sacrifice of some few lives was anticipated, the circumstance was thought to be inconsiderable when weighed against the danger that was so much dreaded.

Whilst this confusion prevailed in the Raven's Nest, intelligence was brought that two men who were the principal evidence against their comrade would pass along a road at the distance of about a mile from the place on their way towards the next town, where their depositions were to be taken against the captured smuggler. To seize upon these men then, and hold them captive till after the day of trial, was their first thought, and as it was considered fair that all should participate alike in what was going to be done, it was agreed that the whole band should sally forth at dusk and waylay the men upon whose evidence the whole proof rested. Gilbert Copley would gladly have excused himself from sharing in this exploit, but the ruffians were determined that there should be no skulkers, and at the appointed time he was forced to accompany them, though resolving in his own mind to take no share in any violence that might be offered.

At length they reached a copse that skirted the road-side, and as this offered them a place of concealment, they threw themselves down upon the long grass, and listened in breathless silence for the first sounds that might fall upon their ears. Here they remained nearly an hour, and voices were then heard at a distance, when each man, springing upon his legs, stood ready to spring forth upon their victims as they passed. In a few minutes the two men were seen at a short distance off; and then, on a signal being given by Mark Harrowby, his comrades sprang into the road, and pointing their pistols at the travellers, commanded them to stop at the peril of their lives.

"Thieves, robbers!" shouted one of the men, and with a desperate effort to escape, he rushed forward, and striking down the man who would have opposed his flight, he continued his way with every chance of eluding the ruffians who had waylaid him. A dozen pistols, however, were at once fired, and the unfortunate wretch, staggering backwards a few paces, fell dead upon the ground. At the same moment the butt end of a pistol laid his companion prostrate, and the murdered man was dragged back to the spot from where he had started when he made his attempt to escape from the ruffians who had stopped him.

"There's one of 'em dead, at any rate," exclaimed Dick Elliot, "and the other has had a crack on the crown that will give him a headache for many a long day to come."

"The fool that's killed brought it upon himself," observed Harrowby; "but let that be as it may, we stand in a fair chance of swinging for it, if something is not done to keep the fellow's death from being known."

"If we stand chattering here in the public road it's not likely the secret will be kept long," interposed Rob Redland, another of the smugglers. "The blood on the road, too, will tell tales; so I, for one, propose that each man takes a separate route, and hides himself where he can, till it will be safe to return to the Raven's Nest."

" And if we do that," exclaimed Hugh Darnton, " the chances are, that most of us will be grabbed before we are a week older. As for the blood you speak of, a heavy rain seems to be coming on, and by the morning there'll not be a trace left of the job that's been done."

" Drag the body into the wood," said Harrowby, " and if a mattock and a few spades can be got from the nearest farm-yard, we may soon find means to put the dead man into a hole where he'll not be found in a hurry. As for the other fellow that only seems stunned, I hardly know what's to be done with him."

" Dead men tell no tales," observed Rob Redland, " and it won't be harder for him to die than it was for his companion."

" For Heaven's sake, let us have no more murder !" cried Gilbert, whose agitation had hitherto deprived him of the power of utterance; " my heart sickens at what has already been done, and rather will I lose my own life than stand by to witness further bloodshed."

" Ho, ho, ho !" shouted Mark Harrowby; " the young gentleman begins to grow qualmish because this trifling accident has happened to a fellow that would have denounced us to our enemies. But we are masters here, I believe," he added, looking round him, " and if I give the word the other man will not have much chance of his life."

" But you will *not* give it, Mark Harrowby !" exclaimed Gilbert, earnestly. " A second murder is not necessary, and a sign or a motion from yourself will save a fellow creature from destruction."

" And pray what is to be done with him," asked Mark, " if we don't kill him ?"

" Let him be conveyed to our retreat," answered Gilbert Copley : " he may be kept in safety there for a time, and if it should be found necessary to remove him, we have the means to take him over to Holland, where a careful watch may be kept over him."

" All that sounds very well," exclaimed Dick Elliot ; " but suppose he happen to escape, what sort of a chance should we have then, think you ?"

" Ay, there would be halters a-piece for us," said Rob Redland ; " and who, I should like to know, is going to risk his own neck to humour this youngster's humanity ?"

By this time the murdered man and his still insensible companion were dragged into the wood, and two or three of the men were sent in quest of the implements to dig a grave that should for a time hide from the eye of the world the crime that had that night been committed.

" The other fellow begins to show signs of life," exclaimed Dick Elliot, as he stooped over the body of the man who had been stunned by the blow. " I was in hopes he was dead, and would spare us any further trouble; but it seems he ain't satisfied with what he's had already."

" It won't be much trouble to dispatch him," observed another of the ruffians ; " and if the office happens to fall upon me, it shall soon be seen which I prefer—his life or my own."

" Let me again entreat you to spare him," cried Gilbert ; " the man has never injured us, and it would be a cold-blooded murder to slay him before we know whether he is conscious of his fate."

" Be advised by me, Gilbert," whispered Hugh Darnton, " and say nothing more about the business. These men will begin to suspect you presently, and then, perhaps, you may meet the doom you are so anxious to save the other from."

" Harkye, young fellow !" exclaimed Harrowby, addressing himself to Gilbert, " you've been among us for some time, and there was a daring about your character that made me think you would turn out a chap after our own hearts. But now you have shown the white feather, and if any more objections are made to our proceedings, I shall begin to think you're going to turn traitor against us ; and then, for our own sakes, we must send a ball through your brain."

" I can die without fear," answered Gilbert ; " but cannot be the witness of a second murder upon an unoffending man."

Luckily for Gilbert Copley, the conversation was here interrupted by the arrival of Rob Redland with spades and a pickaxe, which he had found in a hovel belonging to a neighbouring farm yard. These were quickly distributed among the men, who set themselves to work, and in a short space of time a deep hole was dug, into which the body of the murdered man was thrown with as little remorse as if it had been that of a dog.

" There's an end of one of 'em at any rate," exclaimed Mark Harrowby, as soon as this had been accomplished, " and it now only remains for us to decide whether the other fellow shall rest by the side of him. What says the general voice ?"

" Let him die !" was the exclamation of all except Gilbert Copley.

" Well," cried Harrowby, " and now, since sentence has been fairly pronounced, where is the man that's willing to be his executioner?"

" The truth is," replied Dick Elliot, " there's not more than one among us that would slink out of the job ; but as the murder may have to be answered for one of these odd days, I don't see why it shouldn't be fairly decided by drawing lots."

" A very fair proposal," exclaimed Mark, " and no one, I should suppose, can object to it. Are all agreed ?"

" Ay, all, all !" shouted the ruffians.

" Then the next thing to be considered," said the leader, " is how the lots are to be drawn for ?"

" Oh, that's easily done," cried Rob Redland. " Let each of us give you his poniard, which you are to hold in your hand, and the one who draws forth the longest shall plunge it into the heart of yonder fellow."

The daggers were immediately surrendered to Harrowby in the way that had been proposed, and that of Gilbert alone remained in his own possession. This fact, however, was soon discovered, and murmurs, mingled with threats, were uttered by his lawless associates.

" Come, young fellow," exclaimed the leader, " we must have no cowardice or shrinking back. You must take your chance as well as the rest of us, so give me your poniard, and if the chance is yours, there's plenty here to see that you do your duty, and if you hesitate your own life will be the forfeit.'"

Gilbert saw that there was no escape for him, and delivering his dagger into the hands of Mark Harrowby, he resolved in his own mind—should the lot fall upon him—to perish rather than take away the life of a fellow-creature. Meanwhile the drawing went on, and when his own turn came, he saw with unutterable joy that the fate so much dreaded had not fallen to him ; the longest poniard was drawn by Rob Redland, who, brandishing the weapon in his hand, declared his readiness to perform the task whenever the word of command should be given.

" And it shall not be long first, depend upon it," exclaimed Harrowby. " The man must die, that's certain ; but we must now decide whether he shall be stabbed while he lies in his stupor, or if it will be better to wait till he revives, that he may have a chance of saying a prayer or two before we send him into eternity."

" Let him die as he is," said Dick Elliot, " for though I'm one of those that wouldn't say a word to save his life, yet I don't see the use of waiting till he recovers, just to add torments to his last moments."

" Is it agreed among you," asked Harrowby, " that Rob Redland perform his task without delay ?"

" Ay, ay," answered the ruffians.

" Then, strike," exclaimed the leader, " and see that your dagger goes direct to his heart."

The ruffian approached to execute his diabolical purpose ; but as the steel was uplifted to strike the fatal blow, the unfortunate man uttered a low groan, and raising himself in a sitting posture, earnestly implored that his life might be spared.

" Ho ! ho !" cried Harrowby, " so the fellow has only been shamming all this time ! But, of course, he has heard what his fate is to be, so there's no occasion for us to announce it to him."

" Mercy !—mercy !" cried the trembling victim ; " spare but my life, and I will endure imprisonment—anything you choose to command, or that may seem necessary for your safety."

" Spare your life, eh ?" exclaimed Mark Harrowby, with a brutish chuckle ; " let you live that you may afterwards turn against us, and bring the whole band to the gallows. No—no, we don't hold our lives quite so cheap as that ; so if you have got a short prayer or two to say, be quick about it, for we can't waste much more time when every moment of delay increases our chance of falling into the hands of justice as one of our poor devils has done already."

" Oh, do not murder me," supplicated the unfortunate man. " I have never injured any one among you, yet you seek my life as if I was an enemy."

" So you are," growled Dick Elliot ; " wasn't you one of the witnesses that was going to swear against our comrade, and can you call yourself anything else than an enemy when you would do the same sort of thing for all the rest of us ?"

" But I have not done so," cried the trembling victim, " and the blood that has been already spilt may surely satisfy the most vindictive among you."

" Your companion," exclaimed Mark Harrowby, " lies at the bottom of this pit, and, as you see, we have made it large enough for two. The other will lie in close companionship with his former friend before we leave this place."

" Alas !" groaned the poor fellow ; " will nothing soften your hearts towards me ?"

" Nothing," answered the leader ; " so waste no more time in useless supplications, but make the best use you can of the brief space that's been allowed you."

" I will," exclaimed the man, who was excited to the highest pitch of desperation, and snatching a dagger from the ruffian who stood nearest to him, he rushed towards Mark Harrowby, and was about to plunge the weapon into his bosom, when he was seized by the throat by Rob Redland, and in another instant a poniard was buried in his heart, and the wretched man was precipitated into the pit beside his unfortunate companion.

" That was a good blow, Rob," cried Harrowby, " for it was struck just in time to save me from a thrust that would have left you without a leader. The fellow has died game at any rate, and now, as it's all over with him, let the hole be filled up as quickly as possible, and then we'll get back to the Raven's Nest, lest this business of ours should be found out."

The men required no further incentive to execute this task, and the earth having been filled in to a level with the rest of the ground, the remainder was carried to a distance, so that no traces should be left of the bloody deed that had been perpetrated. The implements that had been borrowed were then returned to the place from whence they had been taken; and when all had thus been completed to their satisfaction, they returned with noiseless footsteps, and took their way back towards their haunt amidst the cliffs. By this time the rain had begun to come down in torrents, and the blackness of the clouds seemed to promise that it would be of some continuance.

"This is the very thing for us, my friends," exclaimed Harrowby, breaking the silence that had been maintained. "It will serve to wash out the blood stains from the road where the first man fell, and if we only keep our own counsel, there is no trouble to be feared for what has been done to-night. But how's this, Gilbert?" he added, turning to our hero; "you seem dumb-founded, man! Has the sight of a little blood frightened you out of your senses?"

Gilbert's brain burned and throbbed at the recollection of all he had that night witnessed, and he could make no reply to the question that had been put to him. Hugh Darnton observed that his step faltered, and grasping his arm firmly, he supported him during the remainder of their way to the Raven's Nest.

CHAPTER XIV.

RIVALRY.—A QUARREL.—THE RETREAT.

For a period of three weeks after the tragical occurrence described in the last chapter, Gilbert Copley was confined to his bed by a brain fever that had seized him in the course of that night. His ravings on the subject were so fearful and incessant that none of the band could venture into his chamber; and during the period of his illness, he was attended solely by Deborah and Martha Darnton, whose little medical skill was exerted to restore him to health and reason. This, however, would have availed but little had he not possessed a naturally strong constitution, and at length, as the fever gradually left his brain, he was able to recognise those to whose attention he was indebted for recovery.

But at the same time came the recollection of all that had occurred on the fearful night when he had last been out, and it required all the soothing powers of Martha to prevent him from falling into a relapse. Sensible of the kindness which prompted her to make so generous an effort in his behalf, he restrained the violence of his emotions whenever she was present, but in his own mind he resolved to quit the retreat as soon as he should be able to endure fatigue, and thus for ever abandon the comrades who had betrayed the remorselessness with which they could sacrifice the lives of their fellow creatures to their own demoniac feelings of revenge.

Deborah, who had observed the watchful attentions of Martha Darnton with mingled sensations of jealousy and hate, vowed in her own mind to endure no rival, and a thousand dark schemes were continually flitting through her mind to rid herself of one whom she loathed as an enemy. Had it been possible to do so without fear of discovery she would have removed the unsuspecting girl by a death of violence, but she stood in some little fear of Hugh Darnton's vengeance should any harm befal his daughter, and as no better plan presented itself, she determined to wait a favourable opportunity, and in the meanwhile to keep a careful watch upon Gilbert and her supposed rival.

It was about a week after our hero had begun to recover from his terrible malady, that, being alone with Martha, he fervently expressed the gratitude with which her kindness had inspired him.

"Nay," he added, after a pause; "gratitude is far too cool a word to describe the feelings that your generous conduct has warmed me with. In truth, Martha, I believe it may be more truly described as love than gratitude."

"—are, Mr. Copley," cried the blushing girl, "if your brain is not still — Gratitude, I'm sure, is a very pretty word, but love you can —el for such as me."

"And why not?" he asked.

"Because you were born a gentleman," she replied, "and I am only the daughter of very humble people."

"And if I was born a gentleman, as you say," answered Gilbert, "I have done enough of late to lower me beneath the level of the poorest rustic. Have I not been the associate of the basest villains, and can any act of my own, however honourable it may be, restore me to the station from which I have madly thrown myself?"

"Why, you have done wrong, it must be confessed," replied Martha; "but it may not be too late to amend the fault. The world cannot lay claim to perfection, and I dare say, if the actions of all men could be discovered to us, we should find that many a man stands high in society who ought to be shunned."

"You are a good comforter at all events, Martha," exclaimed Gilbert Copley, "and I will try to think it is not yet too late to amend. This place shall be my home no longer than can be helped, and once free from my comrades, I have only to ask your love to make me one of the happiest fellows alive."

"Ah!" cried Martha, "you only say this to me now, because your head don't happen to be quite right yet."

"Nay, I swear it upon this hand."

Gilbert pressed her unresisting hand to his lips, and as he did so, Deborah, with flaming eyes and furious countenance, presented herself before them.

"So!" she exclaimed, as well as her quaking voice would permit; "there's very pretty doings going on here, I find. You, Gilbert Copley, ought to be ashamed of yourself for letting yourself down to notice a paltry draggletail hussey like this; and as for you, ma'am," she added to Martha, "I'll take care that you have no more love-making in this place. For two pins, I'd turn you out this very moment, and stand the racket for it when our people came home."

"Indeed, Deborah," cried Martha, "it's no fault of mine. The young gentleman would kiss my hand in spite of everything."

"And where's the harm if I did?" exclaimed Gilbert, with an angry look towards Deborah. "This maiden and I have been acquainted with each other long before we met in this place, and if I can't use the privilege of friendship, it's very strange."

"But you never kissed *my* hand," cried Deborah, "nor said half the civil things you've thought proper to utter to this forward minx."

"Had I liked you half as well," replied Gilbert, "it is likely I should have told you so long before this. You now know that my heart is engaged to another, and if you must needs have a lover, there are plenty belonging to the band who are more worthy of your regard than I can ever hope to be."

"Let me advise you not to put me in a passion," cried Deborah, furiously. "You've never seen what I can do when my blood's up, and I can perhaps use a knife as well as the best among the crew. Love will sometimes turn to hate, and when it does, there's no saying where the mischief will end."

"You threaten me, woman?"

"I only speak my mind freely, that you may know what to expect," answered Deborah. "I don't want to harm you, but an angry woman is not a foe to be despised. You must either look coldly upon this girl, or the consequences will be worse than you think for."

"He does—he will look coldly upon me," cried the terrified Martha. "If he regards me, it is only as a sister, for we were brought up together, and he esteems me for old acquaintance sake."

"'Tis false!" exclaimed the woman, furiously. "I overheard enough to convince me that the young fellow would cast me off, because there's one that is younger and, it may be, prettier, that's to be had for the asking."

"Woman!" ejaculated Gilbert, wrathfully, "you presume upon a temper that you have never yet seen in its worst light. I have endured more than I ought, but it is now my command that you leave the room before my anger drives me to desperation."

"Your command!" she returned scornfully; "and pray who is Gilbert Copley, that he takes it upon himself to say so much to one who cares not for his threats? Leave the room, too! ay, ay, so I will, but it shall not be till this hussey goes with me."

"Martha Darnton remains where she is," replied Gilbert. "I have something yet to say to her, and she is not to be driven away merely because it is your will that we shall not be left together."

"You have heard me," exclaimed Deborah, addressing herself to the terrified girl, "and it now remains for yourself to say whether I am to be obeyed or not."

Martha shrunk from her in alarm, and the woman seizing her by the arm, snatched up a knife that was lying upon the table, and waved it threateningly above her head. Gilbert knew her fierce nature too well to

No. 8

doubt that she was capable of any crime, and taking from beneath his pillow one of the pistols that he always kept loaded by him, he presented it at the infuriated woman, exclaiming,—

"Release your hold, foul hag, or by the Heaven above us, I swear to send a brace of bullets through your polluted heart. Take off your hands, I say, or your blood shall answer for this violence!"

Deborah saw by the flashing of his eye that this was no time to stand parleying with a desperate man, and dropping the knife upon the ground, she at the same moment relaxed the grasp with which she had held Martha Darnton.

"What a coil is here," she exclaimed, "for what, after all, is nothing but a jest. I don't want to harm the girl, but I couldn't stand by and see you prefer her to myself, who have always been your friend."

"I never asked for your friendship," replied Gilbert, "and since matters have come to this pass, I must candidly confess that I would rather not have it."

"Well, then, give me back the present I gave when I thought your love was worth the having," she exclaimed. "If we are to quarrel, you can't want anything to remind you that your own folly has made an enemy where you might have had a friend."

"Take back your poniard, woman," he exclaimed, throwing on the table the weapon she had given him some time before. "The gift was not asked for, and, to confess the truth, I never esteemed it, seeing that it came from the hands of one whose connexion with this band made her hateful to my sight."

"Yet it was not to be despised, either," answered Deborah; "the day may come, young man, when such a weapon as this would save you from the gallows. Hah! you start at the sound of that fearful word; but I tell you, many a pretty fellow, that once belonged to our band, has swung upon the gibbet, and, doubt not, it will be your turn one of these days."

"Out, witch!" exclaimed Gilbert, furiously.

"Ay," she replied, "the truth is seldom palatable; yet for all that, you have heard it from my lips. I can see into futurity, and my words are not to be treated with scorn by one whose fate is already sealed."

"My fate," said the young man, "is to live and see you hanged."

"It may be so," exclaimed Deborah; "but it will not change your own doom. I myself know something of your history, and if you would learn more, seek it of Hugh Darnton, who could tell you that which you never dreamed of. You have been the companion of smugglers and robbers, yet, when the hangsman claims his due, it will be to put a rope round the neck of one of England's titled ones."

Astonished at the ambiguous words she had uttered, Gilbert Copley was about to demand an explanation of them, but ere he could do this, the door was suddenly burst open, and Harrowby, followed by Hugh Darnton and nearly the whole of the band, rushed tumultuously into the room.

"Gilbert," exclaimed the leader, "if your life is worth the caring for, make haste to save yourself. The devils of officers have raised a hue and cry, and, as some villain has betrayed our haunt, the pursuers will be upon us before we can make preparation for our defence."

"Whither do you propose going?" demanded Gilbert, who, during the time occupied by this speech, had been arming himself with all the weapons he possessed.

"It matters not where we are going," replied Mark; "for, turn which way we will, there can be no greater danger than in remaining where we are."

"Do you travel on horseback?"

"No. England is too hot to hold us just now," answered Harrowby;

" and so I've ordered the lugger to be got in readiness, and by this time she's waiting near the shore, at the bottom of these cliffs. But, how's this, Deborah?" he exclaimed. " You don't seem to be in any hurry to get yourself prepared for accompanying us."

" That's because I intend to stay where I am," she replied, sullenly.

" What! to run the chance of being taken and hanged as one of our band?"

" I care not what becomes of me," exclaimed Deborah; "for I'd rather risk my fate than go on board the lugger, when there'll be two in it that I hate. Let 'em hang me if they like, but there'll be one consolation for my last moments, which is, that I know another one, who is not far off from me, that will come to the same end before very long."

" You look very hard at Gilbert," said Harrowby; " but surely you don't mean to say he'll ever swing at the end of a rope?"

" But I do say it," she replied; " and when the time comes, perhaps he may recollect there was one that would have saved him, but was made an enemy by his own haughty conduct."

" And so you won't go with us, because he happens to be part of our company?"

" No," she replied, " I stay here, and if the officers show their faces at the Raven's Nest, I'll shew 'em a trick that shall make matters even between us."

" Why, what can a woman's arm do against half-a-dozen resolute fellows?" demanded Harrowby.

" I'll tell you what it can do," she replied; " it can throw a blazing brand into the gunpowder that's below in the vaults, and though my own life will be sacrificed, I can willingly yield it up for the sake of revenge."

" Well," exclaimed Mark Harrowby, " you've got a bit of spirit in you, it must be confessed, and if it's any consolation to have company with you, there's three of our band wandering somewhere about, and I suppose they'll be back in the course of an hour or two. Till we return here again, if things go on pretty quietly, and if you shouldn't blow up the old place, we may meet together by-and-bye and carry on matters as we've been used to do. So, boys, let's have one more carouse before we go, and then hey for new quarters till we find out how the land lies."

Brandy was now produced by Deborah, and each man drained three or four glasses successively, as if to inspire him with courage, and then leaving the house, they slowly descended by a winding path to the beach. Favoured by the moonlight, they were enabled to do this with tolerable ease, and then making their way towards a small cave that ran some distance into the rocks, they found a boat, into which they all stepped, and were rowed off towards the lugger which was lying about a mile from the shore. This they soon reached, and the sails being set, they pursued their way across the pathless bosom of the deep.

CHAPTER XV.

MATERNAL FEARS.—A TRAGIC OCCURRENCE.—THE DECLARATION.

LEAVING the smugglers for awhile to pursue their own course, we must now return to the mansion of Sir Lionel Dacre, where events had made considerable progress since we last left it. In less time than had been expected letters were received from Henry Markham and his father; the one announcing that he had received permission to pay his addresses to Eleanor, and the other expressing the highest gratification at the prospect of a union between the two families.

Thus far affairs were going on favourably enough; but the happiness of Agnes Evered had been for some little time upon the wane, for there was an evident coldness in the conduct of Lady Dacre towards her, and even Sir Lionel himself seemed not to treat her with the same cordiality that he had done when first she became an inmate of their house. At the beginning of this change Agnes was at a loss to discover the cause; but at last the truth flashed upon her mind, for Vivian had of late paid her a very marked attention, and it was, therefore, plain that his parents were displeased at the prospect of his uniting himself in marriage with a female whose prospects in life were far inferior to his own. Under these circumstances she determined to seek an asylum in the house of a relative, who had frequently offered her a shelter; and at the earliest opportunity that presented itself she informed Eleanor Dacre of the determination she had formed. From Eleanor the news, of course, soon passed to Vivian, and no sooner did he hear of what had passed, than he determined to see his mother upon the subject, and ascertain whether it was by her wish that Agnes was to leave a house which she had been taught to believe would be a permanent home. He was still bewildered with these thoughts when Lady Dacre entered the room to pass into the one adjoining.

"Stay, mother," he exclaimed; "you were the last person in my mind, and I would be glad if you will favour me with a few minutes' conversation."

"And pray what have you to say that is of so much importance?" asked her ladyship, with a smile at the impetuosity of his words.

"I would ask," he replied, "if you are aware that Miss Evered thinks of leaving our house?"

"Indeed, my dear Vivian!—this is the first I have heard of it," replied her ladyship, with surprise. "May I ask if you are aware of the reason that has prompted her to so sudden a resolution?"

"I am," answered Vivian;—"she believes there is a coldness on the part of Sir Lionel and yourself towards her, and rather than interfere with the happiness of our family, she has made up her mind to seek an asylum somewhere else."

"Surely," said Lady Dacre, "the foolish girl does not think we are tired of her?"

"I don't know that she thinks that," answered Vivian; "but it is certain she believes there is a marked difference in your conduct towards her of late, and with a proper spirit she has resolved to remain no longer where her presence is regarded as an intrusion."

"And has she really said there is a change in our conduct towards her?" demanded her ladyship.

"I have perhaps uttered more than I have a right to do," exclaimed Vivian, "for Miss Evered has too good sense to speak against those, who she justly conceives have been her best friends. That she believes her longer stay here would be an intrusion is true, and I would therefore ask of you whether there is any cause for a change of conduct that I, myself, have not failed to observe?"

"My actions are not to be questioned," answered Lady Dacre, "even if there were any grounds for the surmises you have thought proper to form. Miss Evered is, of course, the mistress of her own actions, and neither your father nor myself will urge her to remain here a moment longer than she thinks proper."

" Then, supposing she has formed an erroneous opinion," exclaimed Vivian, " you will not endeavour to remove it, though a few kind words would be sufficient to convince her that she is mistaken ?"

" It would be making a concession," replied Lady Dacre, " that I conceive to be quite unnecessary. If Miss Evered felt herself aggrieved, it was her duty to have mentioned it to me ; but since she has thought proper to let me hear of it in this roundabout way, I shall let affairs take their own course."

" And you will suffer an innocent and unsuspecting friend to suffer for a fault that arises entirely from her youth and inexperience ?"

" She has only herself to blame for it," answered her ladyship; " and if people will take such groundless notions into their heads, they must suffer for it."

" Have I your permission to tell Agnes that she is mistaken ?"

" Certainly not from me, Vivian," she replied. " Miss Evered found a home here when none other presented itself, and if she has grown dissatisfied with it there can be no wish on my part to persuade her to remain a moment longer than she wishes."

" Indeed, mother, you are unnecessarily angry with her," exclaimed Vivian, earnestly. " If there be any fault, let it remain with me, for Agnes knows not that the subject would be mentioned, and it is likely I have exaggerated her feelings upon the matter. Certain it is, however, that she has observed with grief a marked change in your deportment, and instead of blaming her for resolving to leave the house, she deserved all credit for making a sacrifice that must be painful in the extreme."

" That *you* would advocate her cause is nothing more than I expected," replied Lady Dacre, earnestly. " I have observed your attentions to her of late, and to confess the truth, Vivian I am not sorry that she has taken it into her head to leave us. I, however, still think she might have told me her intentions without desiring them to come through another channel."

" Again you are doing her an injustice," exclaimed Vivian, " for Miss Evered is quite unconscious that I had a notion of seeing you upon the matter. She knows not that I am aware of the uneasiness that has prompted her to this alternative, and if any one is to blame it is I alone who ought to bear it."

" How did you know her thoughts then ?" inquired Lady Dacre.

" From my sister Eleanor," replied the young man. " She is the confidant of Miss Evered, and I have perhaps been guilty of an indiscretion in mentioning that which was told me as a secret."

" Blame yourself as you may, Vivian," exclaimed his mother, " it will not remove from my mind the impression that Miss Evered has acted in this affair with a total want of candour. Why, instead of telling her troubles to your sister, did she not come to me and state what she has thought proper to repose in others ?"

" I am unable to answer your questions," replied the young man, " but a thousand excuses may be formed, unless your prejudices happen to stand in the way."

" Believe me, Vivian, I have no prejudices," exclaimed Lady Dacre, " nor is my regard for Miss Evered diminished, though it must be confessed some things have happened that I cannot but regret."

" May I inquire what it is you allude to ?" asked Vivian, earnestly.

" At present I must decline giving any explanation," replied her ladyship. " But pray tell me when did this conversation take place between your sister and Miss Evered ?"

" Two days ago."

" And you were immediately informed of it, I suppose. by your sister ?"

" No," replied Vivian, " I did not hear of it till this morning, and feeling naturally anxious to discover whether there was any ground for the belief that had taken possession of her mind, I seized the first opportunity that offered to mention it to you."

" And Miss Evered is determined to leave us ?"

" She is," replied her son ; "that is, unless you will condescend to assure her, that there is no ground for the idea she has formed."

" Which I shall certainly not do," replied Lady Dacre.   " Indeed, to tell you the truth, Vivian, there are reasons why I would rather she does leave us for a time, and by-and-bye I may be induced to tell you the cause of my altered opinion with respect to the young lady."

" But, surely," exclaimed Vivian, " you will not be so unjust as to let her leave our house without an explanation taking place ?"

" If an explanation is to take place," answered Lady Dacre, haughtily, " it must come from Miss Evered herself. Sir Lionel and I have acted as generous friends to her, and I must say she has shown a want of gratitude in adopting such a course as she has."

" Alas !" cried Vivian, " you know not the feelings that may have actuated such a heart as hers. She is most grateful for all the favours she has received, and her quitting your protection is only a proof that she is unwilling to remain longer with those who have lost their former confidence in her."

" You are warm in her praises, sir."

" And if I am so," he replied, " the warmth has been occasioned by seeing a young and friendless orphan suffering through the misconceptions of those she has ever regarded as her best friends."

" I am glad," exclaimed Lady Dacre, " to hear that there is no other cause for the interest you have manifested."

" There can be no better reason," answered her son, " than that which prompts a man to lend his assistance for the protection of the helpless. But we will not cavil, mother, about trifles ; an unfriended girl is rendered unhappy by circumstances over which you have control, and the only favour I ask of you, is, that I may have your permission to see Miss Evered, and explain away the error which has led to a resolution we may all of us afterwards deplore."

" I shall give no permission of the kind," replied her ladyship.   " But to convince you that my feelings towards her are unaltered, you may inform her that I shall be happy at any time to give her an interview, to assure her that however hasty she may have been in her judgment, I am still inclined to be her friend."

" And will you try to prevail on her to live with us on the same terms as before ?"

" That I cannot do, Vivian."

" Then you will send forth an orphan to feel the harshness which the world is too apt to bestow upon those who are friendless."

" Miss Evered is not without friends," exclaimed Lady Dacre ; " and the one she is going to will, I dare say, afford more satisfaction than we have been able to do.   There is Mr. Blundell, for instance, whose wealth is said to be immense ; surely, he will not refuse to give shelter to the orphan daughter of his late brother ?"

" And what does she know of him ?" demanded Vivian.   " He has lately returned from India with a fortune that he has made there ; but we have too many proofs that such men are harsh and ungenerous to their poor relations. It is true, I have no right to say so of Mr. Blundell, but, as we know not at present what he is, it would be cruel to trust Agnes with him, till she has been invited to partake the shelter of his roof."

" Mr. Blundell appears to be a good sort of man, I'm sure," returned Lady Dacre ; " and even if he should not be all that we could wish, I don't see how I can possibly make things better."

" At any rate, you can prevent them getting worse," answered Vivian. " There is no reason why Miss Evered should go away from us, and a word from you would prevail upon her to stay, and we should once more see her happy, as she used to be before this unfortunate coldness took place."

" You speak without consideration, Vivian," said her ladyship. " Miss Evered is the uncontrolled mistress of her own actions. The step she is about to take is the result of her own deliberations, and it would be quite ridiculous for any one to attempt to persuade her after she has once made up her mind. For my own part, I am not inclined to run the chance of a refusal ; so, as she is resolved, the best way is to let her go, and if at any time she would like to return, I give you my word, that there shall be no opposition on my part. But enough has been said upon this subject, and, as I am not inclined to argue upon it any longer, I shall take my leave of you, Vivian, with a hope that you will let matters take their own course."

Lady Dacre left him with these words, and never did Vivian feel more grief than when he found that all he had said was of no avail. For some time past he had buoyed himself up with a hope that no opposition would be offered to his union with Agnes Evered, and now his every prospect had been blighted by a prejudice that was as unjust as it was cruel. On the score of family connexions there could be no objection to the marriage, and if money was an object to be desired, she was not without prospects from the wealthy uncle who had just returned from India, and whose only son was afflicted with what had been pronounced to be incurable insanity. It was therefore with a broken and perturbed spirit, that he retired to the privacy of his own chamber, to reflect upon his blighted prospects, and devise further means for healing the difference which had broken out between his family and their young protege.

Vivian passed a restless night, and it was not till nearly dawn that he fell into a slumber, to dream over the troubles which had afflicted his waking fancy. Scarcely, however, had he slept an hour, when a violent knocking at the door aroused him, and the voice of one of the servants was heard without, announcing that a fire had broken out at the house of Simon Stripes, and that a report was spread abroad that the old man and his servant had been murdered during the night. Upon hearing this startling intelligence, he leaped out of bed, and hurrying on his clothes, proceeded to the scene of conflagration, where he quickly ascertained that the news was but too true in all its details.

The house, which stood in a lonely situation, had been discovered some time before to be in flames, by a labourer who was passing near on his way to a neighbouring farm-house. An alarm was instantly raised, and the door being broken open, the body of Simon Stripes was found in a room which the flames had not yet reached, and from the marks of blows upon the head of the unfortunate man, there could be no doubt that he had been murdered, and the house afterwards set fire to in order to conceal the guilt of the assassin. A search was then made for the servant girl, but it was not till after the lapse of a couple of hours, that the body, nearly consumed, was found beneath the ruins, but so dreadfully had it been mutilated by the fallen ruins, that there was no possibility of judging whether her death had been occasioned by fire or violence. The general opinion, however, was that she had shared the fate of her master, and that she had fallen by the same ruthless hands that had deprived the old man of life.

Of course, the occurrence occasioned a great deal of noise and speculation. Everybody was anxious to afford assistance towards discovering the authors of so diabolical a deed. Large rewards were offered for the apprehension of the murderer, and constables were sent off in every direction to ascertain if any suspicious persons had lately been lurking about. All, however, was in vain, no clue whatever could be found, and it seemed that the murder of Simon Stripes and his servant was doomed to become one of those impenetrable mysteries that sometimes occur in the annals of crime.

Leaving this fearful subject for a time, however, we must now return to Vivian, who, on returning home again, gave way to the thoughts which had so deeply afflicted him throughout the night. He would have sought an interview with his father, to try whether his influence might be obtained in behalf of Agnes Evered, but reflection convinced him that the effort would be useless, and leaving the house he strolled into the pleasure grounds, where, to his infinite joy, he found Agnes walking by herself. In an instant he was by her side, and uttering a hasty apology for his intrusion, he falteringly inquired if the news was indeed true, that she was about to leave them.

" It is," replied Agnes, with a sigh, that she in vain endeavoured to suppress.

" And is it by your own wish that you do so?"

" Certainly."

" May I ask the motive that has induced you to come to such a resolution?"

" I would rather the secret remained within my own bosom," she replied. " The reason that actuates me is one that deeply afflicts me, since it has cost the friendship of those whose esteem was most valuable to me."

" Then let me entreat you, my dear Agnes, to reflect, ere you take a step that may be productive of much unhappiness. I speak selfishly, perhaps, and yet I cannot resist the impulse that bids me urge you to remain with us a brief time longer."

" And why should I do so," she asked, " since there are those who consider my presence here an intrusion?"

" Be assured, Agnes, you have deceived yourself," he exclaimed. " As an orphan you were invited here, to share the shelter of our roof. and there are none but would regret your absence as one of the greatest misfortunes that could befal us."

" There is, indeed, deep cause for my gratitude to those who have afforded me protection," she replied; " yet I have at length found, that for the happiness of all parties, it will be better for me to adopt the plan I have proposed. Bitterly do I regret the necessity, but, since no other alternative remains, I must sacrifice my own wishes to what I consider an imperative duty."

" Nay," said Vivian; " you have judged too hastily in this instance, and a short time will serve to convince you that your presence here is as welcome as ever it was. Some fancied slight has been the cause of this, and all I implore of you is, to remain with us a few days longer."

" That I must do," answered Agnes; " for the gratitude I bear your father and mother forbids me to quit their house with any appearance of anger. I may probably stay here a fortnight longer, but at the end of that time, I take my leave of them, in all probability never to return."

" A fortnight," exclaimed Vivian, " may effect such alterations, that you will not think it necessary to put your present design into execution. The ardour with which I urge you to remain with us, arises partly from selfish motives; for I feel, Agnes, that to part with you would be to involve me in an abyss of misery from which there could be no escape."

" Vivian," cried Miss Evered, " your words recal me to a sense of that duty which you would fain make me forget. I should have avoided this interview, for does not what has just passed warrant Lady Dacre for the coolness

with which she has of late regarded me. She has feared an avowal such as you have uttered, and it was to avoid your presence that I resolved to quit this house for ever."

"Then you bid me give myself up to despair!" exclaimed Vivian, reproachfully.

"I would rather bid you forget one," answered Agnes, "whose greatest cause of unhappiness will be the reflection that she has brought sorrow to those who have been her generous friends. I saw not the fatal error, however, till it was too late, and now the cup of bitterness has been filled to the very brim. But be warned in time, Vivian, for it is not yet too late to escape from a danger that threatens your future peace."

"Will you then afford me no hope," he exclaimed, "that the time is not far off when I may be happy in the possession of her who alone can render my life of value to myself?"

"You have heard me," she replied, "and, oh, do not urge me further upon a subject that I dare not speak of."

"You love me not, Agnes," cried Vivian, "or my passion would have met with a far different return."

"I feared your reproaches," answered Miss Evered, "and it wanted only that to complete my misery. My duty to those who sheltered me has led to the resolution you have heard; and the only consolation that remains for me is the certainty that I have sacrificed my own feelings to the wishes of others."

"Has my mother ever mentioned the subject to you?" asked Vivian.

"She has not."

"Then how know you that she would be opposed to our union?"

"I have observed the change that has taken place in her conduct towards me," replied Agnes; "and my own heart told me the cause; I have lost the

No. 9

friendship of those I love, but they shall at least see that I can yield myself obediently to their wishes."

"And have you forgotten," asked Vivian, "that by adopting this course
you have plunged me into a sea of despair that death only can terminate ?"

" Alas ! there is no help for it," cried Agnes ; "for had I yielded to my
affection for yourself, it would have been at the cost of losing those friends
to whom I am most deeply indebted. Had there been no such obstacles in
the way I could have given my hand where my heart has long since been bestowed."

"Your words inspire me with fresh hope," exclaimed Vivian ; "for, since
I am not despised, I will look forward to the period when all restraint will be
removed. Sir Lionel regards my happiness far more than he does his own,
and he will yield to my earnest entreaties."

"And your mother ?"

"Will learn to subdue her own feelings when she sees the happiness of her
son depends upon it," answered Vivian.

"You would fain believe so," returned Agnes ; "but be assured, 'tis only a
delusion that will afterwards make the disappointment more bitter. Lady
Dacre looks forward to a high alliance for her son, and never will she consent
to receive into her family a poor orphan, who has been the object of her
bounty."

"Do you afford me no hope ?" exclaimed Vivian, in a tone of deep despondency.

"To do so would be an act of cruelty," she replied, "for my heart assures
me that there is not the most distant chance of my ever being received into
your family. This meeting should have been avoided, but since it has unfortunately taken place, let us now separate, and forget the subject of our
separation. We may meet again, perhaps, before I leave ; but, if we should
do so, let me entreat you to speak no more upon an affair that must now be
brought to an end."

Agnes Evered hurried from the room ere Vivian could prevent her departure, and for some minutes he remained as if deprived of all power of motion.
Upon collecting his scattered thoughts, however, he resolved not to yield
himself to despair until every hope of success had entirely failed him.

CHAPTER XVI.

AN EXPLANATION.—THE RETURN.—IMPORTANT NEWS.

ON the day succeeding the interview described in the last chapter, Agnes
received a message from Lady Dacre, requesting to see her with as little delay
as possible. She trembled at the thought of meeting with one whom she had
reason to believe was displeased with her ; but, on entering the room where
her ladyship was waiting for her, she was agreeably surprised by the warmth
and unusual kindness with which she was greeted. Agnes soon recovered her
composure, and, having taken a seat next to Lady Dacre, she said,—

"I believe your ladyship wished to see me upon business of importance ?"

"I did," was the reply. "In fact, I have for some time desired an interview to discuss an affair that has occasioned a good deal of trouble to Sir
Lionel, as well as myself. You can perhaps guess that I allude to my son,
whose future destiny may be in your own hands ?"

"Alas !" cried Agnes, "this subject is, indeed, one that I would have
gladly avoided. It has been the source of much unhappiness to me, yet the
step I am about to take will, I trust, procure for me the approbation of both
Sir Lionel and yourself."

"You are prepared, then," said Lady Dacre, "to sacrifice your own feelings rather than wound those of others?"

"My purpose is already fixed," answered Miss Evered, "and in a few days I shall quit a house where I fear my presence has excited too much uneasiness."

"This is exactly what I expected from you," exclaimed Lady Dacre, "and if I show too steady an acquiescence in your plans, I hope you will do me the justice to believe that it is from no desire to lose the society of one whom I could regard as a daughter, were it not that I foresee much misery in the event of my son forming an imprudent alliance. Sir Lionel has expressed his disapprobation of such an union, and it must be confessed that I also have objections, though, had circumstances permitted it, I could have rejoiced to see you more closely allied to our family."

"I have been to blame for remaining here after there was no longer a doubt of your son's partiality for me," replied Agnes. "My own want of fortune is a sufficient barrier to such an union, and it now only remains for me to adopt a course that shall at once relieve my friends from the anxiety my presence here has given rise to."

"May I ask where you intend to reside?"

"With my uncle."

"But Mr. Blundell," observed her ladyship, "may not be inclined to make so great an alteration in her family arrangements."

"I have already written to him on the subject," answered Agnes, "and no doubt he will be here within a few hours, to take me with him; still, however, your ladyship may rely upon it I shall never forget the gratitude I owe to those who have extended their kindness to an almost friendless orphan."

"And you may also be assured," added Lady Dacre, "that the generous course you have adopted will secure for you the esteem of those who know the sacrifice you have made in their behalf. Vivian will soon learn to forget his boyish passion; and, when his heart has been given to another, I hope we shall resume the intimacy that has been thus suddenly broken off."

"Rather let me be forgotten, as if it had never been my misfortune to bring trouble on your house," replied Agnes. "The favours I have received can never be effaced from my memory; yet reflection will bring bitterness to my soul when I think that there are hearts left behind that will feel pain in consequence of what has passed."

"Vivian will, no doubt, experience grief when you leave us," answered Lady Dacre; "but time will serve to subdue his sorrow, and, ere long, we shall see him resume all his former gaiety and spirits. He has ever been submissive to the will of his father, and cannot but see that what is now done is solely from an anxiety for his own happiness. In truth, Sir Lionel has ever looked forward to a high matrimonial alliance, and though the present steps may appear harsh, the reasons which have produced them are of great and permanent importance."

"And shall be respected, my kind friend," exclaimed Miss Evered. "The obstacles are such as I can never hope to overcome, and no selfish motives shall ever induce me to bring dissention into a family that I have so many reasons to respect."

At this point of their conversation they were interrupted by the entrance of Sir Lionel Dacre, and in a few minutes afterwards Agnes took an opportunity to leave the room in order that she might, in the solitude of her own chamber, give way to those tears of sorrow which she had with difficulty restrained during her interview.

For two days after this Vivian was unable to see her alone, for she cautiously avoided giving him an opportunity to renew the entreaties which she had promised to listen to no longer. Half suspecting what had occurred, he several times determined to speak to his father upon the subject ; but wishing to see Agnes first, he deferred his plan in the hope that she might have something to communicate which would afford a brighter prospect than his fears had led him to anticipate. At length he resolved to see his sister Eleanor upon the subject, and having succeeded in finding her alone, he recounted the doubts that perplexed his mind, and in conclusion demanded from her, as the confidant of Miss Evered, whether he had any chance of succeeding in his suit.

" Why, to tell you the truth," she replied, after hearing him to an end, " I scarcely know what opinion to give upon an affair that is full of perplexity. That Agnes regards you with somewhat more than a sisterly affection is very certain ; but there are obstacles in the way that I fear will not be very easily surmounted."

" What are the obstacles you speak of ?"

" The prejudice of a father and mother, who look forward to a high alliance for their son," answered Eleanor. " They are not free, as you are aware, from pride of birth, and as there is a sort of mystery connected with the mother of Agnes Evered, they are but too ready to put the worst constructions upon it."

" But," exclaimed Vivian, " they know her father to have been an honourable man, and a soldier, and surely that is a consideration that ought to weigh down all other feelings upon the subject."

" Very true, my dear brother," she replied ; " yet your arguments, I fear, would go but little way towards convincing them that they ought to sacrifice their own opinion in favour of yours."

" At all events, I will see them upon the subject," answered her brother, " and should they prove as resolute as you seem to imagine, it will then be for me to assert my own rights in an affair that so nearly concerns myself. They may be prejudiced against Agnes, but it does not follow that I may not be able to convince them that they are doing her an act of cruel injustice."

" To speak my mind more freely," returned Eleanor, " I believe your chance in that respect is a very feeble one. Agnes has already had an interview with our mother, and the consequence of it is that she has resolved to quit the house with as little delay as possible, and thus remove herself from the presence of one whose society has been strictly forbidden."

" Then she loves me not ?" cried Vivian.

" Nay, there you wrong her," answered his sister, " for I can take it upon upon myself to declare that her heart is yours, and yours only."

" Why then does she resolve to leave our house," demanded Vivian, " when she knows that by such a step she will render me a slight that must embitter my future life ?"

" And do you forget," asked Eleanor, " that by the same step she consigns herself to a degree of sorrow that may last during the remainder of her existence ?"

" How easily, then, she can avoid it," exclaimed Vivian. " Let her remain where she is for the present, and I have little doubt that the difficulties which environ us will be removed more easily than she expects."

" But her word has been given, and Agnes is not one to break a promise, however painful it may be to keep it."

" The promise was given hastily," answered her brother ; " and, therefore, may be broken without reproach."

" So, at least, thinks not Agnes Evered," exclaimed Eleanor.

" Nay, I am sure that you, on calmer consideration, would not ask her to do that which would render her dishonoured in her own sight. That she will endure much pain from the separation I well know, yet all will be suffered with resignation rather than forfeit a promise that has been solemnly given."

" Eleanor," exclaimed her brother, with more sternness than he usually manifested towards her, " I had hoped to have found in you a friend who would rather assist me than throw a damp upon my fondest hopes."

" And my assistance you shall ever have, my dear Vivian," she replied ; " but I cannot counsel Agnes Evered to do that which all of us might afterwards regret. She knows the feelings of your family upon the subject, and, in my opinion, has acted a praiseworthy part in adopting the step she has chosen."

" What !" he cried, " even though it may consign me to a life of misery ?"

" There is no reason why you should take it so much to heart," replied Eleanor ; " and, in a little while, I have no doubt, you will think as I do upon the subject. Our father and mother hold you in their tenderest regard, and when they see that your happiness depends upon a marriage with Agnes, they will yield up their own prejudices, and consent to receive her as one of our family."

" *You* think so," answered Vivian ; " but unfortunately *I* have reasons to believe they will never consent to it. The altered behaviour of my mother towards Agnes proves that a strong antipathy has grown up, and it is owing to this change of conduct that Miss Evered has determined to quit our house."

" Yet she may only do so for a time," observed Eleanor, " and when she returns to us it will be as the destined bride of my brother. Your languid smile, Vivian, tells me that you put little faith in my prophecy; but such is my firm belief, and it is my most earnest wish that you should think as I do."

" What does Agnes herself say to it ?"

" It is unfair to ask me to disclose that which has passed in confidence," answered his sister.

" But does she appear to grieve at the prospect of our speedy separation ?"

" Ay, deeply."

" Yet persists in her resolution ?"

" How can she do otherwise ?" asked Eleanor. " She fears being the cause of a quarrel in the family which has afforded her an asylum, and has, therefore, adopted the generous course of plunging herself in sorrow rather than be the cause of bringing it upon others."

" And yet her generous conduct makes no impression upon those who have driven her to the painful alternative ?"

" To tell you the truth," replied Eleanor, " I rather think neither our father nor mother have a notion of the intensity with which you love each other. They are absorbed in their own worldly considerations, and can think only of the high alliance for which they have destined their son."

" Without troubling themselves to think," exclaimed Vivian, " of the wretchedness to which their cold, worldly conduct must bring him. I will, however, see them on the subject, and should it not be possible to change their determination, I will purchase a commission in the army, and spend the remainder of my life abroad."

" Nay, let me entreat you not to be too rash in taking such a step," cried his sister, earnestly. " Agnes will not leave us for a day or two, and in the meantime circumstances may arise to remove some of the difficulties that have been cast in your way. Those who are opposed to your marriage with my friend may see reason to change their opinions, and even if that should not be the case, you may then seek an interview with them, and state the determination you have just expressed."

" And, in the meantime," exclaimed Vivian, " you will perhaps see Agnes, and learn from her whether, in the event of no favourable change taking place, she will consent to become mine, and thus risk a displeasure which I hope would not be of very long duration."

"I am convinced she would not listen to such a proposition," answered Eleanor.

"Yet you say she loves me?"

"She has confessed as much to me," replied his sister, "and it is for that reason that I feel assured she will take no step that must bring upon you the anger of those whom it is your duty to obey."

Vivian was about to reply to this, when the door flew open, and, to his mingled joy and surprise, Henry Markham entered the room. The alternate changes of colour visible in the countenance of Eleanor showed that she was no less gratified than her brother; but anxious to conceal the emotion this unexpected return of her lover had given rise to, she in faltering accents begged permission to retire, and quitted the apartment to seek out Agnes, and communicate the conversation that had just passed.

"You are surprised to see me return sooner than I was expected," said Markham, as soon as he and his friend were left alone; "but the truth is, love has made me restless, and I could not endure a longer separation from your sister."

"Matters seem to run more smoothly with you than they do with me," exclaimed Vivian, with a feeling of bitterness that he could not restrain.

"Everything is as I could have wished," answered Markham, without heeding the momentary vexation of his friend. "There are no objections to my marriage with your sister; and, believe me, one of the chief sources of my happiness, while returning hither, was the hope that I should hear there was no impediment in the way of your union with Agnes Evered."

"The subject," replied Vivian, "is a painful one to speak upon; yet, as we have no secrets from each other, I may as well tell you at once that a positive interdict has been put upon our marriage."

"May I inquire upon what ground?"

"The want of fortune is one cause," replied Vivian; "and another is, Agnes Evered does not come from a family high enough to make her a fitting match for the heir of a baronetcy."

"Indeed! and how can that be said when nobody knows from how proud a descent she may have come from her mother's side. You shake your head, Vivian, but there has always been a mystery respecting the wife of Captain Evered, and to keep you no longer in suspense, I have, within the last few hours, heard enough to convince me that she was the daughter of a nobleman."

"Agnes's mother the daughter of a nobleman?"

"Ay."

"Where heard you this?"

"The story is rather a long one," replied Markham, "but I will bring it into as small a compass as possible. The truth then is, that on my return I stopped at the inn where you and I called on the day when we were journeying hither from the university. The conversation between the host and myself naturally enough turned upon our singular encounter with the madman, and that led me to speak of Agnes Evered as being nearly related to the party we were talking about. Dawson's countenance changed a good deal at this part of our conversation, and after a great deal of pressing, I got him to confess that he knew more about the family than he at first seemed willing to admit. In short, I heard quite enough to convince me that, on the mother's side, Miss Evered is descended from a family of higher birth than has been hitherto suspected."

" For Heaven's sake be brief in your narrative," exclaimed Vivian, as his friend paused.

" So I will," answered Markham; " but as Dawson was rather prolix in his story, it takes some little time to bring its chief points within a narrow compass. However, it appears, that Dawson had once been much better off than he is at present, and lived in London, where he and his wife kept a house in very good style. Things, however, began to grow worse with them, and as no other alternative presented itself, they opened their doors to families who make the metropolis an occasional place of residence. But it seems things still continued to go on crossly with them, and had almost arrived at the last extremity, when a certain Ensign Evered went to take lodgings there, and took with him his beautiful young wife, to whom he whom he had been recently married."

" And this was the mother of Agnes ?"

" Exactly so," replied Markham; " the marriage was a runaway one, and though the bride came of a highly distinguished family, both she and her husband were so short of money, that they were obliged to live with the greatest economy, in order to avoid getting into debt."

" In consequence, I suppose," observed Vivian, " of the young lady's friends being angry at her having formed a matrimonial alliance of which they did not approve."

" That was it," replied his friend, " and their rage was the greater, because they had arranged for her marriage with a nobleman whose fortune offered a golden bait that was not to be resisted. But it happened that his age was about double that of the intended bride, and we can therefore scarcely wonder that she chose for her husband a young, handsome fellow, whose good looks she preferred to either wealth or title."

" Did the young couple live long in the house of this Dawson?" inquired Vivian.

" Four or five months, I believe," replied the other, " and at the expiration of that time, Ensign Evered was called upon to join his regiment, which had been ordered abroad. The parting was a most reluctant one on both sides, and as no better home offered just then, it was arranged that the wife should remain at Dawson's till it should be known whether her friends would be reconciled to her. This being the only thing that could be done, he took a sorrowful leave of his wife, and the next day left England, to be absent longer than he had expected. Their parting was the more painful, as Mrs. Evered was then in a situation that promised in due time to make an addition to her family."

" And did this Dawson behave kindly to her after she was thus left alone ?"

" The truth is, he was at heart a great scoundrel," answered Markham; " but of that part you will presently be able to judge for yourself. As I was telling you, the ensign quitted his native land, and he had not been gone many days, when an elderly gentleman called at her lodings, and from what passed, it seemed that he and Mrs. Evered had been previously acquainted. She was not, however, very glad to see him, for Mrs. Dawson, who had a habit of listening at doors, overheard a few words that were just sufficient to serve as a foundation for certain little surmises of her own. But be this as it may, when the old gentleman went away, he left with the master of the house a sum of money sufficient to support the poor lady for some time to come."

" Had they any idea who he was?" asked Vivian.

" Why, at first it was supposed to be her father," answered the other; " but at length, by dint of listening and other contrivances, Mrs. Dawson discovered what she considered to be a very important secret."

" That is to say, the name of the gentleman, I suppose ?"

" Yes ; and who do you think he was ?"

" I am unable to guess."

" Well, then, to end your suspense," answered Markham, " the mysterious visitor was no other than my uncle, the Earl of Belfast, who it seems had been the lady's elderly lover, and who, it further appeared, she had run away from when she gave her hand to Ensign Evered."

" Did you ever happen to hear anything that may serve to corroborate this extraordinary statement ?" asked Vivian.

" Oh, yes," replied the other. " It has often been mentioned in my presence, that the earl was disappointed in a love affair, but as there was so great a difference between his own age and that of his intended bride, it was generally admitted that he had no great cause to complain. However, the result of it all was, that my relative gave up all further idea of marriage, and I suppose he afterwards sought out the young lady under the idea of retaliating upon Ensign Evered for the disappointment he had occasioned."

" And you are certain the lady you speak of was the mother of Agnes ?"

" There can be no doubt of it," answered Markham. " The child was born in Dawson's house, and the man himself is ready to come forward at any time to repeat the story I have been telling you."

" Yet he knows not who the lady was ?"

" That was a mystery he could never penetrate," replied Markham ; " because his lodger was resolutely silent upon that particular subject. But from what little he could gather, he feels quite satisfied that she was the daughter of a nobleman."

" How long did she remain at Dawson's ?"

" Why, the truth is," replied Markham, " the poor lady's health began to decline from the period of her giving birth to the child, and within a few months after she died. Mr. Dawson appears to have acted a cruel part, for the letters that came from the ensign were witheld, and her last moments were embittered by the thought that her husband's affection had been alienated from her."

" And she never heard from him ?"

" Unfortunately, the schemes against her were but too successful," answered Markham, " and she died in the full belief of having been forsaken by the man for whose sake she had forfeited the regard of her family. A few weeks afterwards, however, a friend of the ensign's called at the house, and having ascertained the fate of Mrs. Evered, he took the child away, and placed it with some persons in humble circumstances, by whom the child was taken care of till the return of her father."

" Who, I suppose," observed Vivian, " never learned the circumstances under which his wife had died ?"

" He knew not that his letters had been intercepted," replied the other ; " and as the war had ended, he sought for a place where he might pass the remainder of his days in peace and quietness.

" The story," observed Vivian, " has a strange air of romance about it, and the worst is, that the facts rest upon the assertions of that consummate villain, Dawson. How can we believe the assertions of a scoundrel who has confessed his share in such an act of monstrous perfidy ?"

" I am inclined to think the fellow has spoken truth for once in his life," answered Markham. " Besides, he has entrusted me with a packet of the intercepted letters, which I am to place in the hands of Miss Evered, and no doubt they will serve in a great measure to confirm the story I have been relating."

" Heaven grant it may be so," exclaimed Vivian ; and then, with a sigh, he

added,—"but, even if it should be so, I see not how the clearing up of this mystery can be of any advantage to me."

"That must, of course, depend upon yourself," answered her friend. "You love the young lady, it seems, and the only obstacle to your happiness is the mingled pride and prejudice of your parents. I would see them upon the subject: open your mind freely, without disguise; tell them the wretchedness you will be doomed to if they oppose this marriage, and I think they will yield to the argument."

"I am sure they will not."

"Well then, I should marry her in spite of their objections," exclaimed Markham; "at all events, see them upon the subject first; and, if your entreaties fail to make any impression, it will then remain for you to decide what course it will be best to adopt."

Vivian was thus prevailed on to try the effect of an appeal to the affection of his parents, and shortly afterwards he left his friend to go and meditate alone upon the arguments he should use on the momentous occasion.

CHAPTER XVII.

PREJUDICES.—AN INTERDICTION.—NUPTIALS POSTPONED.

The mind of Vivian was soon made up, and within half an hour after his conversation with Markham, he entered the room where his father and mother were seated alone. The subject nearest to heart was briefly, but firmly explained; and, in order that a perfect understanding might take place, he declared that he was resolved either to marry Miss Evered, or remain single

No. 10

for life. Sir Lionel Dacre listened to him with tolerable composure; but her ladyship could not so well repress her emotions, and in a haughty, imperious tone she demanded if he had reflected on the consequences of acting in opposition to the will of his parents.

"I have," he replied, "and must beg respectfully to suggest that my own feelings should be consulted in an affair upon which my future happiness or misery depends. I believe you cannot entertain one unkind thought of Agnes, and therefore the only objection you can raise against our union is the worldly one, that her fortune is small. That it is so cannot be denied; but I have lately ascertained that she is descended from a noble family, and thus one of your chief reasons for opposing our marriage is at an end."

"What proof have you that she is of noble origin?"

"The proof I believe will very soon be produced," answered Vivian, "and then I should imagine you will no longer take into consideration the smallness of her fortune."

"And why," demanded Lady Dacre, "should you still seek the hand of Miss Evered, when you see how much it is against our wishes?"

"Because I feel that my future felicity is dependant upon our destinies being united," answered her son.

"This is the weakness of a love-sick boy," exclaimed Lady Dacre, "and may be controlled with a little effort on your own part. Wait a few months before any decisive step is taken in this business, and during that time you will, I hope, see some other female, whose beauty will drive from your remembrance the image of one whom I can esteem as a friend, though I cannot consent that she should become your wife."

"Do not believe that I can ever forget her," answered her son, earnestly. "My heart cannot prove aithless to its first attachment; and I will either marry Agnes Evered, or never wed at all."

"My dear Vivian," exclaimed Sir Lionel, "subdue, I entreat you, this wild infatuation, that, if persisted in, can only end in your own destruction. Wait till you have more experience; and, if at the end of twelvemonths, you are still bent upon this alliance, I will seriously consider the subject, and may perhaps be induced to yield rather than thwart you further."

"If he will only consent to that," cried Lady Dacre, "I feel assured that he will see the duty of yielding to the earnest entreaties of those who are only anxious for his future happiness and welfare."

"Nay," he exclaimed, "I would not have you depend upon my fickleness, since I feel thoroughly assured that my heart can never be given to another. At present I will not urge the point any further with you, because I see it is impossible just now to remove this unfortunate prejudice. Another time, however, we may refer to it again, and you will then see that my heart remains unchanged in its love for Agnes Evered."

Here the conversation ended, and Vivian was obliged to acknowledge to himself, with a sigh, that he had made but little progress in the object that was most dear to him. The only thought which consoled him, was, that his views were now fully explained; and, as his father did not seem to be quite so opposed to the marriage as Lady Dacre was, there might be some faint hope that he would be able to prevail over the scruples which had unfortunately forced themselves on her mind. They had now heard from him that his happiness depended on the determination they might come to, and surely, he thought, they would not blight his fairest hopes when, by a word, they might render him happy in the possession of an inestimable woman.

It was nearly a week after the return of Henry Markham, that Miss Evered left her own chamber, to mix, as usual, with the family. Her countenance had assumed a pale and melancholy expression during the period that she had secluded herself; but, on seeing that this was observed by Vivian, she attempted to appear more cheerful. The effort, however, was painfully apparent, and the lover perceived, with anguish, that she was a prey to the same griefs that had taken possession of his own heart.

Her reception by Lady Dacre was kind, as usual; but it was easy to see that there was a constraint which she in vain tried to conceal. Sir Lionel was as kind and warm-hearted as ever; he expressed great pleasure at seeing her again, and regretted with sincerity the illness which had deprived them of her society. As for Vivian, he now felt certain of having an opportunity to speak with Agnes on the subject of their ill-starred love. But, to his chagrin, she avoided him whenever they were likely to be left alone, and he was thus left to form a thousand jealous suspicions, either that her love towards him cooled, or that she was afraid of giving offence to Sir Lionel and Lady Dacre, by encouraging the addresses of their son.

Henry Markham, however, found an opportunity of giving into her possession the packet of letters which he had received from Dawson. In as brief a manner as possible he explained the circumstances under which they had come into the hands of this man, explaining the motives which had induced the fellow to retain possession of them, and offered his most zealous services, if he could render any, towards removing a mystery which had so long involved her.

Her father had sometimes slightly alluded to the circumstances attending the earlier period of his life, and after his funeral, she found among a heap of other documents, a letter, evidently written by the person who transacted his business, detailing all that had occurred upon visiting the house where her unfortunate mother had died. Upon the margin of this letter were a few lines in the handwriting of her father, in which he denounced curses on the heads of her oppressors, and vowed to be revenged on them as soon as he could return to England.

The parcel which she received from Henry Markham contained half-a-dozen letters, three of which were from her mother to her father, and the other three from him to her. All of them were expressive of the greatest attachment to each other; the principal grief of the writers seemed to be the long interval that separated them, and the probability that they might never see each other again in this world. Agnes wept over these sad memorials of those who were now lost to her for ever, and sinking back in her chair, she gave way to the grief that had been occasioned by the perusal of the letters.

It was during this time that Eleanor came bounding into the room with a joyful countenance, to inform Agnes that her uncle had just arrived at the mansion. The intelligence was most welcome to the sorrowing girl, for so long a time had passed since she wrote, that she began to have serious doubts as day after day passed by without receiving any answer from him. Now, however, all her doubts were removed, and with a lighter heart than she had felt for many a day before, she accompanied Eleanor to the room where the old gentleman was impatiently awaiting her arrival.

"My dear little Aggy," he exclaimed, after the first salutations were over, "I have come to take you away from our kind friends, unless any reasonable cause can be shown to the contrary. I suppose you thought I had forgotten you, my love; but the truth is, I knew you were a welcome visiter here, and so I deferred coming till it was perfectly convenient to myself."

"When do you think of taking your departure?" she eagerly inquired.

"Humph!" he replied, in an undecided tone; "perhaps to-morrow or the next day."

"Can it not be immediately?"

"What, to-day?"

"If convenient to yourself, I should like to go immediately," replied Agnes.

"Are you tired of your visit?"

"No," she replied, with some confusion; "but, as it is decided that I am to leave my kind friends, I care not how soon the pain of parting from them is over."

The truth is, however, that both Vivian and his friend happened to be out at the time, and Agnes was most anxious to take the opportunity in order that she might be spared the affliction of a parting from her lover. She, therefore, hastened to her room, wrote a short farewell letter to him, which she confided to the care of Eleanor, and as the carriage was by that time ready, she bade adieu to her friends, and immediately afterwards was hurrying far from the scene where had passed so many, yet sad incidents of her life. The separation cost her more pain than she had imagined it would, and giving way to the tears that forced their way to her eyes, she remained silent and thoughtful till her melancholy reflections were broken in upon by the good-humoured raillery of her uncle.

When Vivian Dacre returned home and heard of the sudden departure of Miss Evered, he remained for some few minutes speechless and without motion. It seemed to him as if every hope of joy had vanished with her, and at length, rushing from the room, he was about to leave the house, when his impetuous steps were arrested by his sister Eleanor. She saw his despair, and guessing the cause of it, endeavoured to console him with an assurance that he would see Agnes again before long. But Vivian's heart was heavy with despair, and he was turning away without making any reply, when she placed in his hands the letter which had been confided to her care.

"It is from Agnes!" he exclaimed, on looking at the superscription.

"It is."

"Did she leave no message for me?"

"None," answered Eleanor; "indeed, she was too much agitated to trust herself to say anything upon a subject that must necessarily have occasioned her so much pain."

"True," he exclaimed; "and yet she might have said something to assure me that I shall not be forgotten."

"I dare say she has told you that in her letter," replied Eleanor. "Poor girl, she seemed unhappy enough at the thought of leaving us, and yet, how could she act otherwise than she has done, when it is but too evident that she was regarded by your mother in no favourable light for having unconsciously gained your affection."

"And now," exclaimed her brother, "I suppose I may consider all chance of obtaining her as being at an end."

"Nay, I should not despair till matters assume a still more threatening appearance," answered Eleanor. "At all events, it is certain that Agnes loves you, and who knows but these prejudices of our mother will yield to the anxiety that I know she feels for your future welfare?"

"She might have yielded, then," exclaimed Vivian, "before Agnes took her departure from our house. Her kindness, I fear, would come too late, for Miss Evered has a high spirit, and will never return to us, lest it should be imagined that she wishes to entrap me into an ill-assorted marriage."

He then left his sister, and entering a room where it was not likely he would be disturbed, he broke open the seal, and perused the letter which had been given him. The contents were such as he had anticipated. Miss Evered frankly acknowledged that the step taken had required all her fortitude, and that she had adopted it in consequence of finding that there was no chance of Lady Dacre's opposition being relaxed. The letter then went on to implore that he would forget the love which had unhappily existed between them, and, as a reason for doing so, she declared it to be her fixed determination never to become his wife. All this was expressed in words that admitted of no second construction; the resolution she had formed was not likely to be broken whilst matters remained in their present state, and, sanguine as Vivian generally was, he saw no chance of any change taking place for some time to come. He was, however, gratified at perceiving that Agnes had expressed no coldness in her farewell letter, and this circumstance afforded him some slight hope that she would not give her hand to any one else whilst the faintest chance remained that Lady Dacre would yield up her prejudices in their favour.

From this period Eleanor received frequent letters from Miss Evered, but in none of them did she allude to Vivian, or the cause of their separation. The better to disguise her own secret sufferings, she wrote in a more cheerful strain than usual, describing the conduct of her uncle to be kind in the extreme, and entering into full particulars of all the amusements he contrived to make her forget the grief which he saw was preying on her mind.

By the time that a fortnight had passed away, Lady Dacre began to see sufficient cause to regret the prejudice which had led to the separation of the lovers; Vivian no longer possessed the buoyancy of spirit which had once rendered him the very life of their domestic circle. His manner had now become grave and thoughtful, and his countenance assumed a wan, sickly appearance, that gave rise to serious fears lest his health should suffer from the grief in which he indulged. He preferred solitude to company, and though various schemes were devised to banish his melancholy, he would stroll out by himself for hours together to pursue the dark chain of thoughts which recent events had given rise to. He had lost her whose love was more precious to him than all the world beside, and now life had become a cheerless void that he would have been glad to be released from.

Shocked at this change, Sir Lionel endeavoured to prevail on Lady Dacre to recal Agnes, and freely consent to a marriage that seemed necessary for the happiness of their son. She, however, still remained bigotted to her former opinion, declaring that his melancholy would soon wear off, as the separation became longer, and firmly maintaining that the honour of their family rendered it necessary that they should, under all circumstances, prohibit a union as unequal as this was. Sir Lionel was so much in the habit of yielding to the more resolute nature of his wife, that he seldom carried these controversies to any great extent, and they usually ended in much the same way that they began.

At length it was proposed that they should visit London for a few weeks. The change, it was believed, would be beneficial to Vivian, who would thus be forced to mix a little more in society; he might, probably, meet with some female of rank, whose attractions would supersede those of Agnes Evered, and thus, as the scheming mother fondly imagined, her own ambitious views would, in all probability, be realized. Sir Lionel yielded to this suggestion, because he knew it would be in vain to raise any opposition; but he had studied the heart of his son, and in his own mind he felt convinced that no attractions could ever draw his love from the fair object upon whom it had been placed. But Lady Dacre had decreed it, and within a week afterwards the whole family had established themselves at one of the fashionable hotels in London.

Vivian had never before been in the metropolis, and for a time the change certainly seemed to have produced the effect anticipated by his mother. He accompanied her to the exhibitions, the theatres, and all other places where amusement was to be found. In short, his melancholy seemed to have disappeared, and Lady Dacre expressed herself exultingly to her husband on the success of the scheme she had devised. But, worldly-minded herself, she little thought that love, when sincere, can never be eradicated from the human heart.

Being thus fixed for a time in London, they cultivated a more intimate

friendship with Henry Markham's father, who was so well pleased at the
prospect of his son's union with Ellen Dacre, that he willingly gave his consent to it, and expressed a hope that the marriage would take place with as
little delay as possible.   But Lady Dacre chose to have a principal voice in
this, as in all other cases, and for reasons that she did not give, the marriage
of the young couple was postponed till after they should have returned to
the Hall.

Within the time originally proposed, Sir Lionel and his family left the
metropolis for home.   The cause assigned for this change in their arrangements was the illness of Vivian, whose constitution, it was imagined, could
not bear the confined air of London.   Orders were, therefore, sent down to
get the house in readiness for their return, and within a few days afterwards
the baronet and his family were once more snugly housed in their own comfortable mansion.

From this period active preparations were made for the nuptials, which it
was agreed should take place within as short a time as possible.   Even
Lady Dacre now condescended to bestir herself in the matter ; she must
always be of the first consequence, and therefore took especial care that not
an order nor an arrangement should be permitted until it had first received
her sanction.   Poor Sir Lionel was obliged to play second fiddle on the
occasion. Expensive articles were purchased for the bride elect, and though
some of the things might appear extravagant and unnecessary, it was more
than his peace of mind was worth to utter a word that might be supposed
to be in remonstrance ; so like a prudent man, as he was, he sat himself
down perfectly resigned to his fate—supplying with a liberal hand whatever
money was required, and never venturing to utter a word of complaint. His
only consolation was, that, some time or other, it would come to an end;
and well pleased was he when at length arrived the day before the one on
which the marriage was to be celebrated.

But on the very evening of this happy day, when the whole family were
seated together, in that joyousness which seems to know no bounds, they
were to receive a shock for which none of them could possibly have been
prepared.   Henry Markham was more than usually cheerful, and seated by
the side of Eleanor, he was describing to her the scenery of the place where
they were to pass the honeymoon, when the door was opened, and a servant placed in his hand a letter which had just been brought by a messenger,
who had ridden with all haste, from London.   Markham recognised at once
the hand-writing of his father, and immediately tearing open the seal, he
discovered that it was a solemn prohibition not to marry Ellen Dacre till
certain inquiries, which were then going on, had been brought to a conclusion.   The writer merely said that a report had reached him which required
the most careful sifting, but purposely omitted explaining what it was till
Henry returned to town, when the affair should receive the most anxious
attention.   The old gentleman expressed his regret that this letter should
have been on the marriage eve, but, he added, there was the most positive
necessity for it, as well as for his son to hasten up to London immediately
after the communication had reached him.

The letter fell from the hand of Henry Markham as soon as he had perused it, and by the change that took place in his countenance it was evident to every one that the news he had received was of a most afflicting nature.   The haste, too, with which he soon afterwards picked up the paper
showed how anxious he was that its contents should not be seen.   Sir
Lionel had watched him with an anxious eye, and unable any longer to
suppress his anxious fears, he eagerly inquired of Henry whether the intelligence he had received was of any serious importance.

"I fear it will entirely disconcert our plans for the present," answered

Markham; "for my father is most importunate in his desire to see me without delay, and commands me to set off for London as soon as I have received his communication."

"Are you going to leave us?" demanded Sir Lionel.

"I am."

"And to-night?" exclaimed her ladyship.

"Alas! madam, stern necessity will, I fear, leave me no alternative."

"But surely," interposed Vivian, "you can postpone the journey till after the ceremony has taken place to-morrow?"

"Would to Heaven it were possible," exclaimed Henry Markham, with a sigh. "The commands of my father are, however, imperative, and all I can promise is to return again as soon as possible."

Eleanor alone was unable to question him upon this mysterious subject. As she gazed earnestly at her lover, a deadly paleness suffused her countenance, and she seemed as if endeavouring to discover from his looks the contents of the letter, which was still grasped in his tremulous hand. Presently, however, a dizziness seized upon her brain, and she would have fallen to the floor but for the timely assistance that was rendered by Henry Markham. His own sufferings were increased tenfold by witnessing the mingled doubt and dread with which she was perplexed.

"Must you then leave us, dearest Henry?" she at length faltered; "is the cup of happiness to be dashed away even at the moment when we were about to raise it to our lips? Cannot a messenger be sent to tell your father that you will obey his summons to-morrow?"

"The imperative nature of his letter admits of not a moment's delay, answered Henry.

"Do you know what the business is, that he calls you to London at such a moment as this?" demanded Sir Lionel.

"I do not, indeed, my dear sir," replied the young man. "He only tells me that I must not on any consideration fail to obey his call, and I must either yield a reluctant obedience or risk his eternal displeasure."

"And it is quite right that children should pay a due regard to the will of their parents," cried Lady Dacre, with a glance towards Vivian. "Experience is not to be expected from youth, and I am always pleased to see young folks show a proper deference to those whose age authorises them to give advice."

"At least," exclaimed Sir Lionel, "I think it would be better for Henry to stay with us over to-morrow."

"Not for the world!" said her ladyship; "the business must of course be very important, or his father would not have sent for him at such a moment as this. Suffer him, therefore, to take his departure, and I dare say in a few hours he will return to us again."

"I shall not be an hour longer than necessity compels," answered Henry Markham. "Every moment will be torture to me, and on my return here you shall know everything that relates to this mysterious business. All I ask is, that you will not form any hasty conclusion, since I believe it will turn out that the unexpected summons is not connected with business of any great importance."

"Well," exclaimed Vivian, "if you must go, Henry, you will at least permit me to bear you company?"

"Nay, I must go alone."

"Oh, do not refuse him this one favour," cried Eleanor; "let him go with you, and I shall feel the more easy during your absence."

Henry Markham could not resist this earnest appeal, and it having been so arranged, orders were immediately given for a couple of horses to be prepared for the travellers. Whilst this was doing Eleanor accompanied her lover to a window at the further end of the room, and in a low voice, that might not be overheard, said,—

"Do not think, Henry, that I have any desire to know the reason that has compelled you to leave me at such a moment as this. It is enough that I believe there is an absolute necessity for it, and that you will return as soon as your father can spare you. But I would warn you to take care of yourself, for there may be enemies abroad who have laid a plot for your destruction. I shall pray for your safety, Henry, and will wait with resignation till you can again return to us."

"And that shall not be many hours first," he replied. "My father cannot wish to detain me long, or he would not have sent this message till after to-morrow."

"Does he object to our marriage, think you?" she asked.

"That is most unlikely," answered her lover, "for if you remember, Eleanor, it was he who, in the first instance, was most anxious to bring it about. No, no, believe me he would rather further the object than throw any obstacle in the way, so that in a short time you may expect to see me return with an assurance that no other delay will take place to mar our happiness."

By this time the horses were announced to be in readiness, and the two young men having taken their leave, were soon galloping towards London. But the forebodings of poor Eleanor were most melancholy, and no argument could prevail on her to endure the departure with fortitude.

CHAPTER XVIII.

SHIPWRECK.—THE RETREAT.—A PROMISE OF GREATNESS.

WE must now return to Gilbert Copley and his lawless associates, who, on their escape from the Raven's Nest, steered their way northward, just keeping the coast of England in sight. Gilbert would have been glad to have been informed where they were going, and what they were next to do; but there seemed to be a determination to keep him in the dark on this point, for though the question was asked a great many times, there was not one of the fellows who thought proper to indulge his curiosity.

It was some time, too, before he could obtain an explanation of the reason which had occasioned their sudden flight; at length, however, one of the men, who was rather more good-natured than the rest, afforded him the following outline of the circumstances which had compelled them to become fugitives from their retreat among the rocks.

It seemed that a person who was out with his dogs, chanced to pass through that part of the country where the bodies of the two murdered men had been buried by the ruffians who had slain them. Observing that the dogs suddenly stopped at a place where the earth seemed to have recently been removed, and that they would not come away at his whistle, he naturally began to think there must be some particular reason for it.

He had frequently heard people speak about the two missing men, and was well aware of the prevalent notion that they had been murdered; at this moment the story again occurred to his memory, and hurrying on to the nearest village, he related what had happened to himself, and the suspicion he entertained that they had been buried at the place where his dogs had stopped. This naturally caused a great deal of excitement; a party of labourers and other persons instantly set out for the place; the ground was dug up, and the

bodies of the two men found, but decomposition had proceeded so far that it would have been impossible to recognize them, but for a part of the clothes which it was well known they wore on the day when they had last been seen.

Upon this suspicion fell upon one man in particular, and he was immediately arrested on a charge of having been concerned in the crime. In this, however, they were wrong, for the prisoner clearly established an alibi, and being immediately set at liberty, he, in gratitude for his own deliverance, gave his own reasons for believing that the crime had been committed by the smugglers, who had so long infested that part of the coast. There were several things to confirm this suggestion, and the consequence was the offer of a large reward for the apprehension of any of the persons connected with the gang. This circumstance happened to come the ears of Mark Harrowby, and feeling no great inclination to risk his life where the hue-and-cry was raised, he hastened back to the cave in the manner we have before alluded to, and without loss of time, set out in their vessel with the greater part of his comrades.

Gilbert no longer wondered at the haste with which they had quitted the Raven's Nest ; their escape seemed to be rather a miraculous one, and not wishing to ask any further questions at present, he walked to another part of the vessel to commence his watch. Soon after this, Harrowby and some few of his favourites, went down into the cabin, where they were soon engaged in a carouse, that threatened to send them all drunk to their hammocks.

Copley heard their boisterous mirth, and now, in the solitude of his watch, he felt heartily sorry that his own wilfulness had thrown him in the way of such a villanous set of companions. Had it been possible to quit them he would have done so at the earliest opportunity that might offer, but he knew that his character was forfeited, and now that there was a charge of murder against his comrades, his own life was of course in danger should it ever be known that he had been leagued with the smugglers.

No. 11

He was still occupied with these thoughts, when the wind, which had been blowing fresh, came on in heavy gusts, and the clouds which were extended over head threatened a storm that might send their frail vessel to the bottom. It was in vain that he went down to tell the revellers what he thought, for they only laughed at his fears, and dismissed him with a facetious assurance that, as they were all born to be hanged, there was no fear of their being drowned.

In less than half an hour afterwards, however, they came to a very different conclusion, as by that time the storm had reached a fearful height, that threatened the vessel with momentary destruction. Harrowby and his companions then rushed frantically upon deck, but it was evident that no human aid could save them, and as they stood gazing around them in mute despair, the vessel struck with terrible violence upon a rock. This catastrophe instantly roused them to exertion—the boat was lowered, and immediately filled by those who could first make their way into her. Even then others clung to the side in the hope of being taken in, but the boat was sturdily urged on by those who had taken the oars, and the poor sinking wretches were left with the solitary hope of being able to swim to shore. Fortunately for them this was at no great distance off, and as soon as Harrowby and his companions had landed on a solitary part of the coast, the boat was abandoned to the fury of the waves, whilst they clambered up the rocks in the hope of finding some place where they might procure shelter till means could be devised for escaping to some place where the law would not be likely to reach them.

Mark Harrowby soon recognized the spot where they had landed, and addressing himself to his comrades in a more cheerful tone, he assured them that a few minutes' walk would bring them to a place where they might make themselves comfortable for a short time.

"Where is it?" asked Hugh Darnton, who, overpowered with fatigue, was leaning for support on Gilbert's arm.

"Oh, close by," replied Harrowby. "It's a cave where I passed two or three years of my time when I first took up this pretty trade of smuggling. The fellows deserted it, however, on its being discovered that the officers intended to pay them an unwelcome visit, so we may have it all to ourselves, without much fear of any one suspecting that it has found new tenants."

"A miserable place, I'll be bound," muttered one of the fellows.

"Not so bad as you think," replied Harrowby; "there's plenty of room for three times our number, and if it has not all the comforts of the Raven's Nest about it, we shall at least be safe from danger."

"How far do you say it is?" asked Hugh Darnton, who really needed rest.

"Why we are at it now," replied their leader, forcing aside some shrubs that had grown up and hid its entrance. "We shall find it dark enough inside, I can tell you, so Patty had better stop outside till we contrive to make it a little more comfortable for her. I know where to find the place we used to stow our wood in, and with the assistance of a pistol flint we shall soon be able to comfort ourselves over a good fire."

By this time Mark Harrowby, followed by his comrades, had made their way into the entrance, which was so narrow that they were obliged to proceed through it in single file. After going some distance they reached a chamber of larger dimensions, where Harrowby desired them to stop while he sought for the fuel; this was soon found, and a heap of it being placed in the centre, a flame was quickly kindled, that gave to the place an air of comfort which had not been anticipated. Gilbert was then despatched for Patty, and on their return each of the men produced a flask of spirits from his pocket, which promised to afford them as jovial a night as if they had been at the Raven's Nest.

"We may make ourselves comfortable enough here, boys," exclaimed Harrowby, smacking his lips after a good pull at the bottle. "No one will ever think of looking after us here, and when quite convenient to ourselves we may seek for other quarters, if indeed there should be any among us so discontented as to desire a change."

"The place is well enough," replied Hugh Darnton, looking about him; "but the chief difficulty that strikes me is how we are to get at any provisions."

"Oh, that needn't trouble you," replied Harrowby, "for there's a large town not above three miles off, and one of us can go as often as need be to get us whatever we want. We have money enough among us to supply all our wants, and we'll take it by turns to go to the town, lest the visits of one person should give rise to suspicion."

"I begin to like your plans very well," exclaimed Hugh Darnton; "for the place seems likely enough to baffle our pursuers, and perhaps by-and-bye the story of the murder will be so far forgot that we may venture out without any great fear."

"We can manage all that easily enough whenever we begin to grow tired of this place," answered Harrowby. "We can disguise ourselves, you know, after it's supposed that we have escaped out of the country, and in that way we may pass from place to place without any one suspecting us to be the persons for whose apprehension so spanking a reward has been offered. A little while ago I began to think the winds and waves had played us a scurvy trick; but now, when I look about me, I fancy we might have gone further and fared worse."

"So we might," said Gilbert; "for, to my thinking, the place is almost as good as the Raven's Nest. And Patty, too, looks cheerful and smiling; so that I think we shall have very little reason to regret the accident that drove us to this spot."

In this way they consoled themselves, and when two or three hours had been passed in drinking and carousing, a bed of cloaks and great coats was made up for Patty in a smaller cave that led out of the one in which they were enjoying themselves. With this simple accommodation she expressed herself quite delighted, and as soon as she had retired the others laid themselves round the fire and enjoyed as sound a slumber as if nothing had occurred.

In this place they remained about five months, and as every care was taken to avoid discovery, there was no one in the neighbourhood who had the slightest suspicion that the cavern was inhabited. Patty attended to the domestic concerns, and, as had been previously arranged, the men took it by turns to go out and procure such articles as were required.

Hugh Darnton and Gilbert having purchased for themselves a couple of fishing-rods, often strolled out to enjoy the pleasures of angling in the neighbouring streams. Darnton had for some time past appeared anxious to speak to the young man upon some subject that preyed upon his mind, and one day, as they were watching their lines, he said, abruptly,

"I don't know why it is, Gilbert, that I have kept brooding over this matter so long, but the long and the short of it is, I have something to say, and may as well out with it at once."

"What do you mean?" asked Gilbert, with surprise.

"Why, to tell you the truth, I'm not exactly satisfied with your conduct to my daughter Patty."

"In what respect?"

"Oh, you have no occasion to ask that question," retorted Darnton, sharply. "You can't be off understanding me, Gilbert; but if you wish me to speak more plainly, I must confess that I have for some time past had a notion that matters were not as they ought to be between you and my daughter. At length I have questioned her upon the subject, and she has confessed that my fears are but too well founded. Don't interrupt me, boy, for I am determined to bring the thing to something like a settlement. If I had not regarded you in the light of my own son, this treachery would have cost you your life. You have had the good fortune to escape, but how long this good-nature will last must depend upon yourself."

"If you have any grievance to complain of," exclaimed Gilbert, "why not tell me plainly how it is to be remedied?"

"Because you ought not to require telling," answered the other. "We have been good friends ever since you were a boy. I would have made any sacrifice for you, but, by Heavens, my daughter's ruin will make me a bitter enemy, unless you make her reparation."

"So Patty has told you all about it—has she?"

"She has."

"Well, then, in that case it would be useless to deny it," replied Gilbert Copley. "The truth is, we love each other, and ——"

"You betrayed her."

"Nay; I have promised, some day or other, to make her my wife."

"Which promise must be faithfully performed."

"Be sure it shall."

"That is manfully said," exclaimed Darnton; "I fancied you might be looking out a little higher in the world for a wife, but as Patty has transgressed for your sake, it is only fair that you should marry her."

"I will."

"When?"

"As soon as you like," replied the youth.

"Ay, that's something like," exclaimed Hugh Darnton. "I thought you an honourable fellow, Gilbert, so give me your hand, and we'll consider this affair as good as settled. I feel all the easier for what has passed between us, and since my daughter is to be made an honest woman of, you and I will be as fast friends as ever."

"There shall be no delay about the marriage, as far as I am concerned," answered Gilbert. "Perhaps it ought to have been thought of before, but better late than never, so make yourself very easy on that point, old boy, and tell Patty that I am ready to fulfil all my promises to her as soon as she thinks proper to name the time."

"I thought you wouldn't ride rusty with me for speaking my mind plainly," exclaimed Darnton, after a pause. "The knowledge of the girl's shame was enough to excite the anger of a parent, but after considering the matter carefully, I thought there could be no doubt of your doing the thing what's right; so, instead of flying in a passion, and sending a pistol bullet through your brain, I took the opportunity of reasoning quietly with you upon the subject, and the affair has been comfortably settled."

"Yes," answered Gilbert Copley, "and you shall have no reason to repent your confidence."

"Have you quite given up all thought of Deborah?"

"Deborah!—I hate the filthy old hag."

"But she don't hate you," replied Darnton; "and if she should happen to find out that you are going to marry Patty, I know not how far her passion might carry her. She has blood to answer for already, and I rather think both you and my daughter would be sacrificed to her thirst for vengeance."

"The old woman and I have had words before now," answered Gilbert; "and she has seen how little I care for her violence."

"Yet she still has hopes that you will marry her."

"The old fool!" exclaimed Gilbert.

"Not so great a fool as you imagine," returned the other. "Deborah is in possession of a secret that you little dream of, and her wish to become your wife is grounded on a feeling of greediness and avarice."

"How can that be when I am as poor as herself."

"So you believe," replied Darnton; "but she happens to know that you can be a rich man whenever you choose to claim your rights."

"What do these words mean?" demanded Gilbert Copley, with surprise; "I have heard her throw out such a hint, but thought it was the mere raving of madness."

"There is some truth in it, however," exclaimed the other, with a look of meaning.

"In that case, why am I kept in the dark?" asked Gilbert, impatiently.

"You shall know the reason all in good time," returned his companion. "The thing has been kept snug among ourselves for years, but it wont be much longer before it all comes out, and you will then see that I have been really your friend. What should you think, Gilbert, if I should be the means of putting you in possession of a noble estate, a score of servants, and money enough to make you the equal of any man in the country?"

"I should consider that you ought to have done so long before."

"But I could give you a satisfactory reason for keeping the secret."

"You speak so mysteriously," exclaimed Gilbert, "that I confess myself unable to make out what you are driving at. I may be the heir of all you are telling me of, and if so, let me know the whole truth at once, and you shall soon see that I can make good use of the favours Dame Fortune has in store for me."

"Don't be in such a confounded hurry, my good fellow," returned Darnton. "I have not been keeping this secret for nothing, and should not have told you so much now only that the words escaped my lips before I was aware of it."

"Then having gone so far you may as well let me know the rest at once."

"I've half a mind to do so."

"Have a whole mind, and out with it all at once," exclaimed Gilbert, impatiently. "You have said enough to excite my curiosity, and never will I cease urging you upon this subject, till you have given me the information I desire."

"Well," returned Hugh Darnton, "I don't know but it may as well be told now as at any other time. What should you think of it, young fellow, if I, by a single word, were to make a baronet of you, and instead of Gilbert Copley—the graceless Gilbert Copley, who is now the associate of smugglers— were to hail you by the style and title of Sir Gilbert Dacre?"

"You are jesting with me!"

"Indeed I am not," answered the other;—"there are strange romances in real life, you know, and this happens to be one of them."

"Then you mean seriously to assert that my uncle's title belongs to me?"

"Exactly so."

"Still I cannot believe you," said Gilbert, after a few moments' consideration.

"I tell you it is all as true as that we are now talking together," replied Hugh Darnton. "This is not a matter for jesting, nor would I fill your mind with hope unless it was in my power to prove my words. Sir Lionel Dacre is a mere usurper; he possesses a title and property that he has no right to, and it is in my power to put you in possession of Dacre Hall whenever I think proper to make a stir."

"And even if it is so," exclaimed Gilbert, "ought I to turn my uncle out of house and home?"

"The house was never his to make a home of," replied Hugh Darnton; "and as for turning him out, it would only be serving him as he did by you."

"Nay, I left it of my own accord."

"Perhaps so, but your life was made so miserable that you would no longer remain there."

"That," replied Gilbert, "was my aunt's doings."

"Then now you have it in your power to punish her for it," exclaimed the other. "She has been a petty tyrant over you, and it will be a glorious revenge to reduce her to beggary."

"I should scarcely pity her," said Gilbert; "but my uncle has shown some little kindness to me, and I should be loth to proceed harshly against him."

"What harshness can there be in claiming your own?" demanded the other. "Look at your present situation, my good fellow;—here you are, living in a cave, when a fine house is ready to open its doors to receive you."

"And what would be the use of taking possession," demanded Gilbert, "when the officers of justice would be at my heels directly afterwards?"

"Psha! there's no fear of anything of the kind," replied Darnton. "No one knows that you have been connected with the smugglers, and it will be your own fault if the secret is ever divulged."

"And that it may be if any of my old comrades take it into their heads to denounce me."

"Pay them well, and you will have nothing of that sort to fear," retorted the other. "You can give them something handsome in the shape of hush money, and I'll warrant the fellows remain quiet enough."

"You, too, will expect something for the information you have given,"

"My dear Gilbert, you will find me one of the most disinterested fellows in the world."

"No doubt of it," replied the young man with a sneer; "indeed I have seen enough already to prove your disinterestedness."

"In what respect?"

"Why, did you not first extort a promise from me to marry your daughter, and after my word is pledged, you tell me I am heir to a title and immense wealth!"

"All which was perfectly natural," answered Darnton. "It is the duty of a parent to look after the interest of his children, and what more have I done? Patty has thrown herself upon your honour; she has lost name and fame through her love for you, and it is nothing more than fair that you should restore both to her. You would have married somebody, I suppose, and the title of Lady Dacre will sit as well upon her as any one else."

"At all events," exclaimed Gilbert, "you deserve credit for your generalship in the affair. You long since determined that I should be the husband of your daughter, because the match was such a one as suited your own ambitious projects."

"Do you mean to reproach me, Gilbert?"

"Not I; but it's as well to let you know that I am not quite so blind as may have been thought."

"The truth is," answered Darnton, "I knew well enough that you would not marry the girl had you entertained the least suspicion of your future rise in the world. To-day you have promised to make an honest woman of her—I rely on your word, because I know you dare not break it, and for the same reason I have told the secret which converts you from a fugitive smuggler, into a man of wealth and title."

"It was a cunning trick, Master Darnton," exclaimed the young man; "but I am not inclined to quarrel with you about it, since I owe you thanks for my information."

"You love the girl, don't you?"

" Yes."

" And she loves you, so I don't know how a better match could have been made."

" Except with respect to fortune."

" Why, I can't give her anything it's true," replied Darnton ; " but you will have wealth enough, so that will make matters square between us. I have helped you to a station that you would never have thought of, and that, I suppose, may weigh against my inability to give any money with your wife."

" Say no more about it," exclaimed Gilbert ; " for my word has been given, and even if I did not love Patty so well as I do, there should be no shirking or putting off in the business. I am satisfied with the altered prospects you have placed before me, and shall not forget to give substantial proof of my gratitude."

" Good," cried Darnton ; " and you will find, my dear boy, that I am not too proud to accept your generosity."

" And the others will, of course, expect to be recipients of my bounty ?"

" Ay, you'll find them hungry dogs, I've no doubt," replied Hugh Darnton. " They'll look for something pretty handsome, and perhaps even then will not be satisfied. However, I shall keep a sharp eye upon the rogues, and if they are too extortionate, I know a way that will soon bring them to their senses."

" At any rate," observed Gilbert, " there will be no occasion to let them know of my change of fortune till after we see how I succeed in the affair. Sir Lionel will no doubt resist my claim, and after all I may never get either the title or the estates."

" But you shall have it though," exclaimed Darnton ; " for it so happens, that I have it in my power to make him give up your rights."

" Does he know that you are aware of the circumstances under which I have been excluded ?"

" Oh ! yes, he knows all about that," replied Darnton ; " for it was in consequence of my threatening him with a full disclosure that made him give me sums of money whenever I demanded a supply. I held a farm under him, too, as you know, and whilst other tenants were obliged to pay to the last farthing, I always got off rent free. Sir Lionel was forced to be lenient to me, and I should have had nothing to complain of, if it had not been for the interference of Lady Dacre."

" She never had any very favourable opinion of you," observed Gilbert.

" I had pretty good reason to know it," replied the other, " for it was through her that the baronet afterwards gave me money but seldom, and even the little I could get was given grudgingly. Then it began to strike me that something else must be done, and I made up my mind that you should not remain much longer in the dark. At first it gave me no little trouble to contrive matters to my liking, but at last I managed to persuade you to leave the village where your uncle lived ; you became one of us, and after awhile became fond of Patty. That was exactly what I wanted, so I let matters go on till you were fairly caught out, and then I charged you with deceiving the girl to her own ruin. You, however, have promised to marry her, and after that I had no wish to keep secret the fact of your being the heir of all the estates which are at this time in the possession of your uncle."

" But do you know enough of the facts to place the justice of my claim beyond a doubt ?"

" I should have been a fool to have left anything to chance," answered Darnton. " I know the whole history of Sir Lionel Dacre, and can relate all the particulars of this case whenever I please."

"Then let me know them," exclaimed Gilbert; "I have a right to demand this much of you."

"Another time you shall know all about it," replied the other; "at present I shall not be able to do justice to the story; but, depend upon it, I will satisfy you before very long. You will wonder how I could keep the secret all these years; but, when a man has got an object in view, he can wait patiently till the proper moment arrives. I was determined Patty should share your good fortune; and, after you had given me a promise to make her your wife, you see how soon I began to let you know the good fortune that may be had for the trouble of seeking it."

"Yet you tantalise me by leaving your explanation to a future period!"

"It's only a short time," replied Darnton; "in a few days I shall have recollected everything connected with this strange tale, and you shall then know by what means Sir Lionel has kept you from your birthright."

He moved away, as if to avoid all further questions upon the subject; and Gilbert Copley, knowing that it would be in vain to urge him just then, followed in thoughtful silence. In less than half an hour they returned to the cave where Patty was waiting to receive them with a joyous smile.

CHAPTER XIX.

A REMOVAL.—THE NARRATIVE.—MARRIAGE.

As there had not been any search made after the fugitives, nor rumours spread in the neighbourhood, they resolved to quit the cave and fix themselves in a residence where they might be more at their ease. With this view, one of the party took a house near the town, and, soon after he had taken possession of it, the others, under various assumed names, went to the same place, as visitors from a distant part of the kingdom. The arrival of so many strangers created some surprise among the inhabitants, and fifty contradictory stories were circulated respecting them; but, as no one could give any sufficient ground for suspecting the newly-arrived people of being otherwise than they had represented, the rumours gradually diminished, and in two or three weeks the mystery was almost forgotten.

Gilbert Copley had frequently requested Darnton to give the promised narrative; but he was as often refused on the ground that matters were not yet quite ripe for being put into a proper train. At length, however, when they were one day left by themselves, Gilbert again urged his request, and with so much effect, that, after a little while, he commenced his story as follows :—

"When I was about your age, Gilbert, I lived servant to Sir Edward Dacre, who was then quite a young man. He was a noble hearted fellow, I can tell you, and was as fine a looking man as you would meet with in a day's walk. If he had lived, it would have been well for those who held estates under him; for he had a free hand when money was in the case, and his every thought was to make people happy and contented; yet, in spite of all that, there were some people that thought he was a little queer in the brain. He might, perhaps, have a few strange ways; but he contrived to do a great deal of good, and never injured any one, by word or deed. At all events, Sir Lionel, his brother, got the benefit from some of his queer ways.

"At length Sir Edward fell in love with Miss Emily Raymond, a very beautiful young lady, who lived with her widowed mother, upon a small fortune that was just sufficient for all their wants. Miss Emily seemed exactly the sort of wife for Sir Edward, and I should say no two people ever loved each other more sincerely."

"He married her, of course?" observed Gilbert.

"Why, the truth is, he was a bit of a rake," answered Darnton; "and, though he was very fond of the girl, he was rather too proud to seek her as a wife. He was rich, and her fortune was limited; he had a title, and she was the daughter of a person who had lived and died in middling circumstances. However, the young lady was virtuous enough to reject a dishonourable proposal; and, as my master could not bear to lose her, they were in a short time afterwards married. The ceremony, however, was performed in private; I alone was let into the secret, and everybody thought she had run away with the baronet without caring whether he married her or not. Poor lady! what a world of sufferings did she afterwards have to endure!"

"Was Sir Edward unkind to her?"

"Lord help you! he loved her as if she had been his household idol. No, no, it was a promise which she gave him before marriage that made her so miserable afterwards."

"What was the promise?" demanded Gilbert.

"Why this," replied Darnton; "she consented to keep their marriage a secret from every one till Sir Edward should think proper to acknowledge her openly as his wife. I, as the only witness to their union, was also made to take an oath to the same effect. The consequence of this was, that people shunned her, and she was looked upon in no other light than as the mistress of Sir Edward Dacre. Such was his foolish whim, and well do I remember, as he came out of church, his saying to me,—' Now, Hugh Darnton, farewell to home and the name of Dacre for some years to come!' Poor fellow! how little did he think at that moment that he would never return to it."

"What reason had he for leaving it?" asked Gilbert.

"Upon my word, I dont know," replied the other, "unless it might be to show his young bride the world. He despatched a letter to his brother, the

No. 12

present Sir Lionel, who was married and had a family, giving him leave to take up his residence for a time at the Hall ; and allowing him to take nearly all the rents, leaving for himself only sufficient to support his assumed character as plain Mr. Hammond.   Under that name he and his wife travelled over the greater part of England ; afterwards they went to France, where they lived three or four years—where *he* was slain, *she* died from grief, and *you*, Gilbert Copley, were born !"

"Sir Edward was my father, then ?" exclaimed the young man, with surprise.

"He was."

"And you say he was slain ?"

"Yes, he fell in a duel."

"Do you happen to know who was his antagonist ?"

"A French officer," replied Hugh Darnton.

"His name ?"

"I have forgotten ; but that matters very little, for he also perished in a duel a few years afterwards.   Your father lived a few hours after he had received the wound, and never shall I forget the dreadful scene that took place when they brought him home."

"Was he able to speak ?"

"Yes, but it was very faintly, though," replied Darnton ; "and from the first he seemed conscious of his approaching end.   On recovering himself a little, he desired me to approach, and having desired every one else to leave the room, said :—' You have been a good and zealous friend to me, Darnton, and on you do I rely for the execution of my last wishes when I am no more. You only are aware of my secret marriage, so that everything will depend upon the manner in which you fulfil my dying commands.   If my boy—meaning you, Gilbert—should obtain the age of twenty-one, then, but not till then, disclose the secret of our marriage, that he may have his birthright.   Should he not live till that age, there will be no occasion to say anything about it, for, as I have always denied my marriage, I do not wish to be convicted of a gratuitous falsehood.   But, should my brother, or any of his family, treat my boy with harshness, let the secret be divulged without delay.   My time in this world grows short, Darnton, or there is much that I wish to say ; you will, however, for my sake, treat the child as if he were your own ; be his protector, should he need one, and keep a careful watch to guard him from the machinations of his enemies.   You know all the circumstances connected with his birth :—when the last breath leaves my body he will be Sir Gilbert Dacre, and it will be for you to see him established in his rights so soon as he has attained the full age of twenty-one.'   I promised most solemnly to fulfil these last injunctions of my master, and his looks expressed the gratitude that it was no longer in his power to utter.   He grasped my hand with a gentle pressure, and in a few moments afterwards was no more."

"You have performed your promise faithfully," exclaimed Gilbert, as the other concluded.   "The task has, no doubt, been a difficult one ; but it shall be my first care to prove that I am not ungrateful.   You shall live with me at the old Hall, all that I have shall be at your command, and my future life shall be devoted to your service, even as yours has been to mine."

"It's not worth while thinking about the past," replied Darnton.   "If I have done my duty well, that's enough ; and, as for my reward, the best I can receive will be to see you take possession of your own house and title.   It will be a glorious day, Gilbert, and, as for your uncle, he'll have very little to grumble about, since he has had the range of the place, to do just as he pleased, for more than twenty years."

"You have not yet told me of my mother," said Gilbert Copley ; "did she live long after the unfortunate death of her husband ?"

" No, a very little time," replied Darnton ; " she had been in a very declining state of health since the birth of her second child, which died when it was only a few days old ; and the grief she suffered on account of Sir Edward's death, hurried her all the more quickly to the grave. Poor thing! she, too, had great confidence in me, for when she found her last moments approaching, she commended you to my care, and entreated that I would see you established in your rights."

" I have a faint recollection of her," said Gilbert. " I stood before her when she was dying, and received the last caresses of my unfortunate parent."

" Ay, your memory serves you very well in that respect," answered the other. " However, before we enter upon any other subject, let me finish my story. After she was laid in her grave, I sent a letter to your uncle, to inform him of what had happened ; he sent me a sum of money to defray any expenses that had been incurred, and desired me to hasten back to England immediately after the affairs were brought to a close. I obeyed his commands, and introduced you to him as the illegitimate child of his deceased brother."

" What did he say on the occasion ?" asked Gilbert.

" Oh, he received you kindly enough," replied the other ; " but Lady Dacre seemed to look anything but pleased at the addition to her family. However, I had no alternative but to leave you at the Hall, and remembering the last injunctions of your father, I determined to keep a pretty strict watch over you. This was made all the easier by Sir Lionel offering me a farm close in the neighbourhood, and I think you cannot but acknowledge that I have performed the duty imposed upon me by Sir Edward."

" You have," replied Gilbert ; " but now tell me when am I to go and make my claim to the estates ?"

" You must not do things in too great a hurry," replied Darnton. " You are only just of age you know, so that we can afford to wait a little bit till things get into a right train."

" But I dare say my uncle will not feel inclined to give up the title and estates on our first application," exclaimed Gilbert ; " so I should think it would be better to begin at once, and if he should set us at defiance, we shall then know how to proceed."

" That's all very well," returned Hugh Darnton ; " but I've had more experience in the world than a stripling of one-and-twenty, and the thing must be managed my own way or not at all."

" What is your plan ?" demanded Gilbert.

" In the first place we must go to London directly."

" Directly ?"

" Yes."

" And what are we to do when we get there ?"

" My first plan," answered Darnton, " will be to see you and Patty married. That must be done before I stir a step further."

" You have my promise to make her my wife," replied the young man.

" True ; but ' safe bind safe find' is my motto. You must be married, I tell you, and then I shall have an inducement to hurry the rest forward."

They were now interrupted by the return of Mark Harrowby and two or three of their companions, so that nothing further could he say about the business on that occasion. Hugh Darnton, however, gave Gilbert a look that warned him not to say a word that might excite curiosity, and then took his departure from the room to prepare his daughter Patty for the journey they were about to take to London.

There was some truth in the account which had been given by Hugh Darnton ; but at the same time there were things stated upon which very little reliance could be placed. Some things he had entirely omitted to state, and others were added, when he found it necessary to mystify his auditor. It is not to be denied, for instance, that Sir Edward had made dishonourable proposals to Miss Raymond, but the offence was not forgiven quite so easily, as might be imagined, from Darnton's recital, for the offence was seriously resented; and Sir Edward was not permitted to see her again till his contrition had lasted some few months. At length, however, a reconciliation took place, and they were secretly married.

The bride and bridegroom went abroad under the assumed name of Hammond, and Sir Lionel was permitted to take up his residence at the Hall, where he took the entire management of all money affairs, sending every quarter the moderate sum which the elder brother had considered would be sufficient for his wants. Occasionally a report was raised that Sir Edward was really married to the lady who had accompanied him; but this, for some reason or other, was denied by the party chiefly concerned; and Sir Lionel had it, therefore, as he conceived, on the best authority, that the female was living with him as his mistress.

Sir Edward fell in a duel, as has already been described, and shortly afterwards his wife died, leaving their only child a friendless orphan. She, however, was not aware that the moment of dissolution was so near, and had even made preparations for returning to England, when a fatal change took place, and she discovered that not a chance of surviving many hours remained.

In this condition she wrote a brief letter to Sir Lionel, declaring her marriage, and informing him where it took place, as well as who had been a witness of the marriage. As a further confirmation she enclosed the marriage certificate, and concluded by imploring protection for her infant.

This letter was intrusted to the care of Hugh Darnton, who surmising its contents, took the liberty of breaking the seal, in order that he might know how to proceed. Of course, neither the epistle nor the certificate ever reached Sir Lionel, but from that moment Darnton resolved upon a plan by which he might advance his own interests. The child was conveyed to his uncle, but was branded with the name of bastard, till the period should arrive when a good bargain could be made by a full disclosure of the secret. He knew that Sir Lionel was too honourable to wrong his nephew, should the truth be revealed, and as nothing was to be got by telling him the truth, he determined to wait patiently till he could see what reward he was likely to get from Gilbert, in return for putting him in possession of his hereditary estates. By hints and insinuations, however, he succeeded in working upon the fears of Sir Lionel Dacre, and as we have seen, forced money from him as often as his extravagance rendered such an application necessary.

At length, as Gilbert advanced towards manhood, the wily schemer began to be afraid lest the prize should slip through his fingers, and to avert such a disappointment it was that he prevailed upon him to leave the protection of Sir Lionel, under a promise that he could put him in the way to find honourable employment. In furtherance of this scheme, he sought out his former ally, Mark Harrowby, and the precious pair soon found a plan that was not likely to be detected by an inexperienced youth. In short, the reader is aware how easily Gilbert Copley became the dupe of these designing villains; he believed them to be devoted to his service, followed them in all confidence, and, when too late to recede, found himself the associate of smugglers.

In a brief period he became reconciled to his new course of life, for he believed himself to have been ill-used by his uncle, and any change seemed preferable to the constraint he used to endure. It was part of Darnton's plan to force a matrimonial alliance between his daughter and Gilbert—for that purpose they were brought into each other's society as much as possible. The young man fell into the trap that was laid for him, and everything now seemed in a fair way to reward the cupidity of Hugh Darnton.

On the day following the last interview between Gilbert and his evil genius, they were again alone together, and the former took the opportunity to urge with even more earnestness his wish that something should be immediately done towards obtaining for him the title and wealth that had been promised. Darnton, however, still wished to postpone proceedings for the present; and in a moment of pique, Gilbert threatened to write to his uncle, explaining all the circumstances connected with his birth, and demanded to be placed in that situation which by law belonged to him.

"So, it has come to this—has it?" exclaimed Darnton, grinding his teeth with rage; "I, who have always been your best friend, am to be threatened and bullied. But write the letter, boy, if you please, and the moment you have sent it off, these papers that I have so long carried about me, shall be thrust into the fire. Here is your mother's certificate of marriage, and other documents of equal importance. Without them, who will believe your story? Sir Lionel for one, will not, since it is not his interest to do so, and all the lawyers in the universe can't help you, unless they have proofs put before them that you are the legitimate son of Sir Edward Dacre. *You*, of course, can tell them the story exactly as I have told it, and people will be found fools enough to believe you. Sir Lionel, convinced of the integrity of his nephew, must needs walk out of his Hall to give you quiet possession of it. You at least think so, I dare say, though, between ourselves, young man, you will find yourself grievously mistaken if you think to play any of your scurvy tricks upon Hugh Darnton."

"I have not said that I would take any such step without your advice," replied Gilbert.

"I know what you have said, and what you propose to do," answered Hugh Darnton; "but I certainly did not expect, after my many proofs of friendship, that you would turn round upon me. But, since it is so, you must abide by the consequences; for my own part, I don't care now how the matter goes, and since you choose to ride rusty, it may happen that you will find I can do the same. As for Patty, you have promised to marry the girl, and I'll take care that no more slippery tricks are played her."

"I have already declared that she shall be my wife," exclaimed Gilbert.

"Yes, and you shall be as good as your word, too, young fellow," replied Darnton; "for if I thought you meant to deceive me, I'd take care to prevent your ever telling lies again. In fact, Gilbert, you are completely in my power. Two men were murdered when you were present aiding and assisting. A reward has been offered for the apprehension of any of the persons concerned in the deed, and a word of mine could send you to the gallows."

"Would you be villain enough to betray me?" cried Gilbert.

"That will depend upon yourself," answered the other. "What I have spoken is only to let you know the sort of man you would trifle with. I have no wish to quarrel further with you, Gilbert, so here is my hand in token of peace, if you will only be content to be guided by my advice."

"I have no alternative," replied Gilbert; "but you will not, I suppose, object to go to London as soon as possible?"

"We start to-morrow morning," returned the other. "Patty has got together what few things are wanted for the wedding, and I mean the ceremony to take place as soon as possible after our arrival there. We are now friends again, and you must not think of the few angry words I just now gave utterance to. They were caused by your own folly in threatening to write to Sir Lionel, but as I dare say you are now sorry for it, I shall pay no more heed to what was uttered without due consideration."

"I admit it was wrong of me," replied Gilbert ; "but you can of course make some allowance for the anxiety I feel to bring this affair to a close. If I have just rights to assert there ought to be no delay in bringing them forward."

"There *shall* be no delay, Gilbert," exclaimed the other. "I have now pretty well made up my mind how to proceed in the matter, and when you hear my plans I think you will admit that I have your real interest at heart. Fail we will not, and for that reason, my dear boy, I am acting cautiously ;— a few weeks—nay, perhaps only a few days, shall see you the master of the old Hall."

At the appointed time, Gilbert Copley, accompanied by Patty and his future father-in-law, set out on their journey to London, which they reached without the occurrence of any adventure worthy of being recorded. The first object that occupied the attention of Hugh Darnton, was the marriage of his daughter, for he was resolved to see her the wife of Gilbert before he took a step towards bringing about the design which was to convert the simple-minded Patty into a lady of title.

As publishing the banns would lead to delay, he went to the expense of purchasing a licence at Doctors' Commons, and every arrangement being by that time concluded, the bridal party went to church on the following morning, and Hugh Darnton returned to the lodgings they had taken, with the gratification of seeing one of his favourite plans accomplished. Patty was now the wife of Gilbert, and it laid within the reach of his own power to hail her before very long by the high-sounding title of Lady Dacre. Besides, he was himself on the high road to wealth, for Gilbert had promised to make him the sharer of his riches as soon as he took possession of his estates.

Having made sure of one thing, he was determined to lose no time in prosecuting his other schemes. To this end he paid an early visit to Mr. Briefly, a lawyer to whom he had been recommended on a previous occasion. The man of law heard his statement with surprise, but there was no reason to doubt any portion of it, for Darnton had gone prepared with proof, and the papers that he threw down upon the table, confirmed every assertion that had been made. The case was certainly a most extraordinary one, but it was clear and straightforward, and as there was a great deal of money at stake, the lawyer saw that a golden harvest was to be reaped. He, therefore, gladly undertook the case, and having made a few notes to assist his memory, congratulated Hugh Darnton on the certainty of having the whole affair brought to an end in a very short time. This was no more than the other expected from his own knowledge of the matter, but he thanked the lawyer for the interest he seemed to take in the cause, and then withdrew to inform Gilbert of the state to which his affairs had been brought.

By a very singular coincidence, it so happened that Mr. Briefly was the attorney usually employed by the elder Mr. Markham, and in that capacity had been recently engaged in drawing up the marriage settlements between his son and Eleanor Dacre. The visit of Hugh Darnton opened his eyes to a most important fact, and no sooner did he learn that Gilbert Copley had a good claim to the estates of Sir Lionel, than he set forth to the house of Mr. Markham, and laid the whole statement before him.

The old gentleman was startled by a statement so extraordinary and unexpected. He had, it is true, consented to the marriage of his son with Miss Dacre, but it was under an impression that she would receive a suitable portion, and now there was every certainty that the father would soon be reduced to a state of absolute poverty. Under these circumstances a letter was immediately written to his son, and despatched by a messenger, with strict injunctions to make no delay till the epistle was given into the hands of the person to whom it was directed. As we have already mentioned, the letter reached its destination on the day before the marriage was to have taken place.

CHAPTER XX.

THE CLAIM.—FALLEN FORTUNES.—THE CLIMAX OF DESPAIR.

LAW, so proverbial for its slow movements in general, can be urged into a good round trot, or even a gallop, when there is plenty of money in the way. In the present instance there was a golden harvest to be reaped, and Mr. Briefly, who always had an eye to himself, set to his task in earnest upon the understanding that he was to receive a large sum of money as soon as he had succeeded in establishing the claim of Gilbert Copley. The papers which had been entrusted to him afforded all the proof that could be required, and in answer to Darnton's frequent inquiries, the man of law declared that no impediment was in the way of a speedy termination of the suit.

But that which was a source of joy to one party, was productive of the greatest dismay to the other. Vivian soon heard from the lawyer the exact position in which his father stood ; there could be no doubt that the claimant would succeed in his object ; everything was so clear that no jury could hesitate to give him a verdict, and in that case what ruin must inevitably follow !   There was but too much reason to know that Gilbert was of a stern vindictive temper, and, once in the possession of the estates, his next course would be to compel Sir Lionel to refund the whole of the money that he had received since the death of his brother.   In that case a prison would ere long become the cheerless abode of his father.

Sir Lionel Dacre, however, did not regard matters in quite so gloomy a light ; he at once saw that Hugh Darnton was at the bottom of all the mischief, and knowing the man's love of money, he believed that the offer of a handsome sum would convert his present enemy into a future friend. But he reflected not that Darnton had his own private revenge to carry out, and that if Gilbert joined his cause he would not fail to reward with a liberal hand the person who had acquainted him with the secret of his birth. Lady Dacre looked at the affair with more alarm than her husband ;—she had long known the temper of Gilbert, and now that he had set seriously to work, there was every reason to fear that he would not rest satisfied with half measures.

At the earnest solicitation of his son, the baronet hastened up to London, and on the morning after his arrival, set out to visit Mr. Briefly, from whom alone he could expect to obtain the full particulars.   On reaching the street where the lawyer lived, he saw Hugh Darnton leave the house, and direct his steps towards him ; it was evident that the fellow had recognized him, for he quickened his pace as if wishing to escape an interview with the person whose ruin he had determined on.   But Sir Lionel was resolved that he should not avoid him so easily.

" Stop, Darnton," he exclaimed, " this meeting is well timed, for I have something to speak to you about."

" What may it be, Sir Lionel ?" demanded the other.

" You have no occasion to ask that question," answered the baronet. " An action has been commenced against me by Gilbert Copley, my nephew.   You, I believe, have some influence over him.   What sum of money will purchase your interest in my behalf ?"

" You have mistaken me, Sir Lionel," exclaimed Darnton.   " Your nephew is the rightful heir to the estates of his father, and it is only just that he should have them.   I am sorry to take part against you, but there's no help for it, since I am only acting according to the last commands of my poor master."

" Psha! do you think I am to be imposed upon by this mockery of yours?"

" Mockery!"

" Ay,—have I not known you for years to be a hypocritical, artful knave?"

" I am sure you have no reason to think so badly of me," replied Darnton, controlling with difficulty the anger that was ready to burst forth.

" There is no necessity for our quarrelling," exclaimed Sir Lionel, " for we know each other well, and should not care much for a few hard words spoken at random. You have always made me your banker,—do so still; and, on certain conditions you will never have reason to complain of my liberality."

" Yet a few moments since you called me an artful knave!"

" I did, and with perfect truth."

" Then the knave will have nothing to do with you," replied Darnton, with bitter sarcasm ;—" he despises, spits at you as one that deserves only his contempt. Your offered bribe I refuse, for there is another whose pay is more certain and liberal than yours. Sir Gilbert Dacre knows the value of my friendship, though *you* have always thought proper to scorn it. And now mark the consequence of your pride ;—I have proof that Gilbert is the legitimate son of your late brother, Sir Edward Dacre ;—the whole story has been related to the young man, and he is now seeking to obtain his rights in consequence of my advice. There is some pleasure in such revenge as this ; but how much greater will it be when the time comes that you are compelled to leave the old Hall a beggar!"

" Have I ever injured you?" demanded Sir Lionel.

" Ay," replied the other, " you have rated me for an idle fellow that would not work whilst I could get a shilling out of you. For a time, to be sure, a few sums of money were doled out with an unwilling hand ; but at length my application was flatly refused, and I was driven from your house to perish from want for aught you cared! But I shall yet live to triumph over you in spite of your former greatness, and never, in your direst necessity, will I put forth a hand to render assistance."

" But Gilbert ——"

" Feels no more pity than I do," replied the ruffian. " Besides, he thinks you have enjoyed enough of his wealth, and is not inclined any longer to live in poverty whilst you are revelling in the enjoyments which by rights should be his. Your lady-wife too, must needs treat him like some scurvy menial about the place when he ought to have been in that station which her husband had usurped. He feels gratified that it is now in his power to retaliate, and should a prison be your fate,—as I have no doubt it will be, —you need not expect any kindness or assistance from Sir Gilbert Dacre!"

Having pronounced this cruel taunt, Hugh Darnton turned away with a look of fiendish exultation, and with rapid steps left the baronet to meditate upon the malevolence he had given utterance to. He, however, went to Mr. Briefly, from whom he learnt that the most conclusive evidence in favour of Gilbert's claim had been collected together, and that consequently it would only be involving himself still further to defend an action of which the conclusion might be so clearly foreseen. Still there were some who would have advised him to go on in the forlorn hope that a favourable verdict might be given ; but upon making inquiries respecting the marriage of his brother, it was found that the assertion was strictly true, and consequently the chief point of the plaintiff's case would be clearly and satisfactorily proved.

From that moment Mr. Dacre—for we must now deprive him of his title —resolved to offer no useless opposition to the claims which were mad

against him. He communicated this determination to Mr. Briefly, and
then arranging the few matters that required his earliest attention, he set
off for the Hall, accompanied by his son and Henry Markham. The scene
on his return home was painful in the extreme, for Mrs. Dacre possessed
not the same fortitude that her husband did, and it was not without the
most acute pain that she could yield to the reverse of fortune which had
overtaken them.

With a tenacity that no one could overcome, she still entertained a hope
that affairs would not reach so terrible a climax if a resolute stand was
made against the claim which had been so unexpectedly raised. Gilbert
had never been a favourite of hers, and she believed he would be guilty of
any baseness that was likely to serve his own ends. She even entertained
the strongest suspicion that Darnton and Gilbert Copley had perjured
themselves in the present instance, and most strenuously did she entreat
her husband not to yield unless compelled to do so by the decision of a
court of justice. Had there been any chance Dacre would have clung to it
to the very last, but so satisfied was he that all would be in vain, that he
resolutely persisted in his determination, and gave directions that immediate
preparation should be made to leave a house that he could no longer regard
as his own home.

And well it was that he had philosophy enough to come to this determination, for on the following day he received a letter from Gilbert, peremp-
torily desiring him to leave the Hall within a week, as he and his wife
intended to come down at the expiration of that period to take possession of
their new home.

"My nephew might have had a little more forbearance, I think," said
Mr. Dacre, as he handed the letter to his wife. "You will perceive, my
dear, that he has commanded us to leave the mansion within a very limited
No. 13

period, and we have no alternative but to obey. We are now at his mercy, and there is not much to be expected from him; we will, at least, spare ourselves the mortification of being driven forth by violence."

"Would he dare resort to such a step?" she exclaimed, bursting into tears.

"There is no reason to doubt it," answered her husband. "Sir Gilbert, —as we must now call him—is undisputed master here, and, be assured, he will not fail to make the most of his newly acquired authority. Let us, therefore, support our misfortunes with firmness and dignity. Driven forth from a once happy home we may be, but the oppressor shall not have the gratification of seeing how deeply we feel the harshness he thinks proper to adopt."

"When do you intend to leave?"

"To-morrow if you can make it convenient," he replied. "We are now living here upon sufferance, and I am sure you would not, any more than myself, receive the slightest favour from a man who does not seem to possess even the smallest feeling of humanity. Let him have possession of the Hall;—for a time perhaps he may revel in all the delights of his new dignity, but you may rest assured that ere long he will writhe under the tortures of a guilty conscience. We go, my love, into poverty, yet I do not envy him the reflections that must, sooner or later, force themselves upon his mind."

At an early hour on the following morning, the whole family assembled in the breakfast parlour to partake of the last meal they were to have in this once loved home. The vicar, hearing what was about to take place, joined them on this melancholy occasion, and great was the concern manifested by the good man at losing the society of friends for whom he had the highest respect.

"This is, indeed, a severe blow," he observed; "and yet, so much does it appear like a dream, that I can hardly think your absence will be for any long time."

"There is no chance of our ever returning," answered Mr. Dacre. "My nephew has certainly brought forward the strongest proofs in favour of his claim, and in justice I could do no otherwise than yield up possession without putting him to unnecessary expense or trouble."

"Your motive is an excellent one," exclaimed the vicar; "would that I could say as much for the person who has taken these extreme measures."

"He has indeed taken a vindictive course," replied Mr. Dacre; "and yet I do not blame him so much as the person who has advised him to adopt this course. It is certain, however, that his friend has a powerful motive of his own for the counsel he has given, and I have some doubts whether my graceless nephew will not by-and-bye, turn round upon him in the same way that he has served me."

"Pray," exclaimed the vicar, "do you happen to know what this Gilbert Copley has been doing with himself ever since he disappeared from the village some time ago? Perhaps it might be useful to learn that fact, and also to ascertain what sort of company he has been associating with."

"I believe that would be difficult to ascertain," returned Mr. Dacre; "there is no doubt in my mind as to one of the persons, but of the remainder, if any, I can form no idea."

"Would not the person you speak of give the information we require?"

"There is no chance of it, for I believe him to be as great a scoundrel as ever lived."

"Then were they well matched," exclaimed the clergyman, "for the conduct of Gilbert Copley gives us good ground to believe that he could find few persons worse than himself. But the wicked do not triumph for ever, and though their evil designs are sometimes permitted to succeed, a change in their fortunes is sure, sooner or later, to succeed."

" At any rate," exclaimed Vivian, " I believe he will find few persons in this neighbourhood willing to associate with him. He will be left in solitude, and perhaps when he sees how his conduct is resented, he will begin to repent the harshness that has driven his earliest friend from home."

" There is little chance of that," interposed Mrs. Dacre, " for Gilbert never possessed one single spark of kindly or generous feeling."

" If he regards his own safety," exclaimed Vivian, " he will be careful never to throw himself in my way. I do not speak from any personal ill-will, but when I see those I love turned forth into the world I cannot restrain the anger which his heartless conduct has given rise to."

" Vivian, if you indeed love me do speak thus," cried his father, earnestly. " My trial is indeed a bitter one, but do not you add to the agony of my pangs by an act of rashness that may plunge us all into the deepest abyss of misery. Gilbert may, perhaps, believe himself justified in all he has done ; he may not regret the ruin he has brought upon us, but the time is not far distant when he will see his error, and then the punishment inflicted by his own thoughts will be as ample as we can possibly desire."

" Nothing," answered Vivian, " can ever compensate the deep and lasting injuries he has done us. Has not my sister's marriage been broken off in consequence of the proceedings he commenced against us, and are not two hearts blighted by the very person whom you fostered and protected ? Had the injury fallen upon myself alone, I could freely have forgiven it, but when those I love droop under the withering influence of this villain, I feel as if even his death could not half satisfy my vengeance."

" I trust you will think of this with more composure after a while," observed his father, mildly. " Our reverse of fortune, it must be admitted, is hard to bear, but it is one of our first duties to endure with patience the trials that are imposed upon us. However, we have said enough on this subject at present. The carriage is now at the door, and I am impatient to begin the journey."

Having taken leave of the vicar, Mr. Dacre and his family entered the vehicle which was waiting for them at the door, and in a few minutes they were travelling with all speed towards London. The moment of departure was a bitter one, but Mr. Dacre reflected that it was necessary to exhibit some little firmness of deportment, and rousing himself to exertion, he endeavoured by assumed cheerfulness to set an example to those who were the sharers in his banishment from a once happy home At the end of a few hours, however, they reached London, and took up their temporary abode at an hotel where economy and respectability might be combined.

As for Hugh Darnton, to whom we must now return, his vengeance was not half accomplished, though, as far as matters went, he had succeeded to the very utmost of his wishes. But he was determined never to leave Mr. Dacre till he had brought him to the very dust ; and to effect this object occupied his every thought. It was with this end in view that he persuaded Gilbert to commence an action against his uncle to compel him to refund all the rents that had been received since the death of his father, and if this could but be accomplished, there would be no resource for the unfortunate victim of persecution but to end the remainder of his days in a prison.

The law-suit thus commenced, went through its various stages, and as Mr. Dacre had no sort of defence to make to it, he suffered everything to take its course, well knowing how the affair must terminate. In consequence of the activity of Hugh Darnton, the cause was pushed on with amazing celerity, and at the end of a few weeks the trial came on, and a verdict being given against Mr. Dacre, he was declared to be indebted to Sir Gilbert in the sum of one hundred thousand pounds!

This was a blow that it was impossible to withstand, yet Mr. Dacre had pretty well calculated the result, and was, therefore, prepared for the worst that might befal him. The sum was far greater than he possessed, now that the estates had been taken from him, yet with what remained, he offered to pay off the whole amount in a certain number of years. But the evil counsels of Hugh Darnton were again at work, and by his advice the offer was refused, with an intimation that he must either refund the whole that had been demanded, without delay, or prepare to wipe off the debt in a prison.

And to a prison, sure enough was he forced by the fiendish persecution of a man whom he had never injured. Nay, so inveterate was the hatred that rankled in Darnton's heart, that on the day when the arrest was to take place, he stationed himself near the Bench in order to have the gratification of seeing his unfortunate victim conveyed within those walls which, in all probability, were to divide him from the rest of the world for ever!

It would be impossible to describe the scene of affliction that took place in the family of Mr. Dacre when it was known that he must either leave the country, or pass the rest of his life in gaol. To see him driven from the land of his birth was melancholy enough; but to know that he would be deprived of liberty was a thought not to be endured. The best of the two alternatives was, therefore, urged, but he resolutely refused to flee from the fate that had been awarded him.

"Can no prayers—no entreaties move you, dear father?" exclaimed Vivian, after he had been for a long time endeavouring to prevail on him to quit England without delay. "Why do you refuse us a favour that may yet make us happy? In a foreign land we may join you, but in a gaol you will be debarred the society of those you love. Deprived of liberty, you will soon perish, and therefore do I again implore you to save yourself from the consequences of Darnton's never ending hatred."

Mrs. Dacre and Eleanor joined earnestly in their entreaties, but nothing could move him to flee from England like one who had been guilty of some heinous crime. He resigned himself patiently to his fate, hard as it was, and resolved to endure in silence the misery to which he had been reduced by circumstances over which he had no control. He was still engaged in this argument with those nearest and dearest to him, when the officer arrived whose duty it was to convey him to prison. The evil was not unexpected, and therefore occasioned very little surprise; but to Mrs. Dacre and Eleanor it came like the death-knell of all their hopes, and the scene which ensued was too powerful for description. The females clung to him in all the agony of despair, and for a moment the hapless man felt his resolution giving way. The weakness, however, was of short duration, and after imploring them to yield with humble submission to a destiny which was not to be averted, he tore himself from their embrace and accompanied the officer to a coach which was waiting at the door. Vivian and his friend Henry Markham were resolved not to leave him, and rushing from the apartment, they entered the vehicle with him, whilst the officer took his seat by the side of the driver.

"Why did you leave your mother and sister?" asked Mr. Dacre, in a feeble voice, as the carriage moved forward. "They are unhappy enough, and need all the consolation you can afford them."

"They would have reproached me bitterly if I had suffered you to go to this cheerless home of yours alone and unfriended," replied Vivian. "The sufferings they endure are indeed severe, but they will soon obtain a mastery over their feelings, and then, my dear sir, you will see that they can endure this bitter trial with as much heroism as you have displayed yourself."

" Most earnestly do I hope it may be so," exclaimed Mr. Dacre; " few women, I believe, possess more firmness than your mother, but this change of fortune is so sudden and unexpected, that I almost fear she will never become reconciled to it. Ruin has fallen upon her family—her husband is thrown into hopeless imprisonment, and every spark of hope has been extinguished by the revengeful passions of a man that I never injured in my life."

" Gilbert cannot long endure the thought of your suffering all this through his means," returned Vivian. " You have ever been a friend to him, and surely that reflection will urge him to restore you to liberty."

" It is not to Gilbert that I am indebted for this cruel persecution," answered Mr. Dacre; " he has an evil counsellor who, for some reason that I cannot explain, has urged him to adopt a course which has ended in my ruin."

" You mean Darnton ?"

" Ay, he is the man who plunged us from affluence into poverty."

" I will see him," exclaimed Vivian,—" he cannot surely be quite deaf to the voice of humanity, and I will never cease urging him till he has promised to procure your immediate release."

" It would be in vain to try him," answered Mr. Dacre; " and even if I was certain that, through his means my prison doors would be thrown open to-morrow, I should resolutely refuse to accept the favour from that villain."

" Do you know why he has so cruelly persecuted you ?"

" I do not," replied Mr. Dacre, " unless it is because I refused to accede any longer to his extortionate demands."

" What demands ?" eagerly inquired the young man.

" The means of supplying his extravagance," answered his father. " From the time that Gilbert Copley was first placed under my guardianship, this man has incessantly threatened me with the ruin that he has at length accomplished. He told me that he knew of something which would bring me to poverty, and I at first laughed at the threat as being uttered only to extort money. At last, however, I placed him in a farm, thinking to rid myself from his importunities, but my yielding thus far only made him the more bold and imperative in his demands. He then insisted upon various occasions, on receiving a large sum of money, and I yielded, though each time with a declaration that I would give him no more. At length I kept my word, and when next he applied to me I angrily commanded him to leave my house. Muttering deep vows of vengeance he took his departure, and you see, my son, the extent to which his thirst for revenge has driven him."

Vivian was about to put further questions, but at the moment the coach stopped, and the prison gates stood darkly scowling before them.

CHAPTER XXI.

SUSPICIOUS VISITERS.—REVELRY.—AN ALARMED CONSCIENCE.

NOTWITHSTANDING the haste manifested by Sir Gilbert to drive its late occupants from their beloved home, he did not make his appearance there at the time he was expected, and great was the wonder among the servants as to the reason which had led to the delay.

It was nearly six weeks afterwards that those who were in charge of the house were rather startled by the arrival of two men, whose costly garb corresponded but indifferently with the coarseness of their manners. They seemed to be much disappointed at hearing that Sir Gilbert and his lady were not yet at the Hall; but, after a good deal of whispering between themselves, one of them, addressing the other as Captain Smith, asked what they had better do.

"What had we better do?" exclaimed his companion; "why, take up our quarters here, to be sure, and make ourselves comfortable, till our friend, Sir Gilbert Dacre, returns home."

"You can walk in, gentlemen, and rest yourselves," said Lancelot Cramp, the steward; "but I have no authority from my new master to entertain visiters till he has taken possession of his house."

"Don't you trouble your head about that, old gentleman," exclaimed Captain Smith; "for, as we happen to be very particular friends of Sir Gilbert, he would be angry were any disrespect shown us."

"He would be more so if I admitted people that I know nothing about," retorted Lancelot.

"You are an insolent scoundrel," exclaimed the captain; "and if I hadn't more patience than falls to the share of most men, you would have had my sword through your body before this time. However, my friend, Lieutenant Jinks, and I intend to remain here till your master's return, so lead the way, fellow, and learn the respect due to gentlemen."

Poor Lancelot Cramp had no alternative when thus urged, and moving towards the room that had formerly been used as a breakfast-parlour, he ushered them in, though not without glancing round to see that no silver spoons were lying about. In fact, he had his suspicions about the gentlemen, notwithstanding their assumed rank, and began to wonder in his own mind how he should account to Sir Gilbert in the event of anything wrong happening. His reflections were, however, disturbed by Captain Smith, who demanded what refreshments he had in the house to offer them.

Lancelot was about to stammer forth an excuse, when he was interrupted by Lieutenant Jinks.

"Come, come, old fellow," he exclaimed, "you would try to make us believe that you have nothing in the shape of good fare to place before us. But, harkye, we are hungry travellers, and have not come on a visit to your master to be told that there's nothing to eat and drink; so stir your stumps, old fellow, and put the best you have before us, or it's likely you'll taste cold steel before you are many minutes older."

"Indeed, gentlemen, I have been so taken by surprise," stammered Lancelot, "that we have nothing in the house to put before you."

"What! nothing to eat?" vociferated the captain.

"Nor to drink?" chimed in his friend.

"Have you no cold chicken?"

"Or a bottle of wine?"

"Or ——"

Here all further questions were interrupted by a loud knocking at the hall-door, and in a second or two more the voice of Sir Gilbert was heard, as he entered the house.

"Thank Heaven!" ejaculated Lancelot, "my master has arrived in the very nick of time."

"It is, indeed, my dear friend," exclaimed Captain Smith, as Sir Gilbert and his lady entered the room. "My dear boy, how happy I am to see you," he added, squeezing the baronet's hand; "we have come I don't know how far to pay you a visit, and should have been sent hungry away, but for this timely arrival."

It is perhaps needless to say that in Captain Smith and Lieutenant Jinks, the baronet recognised Mark Harrowby and Dick Elliot, two of his former associates, and the very men of all others whom he would least wish to have seen. He, however, knew that coldness towards them would operate to his prejudice; and, having learned from them, in a whisper, the names they had assumed, he welcomed them with an appearance of cordiality that restored them to their good humour. By this time, too, they were joined by Hugh Darnton and Rob Redland, the latter of whom passed as Squire Byfield; and, the ceremony of an introduction having taken place, the pseudo Captain Smith said,—

"My dear Sir Gilbert, you have no idea how glad I am to see you return. The reception given us by your steward was rather a cold one, and we should have gone hungry away but for your opportune arrival."

"Lancelot must learn in future to treat my friends with more respect," exclaimed Sir Gilbert; "at any rate, it shall be my pleasing task to give you a hearty welcome; and though, owing to the unexpectedness of my return, our feast to-day may not be worthy of the occasion, you shall find that I have not forgotten the many cheerful hours we have spent in each other's company."

The house was not quite so bare of provisions as Lancelot would have made it appear; and the domestics, having been put upon the alert, a substantial repast was prepared, to which the host and his guests sat down with a hearty good will. As listeners, however, were not desired to overhear the conversation that might take place over their wine, the servants were ordered to withdraw as soon as the meal was finished; and then, breaking from their restraint, they gleefully talked over the exploits of former days.

"They were merry times for us, indeed," exclaimed Dick Elliot; "and who would have thought, when we were living in the cave together, that one of the number would come to be a baronet?"

"I knew it all the while," said Hugh Darnton; "but it would have been madness to blab the secret before I was sure how matters would turn out."

"Ay, ay," exclaimed Rob Redland, "I would have sworn you knew all about it, or you would not have been so anxious for him to marry Patty. Her ladyship must excuse my familiarity, for I can't forget when we were companions together."

"It will be better not to get upon that subject now," observed Darnton, "lest we should get into words about it, and so let out too much among the servants. We must be mum for the present, or the officers of justice may get upon our wake."

"That's not very likely, Hugh," exclaimed Harrowby, "for we are known here only as officers in the army, and who would ever suspect Sir Gilbert Dacre of harbouring men that are under the ban of the law."

"Hush!" interposed the youth; "and, remember, there may be listeners about when we are not aware of it."

"If I thought so," muttered Harrowby, "the knaves should meet with a dog's death; there should not be much fear of chattering if I only knew the man that would betray us."

"Violence would but serve to ruin us all," returned Sir Gilbert; "and, for my sake, I charge you to support the characters you have assumed, in order that no suspicion may arise as to who my visitors are. Here all may be safe, and will so long as you conduct yourselves with decorum; but, if you betray yourselves, we shall all be in a dilemma together."

"Do you suppose we don't think of our necks?" exclaimed Dick Elliot; "that we should be fools enough to let the folks hereabouts know who and what we are? The truth is, we want shelter from the devils that would like to send us all to the gallows; and, as your house must be our quarters for the present, we shall take care to conduct ourselves so as to keep our necks in safety."

"Do that, and you are welcome to my hospitality," replied Sir Gilbert. "In truth, I have been used to your company so long that I could find little pleasure in the society of what the world calls respectable men."

"Spoken like a lad of mettle!" exclaimed Mark Harrowby; "you were always a trump, Gilbert, and I'm glad to see that you have come into such a pretty estate as this. 'Tis a pity, too, that it's not nearer the sea coast, because we might have carried on the old game snugly enough, without anybody suspecting us."

"I tell you it wouldn't have done, Mark," interposed Darnton; "you must remember my son-in-law has a character to support now, and if once people began to make their remarks about him, or the company that's here, it might lead to an awkward discovery. Let well alone, say I, and then matters will go on comfortably enough."

"Why, you ain't beginning to grow shy of us, are you?" exclaimed Mark Harrowby.

"There's no difference in me," replied the other, "only that I don't want to see harm come to Sir Gilbert, whose risk is a great deal more than ours."

"Why he can only risk his life, can he?" demanded Rob Redland; "and that we've all of us done for him many a long day."

"The truth of it is," said Harrowby, with a sneer, "our old friend, Hugh Darnton, is afraid of his daughter being made a widow of if we don't steer clear of the gibbet. The girl happens to have tumbled upon her feet, and her father expects to make a pretty good thing of it for himself, if Sir Gilbert lives long enough."

"If you had drank less," exclaimed Darnton, "you wouldn't have dared say so much."

"Not have dared!"

"Ay, those were my words, Mark, so you may take them any how you please. But I don't want to quarrel with you to-night, so I'll away to my roost, and to-morrow, when you are more sober, I shall be ready to talk to you, if what I've said sticks in your gizzard."

Saying this, he snatched up a candle, and left the room, when he was met by Lancelot Cramp, who, leading him to the chamber he was to occupy, was about to retire, when the voice of Hugh Darnton called upon him to remain where he was.

"Stay," he exclaimed, "for you and I have been friends before to-day, and I should like to have a few words with you about the remarkable change that has taken place in this family since we last saw each other."

"It is a sad change, indeed, Master Darnton," sighed the butler.

"And why is it a sad one?" demanded the other. "Mr. Dacre, or Sir Lionel,—as they used to call him,—never had any right to the property; and, of course, it was only fair that his nephew should come in for his own just inheritance."

"That may be very true," replied the steward, submissively; "but it strikes me that if Gilbert really was the heir, you can't have acted exactly right in keeping the secret to yourself for such a time."

"Psha, man," returned Darnton, "I did it out of kindness to Sir Lionel. I didn't want to turn him out of house and home if I could help it; but conscience began to prick me at last, and I couldn't bear to see a young fellow languishing in poverty when I knew a title and good estate belonged to him. Besides, I was breaking my word to his poor dead father, and my heart smote me whenever I thought of it."

"Well, you know best about that, Darnton," exclaimed the steward. "Perhaps it was your duty to act as you did; yet, for all that, some little notice might have been given to Sir Lionel, instead of letting it come upon him like a sudden clap of thunder."

"You mustn't blame me for that, Lancelot," replied the hypocrite, "for the matter was put into a lawyer's hands, and when he saw how right the case stood, he went to work slap dash, and all the mischief was done before I thought proceedings had commenced."

"I'm glad to hear you were not so much to blame as I thought for," answered Lancelot. "It seems, however, that matters ain't yet come to the worst, for the folks hereabouts say that Sir Gilbert is not satisfied with what he's got, and that he's going to proceed against his uncle for all the money he has received for I don't know how many years past."

"Ah!" exclaimed the other, "that again is all the lawyer's doing. He would insist upon carrying the thing to the very farthest, though I tried all in my power to prevent it, and the consequence is ———"

"That poor Sir Lionel will have to go to a prison."

"He is in one already."

"My poor master in a prison!" exclaimed Lancelot, with indignant surprise.

"Yes," replied Darnton; "Sir Lionel, as you call him, has been arrested, and, between ourselves, I see very little chance of his ever coming out of it."

"And yet his nephew can sit down and enjoy himself as he has done this evening."

"Sir Gilbert can't help himself, my good Lancelot," answered Darnton. "It was all done without his knowledge, and I dare say he feels for his uncle as I do myself."

"Which is not much, I suppose, if the truth was known," observed the steward.

"Nay, there you wrong me, old friend," exclaimed the hypocrite; "for, though the world may believe me to have been excited by malicious motives, I am happy to say that my conscience will clear me from all blame in the affair.

No. 14

But we'll not say any more upon this subject, Lancelot ; so tell me, how are all the folks that I once knew in this neighbourhood ?"

"Do you include your wife and family among the number you ask after ?"

"Certainly ; how is my dear wife, and the children I was so fond of ?"

"Your wife is in the poor-house," replied Lancelot, "and the children— except one,—have, I hope, found better quarters in another world."

"This is sad news, indeed," said Darnton, pretending to wipe away his tears ; "and my boy—what has become of him ?"

"He has been taken care of by some one who seems to have been more thoughtful of him than his father was."

"Lancelot, don't reproach me, there's a good fellow," exclaimed Darnton, with affected earnestness. "I have suffered a martyrdom since I went away, and if my poor wife has been plunged in affliction, how much more I must have been grieved at knowing that my own conduct had served to bring it on."

"Well, I'm very glad to see that you have come back so repentant," returned the steward ; "for a man that has done wrong can't do more than see the folly of his ways, and try to amend them."

"They shall be amended, my good Lancelot," said Darnton ; "and those who have been loudest in my abuse shall find reason to acknowledge that they have wronged me. But, tell me, Lancelot, how are all the old friends that I left here when I went away ?"

"Much as when you saw them last," replied the steward ; "except, indeed, poor Simon Stripes, who ——"

"Hah ! Simon Stripes ! Well—well, what of him ?"

"The poor old gentleman was murdered."

"Murdered !" exclaimed Darnton, with agitation ; "how do the people know he was murdered?"

"Ah, there lies the wonder," answered the steward. "The villain that did it thought to conceal the crime by setting the house on fire ; but, luckily, the flames were discovered in good time, and when the neighbours rushed in, there was poor Simon Stripes lying murdered upon the floor."

"You are sure he was murdered ?"

"There can be no doubt of it," answered Lancelot ; "and so all the people hereabouts say as well as myself. The poor servant girl, too, shared a similar fate, at least it's supposed so ; but her body was so much burnt that it was impossible to be quite certain as to the cause of her death."

"'Tis a pity but the body of the old man had been burnt as well," muttered Darnton.

"Lor ! sir, what makes you say so ?"

"Why, because there would have been an end of the wonder at once," answered the other, endeavouring to recover his composure. "I'm sorry to hear of poor Simon's death, but I can't believe anybody could have been found base enough to murder such a harmless old fellow as he was."

"You may depend upon it he was murdered, though," replied Lancelot ; "and I'm very much mistaken if the whole affair is not found out some of these odd days."

"Is there any sort of clue, then ?" demanded Darnton, anxiously.

"Why, I don't know that I'm doing right in saying so much," answered the other ; "and so, with your leave, I'd rather not speak any further upon the subject."

"Psha !" ejaculated Darnton, "what does it matter, since we are such old friends ? You were speaking about the likelihood of the truth coming out one of these days ; do you happen to know whether anybody guesses by whose hand the deed was done—that is to say, supposing the old man was really murdered ?"

"I do know it, Hugh Darnton."

" Hah !"

" You seem agitated."

" No, no—not in the least, old friend," replied the other ; " but I knew poor old Simon well, and the news of his melancholy death made me feel a little nervous, that's all.   By-the-bye, I forgot to ask if *you* have any notion who committed the murder ?"

" I have had my suspicions of three or four," answered Lancelot ; " but as there's no proof against any of them, it would be hard to judge too hastily."

" You are right, my friend ; the innocent should not suffer even by an unjust thought ; and now let me ask who it was you were speaking of just now that was in hopes he should find a clue to the crime ; if, indeed, the old man met his death by violence ?"

" My old master."

" What ! Mr. Dacre ?"

" Yes, Sir Lionel Dacre."

" Well, *Sir* Lionel, if you will call him so," exclaimed Darnton impatiently, " and, pray, what chance has he of knowing anything more of this matter than either you or I do ?"

" It was not my business to ask him any impertinent questions," replied Lancelot ; " but he would sometimes speak to me in confidence, and more than once he has hinted that he had got something or other by him that might prove the means of bringing punishment upon the murderers of poor old Simon Stripes."

" I should say that was very unlikely."

" And why so ?"

" Because he would have made a stir about it before now, Lancelot."

" Then you and I differ," replied the steward ; " for what would be the use of his making a stir till he has got together sufficient evidence ?"

" Very true," answered Darnton ; and then after a pause he added, " you spoke just now of Mr. Dacre having something in his possession that is expected to lead to a discovery of the murderer ; you don't happen to know what it is, do you, my dear friend ?"

" My master was too cautious to tell me that," replied the steward ; " but as he was never a man given to vain boasting, I feel quite satisfied that what he said was nothing but the truth."

" I wonder he didn't let you more into the secret, Lancelot."

" I should have wondered a great deal more if he had," replied the old man, " for gentleman are not apt to tell all their secrets to their servants, and in the present instance it seems to be very necessary that everything should be kept snug and quiet till the proper time arrives for making a stir. And when the moment does come, Master Darnton, you may depend upon it the murderers, whoever they are, will have reason to tremble in their shoes."

" I should like to have known what sort of proof your master 's in possession of."

" Why what does it concern you ?"

" Not much to be sure," answered Darnton ; " only I was thinking that I should be very glad to give my assistance in the event of its being required.   However, it don't matter much that I know of ; so good night, my friend, and if you should ever happen to hear anything more about this, just let me know of it immediately."

Some few weeks elapsed after this conversation, and the scenes that were witnessed at the mansion were such as to create a great deal of surprise and conversation among the neighbourhood.   Not that anybody suspected the real character of the strange people by whom the new baronet was surrounded, for it was imagined that he had fallen into low company after his abrupt departure, and the consequent supposition was that his strange visitors were gamesters and other dissolute characters, whose society he preferred to persons of more honourable pursuits.

The consequence of this was that Sir Gilbert saw himself shunned wherever he endeavoured to form an intimacy, and in some instances the coolness manifested towards him was so marked as to leave no doubt upon his mind that an evil impression had got abroad respecting him. His disposition then began to grow morose even towards those with whom he had been upon terms of the closest intimacy; seldom associating with them except at table, and sometimes even venturing to throw out hints that their visit had been quite long enough. But such men as these were not likely to be easily affronted when self-interest stood in the way, and affecting to take no notice of his change of manners, they stuck to him like so many leeches, determined to remain where they were as long as it might suit their purpose.

The union which Sir Gilbert had formed with the daughter of Hugh Darnton also became another source of discontent to him. The vulgarity of her manners began to fill him with disgust, and knowing as he did that the marriage had been brought about by her father to accomplish his own ambitious views, he resolved to end the connection at the earliest opportunity, and rid himself of what was now an incumbrance to him, by allowing her a separate maintenance. This, however, was not to be done too hastily, lest the vengeance of her parent should fall upon and crush him.

Nor was Hugh Darnton unmindful of what was passing in the mind of his son-in-law, for he was able to discover a great deal in the expressions that occasionally escaped the lips of Sir Gilbert Dacre, and anticipating what was to follow, he set his wits to work to devise fresh schemes to avert the threatened mischief. But the more he thought it over in his mind the greater appeared to be the difficulties that presented themselves in his way. Sir Gilbert was the free and uncontrolled master of his own actions, and Darnton now began to curse himself for not having made an ample provision for himself at a time when it would have been easy to have done so. Solely dependent upon the liberality of the man he raised to fortune, it behoved him to act with caution, and to take no steps without due consideration. Bitterly did he curse his own folly in not having taken care of himself when it was in his power to have done so; but he was not a man to be easily thwarted, and it was, therefore, his determination to watch every opportunity that might give him the desired advantage.

CHAPTER XXII.

AN EXPEDITION.—THE ROBBERY.—THE AMAZON.

AFTER some time had been passed at the Hall, the visiters began to grow weary of the monotony of their every day life, and it was then seriously argued among them whether they might not return to their former quarters to see what had become of Deborah, and the comrades who had been left behind when they had been compelled to make their hasty retreat. This proposition was at first regarded with great favour, and a day was even named when they should take their departure; but Mark Harrowby was not a man to do things in too great a hurry, and having considered the subject with his usual deliberation, he pointed out the danger of their going in the way proposed, and suggested that one or two of their number should be deputed to undertake the mission, after which the rest could act upon their report.

Accustomed to receive his opinions with deference, the others readily yielded to his proposal, and lots having been cast to decide who should be the envoys, they fell upon Rob Redland and Dick Elliot, the former of whom was to travel under his assumed name of Squire Byfield, and the latter to follow in the capacity of his servant, under the designation of Tom Brand.

The announcement of this plan was received by Sir Gilbert Dacre with secret satisfaction, since it afforded him a hope that he should soon be rid of his unruly companions. He, therefore, supplied them liberally with money, provided them with a couple of horses for their use, and having seen them start on their journey he congratulated himself upon the chance that he should at length be rid of companions, for whose society he had long since ceased to have any relish.

During the former part of their journey nothing particular occurred that is worthy of notice, for the characters they had assumed were pretty well supported, and at the various inns where they halted to rest, they managed so to conduct themselves as to avoid any suspicion that might have been likely to involve them in difficulties. To be sure on one occasion, Dick Elliot was strongly tempted to put a few silver spoons in his pocket, but the threats of his companion forced him to be honest against his will, and with some little grumbling, he left the prize behind him.

On the second night they found themselves within ten miles from the cave, when a consultation took place as to whether they should proceed there at once or rest at the next inn, where it might chance that they would hear whether anything had taken place at the retreat during their absence. The latter alternative was decided on, and entering the first house of entertainment they came to, their horses were given to the care of a groom, and beds secured for themselves for the night. Nothing, however, was said upon the subject they were anxious to be enlightened on, and as any inquiries might give rise to awkward suspicions, they forebore speaking about it, and at an early hour retired to rest.

At breakfast time on the following morning, Redland was surprised at not seeing Dick Elliot, and upon making inquiries of the host his wonder was changed to alarm at hearing that his companion had left at an early hour, without saying where he was going to or whether he was to return. This conduct, to say the least of it, was very suspicious, and it was not without a feeling of dread that Redland waited two or three hours, half suspecting that his comrade might prove false, and by giving information against him, make sure of his own safety.

So thoroughly at last did he become convinced of something being wrong, that, anxious to escape the anticipated danger, he ordered his horse to be got in readiness, and having settled his tavern bill, rode away almost dreading whether he might not have delayed too much time in waiting for the return of Dick Elliot. He even feared that a pursuit would take place before he was sufficiently advanced on his journey, and was about to urge his horse to greater speed, when the well-known form of Elliot was seen galloping towards him as if half the people in the country were at his back. For a moment Redland paused to reflect whether it would be better to advance or retreat, but seeing that his companion motioned for him to remain where he was, he took heart, and reining in his steed, waited till Elliot came up to him.

" Dick !" he exclaimed, " what knavish trick is this you have been playing me ? Speak, scoundrel ! or a brace of bullets through that plotting brain of yours shall be your reward."

" Come, come, Rob," answered the other; " if I suffer you to play the

master over me before other people, it don't follow that you are to do so
when we are by ourselves. Besides, I've been doing business since I last
saw you, and here's a tolerably well filled purse to prove that I'm telling
you the truth."

" How is this?" demanded Redland ; " have you been at some of your
old tricks again ?"

" I can tell you all about it as we ride along," answered the other, " so
don't let us be standing here like a couple of fools when we know not
who may be upon the look-out for us."

" Tell me," cried Redland, as he urged his horse forward, " have you
been committing a highway robbery ?"

" No, there would have been too much danger in that," replied Dick,
" else I've had two or three pretty chances this morning. Yet it's vexatious,
too, when a good opportunity slips through one's fingers."

" How came you by that purse, then ?"

" In the easiest way you can imagine."

" That is to say you have robbed some poor devil of it ?"

" The fact is simply this," replied Dick. " I couldn't sleep last night
for thinking of one thing or another, so, soon after it was daylight, I got
up, and taking my horse from the stable, rode out to see if something
couldn't be gathered about what's been going on at our old quarters since
we've been away. At last I found a public-house open, and having tied
my horse to a tree I went in and saw a party of countrymen sitting round
a table at breakfast. The fellows were civil and chatty enough, so I made
free to invite myself to be one of their party, and as money came to be the
subject of conversation, I soon drew from one of them that he had a few
odd guineas in his pocket that he was going to place in the bank for
safety."

" Which you have taken care of for him ?"

" How could a man like me resist such a temptation ?" demanded Elliot.
" I did think it rather hard to rob him, it's true ; but then my fingers itched
to touch his gold, so I grew very liberal all of a sudden, and having ordered
sundry glasses of brandy-and-water, I at last began to see that my generosity was likely to be rewarded, for the yokels grew very talkative, and at
last they one by one went away, leaving only the poor devil that I had a
design upon."

" And how did you manage to rob him ?"

" Why I made him as drunk as a lord, and then, pretending to be very
much concerned for the old boy, I offered to see him home. On the road,
however, I eased him of his purse, and then bundling him into a dry ditch,
I left him to the enjoyment of his nap without any fear of his being disturbed."

" It will be discovered, Dick," exclaimed Redland, " and if a pursuit
takes place, we shall be lost."

" Oh, there's no fear of that," replied Elliot, " for I returned to the
public-house for my horse and told the landlord that I had seen the old
gentleman safe home. Then riding away I took an opposite direction to
that I intended to come, and after a little while turned across the fields
and came out at a place about a mile ahead of us. So even if a pursuit
takes place at all, they'll take a road that will never bring them in our
track. Now that's what I call managing a job very cleverly, and as we
are comrades together, Rob Redland, you shall go shares with me in whatever the purse may happen to contain."

" How much is there ?" asked Redland, somewhat appeased by the proposition.

" Something above twenty pounds, I believe," replied the other ; " but if you'll dismount for a few minutes, we'll go into yonder barn, where we may count the money and divide it like honourable men."

Redland would rather not have submitted to any delay just then, but thinking there was no time like the present when a division of booty was to take place, he assented to the proposition of his comrade, and both of them having secured their horses, they entered the barn, and seating themselves upon a heap of straw, began to count over the money and apportion it in equal moieties. This done, they were about to quit the place when a rustling among the straw startled them, and before they could effect their retreat, a wild looking man emerged from the place where he had made his bed, and stretching forth his skinny palms towards them, demanded his share of the money.

"Your share!" exclaimed Elliot, with alarm.

"Ay," replied the other, "what has poor Dan of the Heath done that he should go without his rights? Give me my gold, I say, or you shall both swing for your evil doings before you are much older."

"I'll tell you what it is, Mr. Dan of the Heath, or whatever your name may be, we are two honest gentlemen that are dividing the profits of our day's work, and before you come in for any share I should like to know by what right you claim it."

"I answer no questions," returned the other. "I am poor and need money; so share with me, or you'll see how long it will be your luck to escape the gallows."

"We are not to be frightened, old boy," retorted Elliot, "and if you must come in for what you call your share, you had better take it, and then see what good will come of your listening to us. By Jove! I've half a mind, as it is, to send a knife to your heart for daring to be present when a couple of gentlemen are settling their private affairs."

"Be quiet, Dick, will you," exclaimed Redland; "don't you see the poor fellow has lost his wits, and it's only throwing away words to talk to him. Let's give him one of these coins between us, and perhaps it may be the means of saving us from further trouble."

Elliot, however, was not disposed to coincide with this proposition, and motioning for his companion to leave the barn, he instantly followed, and then closing the door, which he took care to lock, he and Redland mounted their horses, and galloped off with all the speed they could. In the hurry they missed their road, and just as the darkness of night was setting in, came to the spot where the two unfortunate men had been buried whom they had assisted to murder a short time before they had been compelled to flee from the retreat. A single glance was sufficient to convince them that the grave had been disturbed, and then dashing forward they sprang over hedges and ditches till they found the right road, and within half an hour afterwards they had reached the place which had been the object of their journey.

Their first care was to secure their horses, and their next to listen at the door and ascertain whether it would be safe to apply for admittance. All was still and silent as the tomb, and judging from this circumstance that no danger was to be apprehended, Dick Elliot ventured to knock gently and call upon the name of old Deborah. For some few minutes, however, no sound was heard from within, and the signal was about to be repeated when stealthy footsteps were heard in the passage, and the voice of Deborah, in a whisper, asked through the keyhole who was there. The usual signal satisfied her that all was right; the heavy bolts were removed, and as the heavy portal turned upon its hinges, the housekeeper was seen by the dull, flickering light she carried in her hand.

"Rob Redland and Dick Elliot, by all that's wonderful!" she exclaimed as they entered, and then closing the door she led the way to the room, muttering as she went along,—" What devil's business are you about now that you come in the darkness of night to terrify a poor lone creature out of her senses ?"

" We come in darkness," replied Rob, " because we feared being seen in the light, and as for the devil's business that has brought us, it was neither more nor less than to know how you've been getting on since we've been away."

" Oh, you're very thoughtful about me, ain't you ?" she exclaimed, as they all entered the room. " I have been left here for months to take my chance, and not one of you has returned to see what's become of me till it's likely there's no more danger."

" Don't be cross with us, Mother Deborah," said Elliot, coaxing, " for we've never forgot you, though till now there's been good reason why we should keep ourselves in concealment. But I see you're living pretty well here," he continued, glancing on the table, upon which a substantial supper had been laid, " and with your good leave we'll sit ourselves down and partake of your fare."

" You'll do as you like about that, I suppose," she replied ; " but I'd rather Mark Harrowby had come here himself instead of sending his underlings."

" Never fear but you'll see him soon enough after he knows how things have been going on," answered Rob Redland, who, with his companion, had by this time commenced operations upon the eatables. " We threw lots, you must understand, and as the chance fell upon us we came to see how our good old friend, Deborah, was getting on."

" You find me alive," she replied, " but no thanks to anybody for it."

" Hah ! you have been in danger then ?"

" I have, and when you've told me how Harrowby and the rest of 'em have managed to escape the gallows, perhaps I may let you into the secret of what has been passing since the night you all went away from this place in such a hurry."

Redland then related every particular of their adventures from their parting to the present moment, to all of which, Deborah listened with sullen silence, except that part which referred to Gilbert Copley and the change of circumstances that had happened to him. Then her whole attention seemed to be absorbed, and when the narrative was brought to a conclusion, she exclaimed with marked emphasis,—

" So ! this is just what I've been expecting to hear. Hugh Darnton has played his cards well ;—his daughter is now a fine lady, and he, I suppose, has taken care of number one for doing what he calls a good turn for Gilbert Copley."

" Sir Gilbert Dacre, you mean, I suppose ?" observed Dick Elliot.

" Ay, Sir Gilbert Dacre, if his fine title suits you better," answered the woman. " It's a grand thing, no doubt, for a man to be a baronet with plenty of money at his command, but let 'em all look to it, for, little as they all think of me at present, the time will yet come when I shall have a a finger in the dish. You may smile, Rob Redland, but I know something that would be worth half Gilbert Copley's fortune to purchase."

" Why you wouldn't harm a young fellow that I always thought you had taken a right fancy for ?"

" I liked him very well at one time," replied the woman, " but he has scorned me because I was not good enough, and now that he has thought fit to make Patty Darnton his wife, I'll see whose turn it shall be to triumph next. The girl's father, too, has been playing his scurvy tricks because I was not near enough to prevent what I've all along foreseen. Yet the

mischief is done;—I have been foiled, Rob Redland, and it shall now be my turn to let 'em see how a woman can be revenged."

"Psha!" ejaculated Redland, " you'll think better of it by-and-bye, Deborah."

"Never!" she exclaimed, dashing her clenched fist upon the table. "I shall yet live to see my vengeance completed, and when that is done there'll not be one of the band left to boast that I've not kept my word."

"Do you threaten us all?"

"Ay, Rob, and *you* in particular."

"Me!"

"Yes."

"And what have I done to deserve your vengeance more than the rest?"

"Why you were the first to counsel the death of those two poor fellows, and it's all through that we have been hunted by the officers of justice. We were quiet enough till then, and now every one of us has as good as got a rope round our necks. Take warning from me, I say, and don't stop here long, or it may be too late to save yourself from your fate."

"Oh, never be afraid about that," exclaimed Redland, " for the gallows and I shall never be more closely connected than we are at present."

"Ay, ay, so many a one has thought the same thing of himself besides you," she exclaimed, " yet the hangman has claimed him at last, in spite of idle boasting."

"Let's have no more of this," exclaimed Dick Elliot, who began to fear a quarrel between these fiery spirits, which would be almost certain to turn in favour of the vixen, who it was well known always carried loaded pistols about her, and which she was not slow in using upon less exciting occasions than the present. "Let's have no quarrelling, Deborah, after our long absence, but forget the past words, and tell us all about what has happened since we have been away from the place."

No. 15

" Well, then," she said, " to begin my story, I must tell you that for some time after Harrowby and all that chose to go with him, had left us, nothing occurred that might give a notion of anything being wrong, and I began to think what fools you must all have been to run away when there was nothing to be afraid of. At length, however, we heard that a large reward was offered for the discovery and apprehension of the murderers of the two men, and from the general excitement throughout the country, there was every reason to believe it would not be long before they found out our retreat."

" That is to say," observed Elliot, " if they could find it, which I should say was rather unlikely."

" Not quite so unlikely as you think for," answered Deborah, " for all on a sudden one of our men was missing, and as I had suspected him to be a traitor for some time before, I felt pretty certain in my own mind that he had only gone away to betray us."

" Who was he?" demanded Redland.

" Ralph Dixon."

" The villain !" muttered Dick Elliot ; " I have had my thoughts about him before, and let him beware how we meet again, for one of us shall die before the strife that's between us is at an end."

" Wait till you've heard my story out," replied Deborah. " Just what I suspected of Ralph Dixon proved to be correct, for it seems that he went to the justice's, and having obtained a promise of pardon and reward, he told them who the murderers were, and offered to lead a party of soldiers to the retreat whenever they might think fit to command his services. His offer was immediately accepted, and that very night our retreat was attacked, two out of our three men were killed, and the other one and I were taken prisoners."

" Who was your fellow captive ?" demanded Elliot.

" Why, poor Tom Henson, and upon the evidence of that villain, Ralph Dixon, he was hung like a dog, though no one could say that he had any hand in the murder."

" Let the villain look to himself," exclaimed Redland, " for if he had ten thousand lives, I would have them all as a punishment for his treachery. But how was it, Deborah, that you happened to escape the fate of our unfortunate comrade ?"

" Why the jury took it into their heads to acquit me," she replied, " and when I left prison I came back here to my old quarters, because there was not another roof in the world where I could hope to find a shelter."

" And solitary enough you must have been, I should think," observed Elliot.

" Not so solitary as you imagine," she replied, " for some of the military often pay me a visit in the hope that some of you may return, and if you and Redland should happen to be caught here, you'll be likely to share the fate of poor Tom Henson."

" They shall not take us very easily at any rate," exclaimed Dick, " for we are both well armed, and, if needs must, a few of them shall die before we suffer ourselves to be dragged off to a prison. But tell me, Deborah, what time was it when the rascals came to pay you this visit ?"

" About midnight."

" And you did nothing to prevent the mischief ?"

" I did as much as you could have done yourself," she replied, " and perhaps a great deal more, for I was as cool as I am at this moment, and my plans were not badly laid out, if I could but have had a little more assistance."

' Did you kill any of the villains that were brought here by your betrayer ?"

" Ay," answered Deborah, " the first fellow that entered the door fell dead as he stepped across the threshold. I was where no one saw me do it though, or they would have hung me up on the same gibbet with poor Tom Henson."

" Was Ralph Dixon with the soldiers when they came?" asked Redland.

" I wish he had been," replied Deborah, " for then he never would have stood up in the witness-box to give his evidence against us. I looked out for him among the crowd,—for I had still another loaded pistol in my hand, and if he had shown his head it should have been to receive a bullet in it as a reward for his treachery. But he was a coward, and dared not look upon the evil work that he had been the cause of."

" Would that I could see him once more," exclaimed Rob Redland, " and I would take care never to let him do us mischief again."

" Perhaps you may see him yet," answered Deborah, in a tone of peculiar meaning. " But come, comrades, you are sitting over long at your meal, and since you are here I have something that you may be able to assist me in. Follow me."

" What is it to do?"

" To dig a grave."

" Hah!"

" Why do you hesitate? I must have done it myself if you had not been here, and you must acknowledge that it's work more suited to a man than a woman."

" Who is it for?"

" Ask no questions, and you shall learn all about it in good time. Will you assist me in the task?"

" Leave it till to-morrow and we will," answered Elliot, " 'tis an ugly job to go about at night, and to tell you the truth, Redland and I are tired of our journey, and want a little rest before we go to work again."

" Well, to-morrow be it then," she exclaimed, " and now, since you want to know who the grave is to be made for, look behind yonder curtain and tell me who it is you'll find there."

Knowing as they well did the character of the woman they had to deal with, both Elliot and his companion felt assured that some horrible spectacle awaited them, and unwillingly approaching the curtain they drew it on one side and discovered the body of a human being, whose countenance was so disfigured with blood, that it was almost impossible to make out a feature.

" Who is this, woman?" demanded Rob Redland.

" Look at him again," she exclaimed, " or is he so altered that you can't remember the features of an old comrade?"

" Hah! I have it," exclaimed Dick Elliot. " This is your vengeance, Deborah, and Ralph Dixon is already punished for his villany."

" You are right," she replied,—" I thirsted for his blood from the night when he betrayed us, and at last destiny threw him in my way."

" Was it your hand then that slew him?"

" Whose else should it have been?" she asked. " Was not my own life threatened by him, and did I ever suffer an injury without having my revenge for it? Had I lived years my rage never would have been appeased till I saw the life blood flowing from his black and guilty heart."

" But suppose you had perished instead of him?" observed Redland.

" Why then I should have died satisfied at having made the attempt," she replied. " But there was little chance of that, for I knew the customer I had to deal with and was prepared for him accordingly. He was a deep, designing villain, but I was determined to be a match for him, let the time come when it might."

"And when did the time come?" asked Elliot.

"Two days ago."

"Did he venture to come here?"

"He did," answered Deborah. "I suspected that there was mischief brewing, and prepared myself accordingly, though he would have made me believe that he had no evil thoughts towards me."

"How did you contrive to overcome a fellow that must have been well prepared for the worst before he ventured to come here?" asked Dick.

"You shall know all about it," she replied, and drawing her stool nearer to the table, she commenced her narrative, but not till she had first gratified herself with a copious libation of brandy.

CHAPTER XXIII.

A TALE OF BLOOD.—WOMAN'S REVENGE.—THE BETRAYER'S DOOM.

"I HAVE told you already," began Deborah, "that when the trial was over and they dismissed me from custody, I returned to this place because I knew of no other where I might find a roof to shelter me. But the very sight of it turned my heart sick, for everything was in confusion, and look round which way I would there was still something to remind me of the night when we were attacked by the soldiers. More than ever did I then hate the wretch that had betrayed us to our enemies, and raising up my hands towards Heaven I swore to have vengeance, and never to cease from my object till I had accomplished my vow.

"The bodies of the two men that were slain had been removed, but their blood lay congealed upon the floor, and the sight of it so unnerved me that it was long before I could gather courage enough to wash away the terrible stains. It was not that I much liked the two men who had fallen, but I hated the treachery of the villain that had caused all the mischief, and the only thought that occupied my mind was the one mad desire for vengeance."

"But it was some time it seems," observed Elliot, "before you had the opportunity you desired."

"It was," she replied, "and the time seemed even longer than it really was. Here I was left in solitude to brood over my own burning thoughts; none ever came to visit the wretched outcast, except the soldiers who now and then came, as I have told you before, to see if any part of the band had yet returned. They would have persuaded me to leave the place and seek a home somewhere else, but I had an object in remaining here that they little dreamt of, and the wealth of all the world would not have tempted me to quit the spot till my vow was fully accomplished."

"Then you must have had a great deal more patience than I ever gave you credit for," observed Redland.

"We can all be patient when we have an object in view," replied Deborah; "at least I have found it so, and many besides myself have done the same. I longed for the hour of my triumph, and at length, when almost despaired of, it came. It was night when I heard the well known signal at the door, and my heart leaped within me at the thought that he whom I most wished to meet, was at last within my reach. His well known voice in answer to my inquiries convinced me that I was right, and as the door flew open the villain stepped in and with a smiling countenance greeted me as if nothing had happened to stir up my hatred."

"And what sort of a reception did you give him?" asked Rob Redland.

" Like himself I acted the part of a hypocrite," she replied. " I bade him welcome; invited him to the shelter he had so basely abused; placed food before him, and acted in all respects as if I had forgotten the baseness he had been guilty of. He was deceived by my apparent cordiality, but, could he have searched into my soul he would have seen the vengeance and hatred that were struggling there."

" Had you no suspicion," asked Elliot, " that he came to betray you as he had done on a former occasion ?"

" I was sure he did," answered Deborah, " and that thought made me the more cautious in my conduct towards him. That the fate of one of us was about to be sealed I well knew, and the consciousness made me the more cautious, lest I should give him the advantage he was seeking."

" Did you venture to ask him why he had been such a villain as to betray his comrade ?"

" No," she replied; " I suffered him to tell his own story, and he made out such an excuse for what he had done, that any one might have believed he was driven to it by necessity. But I knew his black heart, and whilst he was trying to deceive me with falsehoods, I sat silently considering how I should make sure of my purpose and prevent his ever leaving the place alive. At length when he had finished, I asked why he had come to see me in my loneliness."

" And a good story he made up for the occasion, I'll warrant me," exclaimed Redland.

" He professed to have repented all his evil ways," answered Deborah, " and had you heard him you would verily have believed he had turned saint. He spoke of his former doings with horror, and solemnly declared that no temptation should ever induce him to commit another crime. But I soon found out what he meant, for presently afterwards he began to talk of the hoards of money that he supposed were hidden somewhere in the vaults, and as I rather humoured him to see what his drift was, he at length boldly confessed that the money would be an excellent thing to begin life with, and proposed sharing the gold with me if I would agree to assist in removing it on board a small vessel that he had close at hand."

" What did you say to him ?" asked Dick Elliot.

" Nothing that would make him suspect I was against his proposition," answered Deborah. " Indeed, I seemed to agree with him, and he was so completely deceived that he made as sure of the money as if it was already in his own possession."

" I dare say he did," replied Elliot, " for when you like, Deborah, you can cheat even the devil himself."

" I managed to cheat Ralph at any rate," she exclaimed, " and having done that I'm quite content. Had you seen how I persuaded him to sit down and drink the best the place afforded, you would have wondered how I could have played the hypocrite so well with a man that I so hated. He swallowed glass after glass in the joy of his heart that all his hopes would be fulfilled, and seeing how readily he took the bait, I spoke to him of the riches we should carry away with us in the morning, and then the roof echoed again with his wild, loud laugh. I think I hear it now, Rob Redland, for there was something terrible in it, especially to me who knew how soon his laugh would be silenced for ever."

" You felt no misgivings, then," observed the person she had last addressed; " no womanly emotions when those thoughts of blood were passing through your mind?"

" Why should I ?" she demanded. " Didn't I know that he had sought my life, and been the means of others losing theirs ? I hated him, and it seemed that every moment he lived was granting him that mercy which he had not shown to his poor comrades. So I watched him, as a tiger does his prey, and when at length he fell asleep, I crept stealthily across the floor, and grasped a poniard that was hanging over the chimney-piece."

" And stabbed him to the heart ?"

" No," she replied, " he woke up and growled out something about honour between us, and it was a long time before I could convince him that he had nothing to fear. At last I left the room, pretending that I was going to bed; but I listened at the door till his heavy breathing told me that he was again asleep, and then approaching on tip-toe, I raised the dagger, and in another instant it was buried to the haft in his body!"

" Did he die at the moment?" asked Elliot.

" Not exactly," she answered, " for with a howl such as you might expect to hear from a savage wolf, he sprang from his seat, and snatched up one of the pistols that he had laid upon the table. I saw my danger and endeavoured to avoid it, but flight would not have saved me if his aim had been steadier, for the bullet passed within a few inches of my head, and then staggering forward he would have strangled me in his death grasp, but that his strength failed him, and uttering a heavy groan, he fell dead at my feet. I can't tell you the triumph that at the moment filled my heart ; I saw my end accomplished, and the foul betrayer was numbered among the dead."

" And a very pretty companion you had made for yourself," exclaimed Redland. " Egad, you must like the company of dead men better than I do, Deborah, or you would have left the place as soon as the fellow was dead."

" I had a thought of doing so," she replied, " but where else to find a shelter I knew not, and so taking courage I determined to put him out of sight as soon as possible. Then taking up the lamp, I went down into the vault below, and with spade and mattock I began to dig a grave wherein to conceal the body of the man I had sent to his long account. But the task was not so easy a one as I had expected, for the ground was hard and stony, so that at the end of three hours I had scarcely reached the depth of two feet, and then the lamp that had been flickering for some time in its socket, went out, and I was left in total darkness."

" A very awkward sort of predicament," observed Dick Elliot, with a shudder.

" It must be confessed I did feel a little terror at that time," answered Deborah, " and though I tried to drive away all idle fears, I could not muster up resolution enough to go back to the room where the dead man was lying. So groping about, I found a few sacks that I knew had been placed in one corner; I threw myself down upon them, and after a time fell asleep. But, oh ! the dreams that then came upon me, who shall describe ? The deed that had been done was again acted as if all was real, but in my vision the victim seemed to have been the stronger, and his hand clutched my throat till I was almost strangled."

" Ah !" exclaimed Rob Redland, in a moralizing tone, " this conscience is a terrible thing, and I only wonder how you could stay here as long as you have."

" Psha !" returned Deborah, " the terror left me when the morning's light returned, and I then entered the room where the corpse was lying with as little concern as if the carcase had been that of a dog. I looked upon his face, and he seemed to frown upon me in anger, so, throwing a cloth over his grim features, I dragged the body behind yon curtain, where I intended it to remain till the grave was ready for its reception. Last night I again laboured at it; but still the pit is not deep enough, and I must now crave your assistance to remove the carrion that is offensive to my sight."

"Ay, ay, we'll help you, Deborah," exclaimed Redland. "The deed was a bold one to be sure, but it was one that couldn't be helped, and Mark Harrowby will almost love you for ridding the band of such a villain as this Ralph Dixon."

"I care not whether he's pleased at it or not," exclaimed Deborah, "for he seems to have forgot his old friends now that he's enjoying himself with this Gilbert Copley, or *Sir* Gilbert, as you please to call him."

"Psha! don't be jealous about such nonsense as that," returned Elliot, "for if you think proper to go on a visit to the old Hall you'll meet with a welcome reception from the baronet."

"If I go there," returned Deborah, significantly, "I shall not be quite so welcome a visitor as you seem to imagine."

"And why not? You were always pretty good friends."

"We might have appeared to be so," replied the woman, "because it suited my purpose to let everything bide its own time."

"You'll not go, then, and see Sir Stephen Dacre now that he's come to be a great man?"

"I will go, though," she replied, resolutely; "for I have something to say that will perhaps surprise him. He's married, you say, but I'll whisper in his ear a secret that he little dreams of, and Hugh Darnton shall see all his fine schemes vanish like so much smoke."

"If you know of such a secret," exclaimed Dick Elliot, "what good will it do you to repeat it merely to make others miserable?"

"Because I don't see why others should be happy when I am not so," she replied. "Hugh Darnton has overreached me, and I dare say glories in it; but let him look to himself, for I have that in store for him that he don't expect. He must marry his daughter to Gilbert Copley that she may be 'my lady' forsooth; and so far he has succeeded to his heart's content. His dream, however, will soon be at an end, and then he'll be sorry that I was not consulted before the step was taken."

"Bah!" ejaculated Redland, "you'll think better of it by-and-bye, Deborah. You've been a little out of temper lately; but when you see how happily they're all living together at the Hall, you won't be able to find it in your heart to go and set 'em all by the ears together."

"Their happiness will be gall and wormwood to me," exclaimed Deborah. "Why should they be enjoying themselves while I'm a prey to wretchedness? I've a murder upon my conscience, and it ain't a trifle that I shall stick at now, I can tell you. So good night, and to-morrow we'll arrange together what shall be done next."

She left the room upon uttering these words, and then Elliot, turning to his companion, said,—

"Deborah talks of to-morrow, but I've a notion she don't mean to let us see it."

"What makes you think so?"

"Oh, there's reason enough for it, I think," answered the other. "We know the secret about the murder of Ralph; she suspects us, perhaps, as much as she did him, and now that her hands are stained with blood, she'll not think much of putting us out of the way as she did him."

"But we are armed."

"So was Ralph; yet there he lies to prove that if her mind is once made up to anything, she can find a way to carry it into execution."

"Let us fasten the door then," said Redland, "and if she makes any attempt to force it open, a pistol ball will find its way through it to her heart."

" If one scheme fails she'll find another that will not," replied Dick Elliot. " She may put poison in our liquor or food, and how are we to guard against that?"

" By leaving the place as soon as we can."

" Why there's a little sense in that," answered the other. " We must get away from this cursed hole, and if there should be anything in her conduct to give cause for suspicion that she means to get rid of us, we must serve her as she did Ralph Dixon."

" Curse her!" exclaimed Rob Redland, " I almost begin to wish it had not fallen to our lot to come on this ugly business. If it was a man that we had to contend against, I should not so much have minded, but a revengeful woman will think of a thousand schemes to gain her end, that would never enter the heads of one of our sex."

" That's true enough," answered Elliot; " so knowing her as we do, we must be prepared to defeat any plans she may have formed against us. I should be loath to raise my arm against a female, but if she comes any of her tricks with us, I'll shoot her with as little ceremony as I would a dog."

" And a dog's death is the only one she deserves," replied the other. " She seems to have set her face against everybody, and you heard what she said just now about going to the Hall for no other purpose than to breed strife and confusion."

" I'd have her beware how she does that," exclaimed Elliot, " lest she should get a rougher reception than she expects. Mark Harrowby has no great liking for her, I believe, though he may be afraid of any mischief she could do through blabbing our secrets, and he would not be very sorry to have an excuse for putting her out of the way."

" If he had done so a little sooner it would have been the better for us all," replied his companion. " However, it's not too late even now to get rid of a troublesome incumbrance, and if he don't like to do the job himself, why I know of somebody that would not mind taking it off his hands."

" Meaning yourself, of course?"

" Exactly so."

" Don't speak your mind quite so loud then," whispered Elliot, " for she may be listening at the door, and if she should happen to overhear what's passing between us we may never see the outside of this place again."

" Psha!" exclaimed Redland, " are you afraid of her?"

" Why not exactly afraid," replied the other, " but I don't want to give her an advantage when we're already quite enough under her power. We must keep a sharp look-out to-night, and if we live to see the morning, we can make an excuse for going away as soon as possible."

" And do you think she won't see through it all?" asked Redland.

" She may," replied the other; " but there's two of us, you know, and it would not be very easy to keep us here against our will "

" I'll tell you what it is," answered his comrade. " Deborah has got the devil's own spirit, and cares nothing about her own life when she's got any particular purpose to serve. Now I happen to remember that there's such a thing as a powder magazine beneath this house, and if she fancied there was anything to be feared from us, she'd blow the whole concern up before we could put out an arm to prevent her."

" What! when she must lose her own life at the same time?"

" Yes," replied Redland, " she's mad enough for anything, and would not care about perishing herself so that she could but have her revenge. I've

often heard her say as much, and she has even bragged that she has laid trains in all directions about the place, so that at any time she can blow up the house and all that's in it without any one being able to prevent the mischief."

"Then why not go away now while she's asleep?" demanded Elliot.

"Because we can't do so without disturbing her," replied the other, "and in her rage she would fire the train and send us all scampering through the air. No, no, Dick; take my advice and be as cool as you can while we're here; it will lull her suspicions, man, and we can afterwards take the first opportunity that offers to wish her a very good morning."

"I'll be hanged if I can be cool," exclaimed Elliot, "when I know that in a moment she can send us both into eternity."

"But I don't think she is likely to do so," replied the other, "unless we do anything to provoke it. We must not let her suspect that we have any doubts about her, and then perhaps we may have a chance of getting away without being either stabbed in the dark or taking a flight through the air."

"Hush!" exclaimed Dick Elliot, "I can hear her footsteps now retreating from the door! She has overheard us, and our fate is decided on unless we make a bold effort to get away from her clutches."

Rob Redland also heard the same sounds distinctly, and his heart began to sink within him at the probable consequences that would result from her having heard any part of their conversation. He motioned his comrade, however, to be quiet, and having sat listening for some time without hearing anything more of Deborah, they consulted together in whispers what had best be done in their present emergency.

"It's all over with us," said Elliot, "unless we make the best use of our time, and get out of her clutches before she has an opportunity to work any of her infernal mischief against us."

No. 16

"I begin to be of your opinion," answered Redland, "and when it seems likely that she's gone to sleep, we'll make our way from the house, and see what service a good pair of heels will be to us. It's certain we can't stay here any longer with safety if she has a notion that we suspect her, and so the sooner we get away the better it will be."

"Then let's set about it at once," exclaimed the other, "for who knows how soon she may take it in her head to set fire to the train?"

"With all my heart," replied Redland, and rising from his seat he stealthily approached the door, which, to his great consternation, he found fastened on the other side. The window was now the only resource that remained, and even this was so barred and secured that it was with no little difficulty they were enabled to open the shutter. At length, however, they succeeded in accomplishing their task, and then, having first looked to their pistols to see that they were in readiness for immediate use, they noiselessly passed through and once more found themselves at freedom. To descend the winding path that led below was the work of no long time, and their steps were then once more directed to the place from whence they had come.

CHAPTER XXIV.

DESPERATION.—AN UNLOOKED-FOR FRIEND.—A SURPRISE.

THE course of our narrative now leads us back to Mr. Dacre, who, it will be remembered, had been thrown into a prison, to satisfy the boundless hatred of Hugh Darnton. Thither his wife and daughters would have followed him, but the unfortunate captive resolutely insisted upon their abandoning such a prospect, and the chief solace he received was in seeing them during the day, and listening to the cheering words with which they endeavoured to drive away the remembrance of his griefs.

The opposition which was offered to the projected marriage by the father of Henry Markham was still obstinately adhered to, and the more so as the situation of Mr. Dacre became daily more and more hopeless, whilst his own condition had been advanced by the death of his relative, Lord Belfast, to whose title and wealth he had succeeded. This, however, had little effect upon Henry, who determined to possess the hand of Eleanor Dacre, whenever an opportunity should offer for claiming the fulfilment of a promise that had been obtained from her in happier days.

As for Vivian, his case seemed now to be a hopeless one, for though he was still certain of the continued affections of Agnes Evered, his pride suggested that in his altered circumstances he was no longer a fitting match for her, who, report said, would inherit no small share of her uncle's wealth. It was not without a struggle, however, that he could prevail upon himself to abandon the one dear object upon which his heart had been fondly fixed, and it was only after long and anxious deliberation, that he finally sat down to write a letter, in which he explained the motives that had actuated him, and the determination he had arrived at to yield up all that he most highly prized. When Henry Markham heard of what had been done, he blamed him for the haste with which so important a step had been taken ; observing that he had no doubt matters would take a more favourable turn before long, and that he would then regret the unfortunate decision, which must cloud his future days with despair.

Nearly a month after this event passed away, and Vivian had given up all further hopes of a return of brighter prospects, when he and Markham were sitting one day together, the door of the apartment was suddenly thrown open, and Mr. Blundell, the uncle of Agnes Evered, presented himself before them.

"Gentlemen," he exclaimed, "I dare say I am the last person you expected to see, and perhaps I ought to make an apology for the abruptness of my visit. You shall, however, hear my business, and then you shall judge whether I ought to be made welcome or not."

"You can scarcely be an unwelcome visiter, sir," replied Vivian, "though it must be confessed I am rather at a loss to conceive the circumstance to which we owe the honour."

"Then you must have a shorter memory than I had imagined was possible," returned Mr. Blundell. "In short, sir, I suppose you have not forgotten a letter that was sent by you to my niece some time within the last month?"

"I recollect the circumstance but too well," sighed Vivian Dacre.

"Humph!" ejaculated the other, "and has it never struck you since it was sent that the course you have pursued in the affair was anything but gallant towards a lady whom you once professed to have loved?"

"I have felt more upon the subject than you can imagine," replied Vivian. "It was long, indeed, before I could collect resolution enough for the purpose; yet the step was an imperative one, and I have only done my duty in breaking off a pursuit which it would have been baseness to continue."

"And you have been actuated in the affair solely by a sense of honour?"

"Precisely so."

"Well, sir, I am inclined to believe you," answered Mr. Blundell, "or my visit here to-day would have been with a very different purpose. In fact, sir, Agnes is breaking her heart at your supposed faithlessness, and as her guardian, and almost only friend, I have travelled up to town, to learn from your own lips the reason of your conduct towards my niece."

"There is no other reason for it, Mr. Blundell," replied Vivian, "but the unfortunate change that has taken place in the fortunes of my family. You, of course, are aware that my father has been stripped of title and fortune, and that, in fact, he is now lying in a prison without hope of ever regaining his liberty?"

"I have heard it, my good fellow, and am heartily sorry for the reverses that have fallen upon your family. Still I see no reason why you should break the girl's heart; and what is more, you shall not do so, if I have the power to prevent it."

"Really, sir," exclaimed Vivian, "I am unable to guess the meaning of your words."

"Then you are more dull of comprehension than I thought," replied the old gentleman. "To be plain with you, then, I desire to know whether you will marry Agnes on condition that my consent is obtained?"

"Can it be possible!" cried the amazed Vivian, "that you will consent to her marrying a beggar?"

"Ay, when I know the beggar to be an honest man," returned Mr. Blundell. "To tell you the truth, Vivian, I am not sorry to have witnessed the honour you have manifested throughout the affair; but as I can't see the poor girl moping and pining about the house, I came up to propose that the marriage shall take place without delay. I will take care to provide handsomely for your wife, and you will then have the satisfaction of seeing her once more as happy as she used to be."

"Mr. Blundell," exclaimed Vivian, "it would be in vain for me to seek for words that would convey the gratitude I feel for the kindness you have manifested in my behalf. Half an hour since I believed myself to be one of the most miserable wretches in existence, yet now I feel that there are few persons in the world so truly happy as myself."

" And I suppose you would like to see Agnes, and tell her so ?"

" So impatient am I to do so," replied Vivian, " that, with your permission, I will journey down to your mansion this afternoon."

" My good young fellow," continued Mr. Blundell, " there's no occasion to take so much trouble. I never do things by halves, and as I guessed pretty well how this affair would terminate, I brought Agnes along with me, and she is now waiting at our lodgings till I return with news of my interview."

" Then I can see her immediately ?"

" You can."

" And she has quite forgiven the pain I inflicted upon her kind, generous heart ?"

" Forgiven !" exclaimed the old gentleman ; " I don't believe she ever blamed you for it. She was sly enough, however, to keep the secret to herself, and it was only by a mere chance that I managed to get at the truth. Poor creature ! she was glad enough when she saw which way my opinion went, and after weighing the matter in my mind, I determined upon coming up to London, and seeking an interview with you. So now, having pretty freely confessed myself, I shall return home without delay, and if you think proper to accompany me, there is a seat in my carriage at your service."

" How," replied Vivian, fervently, " can I ever repay the kindness that has been thus unexpectedly conferred upon me ?"

" Oh ! we'll talk about that another time," replied the old gentleman. " To tell you the truth, Vivian, I am not very fond of mere words, so say no more about it ; and if matters go on as flatteringly as they commenced, I shall see happy faces about me, and that will more than repay me for any trouble I may have had in bringing this marriage about. I have another source of pleasure, too, that you have not yet heard ;—my son has been restored to his reason, and that, I am happy to add, with every prospect of remaining so."

" And he," interposed Markham, " has, I suppose, accompanied you in your journey to town ?"

" He has," replied Mr. Blundell ; " a constant change of scene has been recommended ; and that, together with the society of a few cheerful friends, will, no doubt, have the desired effect."

" And has Vivian no reason to fear that he may meet with a rival in him ?" asked Markham, with a smile.

" If I thought so, he should not have been trusted so long in her company," answered Mr. Blundell. " No, no, the poor fellow still dwells upon the memory of the wife who was ruthlessly murdered before his eyes, and it seems likely enough that he will pass the remainder of his days in contemplating the sad fate of one that he loved with a most ardent affection. Besides, I know he will rejoice in the happiness of his cousin, and to see her bestowed upon the man she loves, will be a source of joy to him greater than you can imagine. In fact, my dear Vivian, we shall all be gratified by an event which promises so much felicity, and even your father will, I trust, forget his own miseries, in contemplating the brighter prospects that are dawning upon his son."

" Yet, rejoicing as I do in the regard of my dear Agnes," cried her lover, " how can I be thoroughly happy, whilst harassed with the constant reflection that my father lies in hopeless captivity ?"

" I have told you before," exclaimed Henry Markham, " that in my own opinion the case is not so hopeless a one as you imagine."

" Have you any foundation for such a belief ?"

" Perhaps not a sufficiently safe one," answered Markham, " for you to build your hopes upon at present. I have, however, as you know, always had a notion that the scoundrel, Hugh Darnton, was at the bottom of the plot ; and, I rather think a little exertion on our part, will serve to prove that I have not guessed very far from the truth. At all events, it shall be my task to make inquiries into the subject, and it shall be no fault of mine if a conspiracy is not clearly proved between Darnton and his associates."

" You think then," exclaimed Mr. Blundell, " that Gilbert Copley, as he used to be called, is not the heir to the title he has usurped ?"

" Such is my own impression," replied Markham, " and I trust you will also be of my opinion before very long. It is certain Hugh Darnton has never borne a very good character, and that circumstance, together with the fact of his having remained silent so long upon the subject, has served to convince me that the claim made by Gilbert was a fraudulent one. However, be that as it may, we are not at present in a situation to prove anything against the parties, and the matter must, therefore, continue as it is till I have succeeded in discovering enough to afford a foundation upon which we may safely go to work."

Here the conversation dropped for the present ; and Vivian, gladly accepting the invitation which had been made, returned with Mr. Blundell, and once more did he find himself in the society of her whom he had never expected to see again.

When Mr. Dacre heard the news of his son's approaching nuptials, it for a brief period served to banish from his mind the gloom and despondency that had settled there. It is true he could see no chance of his own liberation from a place which became each day more and more irksome to him ; but the alliance of his son and Agnes Evered held out a hope that joy was not entirely driven from his family ; and, consoling himself with this thought, he resigned himself to a fate that at one period of his existence he could not have contemplated without a shudder.

Passing over the brief intervening period, we will merely say, that on the appointed morning Vivian Dacre became the husband of Agnes, and as the father of the bridegroom could not otherwise join the happy party, they all returned to the prison, where a handsome banquet had been ordered by Mr. Blundell. The place where the nuptial feast was given was not, to be sure, such an one as would have been selected, had there been any choice in the matter ; but the presence of Mr. Dacre could not, on any account, be dispensed with, and the gloominess that ever surrounds a prison was forgotten on the joyous occasion which had thus called the party together. Even the unfortunate captive himself, for a time, lost the recollection of his misery, and though the door to liberty was still firmly closed against him, he could willingly endure a life of imprisonment, now that he saw one of his fondest hopes realized.

Mr. Blundell, too, took care that the conversation should refer as little as possible to subjects that might be fraught with pain ; and so well did he succeed in his benevolent design, that the day passed off pleasantly enough, and evening was just setting in, when the servant of Mr. Blundell entered the room to announce that a strange female was without, who demanded to see Mr. Dacre without delay.

" Did she tell you her name ?" asked Vivian.

" No, sir, she would not do that," replied the man, " so I told her Mr. Dacre was particularly engaged just now, and that if she wanted to see him she must call another time."

" And what said she to that ?"

" Why, she rapped out a bit of an oath, sir, and declared that she would see him if five hundred persons stood in the way to prevent her."

"She must be mad," exclaimed Mr. Blundell.

" Perhaps her business with me is really of consequence," observed Mr. Dacre, " and if so, it would be advisable to humour her. With your permission, therefore, the woman shall be introduced to us, and we will hear the business she is so importunate to disclose."

Against this no objection was raised, the servant was dismissed with a message, and immediately afterwards, who should stalk into the room, but Deborah, the associate of Mark Harrowby and his band, and the person who, of all others, could throw most light upon certain events which were at present involved in mystery. She was unknown to all of those before whom she stood, and making an awkward curtsey, she demanded which was Mr. Dacre.

"He who sits on my left hand," replied Mr. Blundell.

"Then in me he sees a friend," answered Deborah, familiarly approaching; "I suppose, though, you scarcely believe me when I say it; but, for all that, I repeat what I've said, and the time is not far off when you will own that this is no vain boast."

"The woman is evidently crazed," whispered Mr. Blundell to his friend, "and I should advise you to dismiss her from the place as soon as you can conveniently."

"I am not crazy," exclaimed Deborah, by whom these words had been overheard, "nor will I leave you till it's my own humour to do so. I came to seek Mr. Dacre,—or, Sir Lionel, as I shall still call him, and if he don't receive me with civility, I shall perhaps be provoked to do that which he'll be sorry for."

"It seems, my good woman, that you have only come to mock me," said Mr. Dacre, "and situated as I am, it is the height of cruelty to heap insults upon one who is already overburthened."

"I came neither to mock nor insult you," she replied.

"Then why remind me of my fallen state by addressing me as Sir Lionel Dacre?"

"Because I know the title is not lost, though you have given it up so easily."

"What mean you by these words?"

"A great deal more than I dare explain at present," she replied. "I know an artful villain has been at work to ensure your ruin,—he has succeeded so far; but let him beware, for the hour of his triumph draws to a close, and I shall yet have it in my power to mock and deride him."

"Of whom is it that you speak?" demanded Mr. Dacre.

"Of Hugh Darnton."

"Then in saying he is a villain you have told us no news," exclaimed Mr. Blundell; "for the truth is, we have known his real character for a long time past. That is to say," he added, "if it is the same fellow who assisted to deprive my friend of his title."

"It is the same man," she replied, "and when all is made known, you will wonder that so great a villain could so long have escaped the gallows."

"If you know aught concerning him, or the means he has taken to bring about all this mischief, I conjure you to reveal it all," cried Vivian, earnestly. "It has long been my own opinion that we have been the victims of a crafty knave and his accomplices, and should a discovery of this plot take place through your means, I can promise a large reward in the name of my father, who has been the principal sufferer through their frauds."

"Young man," she replied, "in its own proper time all shall be known, and the guilty brought to punishment. Till then have patience; and let it be your chief consolation to know that I am not unmindful of my word when vengeance is the object of my pursuit."

"Why did you visit us now, if it is your determination to leave us in a state of uncertainty worse far than that we suffered before?" inquired Mr. Dacre.

" Because I wished to see to how low a state of misery Darnton could reduce his victims, before his hatred towards them was satisfied," she answered.

" And whence," asked Mrs. Dacre, " has all this cruel persecution arisen ?"

" Chiefly through your own fault," replied Deborah. " There was a time when Hugh Darnton could get money from your husband for only the trouble of asking for it. You, however, raised objections against him, and when he began to find that his extortions were not so readily complied with as they had been, he determined to work the ruin of your family. He swore to do it, and you have witnessed how well he has kept his oath."

" But the wretch may yet be within my grasp," exclaimed Mr. Dacre ; " and should I once stretch forth my hand, he shall find that my own power of vengeance is at least equal to his. For the sufferings I have endured through his malice I care but little ; but never can I forget the bitter adversity he has brought down upon those I most dearly love."

" If you take my advice," returned Deborah, " you will take no proceedings in the matter till I have seen him."

" But how do I know how long I may be kept in this dreadful state of suspense ?"

" Be assured it will not be of very long continuance," answered Deborah, " for I am now on my way to your former mansion, where it's likely I may not be a very welcome visiter to Sir Stephen."

" And is it upon this business that you are going ?" asked Mr. Blundell.

" It is."

" May I ask what reason you have for taking up the affair so warmly just now ?"

" There's a bit of private revenge at the bottom, it must be confessed," answered the woman, with hesitation. " Hugh Darnton has thought fit to carry the business all his own way when I ought to have been consulted in it. He has taken away a title to bestow it upon another ; but he forgot that in so doing he has made an enemy there will yet be reason to dread."

" It seems, then," observed Mr. Blundell, " that if my friend here is once restored to his rights he will owe it entirely to a quarrel that has broke out between yourself and this Hugh Darnton ?"

" Does it matter to what circumstances he owes his good fortune ?" demanded the woman, sullenly. " I have my own reasons for acting as I'm going to do, and if your friend is dissatisfied with them, he can remain a prisoner within these walls till Darnton's heart relents, and that will be a long time first, I can promise you. What say you, Mr. Dacre ; shall I give you my assistance or not ?"

" My father," said Vivian, eagerly, " will gladly avail himself of any advantage it may be in your power to bestow upon him. Keep but your promise, and the reward shall be fully equal to the service performed."

" That's spoken sensibly," exclaimed Deborah ; " and you shall now all find that no boasting words have been uttered which I am unable to fulfil. From this place I take my road to the old mansion, and it is likely that before any long time passes away, you will be summoned to take up your abode once more beneath the roof you were driven from."

Deborah again curtseyed awkwardly to the company, and left the room without deigning to answer the next question that was put to her. A dead silence then ensued, which was at length broken by Henry Markham, who said, abruptly,—

" The visit of this singular woman serves to make good the prognostications I have lately uttered. She seems to be aware of some secret or other, the divulging of which will expose the villany of Darnton and his associates,

That will be one great end gained, and then I shall have the happiness of seeing my friends restored to the home from whence they were forced to flee through the machinations of evil men."

"I fear, my young friend," exclaimed Mr. Dacre, "your good wishes prompt anticipations that will never be realized. That there was some villany connected with the affair I always suspected; but, on the other hand, it must be admitted, that proofs of Gilbert's right to the title and estates were brought forward which it would have been in vain to combat against. Under these circumstances I yielded to the demands made upon me, and I now leave you to judge whether any change in my favour can have taken place since?"

"That will depend entirely upon the secret this woman boasts of possessing," answered Markham; "she seems confident, and, for my own part, I am not inclined to doubt that she is acquainted with a great deal more about Hugh Darnton than he would wish to have disclosed."

"In which case," said Mr. Dacre, "he will find means to keep her silent upon the matter. A bribe will be sufficient for the purpose, and my nephew will not grudge a few hundred pounds, when the stakes he is playing for are so heavy."

"But she seems to be actuated by a feeling of revenge," observed Markham, "and that is a passion over which money does not at all times possess influence. She seems to hold this man, Darnton, in utter hatred, and in order to defeat his plans she may be urged into doing an act of justice."

Another pause occurred at this juncture; and, after a short time, Mr. Blundell changed the conversation into a more light and agreeable channel. At length the carriage was announced as being in readiness, when the bride and bridegroom, accompanied by Mr. Blundell, quitted the prison to return home. Mrs. Dacre and her daughters remained with the captive till the latest moment that was allowed, and then, escorted by Henry Markham, they quitted the abode with hearts lighter and happier than they had been for some time before.

CHAPTER XXV.

MATRIMONIAL DIFFERENCES.—A REVEL.—AN INTRUDER.

In the meanwhile affairs at the ancient mansion of the Dacres were rapidly advancing towards a climax, for Sir Gilbert grew weary of the companions who had forced themselves upon his hospitality, and gladly would he have been rid of them, but that it was too dangerous an experiment to try till he could thoroughly ascertain how far he could depend upon the continued favour of Hugh Darnton.

As we have before observed, too, he no longer regarded Patty as he did when fortune had smiled less kindly on him, for he felt that she would be a bar to his entering any society higher than he at present kept. The disinclination shewn in every direction by respectable people to form an intimacy with him, could only be attributed, he thought, to the vulgarity of his wife, and as all respect for her had ceased, he determined to be rid of her as soon as an opportunity presented itself.

Hugh Darnton had long since observed the growing coldness of the young baronet towards his wife, and many an uneasy moment did he pass when reflecting on the loss of influence he should soon sustain. The chief object which had urged him to seek this alliance was the power it would give him over Sir Gilbert, and never recollecting that forced marriages are seldom

attended with happiness, he exulted when the ceremony was completed which made his daughter the bride of a man of title. Great, therefore, was his chagrin when he saw the bonds of love gradually dissolving, and as there appeared to be no hope of a perfect reconciliation taking place, he resolved, on the first occasion that offered, to speak to Sir Gilbert on the subject, and demand an explanation of his intentions. It was not many evenings after he had formed this resolution, that, remaining behind after the rest of his companions had gone drunk to their beds, he found himself alone with his son-in-law, and disguising his rage with what skill he could, he opened the subject by inquiring whether he was mistaken in fancying that an alteration had taken place in his conduct towards his wife.

"Why do you ask me such a question?" demanded Sir Gilbert, with surprise.

"Merely for my own satisfaction," was the calm reply. "I had hoped to have seen my daughter the happy wife of the man I have befriended; and it has lately caused me a great deal of uneasiness to see that she begins to be regarded with indifference."

"You should have thought of all this before you took so much pains to bring the marriage about," answered Sir Gilbert. "For my own part, I would fain have avoided the union; but you seemed to think your daughter's honour was concerned, and I agreed to make her my wife, though it was scarcely to be expected that I could be forced into giving her my heart."

"I am to understand, then," exclaimed Hugh Darnton, with more warmth than he had hitherto displayed, "that the poor girl is to be cast aside to make room for some favoured paramour?"

"You can put what construction you please upon my conduct," answered the other haughtily. "I am my own master in my own house, Darnton, and if anything displeases you, the easiest remedy will be for yourself and Patty to take your leave of me."

No. 17

" These are bold words, Sir Gilbert, to the man that has made you what you are," exclaimed Darnton, as he dashed his clenched first upon the table. " Remember it is I that have been your friend, and as easily as I raised you from poverty to wealth, I can bring you down to the level from whence you sprang. Nay, more,—an angry man knows no bounds to his vengeance, and were I to utter a few words abroad, you would mount the scaffold where many a more honest man has preceded you."

" But the few words you might speak," answered Sir Gilbert, tauntingly, " would bring *you* to a shameful end as well as me."

" True ; but desperation, I have heard, is a species of madness," returned Darnton, " and if once I am urged to that point, you will find that I have resolution enough to dare any danger rather than permit another to triumph over me. The weary, anxious hours that I have passed for years back are not to be repaid with disappointment ; or, if I am to be foiled, it shall not be without the satisfaction of revenge."

" You think to intimidate me, it seems."

" Why, as for that, Sir Gilbert," replied the other, " you can think of my motives as you please, only that it must not be forgotten that I have never been used to vain boasting, and in the present instance I have good cause for keeping my word should you carry your designs against my daughter into effect."

" Your daughter has no ground of complaint against me," exclaimed Sir Gilbert, " and even if she had, her father is the last person to whom I should feel inclined to account for my actions."

" Who else can she look to ?" asked Darnton ; " is she to be forsaken by all the world because her husband thinks proper to forget the obligation he swore to at the altar ?"

" Truly, this is the devil reproving sin," exclaimed the other, with a sneer, " and I could laugh to hear your words, but at this moment I am in no humour for mirth. The marriage with your daughter I was trapped into, and it can surprise you but little if I now see my folly, and try to escape from the consequences of it."

" Speak the truth fairly, and we shall understand each other all the better," replied Darnton. " The fact is, you begin to get high notions now that a title has been added to your name, and, forgetting who it was that made you what you are, my daughter is no longer considered to be a fitting match for your greatness. But the knot has been tied, and I will defy you to release yourself from it, in spite of all your efforts."

" Beware how you irritate me with your insolence," exclaimed Sir Gilbert, furiously, " or I may be tempted to do that in my passion which I should afterwards be sorry for. Leave me, and when we next meet together, forget not the respect you owe to a superior."

" A superior !"

" Ay."

" Then look to yourself, proud upstart," exclaimed Darnton, " for from this moment I no longer regard you as worthy the esteem I have bestowed upon you. We have been friends,—now we are enemies, and you have yet to learn that I can be as bitter in my hatred as I have been faithful whilst I thought you deserved it."

" Whatever service you have done for me has been long since cancelled," replied the other. " Your own interest was the chief motive that urged you to assist in recovering my birthright, and having drawn me into a marriage with your daughter, you must now rate me because I cannot love her as you think I ought."

" I care not whether you love her or not," exclaimed Darnton ; " but there is reason to believe that you intend to send her away from the house as a cast-off wretch whom you have learned to despise. But have a care, Sir Gilbert, how you take such a step, for she has one friend remaining in the world, and he will take care to see that a weak woman is not to be trampled in the dust."

"Your threats will have little influence over me," returned the other, "since I am under no control, and shall act in whatever manner may best suit me. It is true I no longer love Patty; and surely, in that case, it will be better for her to live separate upon the handsome provision I shall make, than to pass the remainder of her days in the consciousness that her presence is no longer wished for."

Before Hugh Darnton could make any further reply, a loud knocking was heard at the hall-door, and whilst they were yet standing in uncertainty and amazement at so unusual an occurrence, a trampling was heard close by, and presently afterwards Dick Elliot and Rob Redland presented themselves to their view.

"How now," exclaimed Darnton, angrily; "why do you make this uproar in the house, when already we are suspected among the servants, and, through them, by the whole neighbourhood?"

"Why, the truth is, Master Darnton," replied Elliot, "we've had cause enough for haste; and if you had been in the same dilemma, you'd have thought exactly about it as we did."

"Are you pursued?" demanded Sir Gilbert anxiously.

"I don't know whether we are or not," replied Elliot; "but we've made our escape from the devil, and if that wouldn't make a man run, I don't know what would."

"What means this foolery?" exclaimed Darnton. "Who have you escaped from?"

"Deborah."

"Humph!—a woman!"

"A devil, as I said before," returned Dick Elliot. "Why, she has committed one murder, at least, since we left the cave, and would have shed more blood if I and Rob Redland had not made ourselves scarce by getting out of the window."

"Psha! you are a couple of cowards."

"Call me what you please, Hugh Darnton," exclaimed Redland; "but the hag seemed to have taken a fancy for our blood, and if we had ventured to sleep in the cave she would have served us as she did Ralph Dixon."

"Ralph Dixon!" vociferated Darnton; "what has she done to him?"

"Killed him, that's all."

"Then the fellow must have proved himself a traitor," exclaimed Darnton, "or she would not have laid violent hands on one of our people."

"Why, the truth is, he turned out to be an infernal villain," answered Elliot, "and there's no denying that he deserved the fate he met with. According to her own account, too, she managed the business very well; but as we fancied she might take it into her head to serve us the same way, we made use of the first opportunity that offered, and escaped from the place to give you warning that she may be expected here in the course of a little while."

"And doubtless," observed Darnton, significantly, "Sir Gilbert will give her a cordial reception."

"If she comes," answered Sir Gilbert, with forced composure, "she shall be received on the same footing with the rest of her companions. It must be confessed, however, that I had rather not have been honoured with the visit, since the eyes of my neighbours are already directed towards my house more than I could have wished."

"We must keep her in doors as much as possible," observed Redland, "and then no one need know anything about her being here."

" Except from the servants," returned Sir Gilbert.

" The servants !" exclaimed Darnton ; " let one of them dare whisper a word that may bring us into trouble, and it shall be the last chance they will have of making mischief against their masters."

" The truth is," said Sir Gilbert, " the woman will come if she has made up her mind to it, and all we have got to do is to prevent any mischief that might follow from her visit. We must appear to give her a hearty welcome to the mansion, and perhaps in a short time we may be able to think of some plan for removing her to a distance."

" And suppose," asked Dick Elliot, " she should find herself so comfortable in her new quarters as to refuse going to any other ?"

" Leave that to me," exclaimed Hugh Darnton, " and I'll undertake to say she shall not give us any very great deal of trouble."

" That is to say you'll serve her as she did our old comrade, Ralph Dixon ?"

" Perhaps so," replied Darnton, gloomily. " I have always owed the woman a grudge, and it would not take much to set me about paying it. She has threatened to blab secrets that might chance to bring my neck to a halter, and if I had not been a fool she would have been silenced long before this time. But come, Sir Gilbert, you and I have had a few words to-night, and as I don't like to lie down to sleep with bitter blood in my heart, suppose we sit down with our two friends here, and finish the night as good fellows ought to do ?"

" That's what I call a very sensible speech of yours, Master Darnton," exclaimed Elliot, " and as I and my companion have had a long ride of it, I don't know that a more acceptable proposition could have been made."

Sir Gilbert would gladly have excused himself ; but, standing as he did, in fear of his lawless associates, he was obliged to comply, and a fresh supply of liquor having been placed upon the table, they passed the night in the same uproarious mirth that had characterized their orgies ever since the mansion had changed masters. It was not until daylight had begun to dawn that they thought of rising from the table, and then the host and his guests went staggering to their beds under the influence of the strong potations they had taken.

The next night saw them all seated round the same board, and revelling amidst the noise and din that usually accompany intemperance. The quarrel between Sir Gilbert and Darnton was apparently forgotten, and all seemed to be the height of mirth and hilarity, when a voice from the further of the room produced instant silence, which was presently afterwards broken by a simultaneous exclamation of " Deborah !"

" Ay," cried the female whose name had been uttered, " it is indeed your old companion Deborah, who hopes her presence will not prove unwelcome after the long parting there has been between us."

" You are just the woman, of all others, that we most wished to have among us," said Mark Harrowby. " Men are but dull company among themselves, my Princess of Hearts ; but, in the society of a delicate female, like yourself, they are softened and moulded into humanity."

" You are joking with me, Mark, I know you are," she replied, seating herself in a chair by his side. " But never mind, you'll find me just what I've always been, so pour me out a bumper of spirits, for I've had a long walk and need refreshment."

A bumper was accordingly poured out, and another followed it with the quickness of thought, which was drank off as if it had been so much water.

" Ah !" she exclaimed, " this puts me in mind of the stuff we used to get down at the cave yonder ;—there's heart in it, my lads, and that's more than you can say for the wishy washy rubbish that pays duty to the king."

"I thought by the smack of your lips you seemed to like it," observed Dick Elliot.

"What!" she exclaimed, "you are here before me, are you? It was a dirty trick, though, of you and Rob Redland to run away as if you thought there was danger in stopping till the morning. But I suppose you were in a hurry to tell Hugh Darnton and Sir Gilbert that I was coming to pay them a visit."

"Pay me a visit," cried Hugh Darnton; "and pray why was I to be so greatly honoured?"

"I see how it is," she said, "you were never very friendly with me, Darnton, and now you're sorry that I've been at so much trouble as to come here. But never mind, there's no great deal of love lost between us; and, bully as you are, I may yet get the best of the quarrel, if you don't take care what you are about."

"Come, come, let's have no words, Deborah," interposed Sir Gilbert. "In this place peace and harmony must reign, or I shall be sorry that you came among us to mar it by your presence."

"Sir Gilbert Dacre will do well not to interfere till he's asked to do so," she replied, sullenly. "Just now I've no quarrel with anybody but Darnton, though how long I shall be at peace with the master of this house will depend upon himself."

"The fairest of Eve's daughters is drunk," muttered Harrowby to himself.

"Not so drunk but she can hear when a fool speaks," answered the amazon. "But Mark Harrowby knows he was always a favourite, and so he can venture to say things that would cost any other man his life."

"Hush!" cried Redland; "don't speak so loud, Deborah, or you'll alarm the mistress of the mansion."

"The mistress of the mansion!" vociferated the woman, in accents of scorn. "Ay, you mean Patty Darnton, or Lady Dacre, as I believe folks now call her. This was a brave plan of yours, Master Hugh, and most artfully was it all brought about. But beware of me, for I hate you as a living pestilence, and will yet turn all these fine schemes to your own ruin."

"Woman! you have pronounced your own death doom," exclaimed Darnton, and levelling a pistol towards her he was in the act of pressing the trigger, when the weapon was struck from his hand by Mark Harrowby, and went flying to the further end of the room.

"Shame on you, Darnton," he cried, "to raise your arm against the most beautiful of her sex. Would you slay a woman, and she too the guest of our noble host?"

"Why did you prevent what he was going to do, Mark Harrowby?" she demanded. "If he wanted to kill me I was ready to take my fate from his hands. But he must have performed his task well though, for if only half a minute of life had been left in me, I would have plunged this knife into his heart, and we should have gone out of the world quits with each other."

Saying this she exhibited a long bladed knife that she always carried about her in case of sudden need; but the weapon was instantly snatched out of her hand by Mark Harrowby, who exclaimed, half in jest, half in earnest,

"I'll tell you what it is, my pretty duck, you and I have always been pretty good friends together; but it's time I should teach you how to conduct yourself before company. Knives are awkward tools to handle when people are in a passion, so you must excuse me for taking care of this till you get a little cooler."

"*He* provoked me to draw it."

"Well, so he did, my bonny lass," returned Harrowby; "but the thing's done and over now, and it's not worth while saying any more about it. Drink with me, thou peerless beauty, and as the liquor flows down thy pretty throat, let it carry away all animosity."

Deborah could not refuse so gallant an invitation, and having quaffed a deep potation, she said, in accents that betokened inebriety,

"Ah, Mark Harrowby, you always know how to quiet me when I happen to forget myself. You are a gentleman, Mark Harrowby ; but as for yonder villain, let him look to himself, for I'll have his heart's blood, even though I die while shedding it."

"The beautiful maid's breaking out again you see, friend Darnton," said Harrowby, winking across to his comrade. "She's rather in a bad humour to-day about something or other ; but don't heed her, man, and to-morrow you'll be better friends than ever."

"Shall we?" exclaimed Deborah, who in the meantime had helped herself to another bumper ; "*you* may think so, but Darnton will find out the mistake. Look how the wretch sits grinning and mocking at me. Give me the knife, Mark Harrowby ;—give it me, I say, for he shall not live to triumph over me. The knife—quick—that I may plunge it in—in his heart !"

Partly overcome by the violence of her passion and partly by the quantity of liquor she had drank, Deborah staggered as she rose from her seat, and reeling a few paces, fell senseless on the floor. With a grim look of hatred Darnton hastily quitted the room, and shortly afterwards the wretched woman was lifted up, and conveyed to the chamber where she was to rest for the night.

"Egad, I thought there would have been blood spilt between them," exclaimed Mark Harrowby, as soon as she was conveyed away, "for she's a very devil when in a passion, and Darnton seems to bear her no good will for some reason or other."

"I observed Hugh's looks when he left the room," said Sir Gilbert, "and they certainly betokened more mischief than has yet taken place between them. We must contrive to get rid of the woman, I believe, or something will happen that may bring us all into a dilemma."

"Why, you don't think he'd murder her in cold blood, Sir Gilbert?" exclaimed Redland.

"There's no saying what a revengeful man may do," answered the other. "Hugh Darnton seems to feel that he is some way or other in her power, and I know enough of him to foresee that there will be mischief unless we find means to separate them."

"Which I fancy will not be a very easy task," observed Mark Harrowby, "for the more you try to persuade her the less likely she is to do as you wish. Darnton, too, is a self-willed fool, and I don't suppose he'll leave your house, lest it should afterwards be said that he turned coward, and run away from a woman."

"Then the only thing we have to do is to watch them both narrowly," interposed Dick Elliot. "We must take care that they don't meet together alone, and then if they should happen to quarrel, we can prevent their coming to blows, as we did to-night."

"Or rather we can try to do so," exclaimed Sir Gilbert, "for, from the specimens I have seen of the woman's violence, I rather think she would prove pretty nearly a match for any of us. As for Darnton, I believe he will be quiet enough if she don't urge him too much with that virago tongue of hers."

"Do you know the cause of the bitter hatred they seem to bear towards each other?" inquired Mark Harrowby.

"Not very perfectly," replied Sir Gilbert ; "but I fancy they each know too much for the other, and both are afraid lest the secret should be let out.

Even when we all lived together in the cave, I have observed the looks of scornful defiance they cast at each other, and on one or two occasions they broke forth, though not quite so violently as to-night. Be the cause of their disagreement what it may, however, they are two such fiery spirits that mischief will surely follow if we look not sharply after them."

"Leave that to me ; and I'll warrant they don't do each other much harm," exclaimed Harrowby. "The woman has certainly a spice of the devil in her ; but somehow or other she submits to my control, and I'll try if she can't be coaxed to leave this place, instead of staying to mar our peace."

"You will never be able to persuade her to move from this place," answered Sir Gilbert.

"Well, then, if arguments should happen to fail, we must try the effects of a bribe," replied the other. "Deborah loves money dearly, and a few hundred pounds would be well bestowed in getting rid of her."

"Let the offer come through you, then," said Gilbert ; "make what excuse you please for wishing to get rid of her, and see that she leaves the house in the course of to-morrow. In the meanwhile, we must take care not to let her and Darnton meet together, or there will be mischief between them, and we shall draw upon ourselves the attention of the whole neighbourhood."

"And why need you care for your neighbours so much ?" demanded Harrowby ; "can't you hold your head as high as the best among them ? and as for their talking, let them say what they please, so long as they don't find out what sort of life we led ere we came here."

"And even that may be discovered if these two fools get quarrelling," replied Sir Gilbert. "The woman is not to be depended on, and as for Hugh Darnton, he would glory in hurling us all into ruin if it was to satisfy a feeling of revenge."

"But he can have no revenge to satisfy ?"

"He may soon have, though," answered Sir Gilbert. "He sees that I no longer love his daughter, and I have already observed the threatening glances he directs towards me. I know him to be a rancorous-hearted villain, and as we are all in his power, we must contrive to keep him in tolerable good humour."

"Why not allow him something handsome to live abroad ?" asked the other.

"It has been suggested to him," replied Gilbert ; "but the fellow pretends that he could not bear to part from his daughter, now that he knows she is unhappy. I told him she might go with him if she liked, and the fierce scowl he gave me afforded a convincing proof that it would be dangerous to repeat such a proposition."

"To-morrow I'll sound him upon the subject," said Harrowby, "and if he seems determined to do us a mischief, I'll try and think of some plan to thwart him. We must look a little to our own safety, and if no other way remains, why I shouldn't mind taking his life."

"And so get ourselves into a worse dilemma than we are at present."

"Why, the truth of it is, that we must not stand nice to a shade or two, when there's treachery to be expected from one who knows so much of our affairs," replied Mark Harrowby. "He can hang us all if he likes to say the word, and it must be our care to prevent the mischief before it is too late."

He left the room immediately after giving utterance to these words, and Sir Gilbert Copley was left by himself to meditate on the new source of uneasiness that had been caused by the unexpected arrival of Deborah.

CHAPTER XXVI.

GUILTY MEDITATIONS.—THE ASSASSIN.—A FEARFUL DISCOVERY.

AFTER quitting the room, Hugh Darnton repaired to the garden, where he paced up and down, revolving in his own mind the crowd of dark thoughts which vengeance gave rise to against the husband of his daughter; he had formed a hatred that nothing could ever quench, for he saw all his own ambitious views in danger of being overturned, and that Patty, instead of being the great lady he had anticipated, would be the cast-off wife of the man who now regarded her with contempt.

The game he played was a deep one, and now he saw himself foiled in every direction; the harvest he anticipated was blighted;—he no longer possessed his once boasted power over the mind of his son-in-law, and his recent quarrel with Deborah had raised him up an enemy whom he had resolved to get rid of without delay. He was aware, too, that all eyes would be upon him in case of the violence he meditated, and that it would be necessary to use extreme caution to prevent suspicion from falling upon himself.

But the impatience with which he looked forward to the completion of his designs urged him to proceed with more haste than might be deemed prudent. He could not endure the thought of suspending the vengeance he had resolved upon; and the more he thought over the project which occupied his mind, the greater appeared the necessity for carrying it into execution before his intentions were suspected by the parties against whom he was plotting.

Whilst he was thus meditating, a light appeared in one of the chamber windows above, and fixing his eyes upon the spot, like a tiger watching for its expected prey, he presently afterwards saw the form of Deborah reflected upon the window blind. An exclamation of fiend-like exultation burst from his lips at the sight, and bounding forward, he was about to enter the house, when footsteps were heard, and the old steward was seen looking about the premises, as if he suspected that some one was lurking about. Fearful of being seen, Hugh Darnton softly crept back towards the shrubbery, where he might remain concealed till after the intruder had given up his search. On one occasion the old man approached so near, that Hugh snatched out his clasp knife, and stood prepared to plunge it into the heart of his victim should a recognition take place. Luckily, however, the steward at that moment turned in another direction; and Darnton, returning the weapon to his pocket, leaned against a tree, as if overpowered by the conflict of passion that agitated his breast.

It was half an hour before he ventured to leave the retreat he had chosen, and even then he did so with extreme caution, for the guiltiness of his purpose made a coward of him, and he feared being seen, lest the circumstance should afterwards be brought against him. On trying the various doors he found them all securely fastened, and it was not for some time that he discovered a window in the rear of the premises which yielded to a slight pressure, and through this he noiselessly effected an entrance to the house. Having arranged everything as it had been previously to his getting in, he listened to satisfy himself whether anybody was about; all, however, was still and silent as the grave, and groping his way in the dark, he reached the staircase, which he mounted, after having taken off his shoes, in order that no sound should tell of his wandering about the house after all the other inmates were in bed.

Oppressed with a sense of his own evil intentions, he entered his own chamber, half irresolute whether to complete his design or leave it till some other opportunity. But revenge became paramount to every other feeling,

and having resolved upon the death of the woman who had so lately threatened him, he rose from the chair into which he had thrown himself, and once more taking out his knife, he opened the blade, and clasping the weapon firmly in his hand, made his way from the room.

Intuitively he made his way towards the chamber where he had seen the light, and which he consequently believed to be the one in which Deborah was to pass the night.   On entering it he paused to listen for any sound that might assure him of her presence, and hearing the respirations of some one who appeared to be asleep, he advanced on tiptoe, with the fell design of immolating his victim.   But the profound darkness with which he was surrounded prevented his seeing who slept there, and it became necessary to observe the greatest caution, in order that the blow he meditated should be sure.   At length he succeeded in finding the bed, and then gently withdrawing the pillow, he threw it over the mouth of his victim, so as to prevent her cries from being heard, and then raising the hand which the fatal weapon was in, he plunged it into the heart of the unfortunate woman.

In a moment all was over ; the last groan of mortal anguish was uttered, and then Hugh Darnton, inspired by terror and an anxious desire to escape, made his way from the scene of blood, and once more returned to his own room.   Here a momentary remorse seized him, but his worse passions quickly returned, and as he tossed himself about on the bed upon which he had thrown himself, he exulted with fiend-like exultation at the death of her whom he hated for the threats she had thrown out.

That night Hugh Darnton, guilty as he was, could not close his eyes in sleep ; frightful spectral objects seemed to pass continually before his sight. They threatened and exulted in the punishment that would follow the deed he had committed, and loud laughs of horrid exultation appeared to ring upon his ears, as if even demons triumphed in the retribution which was to succeed the foul deed he had accomplished.

No. 18

Never was night so long and full of horrors as that on which Hugh Darnton had hurried his hapless victim to a premature grave. At length, however, the first grey tints of morn began to appear, and then springing from his bed, he was horror-struck at perceiving that his hands were crimsoned with the gore of her whom he had destroyed. His first act was to cleanse them from this horrible witness of his crime, and having done this, he once more made his way into the garden, in order to allay the burning heat that was consuming his brain. No one was yet stirring in the house, but as he directed his eyes towards the window of the chamber where the deed had been committed, his heart sickened with apprehension, and he shuddered as if but too conscious that he would be suspected of the murder.

At last, entering a summer-house, he threw himself upon a seat, and burying his face in his hands, remained in a state of mental torture that is not to be described. In this condition he remained for some time, when approaching footsteps were heard, and looking up, he discovered, to his horror and amazement, that Deborah, the woman whom he supposed he had slain, was standing before him! She was accompanied by Mark Harrowby, and by the gloom that was apparent in their faces, it was evident that they were bearers of melancholy intelligence.

"You seem sad this morning, Hugh," exclaimed the woman, "and of a truth there is reason enough for it. Of course you have heard of what has taken place in the course of the night?"

"What mean you?" demanded the culprit, in a hoarse discordant voice. "Have the officers of justice at length tracked us to our lair?"

"No, but they soon will though," she replied; "there has been a foul crime committed, and the whole neighbourhood will soon be in arms against us."

"Of what crime do you speak?" asked Hugh Darnton, with affected surprise.

"Only a murder," she replied, darting a keen, searching look towards him. "There has been bloodshed in the house whilst we were all sleeping in our beds!"

"What's the use of making such a mystery about it?" interposed Mark Harrowby. "The truth is, Darnton, a woman has been stabbed to the heart! and that woman is no other than your own daughter, Patty!"

A cry of the most thrilling agony burst from the lips of Hugh Darnton, and sinking back upon his seat, he appeared for some few moments as if deprived of life by the suddenness with which this terrible announcement had been made. As he gradually recovered, however, the fearful truth disclosed itself in all its horrors; in the darkness of the night he had mistaken the room in which he supposed Deborah had retired to rest, and his own child had fallen a victim to the all-absorbing vengeance that had taken possession of his heart. He groaned in mental agony as he thought of the crime he had committed, and in wild, broken accents, exclaimed,—

"'Tis false! she lives! my Patty lives! she had no enemies that would have committed so foul a deed! This is but some trick to inflict torture upon the heart of her unhappy father!"

"Ah, you writhe under the infliction, do you?" exclaimed Deborah, exultingly. "This is as it should be—you have plotted against another, and the blow has fallen upon yourself. You loved the girl, Hugh Darnton, though your heart was steeled against every one else; she is now dead, and I leave you to enjoy the comfortable reflections. Lady Copley has just been found murdered in her bed; they say no one has forced an entrance into the house, but, perhaps, you may be able to afford a clue when you come to rub up your memory a little."

"Hag! would you goad me into madness?" cried Darnton, furiously. "Is it not enough that I am to be told my daughter has been murdered, but you must now add taunts and gibes to lacerate my heart still further ? Avaunt! leave me, I say, or the crime you have come to tell me of will not be the only one committed to-day in this place."

" Your threats will not frighten me," she replied, " for it so happens that you are more in my power than I am in yours. Often have you threatened me with your vengeance ; but the tables are now turned, and before long you shall be made to feel that, as an enemy, I am to be as much dreaded as the sweeping pestilence."

" Come—come," exclaimed Harrowby, " let's have no quarrelling when we had better be thinking how we had best contrive to get out of the trouble we have fallen into. The servants have before now spread abroad a report of this murder, and presently we shall have magistrates and policemen coming to make inquiries into the affair. The eyes of the people hereabouts have been upon us for some time, and it will not be an easy task to convince the world of our own innocence."

" Let him that is guilty of the murder tremble for the consequences," said Deborah, with another of her searching glances towards Darnton. " For my own part, I had no ill feeling towards the girl, and, therefore, cannot be suspected of having committed the crime."

" This news has come upon me like a thunder-clap," cried Hugh Darnton ; " yet still would I fain believe it is a falsehood, devised for no other purpose than to wring my heart with agony."

" Then the sooner you get rid of that notion the better," exclaimed Harrowby ; " for I have myself seen the body, and can answer for it you have heard nothing but the truth. Nay, if you think we have told a falsehood, it will be easy to convince yourself by going to the room where the body still lies as it was left by the murderer."

" I cannot go yet," returned the trembling culprit. " My heart would sicken at the sight were I to look upon the bleeding form of my hapless daughter."

" Well, you know best what your own feelings are," said Deborah ; " but for my own part, I think it seems rather strange that you should be afraid to go into the room where she lies. By-and-by there may be ill-natured people who will say that you know more about the murder than you would be willing to admit."

" Hah !" exclaimed Darnton ; " is there any one that would dare suspect me of taking away the life of my own child ? Have I not ever loved her, and can any one believe me guilty of this horrible crime?"

" Ay, Hugh Darnton," she replied, " there are many that will have such a notion, though it may not be very easy to produce facts against you. It is plain enough that Patty has been slain in mistake, though you alone may be able to say how the mistake occurred."

" You are rather too hard upon him, old Mother Devilskin," exclaimed Mark Harrowby, as he observed the furious passion these words had given rise to. " That a murder has been committed there can be no doubt, but how the assassin contrived to get into the house is a matter that I own somewhat puzzles me. The wound must have caused instant death, and, if we may judge from appearances, it was inflicted in the dark. The villain was a bungler at his work, or, it may be, was disturbed by some of the servants moving about the house."

" Whoever did it must have remained in the place all night," said Deborah, " for all the doors and windows were found securely fastened up, exactly as they had been left when the house was closed."

" It certainly is a very mysterious affair altogether," added Mark Harrowby ; " for it is quite certain the murderer, whoever he may have been, was pretty well acquainted with the premises, since he was able to find her room so easy. Now there's no denying that we have some queerish chaps among our companions, yet among them all there's not one that I could fix upon as likely to murder such an inoffensive creature as poor Patty. There could have been no motive for it that I know of."

"There is but one person that I can suspect," exclaimed Hugh Darnton, after he had given some few minutes to reflection.

"And who may that be?" demanded Harrowby.

"I shall not mention his name at present," replied the other, "lest I should be as unjust in my suspicion as Deborah has been towards me."

He paused a second or two, and then inquired where Sir Gilbert Copley was.

"That we none of us know," replied Mark Harrowby; "but he was up soon after daybreak, and rode away on horseback towards the London road."

"Humph!" ejaculated Darnton; "it is somewhat unusual for him to leave the house at so early an hour. Do either of you know whether he has any very particular business on hand?"

"Sir Gilbert has grown so reserved of late, that we know little about his affairs," answered Harrowby. "But see, he is galloping up the avenue, so, if you have any questions to ask, you will soon have an opportunity."

"I will myself go and break this news to him," exclaimed Deborah; "for the poor fellow will need some one to console him under his severe affliction, and I have always had more influence over him than any one else. He will be dreadfully shocked when he hears of it, though he and his wife were not very good friends, and the assassin had need tremble, for he may depend on it Sir Gilbert will not leave a stone unturned till he has brought the perpetrator to justice."

These words were threateningly addressed to Hugh Darnton, and having given utterance to them, she hurried away to fulfil her design.

"What does yonder hag mean?" cried the conscience-stricken culprit, as soon as she was out of hearing. "Her eyes glared upon me with fiend-like exultation, and I almost think she suspects me to be the murderer of my own daughter."

"It matters very little what she thinks," returned Mark Harrowby, "for we all know she's a little queer in the head, and says things that only serve for us to laugh at for their folly."

"But it will be no laughing matter if people should happen to believe her ravings in the present instance," answered Darnton. "It is a charge more easily made than disproved, and my life may be sacrificed if means are not found to quiet her."

"There are more ways of doing that than one," said Mark Harrowby. "Surely you don't think of murdering the poor wretch for what she has just said?"

"No—no," answered Darnton, quickly; "of course I can have no wish to run my neck into a halter; but something may be thought of to keep her quiet. I have not much money of my own to bribe her with; but Sir Gilbert must be spoken to, and I dare say he will lend me a helping hand."

"At any rate he ought to do so," exclaimed the other, "for I have pretty good reason to suspect that it is he who has got into this dilemma."

"What mean you?"

"If I dared trust you, Harrowby, you should immediately know my thoughts."

"Nay, speak out man, and take my word for it, there shall come no harm from it."

"Well, then," said Darnton, "I was going to ask if there is any person in particular that you would name who is likely to have committed this murder?"

" Indeed, I cannot," replied Harrowby, " for there is not a soul I know of that could have had the heart to kill so inoffensive a girl."

" Yet there is one that I have good reason to believe has for some time past wished for her death."

" Who is it ?" demanded Harrowby, quickly.

" Her husband."

" Sir Gilbert Copley ?"

" Ay," replied Darnton, with a ghastly smile ; " is he not more likely to have done it than anybody else? He has grown proud since fortune has been more favourable to him, and his wife, whom he married in adversity, is no longer considered a fitting mate, now that he has a title and wealth to support. They have lived separate for some time, though dwelling beneath the same roof ; his dislike has lately grown into hatred, and more than once he has used expressions in my presence that serve to convince me he would not stop at any crime if he could only get rid of her for ever. He rose this morning at an earlier hour than usual, and has taken a ride out in order to get rid of the suspicion that he knows must be directed towards him."

" You must bring some more convincing proof of his guilt before I can believe such an accusation," said Mark Harrowby. " Just now, when he rode up to the house, he looked as cheerful as ever I saw him, and that would not have been the case if thoughts of crime had been in his mind."

" You don't think, then, that he is guilty of murdering my poor daughter ?"

" I am sure he is not."

" In that case you, perhaps, suspect some one else," said Darnton, again trembling with apprehension lest the truth should be guessed at. " May I ask who you think could have had the heart to do this deed except himself ?"

" Why, the truth is, I don't want to get into a quarrel with you, old fellow," returned the other ; " but I have lived long enough in the world to know that when a man has done anything wrong he will try to shift the suspicion from himself to some one else."

" And do you believe that to be the reason why I have said that Sir Gilbert is the murderer of my child ?"

" A man can't help the notion that comes into his head," replied Mark Harrowby, " and if I have made any mistake in the present case, you must forgive me, since I have told you the reason why I think Sir Gilbert is innocent."

" But you know he has been cold and indifferent to her for a long time past. He married her because I insisted upon it as the only terms upon which I would get him his title and estate. I have, as you know, performed my promise, and then, like an ungrateful vagabond, as he is, he turns round and threatens me that he will get rid of her."

" Ay, but he didn't mean that he would murder her."

" How are we to know what he meant ?" demanded Hugh Darnton. " The girl is found stabbed to death in her bed ; no one but Gilbert was likely to enter that room, and yet you must needs believe that he had no hand in the crime."

" You have no proof that he had."

" There is no direct proof, certainly," replied Darnton ; " but there are many things that may lead us to such a belief. For instance, it is quite certain the crime was committed by some one belonging to the house."

" Well, that may be, although I do not feel quite so certain about it as you seem to do."

" If any stranger had come into the house," resumed Hugh Darnton, " he would not have left it without taking away some of the jewels that she always kept in the room."

" And how do you know that nothing was taken away?" demanded Harrowby, quickly.

" I—I—merely supposed Deborah would have mentioned it if there had been robbery as well as murder," replied Darnton, stammering, and sorely puzzled what answer to make. " Besides, there is another fact that makes me suspect Sir Gilbert more than any one else ; no doors nor windows were broken open, and it stands to reason that if the crime had been committed by a stranger, his entrance could only have been made by force. So that you see ——"

" I see nothing to convince me that we ought to think your son-in-law guilty of murdering his own wife," interrupted Mark Harrowby. " Of late he has grown cool towards her, I admit ; but it don't follow that he should wish to obtain a divorce by plunging a knife into her heart."

" Well, then, what think you of its having been done by that accursed hag, Deborah ?"

" Deborah ?"

" Ay," replied Darnton ; " didn't she come into the house only last night, and a few hours afterwards my unfortunate daughter is found murdered."

" But where could be her motive?"

" Why, jealousy, of course," answered the culprit.

" Psha ! an old woman like that be jealous ?"

" To be sure she was."

" Of whom ?"

" Of my daughter," replied Hugh Darnton. " You surely can't forget how troublesome her loving attentions to Gilbert were when first he lived among us. Deborah has often said she was sure he meant to marry her, and never shall I forget the dreadful rage she flew into when it was made known that Gilbert and my daughter were to make a match of it. In short, I have always expected that some terrible act of violence would follow, and now, upon second thoughts, I am inclined to believe that the murder was planned by Deborah and Sir Gilbert Copley."

" Humph !" retorted Mark Harrowby, " at any rate you seem very anxious to fix this crime upon some one. For my own part, I don't know what to think of the matter ; so, for the present, I shall content myself with lending a ready hand to assist those who try to find out who the real assassin is."

" I see how it is," exclaimed Darnton, chafing with ill-suppressed rage ; " that woman has prejudiced you against me, and you believe that I am the murderer of my poor daughter. But let the old hag beware how she tempts my fury ; for, if she dares utter a hint against me, it is likely I may become the assassin she would fain make me out."

" Why, would you harm one that has belonged to our band?" cried Harrowby.

" Let her mind what she's about, then," exclaimed the other through his clenched teeth. " She thinks to bring me to the gallows by pointing me out as the person that committed this dreadful crime."

" And what need an innocent man care for the sayings of an old woman?" asked Mark Harrowby. " They would not find you guilty upon her unsupported charge, when it is considered that the unfortunate victim was your own daughter."

" But isn't it something to be suspected ?"

" Psha ! who knows what a few hours may bring out?" exclaimed Harrowby. " Wait till the inquest takes place, and then I'll be bound we shall find out more than we know at present."

Mark hastened from the place when he had said this, but there was an expression upon his countenance that served to increase the alarm of Hugh Darnton.

CHAPTER XXVII.

A NEW SCHEME.—THE CORONER'S INQUEST.

THE situation in which the miserable culprit found himself was desperate in the extreme ; he knew that the vindictive spirit of Deborah would urge her to the utmost extremes ; and, conscious as he was of his own guilt, he gave way to the paroxysms of fear with which he was seized. It served but little to mitigate his remorse, that the blow which deprived his daughter of life was not intended for her ; he had entered the chamber for the purpose of committing a murder, and the death of Patty seemed to be the punishment of his meditated crime.

After some little time had been occupied in these torturing thoughts, he rose from the seat upon which he had thrown himself, and with hurried steps paced along the winding walk that led towards the shrubbery which had concealed him on the previous night. He, however, started as this came within his sight, and, turning abruptly off, came to a small piece of water that ornamented a portion of the grounds. He paused a few minutes, to gaze upon the unrippled surface which reflected his own pale, distorted countenance, and he thought how easily he might terminate that agony which a guilty conscience had given rise to. But crime had made a coward of him ; he shuddered at the thought of rushing unbidden into the presence of his offended Maker, and, fleeing as if from the pursuit of his own fearful thoughts, returned once more to the summer-house where his late interview with Mark Harrowby had taken place. Here he once more resumed his seat, and again did his thoughts wander to the dreadful catastrophe that he would have given worlds to have been able to drive from his memory. Still, however, the same appalling scene was presented to his view, and, unable any longer to endure the torture of his own reflections, he was about once more to leave the place, when the form of Deborah was again presented before him. The look she directed towards him was full of malicious triumph, and, having sufficiently long enjoyed the agony which she well knew he felt, she exclaimed,—

" It is in vain, Hugh Darnton, that you try to evade the consequences of your guilt. I am well aware of all the schemes you will practice to throw suspicion upon those who are guiltless of this heinous crime. You think to evade the halter ; but, so surely as I now tell you so, your moments in this world are numbered."

" What mean you by these words ?" he said, in a tone of conciliation.

" That you are the murderer of your daughter !"

" 'Tis false !" he exclaimed ; " you would destroy me with a false accusation, though you well know that I loved Patty too much to have committed this sinful violence, and only seek to bring the real perpetrator to justice without loss of time."

" And who is it you would accuse ?"

" That I have not yet been able to determine upon," he replied, after a pause.

" Base villain ! you think to deceive me !" exclaimed Deborah, fiercely. " You are plotting against those you know to be innocent, and are only waiting your time to make the lying accusation. But I know the secret thoughts of your heart ; I have watched your every look—your every movement, and I now warn you to beware how you arouse my further fury. You are laying snares for the destruction of your former associates, yet is it possible you may yourself be caught in them."

" I am forming no plans," he replied, " but such as will be necessary to prove my own innocence, should you carry your threats into execution."

"Dare you deny being the assassin of your unfortunate daughter?" demanded his tormentor.

"I do."

"Then your miserable evasion will not succeed," exclaimed Deborah; "for I have sworn to bring the culprit to justice, and it is seldom that I fail to keep my word. I know more than you think for, Hugh Darnton—the knife was meant for my heart, and I should not have been here as your accuser but for the circumstance of your daughter having last night changed her sleeping chamber. You stole into it with murder in your thoughts, and left it the assassin of your own child."

"Nay, by my soul, I swear——"

"Would you add perjury to your other crimes," interrupted Deborah, sternly. "Is it not enough that you are a shedder of human blood, but you must utter a falsehood to conceal the deed? Hugh Darnton, it is in vain that you seek to deceive me. I know enough to hang you—and the words shall be spoken too, that such a monster may meet with his deserts."

"I repeat to you, Deborah, that your suspicions are ill founded," he exclaimed. "Have I not ever loved my daughter, and is it likely that I should take away the life I gave her?"

"Have I not told you before that it was done in error?" she retorted. "You dreamed not that it was Patty, who lay unconscious of her danger before you, or your arm would have shrunk back from the cruel task you had undertaken. That, however, matters not—you intended to take away a life—the crime was accomplished, and now I exult in the remorse you must suffer on discovering the fatal mistake you made."

"Why do you still persist in accusing me of this fearful deed?" asked Hugh Darnton, in a tone of remonstrance. "Is it not enough that I have denied all knowledge of it, but you must still further wound my feelings by an accusation so horrible? Come, come, Deborah, you and I had better be friends. Each may injure the other should this ill-feeling last any longer, but if we both keep to one story we may defy all the world to prove aught against us."

"Ho, ho! you begin to fear me, then, it seems," exclaimed the woman. "You are not quite so confident of throwing the blame upon me as you were before we had this interview together. You feel that my power over you is too great to be despised."

"What have I to fear from you?" he asked. "Even if I had been the assassin you would make it appear, there could be little to dread from any evidence you may be able to give. Whoever gave the blow, you were not present to witness it, so that your testimony would not be received in a court of justice."

"But I have such testimony as you little think of," answered Deborah, eagerly. "I have just come from the chamber where poor Patty lies weltering in her blood. By chance I raised her hand, and found fast clutched in it a something that will go far to confirm the accusation I am about to make."

Anxiously did Hugh Darnton implore her to say what it was she had found; but Deborah was to be moved neither by his prayers nor threats, and directing towards him another look of menace, she hurried away.

The culprit now found himself more than ever a prey to fear. Conscience told him that her words might be fatally true, and when he had in some degree conquered the despair with which he had been seized, he began to reflect how her designs against him might be best counteracted. All hopes of conciliating her in his behalf were completely at an end, for her rooted hatred had been openly expressed, and no chance remained of appeasing her deadly hatred.

It, therefore, became necessary to devise other schemes that should have for their object the entangling her in some web from which she should not find it easy to extricate herself. Her destruction indeed seemed to be essentially

necessary for his own safety;—living, he had to fear her more than any other mortal, and it was only by accusing her of the crime he had himself committed that any chance would be afforded of throwing discredit upon the testimony she threatened to give.

It seemed to him necessary also that Sir Gilbert Copley should be included in the same charge; for some time past he had formed a most bitter hatred to him, and so intense had it now become, that he determined to sacrifice him by the accusation that he had participated with Deborah in the murder which had been committed. He would thus remove two of those persons against whom he was prejudiced, and at the same time might himself expect to escape a punishment that he looked forward to with horror. The successful execution of this plan seemed to promise but little difficulty, and he even began to anticipate with a feeling of certainty the successful termination of his nefarious schemes.

On returning to the house, after his villanous plans had been resolved on, he was met by Sir Gilbert Copley and Mark Harrowby. The former seemed to be suffering much anguish from the melancholy event which had deprived Patty of life. That his love for her had much diminished of late is certain, but his heart was not wholly lost to feeling, and no sooner had he been informed of the murder which had taken place beneath his roof, than he gave orders that every effort should be made to discover the assassin. Information had already been given to the magistrates, who, without delay, sent officers to make a strict inquiry, and an inquest had been appointed to take place on the same afternoon.

When Hugh Darnton entered the room where Sir Gilbert and Mark Harrowby were conversing, he started with conscious guilt, and would have retreated hastily. His intention, however, was prevented by the former, who taking him by the hand, spoke feelingly of the dreadful circumstance that had just thrown so solemn a gloom over the mansion.

"I am glad we have met, Darnton," he exclaimed, "though I fear you must bitterly feel the awful catastrophe that has befallen us."

"Can it be possible," retorted the other, "that you regret the death of one who, when living, you despised?"

"You wrong me," cried Sir Gilbert, earnestly; "for, on my soul, I never despised the hapless girl, whose death has been so fearfully sudden."

"Humph! you would fain persuade me, I suppose, that you loved her to the very last."

"I have never ceased to regard her with esteem," replied Sir Gilbert. "Our marriage was unfortunately a forced one—you, yourself compelled me to make her my wife, and hence arose the unhappiness that followed. I found her kind and affectionate as a wife, but our dispositions were at variance, and when fortune raised me to a higher station, we were no longer equally mated. In that respect you have only yourself to blame, though it is not my wish, at such a moment as this, to increase the affliction into which you have been thrown."

"Your kindness is more than I expected," said Hugh Darnton, with a sneer. "However, a truce with all vain commiseration; I would have avoided you if possible, but since we have met, I would ask if you can form any notion as to the person by whom this black deed has been perpetrated?"

"I can make no guess," answered Sir Gilbert, "and was about to ask you a similar question."

"Me!" exclaimed Darnton, with trepidation that was apparent; "why should I be asked a question, that you must suppose I cannot reply to? You are much more likely to form a tolerably correct notion as to the murderer of my hapless child."

"'Tis in vain that I have attempted to do so," replied Sir Gilbert. "I do not know that she had any enemies, and even if she had, there are few, I should imagine, who would seek so cowardly a means of revenge. I therefore imagine that robbery was the chief object, and that, upon her attempting to make an alarm, the villain slew her to prevent the danger with which he was threatened."

"But as I have been told that nothing has been taken from the room, your surmises at once fall to the ground," exclaimed Darnton. "Besides, it is quite clear that no one can have passed either in or out of the premises after the house was closed for the evening."

"In that case, the villain must have concealed himself in some part of the mansion."

"I know nothing of how that might have been," answered Hugh; "but if the murderer should flee to the uttermost parts of the earth, I would follow in pursuit of him."

"Yet you can form no idea of who is the assassin of your unfortunate daughter?"

"I will not say, but I have my eye upon one or two persons that I suspect," answered Darnton with peculiar emphasis. "At present, however, I shall not explain myself further; in a short time the coroner's jury will assemble, and then perhaps I shall surprise some of the persons who meet there with an accusation they are least prepared to hear."

"May I not have your confidence in a matter which so deeply interests me?"

"The short time that will intervene can make but little difference," replied Hugh Darnton; "I shall bide my time quietly and patiently, and you must do the same. In short, Sir Gilbert, the ends of justice require that I should keep the secret to myself for the present, but I promise you shall know all as soon as the proper moment arrives."

With a sullen and haughty air he left the room, and once more sought the solitude of the garden, where he might roam about by himself till his presence was required before those who were to assemble to make a solemn inquiry into the fearful tragedy that had spread dismay through the neighbourhood.

At the appointed time in the afternoon, the persons who had been summoned on the jury arrived at the mansion, and having viewed the body as it lay on the precise spot where the crime had been perpetrated, they repaired to the presence of the coroner, who, in a brief address, explained the difficulties that might happen to arise during the investigation. This being done, the various persons who were to give their testimony withdrew from the room, and the solemn inquiry began by obtaining evidence that the deceased had retired to rest on the previous night in her usual health. The next witness deposed to finding the body in the same state that it had been seen by the jury, and it was further added, that Lady Copley had shown no symptom of insanity, so that there was not the least ground for supposing that she had made away with herself.

Sir Gilbert was himself present at the investigation, but from a desire to avoid giving him all unnecessary pain, it was resolved not to subject him to an examination unless it should appear to be necessary for the clearing up of any particular point in the evidence that had been already heard. The next person, therefore, whose name was called upon, was Hugh Darnton, who, acting his part with consummate skill, appeared to be as much overcome with emotion as scarcely to be able to rise from his seat. Nor was this entirely thrown away upon the spectators in the room, for a buzz was heard running round the place, and every one looked with an eye of pity upon the man who they supposed was suffering the most intense anguish for the unfortunate event that had deprived him of a beloved daughter.

At length, when silence had been obtained, the coroner, addressing himself to Darnton, explained to him the solemn nature of the duty he was called upon to perform.

"It would be expected from him," he said, "that no fact should be withheld, but that every circumstance tending to throw a light upon this mysterious affair should be related in a straightforward manner. He was, in short, to relate all he knew in any way connected with the case, even though by so doing he should involve his dearest friend or relative in suspicion."

"I am here for that, and no other purpose," replied Darnton, impatiently, when this address was concluded. "The feelings of a parent may be judged when they have been outraged by such a crime as this, and I am determined that no effort of my own shall be wanting towards bringing the guilty parties to justice."

"Are you aware of any facts that may serve to discover who the assassins are?" asked the coroner.

"I think I am."

"Then it now becomes my duty to caution you against making any statement that may not be hereafter proved," said the coroner. "I am aware that, during the period of first excitement, opinions may be formed that afterwards turn out to be erroneous. You are, it seems, about to mention parties who you believe to be implicated in this crime. Your conclusions may, however, have been too hastily formed, and I therefore feel it my duty to weigh carefully what you are going to say, lest innocent persons should lose their name and character through an accusation that involves so awful a penalty."

"I am quite aware of all that, sir," replied Hugh Darnton; "but I am here to speak the truth, though my dearest friend should suffer for it. My child has been murdered, and I will have vengeance on the offender."

"You shall have justice, though I cannot promise you *vengeance* in the terms that you mean it," said the coroner. "Are the persons of whom you speak in the custody of an officer?"

"They are not."

"Are they within reach?"

"They are both in the room at this moment."

"Point them out," said the coroner; "and when means have been taken to prevent their escape, we will proceed further in this investigation. What are the names of the parties you accuse?"

"Deborah Ratcliffe is one," answered Darnton, pointing towards the old woman, who was standing at a short distance in advance of him.

"Let the woman be taken in charge," said the coroner; and immediately afterwards a couple of officers were stationed by her side.

Deborah now became an object of general scrutiny, and her harsh, masculine features seemed to render the accusation an extremely probable one. The woman, however, took little notice of the attention that was bestowed upon her, though it was observed by every one that she directed a look of scornful defiance towards the person who had thus charged her with the commission of a dreadful offence. Hugh Darnton could not endure the fixed gaze that she directed towards him; his very soul seemed to shrink appalled within him, a deadly paleness overspread his countenance, and so absorbed was he in fearful thought that he heard not the next question put to him.

"You have charged one person with being concerned in the murder of your daughter," repeated the coroner; "and it is my next duty to inquire who the other person is that you believe to be implicated with the woman?"

"He is sitting near your right hand," answered Hugh Darnton, with the same effrontery that he had assumed at first. "Sir Gilbert Copley is the other person who I believe was concerned in this tragical affair."

"Sir Gilbert Copley!" murmured the crowd; and the looks of every person present declared how much they doubted the charge that had been so unexpectedly made.

As for the person who had been thus accused, he became immediately so much agitated that any one might have imagined him really guilty of the deed alleged against him. His whole frame was convulsed with emotion, and then, somewhat recovering his fortitude, he directed a glance towards his accuser, that seemed to ask if it was possible he could be serious in giving utterance to the words that had just fallen from him. But Darnton maintained a fixed and rigid countenance. He might experience remorse in his soul, but no indication of it was suffered to appear, and presuming on the impression he had made upon his auditors, he inquired if it was the will of the coroner that he should proceed with the testimony he was prepared to give against the accused.

"I was about to ask you," replied the person he had addressed, "what grounds you have for believing that either of these two persons were concerned in the crime we are now inquiring into?"

"In my own mind I am sure I have not falsely charged them with the crime," answered Hugh Darnton. "The male prisoner and I have been acquainted for some time past: an affection sprung up between him and my poor daughter, which terminated in their marriage. At that time Sir Gilbert had no expectations of succeeding to his present title and estate, and well would it have been for them both if he had not done so, for, from the moment that he found himself elevated in rank, he began to treat his wife with many marks of growing disregard. At length they separated, though still living in the same house, and it became evident to me that he intended to get rid of her without delay."

"But that," observed the coroner, "does not imply that he would take away the life of the woman he had solemnly vowed to love."

"There is no saying what a man will do when he becomes excited with passion," returned Darnton. "I have known Sir Gilbert a long time, and can affirm that there is no act of violence he would pause at, when any favourite object is likely to be marred. My daughter, being no longer loved by him, was an incumbrance that he would gladly remove out of his way. Whilst she lived, however, that was not to be effected very easily; but with the aid of an accomplice he found little difficulty in executing a deed which removed from him the wife who stood in the way of a more exalted alliance."

"Villain!" exclaimed Sir Gilbert, unable to control his passion any longer, "dare you stand up, and in the face of Heaven declare that you believe me guilty of having murdered your daughter?"

"I dare maintain all that I have said," replied Darnton. "I am now on my oath, and I call upon the coroner to protect me from the violence you seem inclined to exhibit towards me.

"Sir Gilbert will, I trust, pay all proper respect to the court," said the coroner; and then when silence was once more restored, he inquired of the witness what reason he had for believing that Deborah Ratcliffe had been engaged in the crime.

"I have been acquainted with her many years," replied Darnton, "and, from several instances that I have witnessed, there is every ground for supposing that even human life would be remorselessly destroyed should she happen to believe there was any necessity for getting rid of one, against whom she has formed a dislike. Besides, she arrived at the mansion only yesterday, and during the night it was that my unfortunate daughter was murdered."

"Am I to understand," asked the coroner, "that you charge her with this crime?"

"If a little time is given to me, I shall be better prepared to do so," replied Darnton; "I may, perhaps, be allowed to observe that she is quite a stranger to the place, and could not possibly have found her way to the chamber unless some one had guided her there. Sir Gilbert is the most likely person to have done this, and therefore do I persist in my accusation till he can satisfactorily prove his innocence."

Had any body particularly noticed the speaker, he could not have failed to observe the trepidation with which Hugh Darnton gave utterance to the vile fabrication. His eyes wandered from place to place, as if fearing to meet the gaze of those who were not inclined to believe his story. His limbs trembled with agitation; but though this was apparent enough to all the spectators, they attributed it to the circumstance of his recent bereavement. The culprit, however, felt that he was treading on dangerous ground, and, appalled at the thought of being detected, he would have given worlds had the examination ended at the point he had brought it to. During this interval, the coroner and his clerk were engaged in a half whispered conversation that seemed ominous to the accuser, who started and turned deadly pale when the former broke off the conference, and, addressing himself to the jury, said:—

"It appears to me, gentlemen, that we shall obtain no more evidence to-day, and it will, therefore, be necessary that we adjourn this inquest. The witness, Darnton, has publicly accused two persons of having committed the murder, but his evidence must be received with extreme caution, as it is entirely circumstantial, and we have at present nothing to corroborate it. We may even suppose that he is actuated by motives of revenge; but whether such is the case or not, it will be your duty to endeavour to discover. A few hours, however, may put us in possession of further evidence, and I therefore declare the further business of this court be adjourned till to-morrow. Sir Gilbert

Copley and Deborah Ratcliffe, however, must enter their own recognizances to appear before us at the time I have named."

The necessary form having been entered into, the court broke up; the coroner and the jury took their departure and Hugh Darnton, unable to face those whom he had unjustly accused, retired to the solitude of his own chamber.

~~~~~~~~~~~~~~~~~~~~~~~~~~

CHAPTER XXVIII.

A CONFERENCE.—THE MENACE.—A TREACHEROUS PROMISE.

HUGH DARNTON had not been alone more than half an hour when he was surprised by a visit from Sir Gilbert Copley, Deborah, and the rest of his former associates. Their presence he knew boded him no good, but having proceeded thus far, it was in vain to retreat, and putting on one of his sternest looks, he demanded why they were thus come to disturb him.

"Methinks you hardly need ask such a question as that," retorted Sir Gilbert, his lips quivering with suppressed rage. "You have thought proper to bring a lying accusation against me and Deborah, yet suppose that we will quietly submit to the villany you would practise."

"How are you to help yourself?" demanded the other with a sneer. "The charge has been made—you and the woman are bound to appear again to-morrow, and you will then see what course I mean to pursue."

"I'll tell you what it is, old chap," exclaimed Mark Harrowby; "there's some rumuns among us to deal with, and, if matters should come to the worst, we know how to serve out a traitor."

"You may call me what names you please," replied Darnton, sullenly; "but, after all, it's only natural that a father should wish to punish the murderer of his daughter. Sir Gilbert and his accomplice have heard me openly bring the charge, and, if they are innocent, let them make it appear to those who will have to judge impartially between us."

"But you must know in your own mind that we are guiltless of the horrid deed," said Sir Gilbert.

"I know nothing of the sort," returned the other. "I only know that poor Patty has been murdered, and who so likely as yourself to have committed the act? You have long hated her because she was not good enough for your present high notions, and you get rid of the incumbrance by despatching her to another world."

"I deny bearing her any malice," exclaimed Sir Gilbert, indignantly. "A coolness had certainly grown up between us, but never could I have contemplated such an act as you have laid to my charge."

"You, perhaps, had not the heart to stab her yourself," replied the other, "but Deborah was a good agent for your purpose, and she it is that I suspect as the one that actually plunged the knife in her heart."

"Dare to say that again," exclaimed the infuriated woman, "and I'll not give you another chance to tell your infernal lies of me. Because I have done such things before, you must need suspect me now; but of your daughter's murder I know *less* than you do yourself."

"It strikes me, old fellow," said Harrowby, addressing Hugh Darnton, "that this affair won't end so well for yourself as you thought for. There's not one of us but what the law can grab hold of, and, if matters come to the worst, you sha'n't escape any more than the rest of your old comrades."

"He had better think of what he is about," exclaimed the woman, "or he'll repent when it's too late. If he snarls and bites, we can do the same; so, if he hasn't quite taken leave of his senses, he'll contradict all that he's been saying to-day."

" I shall keep to my story without altering it in the least," answered Hugh Darnton, folding his arms with an air of determination.

" Then you will afterwards repent the madness," exclaimed Sir Gilbert; " for, if any of us must be brought to the gallows, I shall make a clear conscience of it by confessing the murder of the two men, and ———"

" Your threats will not change my purpose," interrupted Darnton; " the scaffold has been before my eyes the last twenty years, and I can mount it without fear of death, so long as I know Sir Gilbert and yonder croaking old hag have gone there before me."

" Then you are an infernal villain for your pains!" exclaimed Mark Harrowby; " however, it's not quite certain yet that your wish will be gratified, for the law don't hang men without evidence, and at present there's nothing against those you've accused, except what you have thought proper to assert."

" Don't make yourself too sure of there being any want of evidence," retorted Hugh Darnton. " My case is not quite so bad as you seem to fancy, but, as I don't mean to let anybody know what I'm going to do till to-morrow, you must be content to remain till then in ignorance."

" Well, I only warn you to look before you leap," continued Harrowby; " there can can be no harm in giving a friendly hint, for, as surely as you play us any of your foul tricks, I shall consider all connection between us as at an end, and you shall be accused before the coroner of a murder that you have long since thought was forgotten."

" Psha!" muttered Darnton; " while fitting a halter to my neck, you'll be bespeaking one for your own."

" Oh, I care not for hanging," exclaimed Harrowby, " so that I bring such a treacherous villain as you to the scaffold."

" Do you mean what you say?" demanded the other, with more trepidation than he had before exhibited.

" I do."

" 'Tis a bold act you have undertaken," exclaimed Hugh Darnton, " and I doubt if you will have courage to go on with it. However, do as you please, —my mind is made up to persist in my accusation against Sir Gilbert and Deborah, and to-morrow you'll see that I am in earnest."

Determined not to be questioned any further upon this subject, Darnton was making his way towards the door, but, before he could reach it, he was seized by Mark Harrowby with a powerful grasp, and hurled to the further end of the room. Darnton's rage now became ungovernable, and, giving vent to a fearful oath, he was about to rush upon his opponent, when the other, presenting a loaded pistol at his head, exclaimed, in a tone of determination :

" If you are not tired of your life, Hugh Darnton, you will not come nearer to me, even so much as a single step. You deserve to die the death of a dog, and, if I haven't sent a bullet whizzing through your brain before now, it's only because I wish you to live and repent the villany you were going to practise against your old comrades."

" And so," growled the other, " I am to be threatened because I am determined to hunt the murderers of my child to the punishment they deserve !"

" Prove that they are what you call them, and I will no longer take part against you."

" I have told you that shall be done to-morrow."

" Well, I'll tell you what it is, Darnton," exclaimed the other, resolutely; " you and I have known each other long enough for my temper to be pretty well known. I am a dare-devil fellow, when once I've made up my mind to a thing, and know as well how to serve a friend as to punish an enemy. This business has begun to grow serious, and, as I see you are determined to act the part of a traitor, it may be as well that we should understand each other.

Sir Gilbert has belonged to our band, he has shared danger with us, and d—n me if I'll see his life sworn away by a cowardly turncoat like yourself."

"What do these threats mean?" demanded Hugh Darnton, trembling with rage.

"They mean," returned the other, "that I'll have a fair, straightforward answer from you before I've done. You boast of having evidence to bring forward to-morrow, against Sir Gilbert and Deborah; it may be that for once in your life you have spoken the truth, and, if so, I demand to know what the proof is that you can bring against them."

"Humph!" ejaculated the other; "and what if I still refuse to answer your question?"

"Why, then, we'll see which of us shall get the best of this quarrel," replied Mark Harrowby. "It must come to open war between us, that's all; and, if that's the case, either you or I shall not leave this room alive!"

"So, you threaten me!"

"I threaten no more than I mean to perform," replied the other. "It's not often that I suffer myself to be worked up into a passion, but I'm in one now, and you may presently find out that I'm in earnest."

"You forget," muttered Darnton, "that in a struggle I may prove a better man than yourself."

"We must both take our chance of that," retorted the other. "You have now heard me speak out boldly, and I want to know what you mean to do. If you don't want to throw away your life, you will at least reflect before you make up your mind to do this villanous action. We are all of us thrown into danger by this mad scheme of yours, and, sooner than be brought to the gallows by the treachery of an old comrade, I'll have your heart's blood, even if I die for it under the hangman's hands."

"Send a bullet through his head without saying anything more about it," whispered Deborah. "The wretch has acknowledged himself to be our enemy, and deserves no better than a dog's death."

"I shall give him just five minutes to make up his mind," replied Harrowby; "and, if at the end of that time, he don't choose to come to terms, I shall know what I have to do."

He withdrew with his companions to a corner of the room near the door, and Hugh Darnton then had an opportunity to reflect upon the proposition that had been made. His rage was unbounded at the situation in which he found himself; but, under the circumstances, he knew that resistance would be useless. Mark Harrowby was a more powerful man than himself should they come to an encounter, and even if that had not been the case, there was little doubt he would have the assistance of Sir Gilbert, in the event of his assistance being required. In this dilemma he determined to have recourse to dissimulation, and, before the allotted five minutes had expired, he said, with pretended submission :—

"I have been reflecting upon what you have said, Harrowby, and, though I am not to be frightened by your threats, I begin to see that it must lead to the ruin of all of us if I persist in this charge against Sir Gilbert and the old woman."

"Ah! you are beginning to grow reasonable, I find," exclaimed the other. "You see the folly of setting yourself up against those who can do you quite as much injury as you can do them."

"Why, the truth is, I feel no animosity against either of them," he replied.

"Then why did you become their accuser?" asked Mark Harrowby. "However, we won't touch upon the old grievance just now; so tell me if you really had any evidence to bring forward to-morrow?"

"It matters not whether I could or not," replied Darnton, " since I've told

you the affair shall drop where it is. When the coroner and jury meet again, they will want to know if I have any evidence to support my charge, and if I tell them I have not, there will be an end of the affair, and, of course, the two accused parties will be discharged without a blemish on their character."

"I don't exactly know how to believe you," said Mark Harrowby; "but if your word is to be taken, you promise to keep back all further evidence?"

"Ay, that is my meaning."

"Well, so far so good," returned Harrowby; "yet how much better it would have been if you had never made a charge at all. It would have saved this bit of a quarrel between us, and you wouldn't have appeared the villain you did just now."

"Don't say anything more about it if you wouldn't bring up old grievances," exclaimed the other. "I've told you the thing sha'n't go any further, so let it rest just where it is."

"Agreed," said Harrowby; and then, turning towards Sir Gilbert, he inquired if he was satisfied with the arrangement that had been made.

"I am," he replied; "Hugh Darnton and I are no longer enemies, though it will be some time before I can forget the injury he tried to do me."

"Well, at any rate you must never speak of it again if matters go on fairly," answered Harrowby. "We have made a better finish of it than I thought for. What say you, Deborah—can you forgive and forget what's past?"

"I haven't quite made up my mind about that," she replied. "Hugh Darnton and I have always led a sort of cat and dog life, so there's no great deal of love lost between us. We would send each other to the gallows if we only knew how, and it's no fault of his that he hasn't done it before this."

"You can't hold your tongue, then, it seems," muttered Darnton, sullenly.

No. 20

"I have just given a promise that I thought would satisfy all parties, and yet you are growling as much now as if I was going to send you to a felon's prison to-morrow."

"Ay," she retorted, "and that's because I don't place any faith in the promise you've made. I know you of old, Hugh Darnton, and have always found you false and deceitful, and a breaker of your promise, however solemnly it may have been given."

"If this is the way I'm to be treated," exclaimed Hugh Darnton, "I may, perhaps, be tempted to break my word as far as you are concerned. Sir Gilbert I shall say nothing against; but, if I am to be railed at by a hag like you, I can hardly be blamed for taking my revenge when they again ask me if I still persist in accusing you of this murder."

"Psha!" interrupted Harrowby; "where's the use of keeping up a quarrel after everything has been comfortably settled? If we all hold our tongues we shall get out of this awkward affair as comfortably as possible; but there'll be the devil to pay if we go kicking up another rumpus."

"Hugh Darnton knows that I care nothing for his ill-will," exclaimed Deborah, tauntingly. "He may say or do against me just what he pleases, and I shall only laugh at him for his pains. He may get me convicted on false evidence, perhaps; but what of that? I shall only have to mount the gibbet a little sooner than I expected. It's been a notion of mine for years past that Jack Ketch and I should shake hands in the last moment, yet nobody ever saw me afraid of it. The truth is, I'm a woman with a man's spirit. I can dare anything if it happens to be in a cause that suits me, and Darnton may yet find out that the hag, as he calls me, is more than a match for him."

"Let us have no more of this," exclaimed Sir Gilbert, as Darnton was about to make an angry retort. "The quarrel has been made up, and we shall only be injuring each other if we commence afresh."

"I don't want to pick up a quarrel," replied Deborah; "but Darnton and I have always pretty well understood each other, and I thought it as well there should be no mistake between us now. I have had my say out, so you needn't be afraid of there being any further rumpus between us."

"Then you and Harrowby had better follow me," said Sir Gilbert, "for there are some few matters that I want to ask your opinion about. Darnton, I dare say, will be glad to be alone, and to-morrow I hope we shall find him still firm in the promise he has just given us."

In a few moments Hugh Darnton found himself alone, and never were reflections more oppressive and discordant than those which now crowded upon his mind. The promise he had given was a mere evasion to rid himself of a danger with which he was threatened. The threat held out by Mark Harrowby had compelled him into seeming acquiescence; but his own thoughts of vengeance were no less intense than they had been previously to the interview. He feared lest suspicion of the murder should fall upon himself, and the only means that appeared to him of averting it was to persist in the charge he had already made against Sir Gilbert and Deborah.

At an early hour he went to bed, but not to sleep; conscience was still busy within him, yet its influence was insufficient to change his diabolical purpose.

CHAPTER XXIX.

STINGS OF CONSCIENCE.—ADJOURNED INQUIRY.—A DILEMMA.

The thoughts which had occupied the waking hours of Darnton were not at all calculated to alleviate the agony of alarm which his perilous situation had given rise to. He saw danger threatening him on every side, in spite of all the efforts he made to avert it; his accusation, too, had brought upon him a host of enemies, each of whom was to be dreaded from the known hatred they felt towards him. Sir Gilbert and he had long since ceased to be friends; Harrowby was not to be relied on unless he faithfully kept the pledge that had been given; and Deborah had exultingly declared that she would bring him to the gibbet.

In short, he could not conceal from himself the fact that the latter named personage more than suspected that the murder had been committed by his own hands. She had broadly hinted her suspicions, and on a recent occasion had even declared that she had found something clasped in the hands of the murdered woman, that would convince the world of who had been the assassin. The more he racked his mind to discover what this could be, the more impossible did he find it to come to a satisfactory conclusion. He knew well enough that nothing he could say or do would in any way appease the vindictive determination she had formed; she had said that she would be more than a match for him when the hour of trial came, and there could be no doubt her words would be fulfilled.

With all these thoughts upon his mind, and with a conscience heavily laden, he rose in the morning with a countenance haggard and care-worn. In his then state of agitation he wished to avoid meeting Sir Gilbert and those with whom he had been used to associate; he knew they would not fail to observe his altered demeanour, and it was but too probable they would form conjectures against him in consequence. With the intention, therefore, of not meeting them till the coroner's court again assembled, he stealthily crept down stairs, and was making his way through the hall when he observed those whom he wished not to be seen by, standing near the door in earnest conversation. They saw him before he could turn back, and conscience whispered to him that their countenances wore an expression of exultation that could only have been occasioned by some plan they had formed to hurl down ruin and destruction upon him who had sought to do the same thing by them.

Stung to madness by the thought, he rushed past them and entered the garden where he hoped to find the solitude he desired. In this he was not disappointed; but solitude only afforded him more opportunity to reflect upon the dangerous situation in which he was placed, and he now began to look forward in a state of terrible suspense to the moment when he was again to stand before those who would observe every word he uttered, and afterwards weigh his evidence so carefully as to detect the slightest discrepancy that might arise. All this served to increase his trepidation, and each moment he felt less able to endure the severe ordeal that in a brief space of time awaited him.

At length he could see, from the bustle going on in the house, that the coroner and jury had arrived, and the thought of what he had to do somewhat restored him to a state of composure. At all events he affected an appearance of firmness if he felt it not, and when a servant approached to inform him that the court had assembled and waited his presence, he walked to the house with an erect mien, as if challenging the suspicion which he in reality believed was already directed towards him, but he only sought to evade the gaze of those he had accused, and taking his place at the table round which the jurymen were assembled, he waited with pretended composure till the business of the court should commence.

At length the coroner, having read over the notes of the previous examination, addressed himself to Sir Gilbert, and inquired if anything had occurred since the adjournment that might in any way assist to unravel the mystery in which this melancholy case was involved.

" I believe, sir," replied the person addressed, " the case remains in exactly the same state as when the court was last assembled here."

"Then I think," said the coroner, "it will be best that we ascertain how far the accusation of Hugh Darnton can be supported by facts. He has declared it to be utterly impossible that Deborah Ratcliffe could have found her way from her own room to that of the murdered lady. By this he would imply that some one must have conducted her to the spot, and for some reason or other his suspicions rest upon Sir Gilbert Copley. It is necessary for the interests of all the parties concerned, that this should be strictly inquired into, and I therefore suggest to the jury that they visit the room in which Deborah Ratcliffe slept, in order that they may satisfy themselves of the probability or improbability of any person finding from thence the place where the unfortunate Lady Copley was murdered."

"If the gentlemen will let me, I will take them to the room myself," exclaimed Deborah, eagerly volunteering her services.

"You can do so," returned the coroner; "but I should wish one of the female servants belonging to the establishment to accompany you."

The housekeeper, being present, was commissioned to perform this duty; and leading the way, she conducted the coroner and jury to the room in question. Deborah, however, was not to be foiled in her design, and keeping close behind them, she proceeded to the chamber they were about to examine. Here a rigid search was made in the hope of discovering some clue, and when every part of the room had been closely looked into, they passed along the passage, and visited the apartment in which the crime had been committed.

Whilst they were absent, a great deal of anxiety was manifested by those who remained in the room below; it was, indeed, expected that some important discovery would take place, and a breathless silence was maintained among the eager throng. Hugh Darnton, during all this time, was in a state of the greatest anxiety; he feared lest the first announcement made on their return should be that suspicion had fallen upon him, and addressing himself in a half whisper to Sir Gilbert, he expressed his regret for the trouble and annoyance the investigation had occasioned him.

"Nay," replied Sir Gilbert, "let that occasion you no annoyance, I beg, for nothing would have afforded me greater satisfaction than to see the care which is taken to investigate this melancholy affair thoroughly. The guilty only need tremble at it; for my own part, I am not the least afraid of the result."

Darnton was about to express a similar feeling of satisfaction, but at the moment the coroner and jury returned, and when all had once more taken their places, the former, addressing himself to the accuser, inquired if he was prepared with any fresh evidence to substantiate the charge he had brought against Sir Gilbert Copley and Deborah Ratcliffe?"

"At present I have none," answered Hugh, after a pause of irresolution. "In fact, sir, the time since the adjournment has been so short, that I can learn but little more than was stated in my last examination before this inquest."

"And, having no further evidence to offer," said the coroner, "are you still of opinion that the crime was committed by the two persons whom you then accused of having murdered your daughter?"

"The truth is, sir," stammered Darnton, after a fierce glance had been directed towards him by Mark Harrowby and Deborah, "I begin to believe that, in the first moment of anguish, I was induced to charge two persons who are innocent."

"In that case," said the coroner, "you have done a grievous wrong to the two persons whose characters have so severely suffered; but perhaps you will now state to me whether there is any reason for having made so great a change in your opinion?"

"I can scarcely give you any satisfactory reason," again stammered Darnton, " unless it is that I have had an opportunity of weighing the matter more carefully in my mind. If I have injured them by words too harshly spoken, I now offer them the only reparation in my power by declaring that I believe them to be quite innocent."

" Yet it seems strange," observed the coroner, " that you should so suddenly have come to a different conclusion than that you arrived at yesterday. The jury and myself have visited the room in which Deborah Ratcliffe slept, and from thence we proceeded to the chamber in which the crime was committed. There is but one opinion among us upon the subject, and that is, that a stranger could not have passed from one place to the other without having been guided by some one else. Whether the persons were Sir Gilbert Copley and Deborah Ratcliffe is a point that will require further investigation to decide."

" There is, indeed, great difficulty in the way, sir," replied Hugh Darnton, scarcely knowing what answer to make; " and you will, therefore, be less surprised that I have unfortunately been led into an error that has thrown suspicion upon two persons whom I now believe to be innocent."

" Am I to understand, then, that you have no further evidence to offer against them ?"

" I have not been able to obtain any ?"

" Yet you told us yesterday that by this time you would be able to substantiate the charge."

" I did say so," answere dDarnton ; " but the inquiries I have since made, convince me that my suspicions were without foundation."

" Then the jury and myself are to understand that you no longer intend to charge these persons with the murder of your daughter ?"

" Exactly so."

" And that you consider the former accusation to be utterly u nunded ?"

" That is my meaning, sir."

" Are you still occupied in your endeavours to find out the perpetrators ?" asked the coroner.

" I shall never cease till that object is accomplished," answered Hugh Darnton. " I am most anxious to bring the murderers to justice, and my most earnest prayer to Heaven is tnat the real perpetrators may be speedily brought to light, and receive the punishment due to their crimes."

" That is what we all pray for," exclaimed Deborah, breaking in upon the momentary silence that had followed Darnton's last words. " I have been accused of being concerned in this crime, yet there is not a person in the room more anxious than myself for the discovery of the miscreant that committed the murder."

There was a peculiar emphasis in the manner of her uttering these words that raised the terror of Hugh Darnton to a higher pitch than ever. He was certain that evil to himself was foreboded by them, and looking earnestly towards her, he endeavoured to discover from the expression of her countenance the thoughts which were brooding in her brain. But Deborah was cautious enough to prevent this, and turning away her head, she seemed to be intently engaged in listening to the summing up of the case.

" You will observe, gentlemen of the jury," the coroner went on to say, " that the inquiry in which we have been engaged has brought out little evidence, and all we have ascertained clearly is that the unfortunate lady has been murdered. There are circumstances that may make it appear probable that the assassin was concealed within the house ; but though a direct charge has been made against two persons, we are without the slightest proof that they are guilty of this heinous offence. The charge may have been made through motives of revenge, and from the fact of the accuser retracting his words to-day, I am inclined to believe that both Sir Gilbert and the woman are as innocent of this crime as any of ourselves. What the motive of the assassin could be we have no evidence to guide us, though it appears robbery was not the object, since neither the money nor jewels that were lying exposed upon a table were touched. If the case is adjourned, I see little probability of any more light being thrown upon the inquiry ; and, therefore, if it meets your own views upon the subject, I think the better way will be to return a verdict of ' Wilful murder against some person or persons unknown.' This will leave the case open, and should any further discovery take place, the accused parties, whoever they may be, can be carried before a magistrate, who will have tne same power to examine the witnesses that we have."

As it really appeared that no further discovery could be made at present, the jury consulted for a few minutes among themselves, and then returned a verdict in accordance with the suggestion thrown out by the coroner.

Thus far matters seemed to have gone on favourably enough for the parties most deeply concerned in this mysterious affair ; but, just as the court was about to rise, the coroner, seeming to recollect himself, once more addressed the jury :—

" It has just struck me," he said, " that we should hardly be doing our duty in dismissing this case, without making all due preparation, in the event of further proceedings subsequently taking place. A charge has been made against Sir Gilbert Copley and Deborah Ratcliffe, which has fallen to the ground for want of sufficient evidence. It is probable, however, that future discoveries may be made, and in order to make sure that all parties will be in attendance, should they be required, I must insist upon each of them entering into securities for that purpose. In fact, I should hardly stand excused in the event of the parties being beyond our reach should their attendance be required at a future period, and they must, therefore, enter into recognizances to meet any charge that may hereafter be made against them."

" With all due deference, sir, I think your proposition a little too hard upon us," exclaimed Sir Gilbert. " I have no friends nor acquaintances in this neighbourhood to whom I can apply to become my surety."

" It may appear hard," replied the coroner ; " but you must remember, Sir Gilbert, that I am myself responsible, and should incur great blame should you not be forthcoming when required. I shall, therefore, insist upon the recognizances being entered into, and in default of your being unable to procure sufficient sureties, I shall be obliged to make out a warrant for the committal of all the parties to the county prison."

" At any rate," exclaimed Hugh Darnton, " I, as the accuser, may be suffered to remain at large ?"

" It is chiefly through your own conduct, sir," answered the coroner, " that I have thought it necessary to take this step. Yesterday you charged Sir Gilbert and the female with the murder of Lady Copley, yet this morning you have, for some reason or other, retracted the accusation. Whether you have been tampered with by interested persons is best known to yourself ; but it has given rise to so much suspicion in my mind, that I have determined to adopt the course you have just heard. The recognizances shall be as light as I can make them, but still they must be sufficiently stringent to meet the ends of justice. With respect to yourself, however, I shall only require your own recognizance, because there is no charge against you. On signing the paper, therefore, you will be at liberty ; but Sir Gilbert Copley and Deborah Ratcliffe will be required to give twenty-four hours' notice of bail, and, consequently, they must submit to a temporary confinement till the necessary forms are complied with."

Three or four constables now bustled their way through the crowd, and Sir Gilbert and the woman were quickly in custody. The former submitted himself quietly, because resistance would have been vain ; but Deborah was of a less yielding nature, and for some little time it was doubtful whether she would not have a struggle for her liberty.

"Surely," exclaimed Hugh Darnton, who began to fear that the turn which matters had taken would go against him, "it cannot be necessary to send a respectable man to gaol merely for want of sureties. Last night you let him remain in his own house under a promise that he would appear again to-day, and I should think you might do the same thing now."

"I did wrong in allowing him to be at liberty when such a charge was hanging over him," replied the coroner; "but it follows not that I should commit a similar fault when I am aware of the error. I am sorry for the situation Sir Gilbert is placed in, but he will see that I have acted with strict impartiality, and most heartily do I hope that he will pass honourably through this severe ordeal."

"At all events," continued Darnton, "you can suffer him to remain here under the care of the constables?"

"I can give no directions to that effect," replied the coroner; "for as every man's house is his castle, it would be too much to expect that I could convert it into a prison. He will, however, be civilly treated, and I hope, for his own sake, his deprivation of liberty will be for a very short period."

"I neither ask for, nor will accept of any favour," exclaimed Sir Gilbert, haughtily. "The whole affair looks to me very like a tyrannical stretch of authority; but I will submit myself to it, though not without a protest against the unnecessary harshness with which I have been treated by one who is armed with a petty authority."

As it was pretty evident a storm was brewing, the coroner and jury now retired. The constables, however, remained to take charge of their prisoners, and convey them to a place of safety.

"You have brought me into a very pretty mess, haven't you?" exclaimed Harrowby to Hugh Darnton. "This is all your doing, and is no more than I expected when first you opened that cursed tongue of yours to accuse Sir Gilbert and Deborah of the murder."

"Fool!" muttered Darnton; "you'll get no good by railing at me now the mischief is done. It's all my fault, and I'm ready to acknowledge it, but you must own I have done my best to give matters a more favourable turn. That has failed, and it now only remains for us to get out of the dilemma as well as we can."

"Your a cunning hand at most things," remarked Mark Harrowby; "so, perhaps, you'll set your wits to work, and show us the way to give these two people the liberty you've been the means of taking away from them."

"I've told you before," exclaimed Darnton, "that this isn't the way to make me your friend in this awkward business. I made the accusation against them under irritated feelings; my child had been cruelly murdered, and nobody could guess by whom. Unfortunately I charged Sir Gilbert and the old woman with the crime; but you also know that I afterwards did all in my power to remove the suspicion."

"And have done very little good, I'm afraid."

"Whether or not," replied Darnton, "I'm heartily sorry for the turn things have taken, and a man can do no more than be sorry for what has happened through his own mistake."

"Humph! you call it a mistake, do you?"

"You don't suppose I would have made such a serious charge unless I had felt pretty certain that I was speaking the truth?" exclaimed Darnton. "We have been friends and companions long enough for me to esteem Sir Gilbert, and as for the old woman, though we sometimes quarrelled a bit, it don't follow that I would swear away her life if I knew her to be innocent, and she knows well enough that I wouldn't harm her for the world."

"Do I?" retorted Deborah, with a sneer; "now it so happens, Hugh Darnton, that I know nothing so certain a sthat you are a cold-blooded villain, that would hang your best friend if it happened to suit your purpose."

"There is a dead set made against me, I see!" exclaimed the hypocrite; "but it shall make no difference in my good intentions. You have both got into a dilemma, and I will get you out of it in the best way, and as soon as I possibly can."

"For my own part, I shall put no trust in you," she replied; "and Sir Gilbert will be a greater fool than I take him for, if he believes a word you say."

"At present I shall give no opinion either way," replied Sir Gilbert, "but will wait till I see how the affair is likely to end. In the meantime, Deborah, you and I must make as light as we can of our troubles; we shall be compelled to take up our lodgings in the gaol, though for how long a time will depend upon whether we can get any good-natured persons to become our recognizances."

"Well, then, to prison let us go," said Deborah, with her usual unconcern; "for my own part, a prison has no such terrors for me, as it has for some people, and, at any rate, I shall have the satisfaction of being in good company. They won't keep us there for ever, I suppose; and, when we come out, I would have Hugh Darnton look to himself, for he knows me of old, and I needn't tell him that I never forget an injury."

"But, if I have done you an injury," exclaimed Darnton, "you must also acknowledge that I have tried all in my power to repair it. I made the charge against you under the feeling that my suspicion was correct, but I have now seen the mistake, and will try all in my power to get you out of trouble."

"Will you, indeed?" cried the woman, ironically. "A very fine promise, truly, after the mischief is done, and when we are going to take up our quarters in a prison; out upon you for a hound, Hugh Darnton, and may your death be upon a gibbet!"

"A truce to this quarrelling," interrupted Sir Gilbert; "angry words will not avail us in our trouble, and, if Darnton's promise may be relied on, he will not fail to obtain our release from the prison he sends us to. I can pardon him the suspicion he entertained against us, and I hope, by his exertions, he will make some recompense for the disgrace and inconvenience he has put us to."

Then the conversation ended; and, when the dusk of the evening was just coming on, a post-chaise arrived from the neighbouring town, in which the two prisoners were to be conveyed to their place of destination. Sir Gilbert Copley, though really downcast in spirits, affected an appearance of unconcern as he stepped into the carriage, but Deborah made no secret of the rage she felt at the turn matters had taken. Her look, on parting from Hugh Darnton, was menacing in the extreme; but, as the post-chaise drove off, she threw herself back upon the seat, and remained brooding over her wrongs till they arrived at the gates of the prison.

CHAPTER XXX.

HIGH WORDS.—UNPLEASANT VISITORS.—A DISCOVERY.

THE good fellowship that had existed between Hugh Darnton and his companions was now broken and destroyed; they regarded him as the cause of all the mischief that had happened, as well as any that might yet be in store for them. Indeed, their situation seemed to be anything but a satisfactory

one, for now that the eyes of people had been drawn towards them, there was no saying how soon they might find themselves in the same gaol to which Sir Gilbert and Deborah had already been sent. It was, therefore, to be expected that, after the departure of the two prisoners, their conduct towards Darnton would not be of a very pacific description, and Dick Elliot, who had hitherto taken but little share in what was passing, seemed determined to pick up a quarrel, if hard words could do so.

"I'll tell you what it is, Master Darnton," he said, breaking in on the silence that had followed the departure of their friends, "you have proved yourself a double-faced villain to your old comrades, and hang me if I don't have my revenge out of your bones. If you have a spark of manhood left in you, you won't hear yourself called a villain without resenting it; so follow me to the lawn, yonder, and let's see if you have any of the courage that you now boast of."

"Are you mad?" exclaimed Darnton; "shall we prove ourselves to be blackguards before the servants here, when we have been at so much pains to make them believe we are gentlemen?"

"I care nothing for what the servants think of us now," replied Elliot; "you have done all you can to open their eyes, and it's strange to me if worse don't come of this before we are many hours older. So accept my challenge, or I'll dash my fist in your face for a coward as you are."

"Come, come, this is carrying matters too far," interposed Mark Harrowby. "We must not let the people here see that we are impostors, or there will soon be the devil to pay among us. The servants have looked at us suspiciously for some time past, and, if we get to fighting and wrangling among ourselves, the news will spread abroad like wild-fire, and then a very pretty situation we should find ourselves in. People would begin to inquire who and what we are, and I needn't tell you, I suppose, that certain awkward disclosures might follow that would send us all in double quick time to the gallows."

" Psha !" cried Rob Redland, " what could they ever find out, so far away from our old haunts ?"

" Why, they might happen to recollect something about that murder."

" You're always frightened lest that should be brought against us," interrupted Redland. " For my own part, I don't think there's any danger to be thought of now, and, if there is, we must face it like men. We felt no terror when we committed the deed, and I, for one, have no notion that a man ought always to be making himself uncomfortable about a thing that can't be undone. At present we are in good quarters, and so let's make ourselves easy as to the future, for I am one of those chaps that think it's time enough to be afraid of danger when it stares us in the face."

" Why, it does that already," answered Harrowby ; " and, when that's the case, it's every man's duty to look after himself."

" You are not going to leave us ?"

" No, no, I'm not such a coward as that," replied Mark ; " but I just want to put you on your guard against giving people room to think queerly of us. There's plenty that would be glad to have us hanged out of the way, and I'm not so tired of life but what the gibbet is a thing that I should like to avoid as long as possible."

" The truth of it is," said Hugh Darnton, " this is an old quarrel that he's trying to bring up ; but it shall be no fault of mine if any mischief comes of it. I have before expressed my sorrow for the misfortunes of Sir Gilbert, and you must all acknowledge that I tried my best to get him through it, though I didn't succeed."

" You must have been either a madman or a black-hearted villain to accuse him of such a crime," exclaimed Dick Elliot. " Was it likely, I should like to ask, that a man, in cold blood, would murder his wife, when there has been no serious quarrel between them ?"

" If there was no quarrel, there was anything but a kind feeling," answered Darnton, " and I happen to know that he had made up his mind to sue for a divorce only a few days before the murder happened."

" Why, man," exclaimed Harrowby, " that very fact of itself ought to be sufficient to convince you that it was not committed either by Sir Gilbert or with his knowledge. If he wanted to get rid of a wife that he no longer loved, it was much more likely that he would have tried for a divorce, than risk his own neck by committing a crime that was almost sure to be brought home to him."

" Well, I'm inclined to think so myself now," returned Darnton ; " but when the news of my daughter's murder came suddenly upon me, I at once suspected Sir Gilbert and Deborah of having planned and executed it. It was not a very unnatural thought of mine, though it has turned out unfortunate ; and, as I've done all I could to repair the injury, it's rather hard that I should be run down by my old comrades."

Hugh Darnton saw clearly enough that nothing he could say would alter the opinion of those who were opposed to him ; and, having no inclination to quarrel when the odds were so greatly against him, he shortly afterwards left the room, and hastened to his own chamber, in the hope of forgetting the horrible events that tortured and harassed his soul. But sleep, as on the previous night, was denied him ; he knew himself to be the murderer of his own child, and the reflection was madness to him. His plan, too, of throwing the suspicion upon Sir Gilbert and the old woman, had partially failed ; he had made enemies of those who had it in their power to bring him to the punishment he had designed for others ; and, from the conversation that had just taken place between them, there was no doubt they were only waiting an opportunity to denounce him as a murderer. The words and looks of Deborah Ratcliffe proved that from her he had no quarter to expect; she had even boasted of being in possession of evidence that would bring the crime home to him; and, though she had hitherto forborne to produce it, there was but too much reason to believe she would do so on the very first occasion when circumstances might favour her.

Feverish, and trembling under the deadly terror that had taken possession of his soul, it is little to be wondered at that Hugh Darnton could not close his eyes in sleep throughout that night of agony and remorse. Each sound that he heard, however slight, startled him, and a dozen times at least did he jump up in his bed, and gaze about in wild affright, expecting to see the room filled with officers of justice. Then, on discovering the utter groundlessness of his alarm, he would endeavour to compose himself, but only to endure a repetition of the guilty apprehensions that had disturbed him. At length daylight once more appeared, and, as his confidence returned, he rose, dressed himself, and strolled into the grounds that surrounded the house, in the hope of appearing less agitated when he again joined his companions.

That morning, too, Mark Harrowby was up at an earlier hour than usual, for he had heard Dick Elliot leave his room, and, wishing to consult him upon various matters, he went in search of him in the plantations, where he frequently resorted with his gun. A loud report close by guided him to the spot, on arriving at which he found the object of his search pocketing a pheasant which had just fallen under his unerring aim. Elliot did not at first observe that he was intruded on; but hearing footsteps, and perceiving who it was that approached, he expressed his gratification at so unexpected a meeting.

"The truth is, my dear fellow, I came on purpose to speak to you about two or three things that concern our present condition. This place, to my fancy, is growing too hot for us; we shall have all sorts of unpleasant inquiries made about us, and, as we shall not be able to give a very good account of who we are, and what we have been doing before we came here, I think we had better make ourselves scarce with all possible haste."

"Upon my life your thoughts and mine are pretty much alike," exclaimed Elliot. "I've been thinking all night that a few hours may bring a hornet's nest about our ears, and so I just took a stroll out with my gun as an excuse to see how the land lies."

"Have you seen any suspicious persons lurking about the place?"

"I've not seen a soul," replied Elliot; "but that makes no difference in my plans, for I'm pretty sure there's mischief in the wind, and so, in spite of the comforts we find here, I shall take my departure, and take care of number one, while the road is clear."

"That's just what I mean to do myself," exclaimed the other. "I have taken the precaution to arm myself, as you see, and, if any one should think it worth while to interrupt me, I shall perhaps have another murder or two to answer for. There are some good horses in the stable, and I shall make bold to borrow one; for, if Sir Gilbert ever returns to his mansion, he can hardly grudge an old friend the use of a steed when liberty, if not life itself, may depend upon it."

"When do you mean to start?"

"Directly," replied Harrowby; "it would be madness for us to remain a moment after we suspect we are threatened with danger; so, if you feel inclined for it, you can bear me company."

"With all my heart," exclaimed Elliot; "I'll leave my gun here, against this tree, and we'll make a clear start of it at once."

"You had better follow my example," said Harrowby; "I have taken care to bring with me all the money I have saved from Sir Gilbert's liberality, and

I would advise you to do the same. We shall need a pretty good supply to carry us along the road, and it may be to take us abroad, in case the pursuit should happen to grow too hot for us."

"Hadn't I better tell Rob Redland what we are going to do, that he may make one of our party?"

"If you stop to do that, it is a hundred to one if we don't get nabbed," returned Harrowby. "I should like very well to have had him with us; but we have not an instant to lose, and though friendship may be all very well in some cases it don't do when one's own neck is in danger. So just go into the house; get your money together, and then return to me as fast as your legs will carry you."

Dick Elliot vanished like a shot, and in an inconceivably short space of time he returned, panting and out of breath with his exertion.

"Well," exclaimed Harrowby, "have you managed to make it all right?"

"Yes, I've got the money in my pocket," he replied. "I have not been long about it, you must acknowledge; though hang me, if I could hardly resist the temptation of waking Rob Redland, to tell him of the new dodge we are going upon."

"It's much better that you acted with caution," returned Mark Harrowby, "for if so many of us had been seen leaving the place at this early hour, it would have given rise to awkward suspicions."

"And pray," asked the other, "may I inquire what has made you in such a confounded hurry to be off?"

"Why, the fact of it is, I have been thinking of our perilous situation all night," replied Harrowby; "and the more I thought the matter over the more did I feel convinced that we should repent it if we suffered our present opportunity for escaping to pass by."

"But what makes you think we are in so much danger?" inquired Elliot.

"There are more reasons than one for suspecting that we can't remain here any longer in safety," replied Mark Harrowby. "In the first place, the folks hereabouts have long looked upon us with an evil eye; and, in the next, it's not at all unlikely that Sir Gilbert, in his extremity, may give in our feigned names as his sureties. Now that would lead to inquiries that we could never stand; unpleasant things would be sure to come out; and, as likely as not, we should be discovered as the very persons that the laws have so long taken so great an interest in. Thus you see, Dick, I have good ground for making this hasty retreat; and now that you know my motives, I care not how soon we make ourselves scarce. In a word, if you mean to go with me, you must start at once."

"Why, if *you* begin to think it necessary to move, I know it's time I should follow," exclaimed the other. "It must be confessed, I should have liked Rob Redland to have gone with us; but I suppose there's no help for it, and so he must be content to remain behind with that infernal villain, Hugh Darnton."

"The scoundrel will deserve all he gets, whatever it may be," returned Harrowby. "As for Redland he will soon take the hint when he finds that we are gone, and I dare say some time or other we shall happen to meet with him again."

They were making their way towards the stable, when the rapid trampling of horses was heard, and turning round they saw a party of mounted soldiers galloping at full speed up the avenue. In an instant Harrowby and his companion concealed themselves behind a small clump of trees, from whence they could observe the intruders, and they then discovered for the first time that at the head of them rode the Rev. Matthew Podgers, who, being a magistrate, had thought it necessary to make himself very busy on the occasion.

"You now see that I was not wrong in suspecting the approach of danger," whispered Harrowby. " These fellows have, no doubt, got warrants against us all ; but they'll be disappointed of part of their errand, for though they may capture some of the parties, there's two that will make their escape in spite of them."

" Do you really think these fellows have been sent to capture us ?" demanded Elliot.

" How can we doubt it, when we see soldiers, and a magistrate accompanying them ?" demanded the other. " However, luckily for ourselves, we got up a little too soon for them this morning, and while they are engaged in searching the house, you and I will make the best of our way from the place. With good fleet nags we shall soon be beyond their reach, and then, my boy, I suppose you will acknowledge that my advice is not always to be scorned."

By this time they had reached the stable, and a couple of strong horses having been saddled and bridled, the two fugitives mounted, and leaving the place by a side gate, that led into a retired lane, they put spurs to their steeds, and set off at a pace that promised to carry them in a short time beyond the reach of danger.

We shall not, however, follow them in their flight at present, but will return to the mansion where the Rev. Matthew Podger and his brother magistrate had alighted, to commence the business that had taken them there. The former of these worthy functionaries had received an intimation that the parties who had been on a visit to Sir Gilbert Copley had formerly belonged to a desperate band of smugglers, and as it was likely a violent resistance would be offered, an early hour in the morning had been chosen for the proposed capture, and a party of the military had been called out to assist instead of the usual civil force. The first thing done was to place a portion of the men round the house to prevent all possibility of escape ; and this being done, the magistrates consulted together, as to how they should next proceed.

Meanwhile Hugh Darnton, who happened to be in the house, became aware of the danger with which he was threatened, and little suspecting how matters really stood, he hurried with frantic speed to the room usually occupied by Mark Harrowby. To his consternation, however, he discovered that the bird had flown ; and, gnashing his teeth with rage, at the thought of having been outwitted, he next hastened in search of Dick Elliot, but with exactly the same result. As a last resource he went to the chamber of Rob Redland, whom he found sleeping as soundly as if life and death were not at stake at that fearful moment. He, however, quickly aroused the slumberer, and in words that were scarcely intelligible, bade him rise without an instant's delay, or all would be lost.

" What the devil's the matter ?" growled Redland, rubbing his eyes. " Are you mad, Darnton, to come and wake a man out of his sleep at this early hour of the morning ?"

" There is danger, I tell you !" exclaimed the other ; " we have been betrayed by some one. The house is surrounded, and we shall be taken, unless you make haste to follow me from this place."

" Who surround the house ?"

" Soldiers."

" Then we are done for at last !" exclaimed Redland, hastily putting on his clothes. " We must, however, try if there's a way to get out without being seen ;—perhaps Harrowby may be able to assist us with his advice."

" Mark Harrowby is a traitor !" muttered the other ; " I have sought for him and find that he has fled, whilst we are left behind to meet our fate."

" Where is Dick Elliot ?"

" Gone with him, I suppose," answered Darnton, " for I have been to his room, and the nest is empty."

"There must be some mistake about this," exclaimed Redland ; "for I am sure neither of them would desert their friends in trouble."

"We have now a plain proof that they care not for our necks so that they save their own," replied Darnton. "They are both of them villains, and I wish I had never seen either of them."

"That's just the very compliment I can pay *you*," exclaimed the other. "You have been a curse to us, and it was only last night that I told you we should get into some plaguy mess through your mad-headed schemes. However, it's no use quarrelling with you now that the gallows is staring us in the face. All we've got to do is to try and get out of the house without being seen by those confounded soldiers."

"That is impossible."

"Then we must defend ourselves."

"What! against such odds ?"

"Odds or no odds, I don't like surrendering, as if we were a couple of cowards. But what is the charge they make against us ? Do you know that ?"

"I do not," replied Darnton.

"Can you guess how they found out that we have ever done anything against the laws ?"

"I know no more about it than you do yourself," replied Darnton. "All I can tell you is that the house is surrounded with soldiers, and I saw just now a couple of magistrates in consultation, underneath my window. I tried to hear their conversation, but they spoke so low that not a word reached me."

"Upon my life, I can't make this out at all," exclaimed the other. "That Mark Harrowby should have deserted us, seems impossible, because he has always stuck to one when you and others have shown the white feather. As for Dick Elliot, he may have taken care of himself, for I never had any great opinion of him if matters should ever take a turn against us."

"Then you have not been deceived," retorted Darnton, "for he is the most black-hearted villain that ever escaped the punishment he deserves."

"Saving yourself, Master Darnton," answered the other, with a sneer. "You are every bit as bad, only that you have contrived to carry it off with a smooth tongue and an unblushing face. This is all your doings—you have been the cause of bringing us into this dilemma, and hang me if I haven't a great mind to send this knife into your heart !"

And it is by no means unlikely that he would have carried this threat into execution, but at the moment footsteps were heard approaching,—a violent push was made at the door, and the two magistrates, with half-a-dozen soldiers, entered the room.

"What is the meaning of this unexpected visit, gentlemen ?" demanded Darnton, with an appearance of his usual composure. "Is any crime charged against us, that the house is to be filled with military ?"

"Your name," said the Reverend Mr. Podgers, "is, I believe, Hugh Darnton ?"

"It is."

"Then I have a warrant for your apprehension, as well as your friend, here, who, I believe, though going under an assumed name, is better known among his associates as Robert Redland."

"Upon what charge ?" demanded the other.

"The most serious," answered the clergyman ; "you are both accused of having been concerned in a murder !"

"Indeed ! perhaps you will next inform us what murder we are charged with ?"

"We are not sent here to answer questions, but to perform our duty," replied Mr. Podgers. "We are charged to convey you both to a place of safety, and as we have sufficient force with us to prevent escape, I would advise you to submit quietly."

"Well, so we will, as we can't help ourselves," returned Robert Redland ; "but perhaps you wouldn't have had quite so easy a job of it if we had all been together, and you had not come with such strong arguments against us. However, it's no use to argufy that just now ;—you tell us we are accused of murder ;—will you be so very kind, old gentleman, as to tell us who we have sent out of the world before his time ?"

"There can be no objection to that, that I know of," replied the clergy-man. "You are accused of having aided and assisted in murdering an aged schoolmaster, named Simon Stripes, who formerly lived in the adjacent village."

"Simon Stripes !" exclaimed Redland. "Never happened to have the honour of his acquaintance. This is some lie of an enemy, you may depend on it. Some one wants to hang us, and so they accuse us of murdering this Mr. Simon Snipes."

"Stripes is the name I mentioned," said the magistrate. "He was well known in this place ; and his shocking death filled the whole place with dismay. A large reward was offered for the assassins, but never were we able to obtain the least clue to them, till accident, within the last few hours, pointed them out among the guests of Sir Gilbert Copley."

"I tell you, we know nothing about the affair," persisted Redland.

"It is my most earnest wish that you may be able to make your innocence clearly manifest," answered the clergyman. "That, however, is a matter that we have nothing at all to do with. The charge has been made, and any defence that you have to offer must be to those whose duty it will be to pre-side at the examination."

"Upon my life, you're very hard of belief," exclaimed Rob Redland, coolly. "My word, I should think, is as good as the chap's that's been informing against us. He says we committed this murder, I say we didn't, and it would hardly be fair to hang us, when we are ready to take our oath that we're inno-cent."

"You will have an opportunity of making any defence you please when the proper time arrives," said the other magistrate. "We are not sent here to decide upon your guilt or innocence, but to convey you to a place where you will be kept in safe custody till the examination of witnesses in support of the charge."

"Then, I suppose you wouldn't take bail, if we were to offer it."

"Bail is never accepted in such cases as this," said the clergyman.

"But I tell you we know no more of the murder of this old Mr. Tripes than you do yourself."

"I earnestly hope it may be made to appear so," replied the magistrate ; "and you may depend upon it every facility will be afforded to enable you to clear your character from this foul imputation. At the same time, however, it is only fair to tell you that the information comes from a source that we put some reliance in."

"Well, sir," exclaimed Darnton, "it's useless to say anything more about it ; so we will submit ourselves quietly, though we both of us protest against the violence that has been perpetrated against us."

"You will find it better to say nothing about that at present," said the clergyman. "I have now, however, another question to ask of you. We also hold warrants against two persons, named Elliott and Harrowby. We have not yet been able to find them ; can you tell us where they are ?"

"Out of your clutches, and that's just what I should like to be myself," said Rob Redland.

"They have escaped, then ?"

" To be sure they have ; and if they never did a wise thing before, I'll give 'em the credit of having done one now."

" Had they any intimation of our intended visit ?" inquired the clergyman.

" We can't tell you that," answered Darnton. " But if they did know of it, I should call them a couple of infernal rascals to leave their friends in trouble, while they themselves got out of it."

" Do you think," asked the other magistrate, " that you could give us any information by which we may be able to apprehend the fugitives ?"

" I don't know whether we could or not," replied Redland ; " but we should be a brace of very pretty villains to turn informers against our old companions."

" Humph," said Darnton ; " you have more consideration for them than they had for us. By their running away they must have known what was coming, yet they leave us to the tender mercies of these gentlemen."

" When did you see them last ?" demanded the Rev. Matthew Podgers.

" Last night."

" Then they must have started at daybreak," exclaimed the magistrate. " In that case they cannot be very far off ; and if active exertions are made, we may hope to capture them before many hours have passed. Let the soldiers divide themselves into parties of three each, and ride over every part of the country for seventy miles in extent. Every place must be carefully scoured, and let no one pass without a close examination, for they have, no doubt, disguised themselves, and will escape us yet, if we are not very cautious in looking after them."

This proposition was no sooner made than put into execution. Parties were despatched in every direction, and when this was done, Hugh Darnton and Rob Redland were secured, and each being mounted behind a soldier, they were taken off to their place of destination.

CHAPTER XXXI.

A PRISON SCENE.——THE LAWYER AND HIS CLIENT.——THE EVIDENCE.

THE news of what had happened at the mansion soon reached the ears of Vivian and his friend, who could not be hypocritical enough to express any sympathy for the troubles of Sir Gilbert Copley and his associates in crime. On the contrary, they rejoiced at the prospect that at length dawned upon them of a change of fortune ; for, like most young men, they were sanguine in their expectations, and believed that now misfortune had fallen upon the enemy of Sir Lionel, the schemes of villany would be discovered, and that ere long the whole conspiracy would be explained.

But Sir Lionel, or Mr. Dacre, as we must still continue to call him, was less ardent in his anticipations. He well knew the temper of his unprincipled nephew, and had no hope that even a spark of honour remained in his bosom. Nor, indeed, did he now care about the restitution of his former rank and wealth. His spirits were broken by the misfortunes that had bowed him down to the earth ; and though a prison was still his home, he had no wish to leave it for the short time he believed remained to him in this world. Besides, he could not forget that Gilbert, base and fallen as he was, was the offspring of his own beloved brother, and the thought of seeing him come to a shameful end occasioned more acute pain to his heart than did all the sufferings and pain he had been made to endure. To those who were most with him, this weakness seemed almost criminal, since his family must share in the privations to which he subjected himself ; but the fallen man would promise no

assistance in the projects that were submitted to him, until he had well considered them.

"And yet," said Henry Markham to him, on one occasion, "I must entreat your pardon for reminding you that the claims of your family should be considered in preference to everything else. The title and estates which have been taken from you will, in the course of time, belong to your son, and surely, for his sake, the villany that has been practised should be thoroughly exposed."

"Of all that I am well aware," replied Mr. Dacre; "yet no feeling of revenge should urge me to adopt a course that must bring ruin and disgrace upon one who, with all his faults, claims near alliance with my family. I may be told that this is a feeling of apathy which I ought not to give way to, since my son must suffer by it. He, however, will, I trust, judge my motives by the conduct he has always seen me observe, and in that confidence I shall for the present be content to remain."

"From me you have no reproaches to fear!" exclaimed Vivian. "I have ever known you to be a lover of justice and impartiality, and no selfish feelings of my own shall now induce me to arraign your motives. My only wish is to see you restored to liberty; and were that desire but satisfied, I could endure poverty and privations without a murmur."

"At all events, my dear son," returned Mr. Dacre, "my apathy in this affair need be no restraint upon any exertions you may think proper to make. All I wish of you is, that you will not proceed in a spirit of vindictiveness. You will first take care to ascertain the exact situation of affairs; and when that is done, it will be for you to proceed according to your own judgment. If Sir Gilbert, as he still persists in calling himself, has indeed fallen into trouble, he may begin to feel the pangs of remorse, and in that case it will be less difficult than you imagine to obtain restitution of the fortune and title he has deprived us of."

No. 22

"Then I see, sir, you still entertain a better opinion of him than I do."

"I should be sorry to condemn any man unjustly," answered his father. "Gilbert, I fear, has fallen into very bad company; Hugh Darnton, for instance, obtained great influence over him, though by what means I have never been able to discover. Certain it is, however, that my unfortunate nephew has been a mere tool in his hands, and from that circumstance have arisen the misfortunes we have endured."

"If Gilbert had not been naturally depraved at heart, he never would have suffered himself to become the associate of a villain," observed Vivian.

"Upon that point we cannot decide at present," returned his father. "All we really know is, that he became partial to the society of Darnton, and from that moment may be dated his ruin. We have, indeed, bitter reason to complain of the ruin he has brought upon us; but he has now fallen into trouble, and we must not pursue him like tigers that are thirsting for his blood."

"Believe me, I am not actuated by feelings of revenge in this instance," replied Vivian. "I believe him to have obtained possession of our property by fraudulent means, and, if that should prove to be the case, it is nothing more than a duty to strip him of his ill-gotten wealth. In short, my dear father, every hour serves to afford additional proof that Sir Gilbert has been guilty of greater crimes than you imagine. It is said that he has been a shedder of human blood,—and, if that should be the case, it will not require the assistance of either you or myself to bring him to punishment."

"And, if punishment should follow," exclaimed Mr. Dacre, "there will be an eternal blot upon our names. At least, Vivian, withhold all unfavourable opinions at present, for much as I dread the result of this inquiry, I would fain buoy myself up with the hope that he has not been guilty of the heinous crime you speak of."

Mr. Dacre become so much agitated that he left the room, and the two young men being left to themselves, consulted together upon the subject of their recent conversation; and, in the end, it was agreed between them that there could be no doubt of Gilbert having been concerned in the mysterious death of the village schoolmaster. As it seemed, however, to be the wish of Mr. Dacre that they should not take any active part in the proceedings, it was arranged that they should merely watch what was going forward, and interfere only if it should appear necessary for the ends of justice.

The feelings of Hugh Darnton upon finding himself a prisoner in the county gaol underwent a remarkable change; he was no longer that bold and reckless villain that he had hitherto been, but yielding to the terrors inspired by his situation, he would have been guilty of any meanness to save himself from the consequences of his long series of crimes. From the consultation he had had with his lawyer, he ascertained that his participation in the murder of Simon Stripes was pretty clearly traced to him, so that he pretty well knew the fate which awaited him, in the event of the whole chain of evidence being completed. The lawyer being himself tolerably well experienced in such cases, saw plainly the state of his client's mind; and, on one occasion of visiting him in prison, he made a desperate effort to get at the facts.

"I needn't tell you, my friend," he at length said, "of what consequence it is that there should be the most perfect confidence between a lawyer and his client in such an affair as this. I am not asking questions for the mere gratification of an idle curiosity, but would possess myself of your confidence, in order that I may be better enabled to prepare your defence."

"What is it you want to know?" demanded Darnton, sullenly; for in spite of the protestations of the other, he could not believe but his intentions were treacherous.

"You must candidly confess to me every criminal affair that you have been concerned in throughout your life," answered the lawyer. "I have to make out the best case I can, that your counsel may be well prepared for the defence. At present the indictment only charges you with being concerned in the murder of Simon Stripes, and there is a possibility that, with hard swearing and good management, we may be able to get you off. But other things may be found out between now and the day of trial, and should we be taken unawares, the consequences would be fatal to yourself. And now I think of it, Darnton, I must ask if the murdered Lady Copley was not your daughter?"

"She was," replied the culprit, sullenly.

"Humph! Well, I dare say you will be glad to hear that circumstances are looking more favourable in that quarter. So much so, indeed, that if it had not been for that awkward affair of Simon Stripes's murder, your son-in-law, Sir Gilbert, would have been set at liberty before this time."

"What do you mean?" demanded Darnton, eagerly.

"I mean," replied the lawyer, "that there is every proof of his being innocent of her death."

"What proof?"

"Ah, that's what I've not been able to get at," answered the man of law. "All I know is, that he would have been discharged from prison, but for that awkward business of old Stripes."

"And Deborah Ratcliff, what has become of her?"

"Oh, she has been told to go about her business as soon as she pleases; but, strange to say, she seems to like her prison quarters, for she has not left, and what's more, she don't seem inclined to do so."

"Why has she been discharged?" asked Darnton.

"Because she has made disclosures that point out the real assassin of Lady Copley."

"The devil!"

"Oh," exclaimed the lawyer, without seeming to notice his agitation, "I thought you would be glad to hear that there is a good chance of punishing the murderer of your poor daughter. The thing has now come to a crisis, Mr. Darnton; the criminal will be sent to the gallows if he don't mind what he's about. So now, perhaps, you will more clearly understand what I meant when I said just now you had better confess to me every crime you have been concerned in."

"What are you driving at?" exclaimed Darnton, with a look that seemed intended to penetrate the inmost thoughts of his professional adviser.

"I must leave you to guess what I mean," answered the other; "but you may be sure I am here only to do you all the service in my power. I must have your full confidence if any good is to be done in this business, and, from what has passed, you may pretty well imagine that I have heard more than at present I mean to state. In short, the affair of old Stripes may be got over, but there is another that will not be quite so easily managed."

"I believe," exclaimed Darnton, huskily after the pause of a few minutes, "you said just now, that the woman, Deborah Ratcliffe, is no longer a prisoner?"

"Exactly so."

"And she has said something that will prove who was the murderer of my daughter?"

"She has both said and done," answered the lawyer; "for though they keep the matter uncommonly close at present, I have heard it whispered that she has produced something in evidence that ——"

"'Tis false!" roared Darnton, taken completely off his guard, "she can produce nothing to criminate any one. The wretch would save herself, and cares not who she charges with the crime!"

Darnton saw by the look of the lawyer that his words had made the very impression he would have avoided, and suddenly pausing, he pondered in his mind how he might best remove the unfavourable [thoughts his words had given rise to. This he knew would not be very easy, and giving it up for the present, he said,—

"You told me just now, I believe, that the woman has not yet left the prison?"

"Oh, yes, she is still here."

"Do you think I could have an interview with her?"

"Humph!" ejaculated the man of law, "I should imagine no objection would be made to it."

"But without any other person being present?"

"Why, it's not very usual to do that," replied the other; "but I think it's quite likely I might be able to get such a favour granted."

But the lawyer knew better, for he saw there was a secret to come out, and he resolved to secret himself somewhere within ear-shot of the parties.

"If you think it's to be done," said Darnton, "let not a moment be lost, but bring her hither."

The other left the room without making any further reply, and Hugh Darnton, for some few minutes became the prey of all those horrible doubts and fears that the recent conversation had given rise to. That Deborah was in possession of the dreadful secret he had but too much reason to believe; her own lips had pronounced the fact on the morning after the murder had taken place, but what the evidence was he could not possibly imagine. He thought of a thousand things, that vanished almost as soon as they rose to his mind, and the suspense under which he laboured had become almost intolerable when the well-known footsteps of his dreaded visiter were heard approaching. This served to rouse him to a sense of the danger in which he was enthralled, and nerving himself as well as he could, he assumed an appearance of tolerable composure, when the woman, accompanied by the lawyer, entered the cell. The latter, however, instantly retired, and went to join some persons that he had told of what was going to take place, and who were already so stationed just without the door, that they could overhear all that was passing within.

"I have come hither at your bidding," commenced Deborah. "They told me you wanted to see me about something, and though I don't owe you much good-will, I've obeyed your wish."

"Answer me one question," exclaimed Hugh Darnton; "have you any wish to send me to the gallows?"

"Why you deserve to go there," answered Deborah; "and perhaps I might not mind lending a helping hand towards giving you your deserts. I have always said the hour of my triumph would some time or other arrive, and now I believe you will own that it is not very far distant."

"Enough of this," exclaimed Darnton, "for there is little merit in trampling upon a fallen man. They tell me you have been saying something about me and the poor murdered Patty, and—and ——"

"Don't haggle so much about it, man," she cried. "They told me you wished to see me; if you have anything to say, be quick about it, for they'll not suffer me to stay here very long."

"I want to make my peace with you, Deborah," he said, in a tone of conciliation. "There never ought to have been any quarrel between us, for I have always desired to be your friend, though, for some reason or other, you have despised my good intentions. Let me hope our late troubles have softened your heart, and that we may yet be friends."

"Don't deceive yourself, Hugh Darnton," she exclaimed, "for you and I can never be friends in this world. I have come because they told me you had something to say of importance, but if you don't quickly unburden yourself I shall quit your company. Is it *you* that dare talk of being friends—

you who meant to have murdered me, only that you mistook my room and went into that of your daughter? And then you must needs charge me and Sir Gilbert with the crime, though well knowing at the time that your own hands had committed it. But I knew you were powerless to injure me while I held a proof that even your own lying tongue dare not deny!"

"What," gasped Darnton, in agony—"what do your fearful words imply?"

"That you are in my power," she exultingly replied. "When the cry of murder was raised, I was among the first to enter your daughter's room, and believing that some evidence of the crime might remain, I was the last to take my departure. When alone, I approached the corpse, and in her hand found ——"

"What?" demanded Darnton, in a voice of thunder.

"Part of a shirt frill," she replied, "and in it a small gold pin that you always wore. You had it on the night the murder was committed. Have you ever seen or worn it since?"

"And this," exclaimed Darnton, trembling with rage, "is the secret that you boast is to hang me?"

"Is it not enough?" she demanded. "I have compared the torn frill with the shirt you wore at the time when your daughter's life was sacrificed for mine, and the piece exactly fits the place from which it was rent, so that there can be no doubt on that point. Now, Darnton, you see that I made no vain boast when I said you were in my power. The proofs are still in my possession, and shall be produced when the proper time arrives."

"And *will* you produce them?"

"Ay, as surely as I now tell you so."

"Then only one chance remains for me!" exclaimed Hugh Darnton; and, springing forward, he fastened upon her throat with the determination of strangling her.

The woman, however, was possessed of herculean strength, and combatting with him, they at length fell heavily to the floor. At that moment those who had been listening rushed in to separate them; but their arrival was too late, for Deborah had come armed with a knife, which she plunged into the body of her adversary, who, with a groan of mortal anguish, sunk back and expired.

CHAPTER XXXII.

A CHOICE OF EVILS.—THE PLAN OF ESCAPE.—A TRAGIC DETERMINATION.

As the death of Hugh Darnton had been caused by Deborah in self-preservation, she was allowed to roam at will over the prison as before. She exulted at having rid the world of a villain; and had any attempt been made to punish her for what had been done, there is little doubt she would have ended her career in the same way.

On the next day she was permitted to have an interview with Sir Gilbert Copley, to whom she related the tragedy in which she had so important a part. She told him, also, of the evidence she possessed to prove that the murder had been perpetrated by Darnton, and as a confirmation produced the gold pin, and a fragment of shirt frill that had been torn from the assassin in the brief struggle that had taken place between him and his victim.

"The villain!" exclaimed Sir Gilbert, when he had heard her to a conclusion, "has met with the fate he merited, though I cannot help regretting that the knife was not plunged into my heart instead of his."

"And why so?" asked Deborah.

" Because, then, my earthly troubles would have been at an end," answered the other. " As it is, I have yet to undergo a trial from which I shrink with terror. I have been present at scenes of blood, but have never taken part in them ; though, it is true, I made no effort to prevent the crime. And now, what is the consequence? There are charges of murder against me ; and should the jury find me guilty, I shall be sent to meet an ignominious death, just at the time when my prospects might have been brightest."

" Yet I can save you, on one condition," replied Deborah. " Let me have the reward I ask for, and this place shall not be your prison many hours longer."

" What reward do you speak off?" demanded Sir Gilbert, looking inquisitively towards her.

" One that you may easily bestow, now that her ladyship is dead," replied the woman. " In one word, Sir Gilbert, I would be your wife."

" My, wife, Deborah! Are you mad?"

" Not so mad as you take me to be," she replied. " We were equal once, though there may be a little difference between us now. Besides, mine is a fair proposition enough, seeing that there is no other way of getting you out of this infernal strong place."

" You are right, Deborah—you are right," he exclaimed, after a momentary silence, for he knew the danger of offending her at such a time as that. " There is but little choice left for me ; but I was thinking whether I ought to let you run so great a risk merely for the sake of getting me out of the scrape into which I have fallen."

" Ah, never think of me !" exclaimed Deborah ; " for I could face death itself for you. I have always loved you, and, as a proof of it, I now offer to ensure your escape from prison before anybody can be aware that we have such a thing in contemplation."

" It is impossible that you can carry such a project into execution," answered Sir Gilbert. " In this place a strict and constant watch is kept over all the prisoners ; and even if such an attempt should be made, it would be sure to end in our own discomfiture."

" You are determined, then, not to trust to me, though your life depends upon it."

" The case is a desperate one, I know," replied Sir Gilbert, with hesitation. " If I remain here, the gallows stares me in the face ; and if I follow your counsel ——"

" You will be sure to get off in safety."

" How know you that ?"

" Because I have formed my plans ; and no watchfulness of your keepers can prevent my carrying them on to a successful termination. So, now that you have heard me, Sir Gilbert Copley, I ask, for the last time, if you will make the attempt ?"

" I—I will."

" Then there's an end of it," she exclaimed. " Our bargain is made, and I shall take your word as much as if you had taken your oath to it."

" You have my promise, and that ought to be enough."

" And you will marry me as soon as we reach a place of safety ?"

" Ay."

" At any rate, we'll have black and white to that bargain," exclaimed Deborah ; and, taking some writing materials from her pocket, she placed them on the table before Sir Gilbert. " I have written out a short contract," she added, " and when your name is written at the bottom, it will be a bargain to hold you to your word."

So confused was Sir Gilbert with what had taken place in this brief interval, that he was scarcely conscious of what he was about. He gazed in silence upon the paper, and then, as if in a fit of desperation, seized the pen, and hurriedly wrote his name at the bottom of the paper. Deborah watched him with exultation, and when this final act was completed, she snatched the document from the table, folded it up, and thrust it into her bosom for safety.

"I have obeyed you so far," exclaimed Sir Gilbert, hoarsely; "what further commands have you for me?"

"At present, this will suffice," she replied. "You have done all that I required, and it shall now be my care to perform the remaining part of the contract. I leave you, Sir Gilbert; and, when next I come, it will be to conduct you to a place of safety."

Cheerless and melancholy as his solitude was, the prisoner felt relieved when she left him to the indulgence of his own dark reflections. He could perceive the art with which she had contrived to bring affairs to this crisis; and, when he thought of the hateful thraldom to which he had bound himself, he bitterly regretted that he had yielded to the urgency of the moment. It was not in his power to retract, and the next consideration was whether to escape from prison with such a penalty attached to it, or refuse to accompany Deborah when she came to conduct him from the house of bondage. These thoughts occupied his mind till long after darkness had set in, and he was just preparing to throw himself upon his miserable pallet, when a slight noise close at hand startled him. He paused to listen, and directly afterwards his name was pronounced in a low whisper.

"Who's there?" exclaimed the captive. "Is it you, Deborah?"

"No; it is a friend, Mark Harrowby."

"I see you not."

"That's very likely," returned the other; "for I am half way down the chimney."

"What would you do?" demanded Sir Gilbert.

"Get you out of the place, to be sure," replied Harrowby; "that is to say, if you can manage to climb up to the place where I am."

"At all events, I'll try to reach you," exclaimed Sir Gilbert; and, in the desperation of the moment, he commenced the ascent. His task, however, was by no means so easy a one as he had anticipated, for the chimney was suddenly contracted at the distance of a few feet from the bottom; and, having almost exhausted himself by his efforts to overcome the difficulty, he was about to descend, when Harrowby again called to him.

"Make haste there below, will you?" he impatiently exclaimed; "we have plenty to do, and very little time to spare; so, if you don't put the best foot foremost, we may as well give it up at once for a bad job."

"We must, indeed, give it up," replied Sir Gilbert, "for I find it impossible to get any higher."

"Wait a bit while I lend you a hand," exclaimed the other, who was descending to see what assistance could be afforded, when the sound of several voices was heard that filled them both with alarm.

"Don't move, for your life!" exclaimed Harrowby; "the people here seem to have a notion of what's going forward, and all depends upon our silence. They may not enter your cell, and in that case we must make the more speed when we begin again."

But Sir Gilbert was by this time so exhausted, that he had no longer the power to assist himself. His strength seemed to have entirely forsaken him; and, slipping from the place to which he had ascended, he was violently precipitated to the bottom. Here his head struck with tremendous violence against the bars of the grate, and, rolling from this into the middle of the cell, he lay bleeding, and dying from the effects of the fall.

The noise made by his rapid descent immediately brought around him the people whose voices had just before been heard; and, as they gathered round the body of the unfortunate man, it was perceived that the wounds inflicted upon his head were mortal. Every effort, however, was made to arrest the approach of death; but all was of no avail, and, after a few convulsive gasps, the wretched man had ceased to exist.

"So much for his own wilfulness!" exclaimed Deborah, who made one of the group that stood around. "He thought his own plans best, and now he's got his reward for it."

"What do you mean?" demanded a turnkey.

"That he has tried to escape up the chimney, and has come down again quicker than he expected."

"How do you know?" asked the same gruff voice.

"Why, it don't want a witch to find that out," she replied; "look at his grimed face and clothes. Ain't they covered with soot like a chimney-sweep?"

By this time the governor of the prison had joined them; and, having ascertained that life was indeed extinct, he gave orders that a strict watch should be kept throughout the place till morning.

"It is plain," he said, "that a desperate attempt has been made to set some of the prisoners free, and, if we are not very careful, the villains will carry their point after all."

"They'll not try any more, sir, depend on it," interposed Deborah, "for they've been disturbed at their work, and the fellows would hardly be fools enough to wait about the place while you send out to take 'em."

"Humph!" exclaimed the governor, "you appear to be fully well up to this sort of thing."

"Why should we have brains given us, if we don't make use of 'em?" she demanded. "If you had kept a more careful look-out to-night, this poor fellow would not have met with such a dreadful accident."

"And yet, after all," said the governor, without heeding the insolence of her remark, "it is perhaps better for him to have met this fate than have swung upon the gallows."

"He was never born to be hanged," retorted Deborah; "and if it hadn't been for his own folly in taking the advice of other people instead of mine, he might have lived to see many a bright summer's day yet."

"I understand," said the governor, "you intended to have assisted him yourself."

"Well, it's no use denying that I did mean to have a try at it," she replied; "but all's over now, so what's the use of talking about it; I've nothing to do with what has taken place, so you can't lock me up for confessing what I intended to have done."

"May I ask what was to have been your reward if you had succeeded?"

"Why, something worth having, you may be sure," she replied. "He was to have made me his wife, and that was the only reward I myself proposed."

"Poor devil," muttered the governor, "he has had a more lucky escape than I thought for."

"You think the match would not have been a good one, then?"

"Why that depends upon what he might have thought of it himself."

"He thought so well of it," answered Deborah, tartly, "that I have a written promise to make me his wife as soon as possible after his release from this place. So you see how much reason I have to regret his death, since wealth and a title have been snatched from me all through his own obstinacy in attempting to make his escape without my assistance."

"Perhaps," said the governor, "he was trying to get away from a bargain that he began to repent of."

"If I thought so," exclaimed Deborah, "I would spurn his carcase with

my foot ! However, I think I knew him better than to believe that he would have dared to deceive me after the promise was given."

"Can you afford us any clue," asked the governor, "as to the persons who assisted him in this ill-advised attempt to escape ?"

"I don't know what I might be able to do if it happened to suit my purpose," replied Deborah.

"And it would suit your purpose," exclaimed the governor, "for I can take it upon myself to promise that you shall receive a proper reward."

"A proper reward—may be in your estimation that would be a gibbet."

"Psha ! you suspect everybody of treachery."

"And for that very reason I'll not turn traitor myself," she replied. "It's likely enough that I could name the very persons that tried to help poor Sir Gilbert out of his troubles ; but I sha'n't do it, though, for I dare say they'll find their way into a gaol quite soon enough without any assistance from me."

"At any rate, they cannot be very far off," said the governor, "and they'll have more luck than they deserve if they manage to make their escape. And now, upon second thoughts, I'll be bound I could name two of the men without much difficulty."

"Indeed !—and who, pray, do your suspicions glance at ?"

"Why, the men that were included in the warrant by which Hugh Darnton and Robert Redland were apprehended," answered the governor. "If my surmise should be correct, we shall soon have them both here, for a hot search is making for them throughout the country, and it was only this afternoon that I heard they were suspected to be lurking at no great distance from us."

"Well, I hope you are mistaken, that's all I can say about it," returned Deborah. "They have been rough and ready chaps enough in their day, but we were all cronies together, and I should be sorry that either of them should be sent out of the world by the hangman's hands."

No. 23

"Humph ! at all events one of your old companions seems likely to meet that fate."

"Ah, you mean poor Rob Redland ?"

"Yes," replied the governor ; "his trial comes on the day after to-morrow, and if he persists in his present resolution they'll hang him as sure as he's got a neck."

"What resolution are you speaking of ?" asked Deborah.

"Why the foolish fellow is going to plead guilty to the charge of murdering Simon Stripes."

"Fool ! and does he know the consequence ?"

"Yes," replied the governor ; "but he is obstinate, and, in spite of all his lawyer can say against it, he's determined to have his own way. To be sure, there's one thing to be said about it—the evidence is pretty conclusive against him, so that it would be quite useless to plead any other way."

"I must see him," exclaimed Deborah, whose thoughts had been too much absorbed to hear these latter words. "The poor fellow wants the counsel of a friend, or he'll throw away his life like a madman."

She strode away upon uttering this, and the governor of the prisoner, having given directions for the present disposal of Sir Gilbert's body, hastened after her to prevent, if possible, the execution of her purpose He was, however, to late, for ere he could overtake her she had obtained admission to the cell of Rob Redland.

CHAPTER XXXIII.

REMORSE.—THE TRIAL.—THE CRIMINAL'S DOOM.

DEBORAH'S visit to the captive proved less successful than she had anticipated, for no arguments that she could use deterred him from the purpose he had resolved upon. Entreaties and threats were alike disregarded ; the former he sternly rejected, and the latter he laughed at as being vain and impotent to a man who counted but few hours on this side the grave.

Being at length desired to leave the cell by one of the turnkeys, she again tried all her powers of persuasion, but with no better result. Redland saw no hope for himself, and reckless of the consequences, he cared little for the doom which he knew to be inevitable. All that Deborah could get from him was a promise that he would make no confession which might in any way implicate those who had been concerned with him. This conversation was carried on in so low a tone, that the man in attendance could not hear what passed ; and finding that she could make no better bargain, she took her departure, with a caution to remember the promise he had given.

On the morning appointed for the trial, Rob Redland was placed at the bar, and to do him justice, he certainly appeared to feel the awful situation in which he was then standing. The indictment, charging him with being concerned in the murder of Simon Stripes, was a very lengthy one, and kept his patience upon the rack for something more than half an hour. At length, however, it was brought to a conclusion, and being then called upon to plead, he did so by proclaiming himself guilty in a firm and audible voice.

"Prisoner," said the judge, "I know not whether you are aware of it, but it is my duty to caution you that such a plea will be of no avail towards procuring a mitigation of punishment. The crime is of such magnitude, that I can hold out no hope of mercy, and you will therefore do well to consider whether it would not be advisable to retract your plea."

"What good should I do by it, my lord ?" demanded the prisoner.

" That remains to be seen," answered the judge. " Your case would have a patient and impartial hearing, and it sometimes happens that an indictment breaks down for want of sufficient evidence. When that happens the prisoner is discharged, and if no other good arises from it, it at least affords him an opportunity to atone by his future life for the sins he has committed in the course of his life."

" I can see no use in going through a long ceremony, when I know well enough that it must come to the same thing in the end," replied Redland.

" Have you consulted your attorney upon this subject ?"

" I have, my lord."

" And did he not endeavour to show you the necessity of throwing yourself upon a jury of your countrymen ?"

" Yes, my lord," replied the prisoner ; " but he also told me the evidence that was to be brought forward, and from that moment I made up my mind that it would be of no use for me to deny the charge."

" We who sit here to try the case," returned the judge, " are supposed to know nothing of the evidence that is to be brought forward ; and even if we did know anything about it, we are solemnly sworn to deal impartial justice between the prisoner and the law.

" I know the worst, and am prepared to meet it without cowardice," answered Redland. " My life has not been a very good one, I confess, but it don't follow that I should go out of the world with a lie in my mouth. I *was* concerned in the murder—more deeply than any of those that were with me, for my hand it was that struck the blow, and sorry enough I've been for it ever since."

A thrill of horror ran through the assembly as Rob Redland made this confession, and a death-like silence prevailed through the court for some time after the prisoner had done speaking. The judge himself was visibly affected, but as he was still anxious that the wretched man should have the benefit of any doubt that might arise in the course of the examination, he again solemnly entreated him to consider before he threw away his last chance.

" My mind is quite made up, and all the consideration in the world will never induce me to alter it," replied the prisoner. " As for a fortunate turn taking place in my favour, it's out of the question entirely, for I have had more than my share of luck already, and to expect any more would only lead to disappointment. As for life, my lord, what pleasure am I to expect from it if I was to see another fifty years pass over my head ? Who would associate with the man that has confessed himself to be a shedder of human blood ? I should be alone in the world, for all my old companions are either dead, or scattered no one knows where. Honesty would be out of the question, and to keep myself from starving, I must return to my former evil courses. In that case, you and I might happen to meet again, my lord, and you would then think it a pity that I was not hanged when arraigned before you for the murder of old Simon Stripes."

" You are determined, then," said his lordship, " not to withdraw your plea."

" I am."

" Then it only remains for me to perform the most painful duty that belongs to the situation I hold," replied the judge. " I should have been glad had it been in my power to alter your determination ; but since my efforts have failed, I have no omission to charge myself with."

He then went through the few remaining formulas, and the record having been made, he proceeded in an impressive manner to pass the awful sentence of death. The address was listened to with breathless silence by the crowded auditory, all of whom were deeply affected by the solemnity with which a wretched fellow-creature was doomed to meet an ignominious death. Rob

Redland himself, however, maintained the utmost composure throughout; not a muscle of his countenance was moved during the whole time the address occupied, and when it was brought to a conclusion, he bowed respectfully to the court, and accompanying the gaoler, went back to his cell with as much unconcern as ever he had exhibited in his life.

On the following day, after the prison chaplain had left him, he was visited by Deborah, who went to him, perhaps as much to reproach him for his obstinacy as to condole with him upon the unfortunate situation to which he had brought himself.

"I'll tell you what it is, Rob," she exclaimed, after the first salutations were over, "you were always a self-willed fool, and you keep up the character even to the end of your existence. What business had you to plead guilty when there was a chance of getting off, as the judge himself told you? I was in court at the time, and I could hardly keep my tongue quiet, though I suppose they would have committed me to prison if I had spoken my mind."

"Now just mind your own business, old woman, and let other people do the same," exclaimed the convict, in no very good humour at the lecture she was giving him. "I knew well enough that there was no chance for me, so what was the use of going through the farce of a trial when I was quite certain the jury would find me guilty? You know I was never backward in speaking my mind, if the consequences were ever so much against me, and now you must acknowledge that I could do so even with death staring me in the face."

"You don't care, then, what becomes of your old comrades," she exclaimed. "This confession of yours will tell against them if they should happen to be taken, and all this evil is likely to happen because you couldn't keep your own counsel. If you had let the trial go on in the regular way, I was prepared with witnesses to prove an *alibi*; you would have been sure to get off."

"I wish you'd be off yourself," muttered Redland, gloomily. "It's no use now talking about what ought or ought not to have been done—the sentence been passed—I'm to be hanged—and I want to be left alone, in order that I may try and prepare myself for what's to follow."

Deborah left the cell, grumbling at what she called the obstinacy of her companion in crime. From that period she saw nothing more of him till the morning on which he mounted the fatal scaffold. The convict appeared to be penitent, though without betraying the slightest emotion of fear, and at length, when the brief preparations were completed, Robert Redland was launched into eternity.

CHAPTER XXXIV.

EXPLANATIONS.

As we have no desire to leave our readers in doubt when important matters require explanation, we will now take a glance at a few recent events, which will serve to render the conclusion of our narrative more intelligible. For this purpose we must return to Mark Harrowby and Dick Elliot, who, it will be remembered, made the best of their way from the Hall on the morning when so unexpected a visit was paid to the mansion by the magistrates and their subordinates. The two guilty confederates saw plainly enough that the part of the country they had been staying in was now too hot to hold them, and having no desire to risk the decision of a jury, they spurred their horses to the utmost of their speed, and stopped not even for a moment till they had reached a place that seemed sufficiently remote from the scene of danger.

Requiring, as they did, a little rest and refreshment, they stopped at a low public-house on the roadside, where, being accommodated with a room to themselves, they began to concert schemes for the future.

At first it was suggested that they should quit England with as little delay as possible ; but, upon reflection, it appeared to be an act of cowardice to leave their companions without trying whether they might not be able to render them a service, and as this could only be done with extreme caution, they determined to leave their horses at the public-house, and after disguising themselves in the best way they could, to return to the Hall, and learn from either the steward or housekeeper how matters had gone in their absence.

This plan was no sooner arranged than means were taken to put it into execution. An excuse was easily made for leaving the place without their horses, and a couple of guineas having been given to the landlord, by way of quieting his suspicions, they set out, promising to return again on the following morning.

After pursuing their way some little distance, chance favoured them beyond their expectations, for in an obscure part of the road they fell in with a couple of trampers, who were easily prevailed upon to exchange clothes with them, as the bargain was evidently greatly in their own favour.   Their silence as to what had occurred was purchased, as in the former case, by a moderate bribe, and being thus disguised so that it was impossible any one could recognize them, they once more resumed their way, stopping every now and then to solicit charity, in order the better to avoid suspicion.

It was nearly nightfall when they entered the park, which surrounded the old Hall, and seeking the covert of a small plantation, they paused to concert schemes for carrying out their intentions.   It then appeared to them that for both to visit the house might give rise to awkward suspicions, and as neither of them wished to share the fate of their comrades, it was at length agreed that Harrowby should go by himself to the Hall, and by cautious inquiries ascertain all that had occurred after their own escape in the morning.

On arriving at the mansion, Harrowby walked boldly up to the door, where he was met by the old housekeeper, who was about to retreat precipitately, when the supposed mendicant solicited charity in the most piteous accents. He represented himself as a ruined tradesman,—described the sufferings of his wife and family, and so far operated upon the kindly feelings of the old woman, that she doled him out a pittance, and desired him to go away as quickly as he could, lest he should chance to fall into the hands of the constables, some of whom were still watching about the house.

" An honest man, like me, needn't be afraid of meeting them," said Harrowby, with a hypocritical whine.

" But they may not be quite satisfied of your honesty, without taking you before the magistrates," answered the housekeeper.   " We have had a good many people in this house lately, that were supposed to be very honest till they were found out, and now some of them have found their way into gaol, with very little chance of coming out again till they go to the gallows."

" I thought such a house as this could only have been inhabited by gentry," observed Mark Harrowby.

" Ah ! so you might well think," answered the old woman ; " but they turned out to be a terrible set of villains ; and I only wish all of them had been taken when the officers were here."

" Some of them escaped, then ?"

" Yes," she replied ; " two as great villains as ever were in being, contrived to get away just before the constables came to the house.   But they needn't think to be at liberty long, for the officers are after them, and I hope they'll come to the gallows with their comrades."

" Serve 'em right," said Harrowby ; " every man ought to be hanged that don't obey the laws ; and if I only knew where these chaps were to be found, you'd see how I'd help to put 'em into limbo. Honesty for ever ! is my maxim, and them as don't like it, ain't any better than they ought to be."

"You are not such a bad chap as I thought you," exclaimed the old woman, completely deceived by his hypocrisy.   "A man needn't be a rogue because he's poor ; so, if you've a mind to earn a few pounds, I can put you in the way of doing it easily."

"How ?"

"By going in search of the two scoundrels," she replied ; "there's a reward offered for their apprehension, and you may as well have it as anybody else."

"True ; but how am I to know them ?"

"Oh, I can describe them pretty closely," replied the old woman. "One of the fellows went by a fine name while he was here ; but it seems he's well known to be one Mark Harrowby, a notorious smuggler, who was afterwards concerned in a murder, for which the police have been looking for him ever since."

"What sort of a chap was he ?"

"Humph ! about your own height, I should say ; but very well dressed when he left this house. There's a hang-dog look about his face that always made me think badly of him ; and one of his hands has got a great scar upon it, that I suppose was received in some of his scuffles with the revenue officers."

Harrowby took especial care to conceal his hand, which had been so accurately described, and then assuming a careless tone, he asked if there was any suspicion as to which way he had directed his flight ?

"No," she replied, "people seem to know nothing about that at present ; but I hope it won't be very long before we hear that both he and his companion are taken.   They are desperate characters, and when Sir Lionel and his family return to the old Hall, they'll not be safe for a moment if these fellows should be still at liberty."

"Then the sooner we make sure of them the better," exclaimed Mark Harrowby. "I'll go and look after the rascals, and if they should happen to fall in my way, I'll lodge them both in prison, and claim the reward."

Having heard as much as was necessary for his purpose, he turned away and walked briskly through the park ; for he was afraid the old woman might take second thoughts, and should she chance to suspect that he was one of the men she had been talking about, a pursuit would instantly be commenced, that would leave him and his companion little chance of escape.   On reaching the plantation he found Dick Elliot enjoying a comfortable sleep, and having roused him, and related all that had passed between him and the old housekeeper, inquired what course they had better adopt under the awkward circumstances in which they were placed.

"Why, look after ourselves, to be sure," answered Dick. "There's danger, ain't there, that Sir Gilbert may peach against us, and in that case, he would save his own neck by getting ours into the halter."

"And for that very reason we must not give him cause to turn against us," exclaimed Harrowby.   "We must try to get him out of prison, whatever may be the risk to ourselves."

"Are you mad ?" demanded Elliot ;—"would you make such an attempt as that when it's almost certain we should be caught ?"

"And ain't it almost certain we shall be caught, any how ?" asked the other. "Haven't I told you that a reward has been offered for my apprehension ? and you may depend upon it they won't give us much chance of slipping out of the kingdom."

"'Tis a wild scheme," answered Elliot ; "yet I should like to know how you think of setting about your task of liberating the prisoners."

"I've had no time to arrange my plan yet," answered the other; "but if we set diligently and carefully about our work, there can be no doubt of succeeding. I know the prison well enough, and can mount any one of its walls as easily as need be. We may not succeed to-day nor to-morrow, perhaps, but we may be getting matters in a fair train, and when the proper time comes we'll get these two fellows out of prison."

"Or ourselves *in*."

"Psha! are you going to turn coward, all on a sudden?" exclaimed the other. "Sir Gilbert and t'other one are in trouble; we have been lucky enough to escape, and it would be cowardly to leave them to the hangman, whilst there's a chance of saving their necks."

"All that's very fine morality, I dare say," retorted Elliot; "but it will hardly convince me that a man ought to run himself into danger after he has been at so much pains to run out of it. We've got our liberty now, Mark, but there's no saying how long we may be able to keep it if we stay in this infernal neighbourhood."

"Well, then, leave me to get through the job myself," cried Harrowby, sullenly. "I want no chicken-hearted fellows to work with me, so go your ways; and perhaps, after all, you may come to the gallows just as soon as if you remained here."

"Then I shall stop where I am, and try to help you through this affair," replied Dick Elliot, who was now shamed into standing by his companion. "You have called me a chicken-hearted fellow, but it shall be seen that I have as much courage as yourself when once my mettle is put up; so now let me know when this attempt to liberate Sir Gilbert is to be made."

"That must depend upon circumstances," replied Harrowby. "In these disguises there's not much fear that any one will discover who we are, especially as people would hardly suspect us of lurking about so near the place where all are anxiously looking out to earn the reward that has been offered for our apprehension."

"Well, you shall see that I'll not flinch from the danger," replied Elliot, "though, to confess the truth, I believe our wisest plan would have been to take care of ourselves. As for getting Sir Gilbert out of prison, I don't see the slightest chance of it; and, if we should happen to be nabbed, there'll be four of us to be hanged instead of two, and we shall have the satisfaction of knowing that we have given Jack Ketch an extra job when it was easy enough for us to have got off scot free."

On the three or four following nights Mark Harrowby strolled round the outside of the prison walls to ascertain which would be the easiest place of access. He saw enough, however, to convince him that the task he had undertaken would be attended with more difficulties than he imagined, and he was at length almost tempted to give it up in despair, when chance threw in his way an assistant, whose services might be of the greatest importance. This was no other than Deborah Ratcliff, who he happened to encounter one evening when he was engaged in his unusual task of exploring the prison walls. The meeting occasioned no little surprise to both of them, and, walking away to a place where they were not likely to be observed or overheard, she inquired why he was lingering about the neighbourhood when an active search was being made after him in every direction.

"You need hardly ask such a question as that," he replied, "when you may suppose I could have no other object in view than the release of Sir Gilbert."

"That's not so easily done as you may expect," answered Deborah. "They've caged him safely enough, I can tell you; and, if there had been a chance of getting him out, you may be sure I should before now have lent him a helping hand."

"Do you think the case a hopeless one, then?"

"Why, what chance do you suppose they'll give us?" demanded the woman. "They've found out everything about the murder of Simon Stripes, that we thought was never likely to cause any mischief, and Sir Gilbert is to be tried for it in a day or two from this time."

"Have they any evidence to prove that he was near when the old man was killed?" asked Harrowby.

"It seems that somehow or other they have found out everything," replied Deborah. "These lawyers manage to fish up evidence where it's least expected, and I believe Sir Lionel Dacre has found a document that throws a good deal of light upon the subject. At all events, people say the business wears a very black appearance, and, between ourselves, I'm afraid young Copley stands in a very awkward situation."

"Then there is the greater need for us to make a desperate push to get him out of it," exclaimed Harrowby. "For my own part, I'm determined not to let an old friend perish for want of assistance; and, if you will lend a helping hand, I think something may be done before the day of trial comes on."

"Well, it sha'n't be me that will throw cold water on any scheme you may have for getting him out of prison," exclaimed the woman. "At present they don't seem to think I have had any hand in the business that has got the others into trouble, and so I'm allowed to go in and out of the place just as I please. They've made me promise not to go out of the way till after the trial, in case I should happen to be wanted to give evidence; but I can tell 'em it ain't much they'll get out of me that will do Copley any harm."

"You sleep in the prison, I suppose?"

"Yes, it's the only home I've got at present."

"Then surely you can think of some plan to assist me," exclaimed Harrowby. "For instance, you might throw a rope over without being seen by anybody, and that would be something towards helping me to get up."

"I'll do it," said Deborah, after a pause; "there's very little fear of being disturbed after ten o'clock, and if you come here about an hour after that time to-morrow, you shall find a rope hanging over the wall on the south side of the building. From thence you may easily reach the roof, and I don't know but it will then be possible to set the captive at liberty."

"How am I to get at him from the roof?"

"Oh, easily enough," she replied; "the way he will have to come is none of the cleanest, to be sure; but beggars mustn't be choosers, you know, and he must e'en be content to creep up the chimney. You can call down to him when you are ready, and I'll warrant he is not long in trying the only means I know of to save his neck from the halter."

"But how am I to know which chimney to call down?" asked Mark Harrowby.

"Oh, it's to be found easily enough," she replied. "It is the lowest one of the stack immediately opposite the place where I shall throw the rope across. You must urge him to make as much haste as possible, and if you are lucky enough to get him outside of the walls, lose not a moment's time, but hurry him out of the country as quickly as possible."

"You needn't fear that," exclaimed Harrowby; "but what's to be done about the others? Are they to be left behind to take their chance?"

"There's no help for it, so don't trouble your head about them," answered Deborah. "I've got Sir Gilbert's promise to make me his wife if ever he gets his liberty, and it's not likely I'm going to throw away such a chance for the sake of liberating a parcel of fellows that I don't care a straw about."

With this understanding they separated, and Harrowby returned to Dick Elliot to tell him of the plan of escape that had been formed. Both of them seemed in extacies at the certainty of success, and at the appointed hour they were at the place mentioned by Deborah. They found the rope thrown over

as she had promised, and Mark Harrowby found little difficulty in ascending. The result, however, is known to the reader, and in the confusion that ensued after the catastrophe, Harrowby found means to effect his own escape over the wall.

CHAPTER XXXV.

THE RELEASE FROM PRISON.—THE WEDDING.

As soon as Vivian heard the news of Sir Gilbert's death, he hastened to the apartments of his friend, Henry Markham, to inform him of the change that had taken place, and seek his advice as to the best method of proceeding. After mature consideration it was agreed that, as a hasty disclosure might be of serious consequence to Vivian's father in his present delicate state of health, a note should be despatched to him in his prison, informing him that important events had recently transpired, and promising to call upon him in the afternoon to put him possession of all the particulars.

"This will, at all events, prepare him to expect something extraordinary," remarked Markham, after a note had been despatched by a messenger. "He may probably even guess that it relates to the restoration of his rights, and then half our errand will be accomplished before we go to announce the unexpected change that has taken place in his fortunes."

"And he will be less gratified by our news than you anticipate," returned Vivian. "We know the bitter reason he has to execrate the name of his worthless nephew; yet, strange to say, I have never heard him utter a complaint at the ruffianly treatment he has received from him."

"That," replied Markham, "is because he believes him to have been mis-

No. 24

led by the evil counsels of that arch] villain, Hugh Darnton; he seems to pity his nephew, and to believe that he would have been all he could have wished but for the instigations of his new ally."

"It must be admitted that Darnton was worthless enough," exclaimed Vivian; "but, on the other hand, I must tell you that Gilbert, from his boyhood, always manifested a disposition that prepared me to expect that he would prove unworthy the kindness bestowed upon him by my father."

"But now, as he is dead," said Markham, "of course your father is restored to the title and property of which he was cruelly deprived."

"That follows naturally enough," replied Vivian; "though I very much doubt whether Sir Lionel—as I may now again call him—will be gratified with the intelligence we are about to convey to him. He has lost all feeling of ambition, and I verily believe would as soon pass the remainder of his days in prison as go back to the mansion from which he was driven by force and violence. My mother, however, will receive the news very differently; and, for her sake and that of his children, he will doubtless go back to the old Hall, though without any of those feelings of pride and satisfaction with which he used to look around him when he was before the owner of those domains."

"Never fear but his old feelings will revive, after a bit," replied Henry Markham. "Grief, we all know, brings down the spirits of a man; but the change from captivity to liberty will soon effect a marvellous change. Besides, he must be of a very different disposition to what I imagine, if he can see unmoved the happiness that this change of fortune affords those whom he best loves. By George, he ought to look upon himself as one of the happiest men alive."

"That he can hardly do if he looks back to the gloomy period of his misfortunes," answered Vivian. "It will ever be to him a dark page in his history, and I much question whether this change to better fortune will make him a happier man. However, that remains to be seen, and as a very short time will serve to prove the effect of our news upon him, we will leave all further speculations upon that subject till we know how he will receive it."

Vivian and Markham had rightly anticipated, when they imagined that Sir Lionel would form a tolerably correct guess as to the nature of the information they had to communicate. His lawyer happened to visit him while he was still cogitating upon this subject, and they were still engaged in consultation when the young man arrived.

"My dear Vivian," he exclaimed, "your countenance assures me that I have guessed the nature of the communication you have to make. There is news from the old Hall, and you would tell me that I am once more its master?"

"True," answered his son; "but can you tell me by what means this has been effected?"

"There is but one way," answered his father—"Sir Gilbert must be dead, or ——"

"He is dead," replied Vivian; "and, luckily for the honour of our family, has escaped the ignominious doom to which he would otherwise have been adjudged. He attempted to break from his prison, and, sustaining a severe fall, died on the spot."

"Heaven pardon his sins!" exclaimed Sir Lionel, fervently. "He committed a grievous wrong against us, my dear boy; but it is not for mortals to pronounce against the motives of others. He was led to the commission of faults through an unfortunate choice of companions, and severely has he suffered for it."

"In my opinion," interposed Henry Markham, "he has not suffered half enough. He committed crimes that ought to have brought him to the gallows; and I, for one, am sorry he has escaped his deserts."

" Do you forget, then," resumed Sir Lionel, " that had such a fate been his, we should have shared in the disgrace ?"

" Do you think the world would be so unjust as to frown upon his unoffending relatives ?"

" The world, in its censures, rarely stands upon justice," replied Sir Lionel. " As it is, however, my reckless nephew has escaped worse consequences; and that reflection somewhat reconciles me to the tragic nature of his death. People will soon forget that such a person ever had existence, and then my family will escape the ignominy which would otherwise attach to our name."

" And, of course," interrupted the loving son, " you are no longer to consider yourself a prisoner within these walls. The action brought against you by your unprincipled nephew ceases with his death, and after a few necessary forms have been gone through, I shall have the happiness of congratulating you on your re-admission to the world."

" It is a change I never expected, nor, indeed, does it afford me so much pleasure as you may imagine," replied Sir Lionel. " I have become careless of liberty ; and I verily believe, if it were not for the sake of my children, I should prefer passing the remainder of my days in this asylum, to which misfortune has driven me."

" But you will think and feel very differently by-and-bye, my dear father," exclaimed Vivian. " You must mix again among your own friends—people who have regretted to see your fallen state as much as they will rejoice to see you once more among them. In their society you will soon forget the sorrows that are past, and, ere many months have glided by, we shall have the happiness of seeing you as happy as when we were a joyous, undivided family."

" I will not deny that there are some good reasons why I may fulfil the anticipations you have formed," replied Sir Lionel. " One of them is, that my fond and faithful wife will be restored to the station from which she was ruthlessly driven ; and the other, that as all obstacles respecting wealth are removed, we may now hope that the union between Henry Markham and my daughter may be looked forward to with some degree of certainty."

" That," exclaimed Markham, " is a subject I should myself have mentioned, but that I thought it might appear like selfishness. Yes, my dear Sir Lionel, every obstacle is indeed removed, and I may now look forward with certainty to the happiness which, but a brief time since, I believed was denied to me for ever."

" This," observed Sir Lionel, " affords a proof of the hollowness of all human friendship. When the cloud of adversity hung over me, an alliance with my family was objected to, but the objection ceases the moment that fortune again smiles upon me."

" Nay," interposed Vivian, " do not give serious utterance to such a reproach ; our friend here will most certainly take it to himself."

" Henry Markham knows too well the respect I entertain for him to imagine that my words apply in even the slightest to himself," replied Sir Lionel. " He has been my firm and steady friend through all the misfortunes that have assailed us, and I can honour him the more for bowing to the dictates of his father, though himself suffering severely from the prohibition that was placed upon his affections. He and my daughter love each other, and nothing will afford me more pleasure than to give my consent to their union if it is also sanctioned by his father."

" Of his approbation I am certain," replied Markham, " and if anything could add to my gratification it would be the having it in my power to convince you that my father's respect for this family has never been diminished, though his command might certainly make it appear so. He has, unfortunately, a notion that marriage, to be happy, should be equal with respect to wealth, and henee arose the objection which occasioned so much misery to us all."

"At all events he shall see that I bear no resentment for what has past," answered Sir Lionel. "The firm bonds of friendship between us shall be renewed, and never will I again revert to a circumstance which is better forgotten than remembered."

"And when," asked Vivian, "may we expect to return to the old Hall?"

"For an answer to that question," replied his father, "I must refer you to my lawyer."

"There need be but little delay," said the person alluded to, "for the matter now lies in a nutshell. In the course of to-morrow I shall be able to go through all the necessary forms for your release, and the next day you may leave the prison at any hour you please. Of course, your son will in the meantime take care to get everything in readiness, so that, if you please, you may set off for the country immediately after bidding adieu to these dreary walls."

"It shall be so," exclaimed Vivian, "for I would not remain in London one hour after my father gets clear of this place. Misfortune has never ceased to follow us from the time of our arrival here, and as better hopes have now dawned upon us we will seek the peace and happiness of our own loved home."

"Let it be even as you have said, my dear boy," cried Sir Lionel. "I am myself no lover of the indolence and follies of a London life, and nowhere else shall I be so likely to forget my troubles as when wandering through my favourite walks round the old mansion. Every spot there will serve to remind me of pleasures that I fancied had fled for ever. Once more established there, and I believe nothing will ever prevail upon me to leave it again."

After a few directions had been given to Vivian, he and his friend took their departure, and most zealously did they set about their task of making all their arrangements for quitting the metropolis. Determined that no delay should intervene, they would not wait till their own carriages could be brought from the country; and others were, accordingly, hired to convey the now happy family to the mansion which they had never expected again to see.

The attorney, too, exerted himself marvellously, so that for once law seemed to move out of its usual sluggish pace. The forms it was necessary to go through were, it is true, not very numerous; but they were accelerated with all possible speed, so that on the evening following Sir Lionel Dacre was informed that, everything being completed, he might on the next day quit the prison as early as was convenient to himself.

It is unnecessary to describe the journey of our happy travellers. All care and anxiety seemed to have taken their departure for ever, and a bright future appeared to rise before them. On reaching the great gates of the park, Sir Lionel and Lady Dacre were met by nearly all their tenantry, who came forth on that happy occasion to hail the return of their beloved master and mistress. The most animated cheers rent the air as the carriage advanced, and in that moment Sir Lionel felt more than recompensed for all the trials and sufferings he had endured.

We have nothing more to add, except that Markham soon obtained his father's consent to his long wished-for union with the daughter of Sir Lionel Dacre. This, though it was anticipated, afforded the most lively joy to all who were concerned in it, and in little more than a month afterwards the old mansion rang with the festivities that followed the union of the two lovers,

THE END.